D1715788

The Temple of the Blind

Book Six

The Judgment of the Sentinels

Brian Harmon

The Judgment of the Sentinels

ISBN: 1484800060
ISBN-13: 978-1484800065

Also by Brian Harmon

The Box
(Book One of The Temple of the Blind)

Gilbert House
(Book Two of The Temple of the Blind)

The Temple of the Blind
(Book Three of The Temple of the Blind)

Road Beneath the Wood
(Book Four of The Temple of the Blind)

Secret of the Labyrinth
(Book Five of The Temple of the Blind)

Rushed
(An Eric Fortrell Novel)

For Sarah

Chapter 1

Thirteen months and a lifetime ago, Albert Cross unlocked his car door and found a small, wooden box. It was only a ten-inch cube, but the object had contained much more than its physical dimensions suggested. That box was where everything began. Everything that came after that singular moment in his life could either be traced directly back to the box or was changed forever the moment he laid eyes on it. Entire worlds had been inside, entire lifetimes. Looking back now, Albert realized that he had essentially found the woman he loved inside that box. And the best friends he'd ever known. Inside that box had been his future, his destiny, even the end of his virginity. Inside that box had been blue eyes and blonde hair and sweet kisses and a warm body pressed against him every night. Inside that box had been adventure and intrigue. But inside that box had also been fear and pain. Inside that box had been grief.

Wayne was dead.

He'd appeared from nowhere, a mystery like all the others that had spewed from the box since that early September evening, out of nothing, and he had hurled himself headlong into an adventure the likes of which none of them had ever imagined. He fought monsters and journeyed across entire worlds to save lives he barely knew. His body battered and bloody, he had soldiered forward with unrivaled courage, enduring without fear or regret, and in the end he had died protecting them all. He was a hero. And now he would forever lie entombed in the relentless darkness of this very passage.

How long had they been walking since they said goodbye? Albert couldn't recall what time that was. It felt like hours ago, though it was probably only half an hour, maybe forty-five minutes. For that matter, he couldn't recall the last time he even glanced at his watch. And he didn't bother now, either. He couldn't seem to care enough to make it worth the effort. It wasn't important.

He reached out with his good arm and took Brandy's hand in his. She turned and looked at him, her blue eyes wet and shimmering. He'd almost lost her back there too. In his mind's eye he could still see her plunging into that darkness. He could still hear her screams as she fell. He thought that his world had ended. But somehow his prayers reached Heaven, even from that dark and endless labyrinth far beneath the earth, and she survived. She was still with him, as though God, Himself, had given her back to him so that he would have the will to keep going, so that he could continue to fight.

Brandy pressed close to him, her cheeks wet with tears. She'd hardly known Wayne, but she knew what he had done for them. He saved Olivia from the nightmare of that horrible forest. He saved her precious Albert from those awful hounds. He'd taken on things she could not imagine, things she would not have been capable of enduring.

He was their hero when they most desperately needed one.

She remembered the way he scooped her up into his arms when the labyrinth began to quake. She remembered the way he held her, not unlike the way Albert held her when he carried her from the fear room all those months ago…when she first knew that she was in love with him, that she wanted to spend her life with him, that she wanted to be his one and only. This was not the way she had felt about Wayne, of course. She was in love with Albert, not Wayne, but by being held that way, she'd felt a little of Albert in Wayne. They shared inside them all the best and most important things. She'd felt his strength, his courage, his compassion. Even with her head pounding with such pain that she could barely focus her eyes, she had felt those things. She knew at that moment, without any doubt, that Wayne was a great man.

But now he was dead and her heart was aching in a way that she would not have believed just a few short hours ago.

Ahead of them, Nicole and Olivia walked side by side. Nicole had finally looked down at her hand. There was a painful hole in her palm and her flesh had been burned by the fire that belched from the stone altar at the top of the tower. Her middle and index fingers were blistered, as were her palm and wrist. Her entire hand was bright red. The pain was constant, both throbbing and stinging, and she had nothing with which to dull it.

Olivia looked at her, her eyes falling on those injuries. She winced. "Are you going to be okay?"

Nicole nodded. She had to be. She didn't have much choice now. God only knew where they were or how far they had traveled from home. There wasn't much chance that this tunnel was going to lead them to a hospital emergency room. She lowered her hand again and kept walking, trying to ignore the pain.

Olivia did not press the matter. She turned and stared into the gloom ahead of them once more. She could feel the wet trails that her tears had left down her cheeks, could still taste the salt on her lips. She felt numb. Wayne had been her hero, her Superman, courageous and strong and, it had seemed, impenetrable. He risked his life to save her, gave his all to protect her, just as he'd promised he would...but now he was gone.

She kept thinking that she would wake up, that any minute now the dream would end and she would be back in her bed, back in the Cube, her alarm clock buzzing, alerting her that it was time for her early class. Misty Redler would roll over with a grumble, her class not for another hour, and she would realize that there was no Wayne Oakley and never had been. There was no Albert Cross. There was no Brandy Rudman or Nicole Smart or Andrea Prophett. Nick and Trish were not lying dead somewhere inside a dark and empty dormitory. They were alive and well and she still had to break off her dead-end relationship with Andy. The world was still turning mundanely and her life was as it always had been because there was no way that things like this could exist. The only worlds besides the one in which she lived were Heaven and Hell and God would not have made a place like the Wood or a creature like the Caggo.

But there would be no waking from this nightmare. Her aching feet were real. Her broken heart was real. These people around her were real. It was so much for her to take. She had actually fallen in love with Wayne Oakley, fallen for him like any girl would fall in love with the man who saved her life, who rode into a dark nightmare as if on a great white steed and carried her away to where everything was okay, to where nothing could harm her.

She could not help but wonder if *she* had killed Wayne. If she had not insisted on coming with him, on helping him, on seeing with her own eyes what all this terror had been about, Wayne might still be alive. He would not have had to wait for her. Nicole would have gone through that opening after Albert. And Wayne would have had time to get away. He would not still have been standing there when…

Fresh tears spilled down her cheeks. She couldn't help it. Poor Wayne. Why couldn't it have been her back there? Why couldn't she have taken his place? He had already saved her life. It would have been worth it to save his in return.

It just wasn't fair.

Andrea walked ahead of them all. She did not want to face them, did not want to look at them. Tears streamed down her face. She couldn't make herself stop crying.

One of them had actually died down here. The reality of that terrified her, but more powerful than the fear was the hurt. Her heart had broken at the sight of Wayne lying there, telling them to go on, to leave him. He actually told them not to tell anyone what happened to him. He wanted them to let him pass into mystery, to vanish without a word.

He'd been right, of course. Nobody would believe them when they returned home. People would probably accuse them. It wasn't fair, but that's the way the ignorant world worked. People refused to believe in anything, much less anything as fantastic as…all *this*.

Wayne's family would never know what became of him. They would never know if he was really dead. They would never be at peace. And they certainly would never know that he died a hero, that he gave his life protecting others. Didn't they at least deserve that much?

Would it have been easier if they hadn't had a chance to say goodbye, she wondered. Would it have seemed less cruel if she had not watched him hand his flashlight to Albert? If she had not had the chance to say goodbye to him, if the thing that speared him through had pierced his heart and dropped him instantly dead, if he had not told her that he was glad to have met her, would it have hurt any less? Would her heart still have been so broken?

A part of her just wanted to stop, to sit down on this cold, hard floor and not take another step, to cry until the pain was washed away. But what was the point? Wayne was already dead. Soon, the rest of them might be too. They knew nothing about what awaited them in the darkness ahead.

Albert put his good arm around Brandy and squeezed her. It was hard, but they had to keep moving. They had to push on. Wayne would not have wanted them to give up on account of him. That would have made his death pointless. He might as well have sat down and let the Caggo kill them all.

He would not let it be that way. He would not let it be for nothing. Wayne knew what he was doing when he made them go first through the opening in the tunnel wall. He knew the risk he was taking, and Albert knew that he would have done it no differently if given the chance again.

He promised Wayne he would take care of these four young women, that he would protect them and lead them safely to their mysterious destination. And he swore to himself now that nothing as meaningless as a broken arm would stop him from keeping that promise.

Chapter 2

The Temple of the Blind was more than any of them had ever dreamed. But all of it, from the first sentinel statues with their grotesque proportions and empty, featureless faces, to the tower with its vast belly full of fire, was only gray stone and shadow. What awaited them at the end of this final passage was far more.

A soft glow greeted them as they approached, like the first light of a new day. But it was no sunrise. They emerged from the labyrinth and stood beneath a sky that was as black and as empty as the tunnels they had left behind them. Rising into this pitch-black sky was a great, gray mountain. The light was coming not from the horizon, lending hope to some distant sun, but from the mountain itself. Columns of fire blazed from hundreds of unseen vents in the stone, illuminating its rocky face in an angry undulation of light and shadow, and from its highest peak spewed a towering inferno of orange and yellow flames.

More fires rose up from cracks in the ground on either side of them, scattering the shadows at their feet and lending a dreadful hue to the path on which they walked. It was as if they had finally descended all the way down into the blazing pits of hell.

"Where are we?" asked Nicole. "What is this place?"

"The Temple of the Blind," Albert replied, still staring up at the burning mountain. It was the most frightful place he had ever seen, far more terrifying than any scene from any movie. "It's inside there. All of it. This is what it looks like from outside."

Brandy gazed up at the mountain, confused. "But the Temple of the Blind is underground…"

"In our world, maybe. Not here."

Andrea turned in a circle, her wide eyes taking everything in. "We're in a different world?"

"We're in the Wood," said Olivia, her voice edged with unmistakable anxiety.

"How can you tell?" asked Nicole.

"It has the same sky."

All of them lifted their faces toward the darkness above them. It could have been nothing more than an overcast night sky, but it wasn't. Peering up, they could somehow tell that it was utterly empty. An eternal abyss filled the heavens here, and looking into it was deeply unsettling.

"I don't like it here," Brandy decided.

"You don't get used to it," Olivia assured her. She recalled cowering beneath the fallen night trees, staring out into this perpetually empty darkness, trying to decide if a place this black could really exist or if she had been struck blind.

Last time she looked into this sky, Wayne came to rescue her. It broke her heart to know that he wouldn't be coming again.

Albert scanned the landscape. A pool of rippling water stood between them and the rocky terrain at the base of the mountain. The smooth, right-angle edges of the temple's interior were not apparent here. This stone was raw, rough, indistinguishable from any other natural formation except for the fire belching from it.

These flames also illuminated the road ahead. It surged from narrow fissures in the stone, hot columns of fire reaching for the sky, lighting the way so that, for the first time since he descended into the steam tunnels the previous evening, he did not need a flashlight to see.

But Albert found little comfort in the light. Inside that mountain was coiled every passage they had traveled during the night, and countless more they never glimpsed. He thought of all that they'd already been through, all that they'd accomplished. And still there was no end in sight. How much farther would they be forced to go? How much more would they have to endure?

Andrea moved closer to the nearest flaming vent, her hands in front of her, cautiously testing the heat. "At least we can warm up out here."

"I think I warmed up enough back there on that tower," Nicole decided. She could still feel the baking heat that had beat down on them as they fled the burning structure. It felt like sunburn on her back and shoulders.

Andrea felt that, too, but it was still nice to know that they now had the option of warming up. They didn't have that inside the temple.

"So what now?" Brandy asked.

Albert looked at her, his eyes washing over her pretty features. He couldn't stop thinking about how he'd almost lost her back there. "We could use some rest, I think. Help me get the first aid kit out of my backpack. We need to look at Nicole's hand."

"Right," said Nicole, annoyed. "The guy with the broken arm is worried about the girl with the scratch on her hand." She'd been trying to hide her injury, determined not to let anyone worry about her. But very little ever got by Albert.

"You kind of *stabbed* your hand," Andrea recalled. "All the way through."

Nicole rolled her eyes. "Not helping."

"Sorry."

"Let's just all take a break for a little bit," Albert said, wincing as Brandy eased the backpack off his shoulders. "We'll get *everyone* patched up."

Olivia stepped toward them. "I can help. I'm not hurt."

"Can't tell it by looking," observed Andrea, staring at her back. "You're covered in bruises."

Olivia looked down at herself. She was still dirty from crossing that awful mud chamber, making it difficult to see exactly how badly she'd been battered, but even so, it was obvious that her arms and legs were spotted with black and purple bruises from her ordeal in the forest. Her belly, too. There was even a blemish the size of her hand on her left breast. She had little doubt that her back looked equally bad. Probably worse.

There were large, blue-black splotches spreading from around the two bite marks. The one on her thigh had grown to the size of a grapefruit. On her arms and legs were a number of long, skinny bruises. These, she realized with something that was almost horror, were *finger marks*. That was where those zombie things had grabbed her and held her down, their hard, bony fingers pressing into her soft flesh with bizarre, desperate strength. She remembered lying there on the cold ground as they swarmed over her, ready to tear her limb from limb and eat her alive.

The memory gave her a hard shudder and sent gooseflesh racing across her entire body. She couldn't help but glance around, half-sure that the shambling dead had surrounded her again and were even now closing in, determined to feast upon her flesh.

"We can switch out those dirty bandages," Nicole suggested.

Olivia nodded, shaking away the awful thoughts. That was probably a good idea. The mud from that room had turned the gauze on her arm and shoulder black. If she survived this day and didn't contract a serious infection, she'd count herself *twice* lucky.

"Let me see your hand," Albert said as he eased himself down onto the ground.

"It's nothing," Nicole assured him. "Take care of yourself first."

But Albert was determined. "Let me see it."

"Seriously, stop worrying about me. I'll be fine."

"I reserve the right to worry about the people I care about. Now show me your hand."

For some reason, this caught her off guard. Nicole stared down at him for a moment. She didn't want to let him fuss about her hand. She wanted him to take care of himself. She almost lost him back there. Him *and* Brandy. But there was simply something about hearing him say that he cared about her that took some of the stubbornness out of her.

Reluctantly, she knelt down and gave him her hand.

Brandy knelt down, too, and helped by shining her flashlight onto her best friend's palm. "Jeez, Nikki…"

"It's okay."

"What did you do?" asked Albert.

Nicole bit her lip as she looked down at the bloody hole and the blistered flesh of her hand and wrist. How did she go about explaining it?

"She slammed it down on a big stone spike up on the tower," Andrea replied for her as she seated herself on the rocky ground nearby.

Brandy winced. "What the hell were you thinking?"

"It was the only way!" argued Nicole.

"It probably was," Albert agreed, examining her hand. "Does it hurt?"

"Not too bad."

"Liar."

"It was actually really cool," Andrea recalled. "*Super* brave. Super gross, too, though…"

"Why would you have to impale yourself?" Brandy demanded.

"'Atop the tower, the secret is blood,'" quoted Albert. "That was the clue."

"My blood dripped down into the altar and something exploded. Fire came out of it. Burned me."

"Same fire that's burning up there now, I'll bet." Albert glanced up at the mountain and wondered how much fuel something like that required. It was like the world's biggest oil rig fire.

"It was stupid," Nicole admitted. "I was just standing there, waiting for something to happen. I should've been getting out of there."

"You didn't know," Olivia assured her. "None of us did." She sat down next to Nicole and began to unravel the filthy gauze from her arm.

"I can make this feel better," Albert promised. "I've got burn gel in the kit. We'll bandage that hole up. Looks like you didn't hit anything important."

"I got lucky."

"That's the attitude."

Nicole gave him a smile.

Brandy pulled the first aid kit out of the backpack and then sat all the way down. Immediately, she gasped at a sharp pain at the base of her back and rose to her knees again.

"You okay?" Nicole asked.

"Yeah... Hurts to sit down."

"Probably banged yourself up when you landed on that platform," Albert reasoned.

"Probably." Brandy turned around. "Am I bruised?"

"I think so," replied Nicole. "Can't really tell how much yet. Your whole back and butt is red."

"I'll bet you'll be bruised tomorrow," predicted Albert. He could already see where there would be coloration on her buttocks and shoulder blades. Those areas were already darkening from the impact.

"Does it really look that bad?"

"They're just bruises," Albert replied. "They'll heal." He looked down at his right arm and saw that his own bruises had spread up to the shoulder and halfway to the elbow. How much of his arm would turn black, he wondered, before this journey was over?

"I'm still not sure how you even survived," added Nicole. She remembered looking down from the tower steps at that very moment.

Every detail remained perfectly clear in her mind. The monster simply lifted her into the air and tossed her out into the darkness. It did it without effort, as if she were nothing more than a child's doll. Horrified, she'd watched as her best friend sailed briefly through the air, turning end-over-end before she was swallowed by the shadows. Her voice wavered a little as she said, "I thought you were gone for a while there."

Brandy gingerly felt at the knot that had grown on the back of her head. It felt huge. "I thought I was, too."

Albert stared at her naked back, recalling the way she looked when he found her atop that platform. She was lying on her back, unconscious, her feet hanging off the edge, just inches above those ravenous hounds. "You must've landed on your butt," he realized, staring at her flushed bottom. "That's probably what saved your life."

Brandy looked over her shoulder at him and frowned. She didn't care for the idea that the only reason she was alive was that she happened to land on her ass instead of her head.

"You probably broke your tailbone," suggested Nicole.

"My uncle broke his tailbone falling out of a hammock," shared Andrea. "My dad still makes fun of him for breaking his butt."

"I heard once that a lot of people walk around with broken tailbones and don't even know it," added Olivia. "I don't think it's anything to worry about. But I'm sure it still hurts."

Brandy nodded. Indeed it did.

Albert studied the marks on his girlfriend's back. If she was bent over in the darkness, struggling to bring herself upright, he considered, she might have struck that platform bottom first and uncurled with the force of the impact. Her back and shoulders would have hit next and her head last, which matched the places where her skin was showing the most bruising. If that was the case, then her body likely would have absorbed most of the impact before her head so that she was knocked unconscious but not killed.

He couldn't be sure that this was what happened, of course, but it made him feel better to analyze it. He preferred the idea that, in her moment of mortal peril, Brandy was saved by her instincts rather than by dumb luck. He couldn't bear the idea that she only remained at his side by an unlikely roll of fate's dice. As it was, she was still incredibly lucky. A million other people would have died from a fall like that, their necks broken or their brains dashed across the cold stone. Just thinking of how fortunate he was to still have her was enough to make him feel sick.

Brandy felt along the bottom of her spine, wincing. "It *is* really tender there…"

"Thank God that's *all* you broke," said Nicole. "You scared the shit out of me."

"I know," agreed Albert. "I thought my heart had stopped dead in my chest."

Brandy lowered herself gently onto the ground again, this time with her legs folded carefully beneath her. "Sorry."

"Not your fault," Nicole assured her. "We blame the Caggo."

"And he didn't end well for it," promised Albert.

"What happened to it?" Andrea asked. She recalled Wayne saying something about feeding the beast to the hounds.

"It was the dumbest thing," recalled Albert. "It tossed me off the tower base, just like it did Brandy. I broke my arm and couldn't get out. That should've been it for me. But the stupid thing jumped in after me." He shook his head. He still couldn't believe his luck. "I guess it got between me and the hounds. They tore it to pieces right in front of me." He could still recall the way the Caggo's blood sprayed everywhere. In fact, glancing down at his arms and chest, he realized that he was still spotted with it.

"That's crazy," marveled Andrea.

"It was," Albert agreed. "It was also terrifying. If Wayne hadn't yanked me out of there at the last second, they would've killed me, too."

Brandy felt her stomach tighten into a knot at the thought of how close she had come to losing him.

Nicole shuddered at the realization of how lucky they *both* were. How close had she come to losing them? They were her best friends. How could she have possibly gone on if they had both died?

Pushing the thoughts from her mind, Brandy opened the first aid kit and began examining its contents. "You bought a big kit, didn't you?"

Albert shrugged. "Wanted to be prepared."

"Good thing," said Nicole. "We're obviously a clumsy bunch." One of those little travel kits that fit in your glove box just wouldn't have cut it.

"What are we supposed to do next?" asked Olivia."

"Good question," replied Albert. "Follow the path, I guess. See where it takes us."

"The Sentinel Queen's doorway?" wondered Andrea.

"It's a fair assumption," reasoned Albert. "Somewhere on this mountain, I guess."

Nicole groaned. "I don't want to. I'm exhausted."

Everyone was.

Brandy checked her watch and saw that it was already lunch time. "I'm *starving*."

"Me too," said Nicole.

Olivia was hungry, too, but she didn't want to say so. It hadn't slipped her attention that she was by far the chubbiest person here. The last thing she wanted was to be the fat girl whining for food.

She hated that they had to be naked. Why? What was the reason? Was it just to torture them? Was *everything* just to torture them?

"I'm mostly thirsty," said Andrea. "Do you think the water's safe to drink?"

"I have no idea," replied Albert as he took some cleaning wipes from the first aid kit. He didn't think *he'd* want to drink the water here. Who knew what might be in it?

"The water is safe."

All five of them turned at the sound of this new voice to find the Keeper standing with them, half-concealed in the shadows with its back to the rocks, as if it'd been there all along and they simply hadn't noticed.

Olivia let out a startled scream and leapt to her feet, covering herself as if embarrassed to be caught naked out here. Andrea sprang to her feet as well, ready to run, although she somehow managed not to scream. Though they had both listened to Albert's description of the strange little creature back inside the labyrinth, neither of them had actually seen the Keeper with her own eyes until now. There was simply no way to prepare for a sight as strange as this. Even Albert, Brandy and Nicole, who had already once weathered the shock of its creepy appearance, were startled to their feet by the abruptness of this unexpected visit.

Clearly, the Keeper wasn't one to call first.

"How did you get here?" Albert asked the little creature. He didn't think it was possible to go back the way they came, and he thought that was the only way out of the labyrinth.

Like before, its voice was clear, but broken and hoarse. Even its vocal cords did not seem to be human. "I didn't."

This reply caught Albert off guard. It didn't make sense. "What?"

Also like before, its head began to rotate, its chin circling toward the black sky, the crown of its head toward the ground. "It's unimportant."

"Of course it is." Brandy and Nicole crowded behind him, peering over his shoulders. Nearby, Olivia and Andrea stood side-by-side as well, ready to bolt should the unusual creature with the oversized skin and the strange little head that tilted on the wrong axis suddenly decide to bare vicious fangs and charge at them. All four remained silent, leaving Albert to address the Keeper alone.

"*Why* are you here, then?"

"I'm here to ensure that you finish your journey."

Albert cocked his head, confused. "Oh. Okay. Well, we didn't exactly think we had a choice in the matter at this point."

"I had no doubt you would keep going," the Keeper clarified. "What I remain unsure of is whether you can survive to reach the top."

"So we don't exactly have your full confidence, then. How reassuring."

Brandy gripped his arm. Albert sounded angry and she was afraid for him. They still had no idea what this "Keeper" was or what its intentions might be. But at the same time, he deserved to be angry. This was all so frustrating.

"The path ahead is treacherous," explained the Keeper. It now wore its face sideways. Its left ear was aimed at the ground. The loose flesh protruding from its jowls and forehead distorted grotesquely as it slid across its features, heeding the pull of gravity. The shriveled mass of dark flesh dangling from its chin jiggled with each word it spoke. "You will be tested."

"Why?" asked Albert. "Why are we here? What's the purpose?"

"The purpose is simply to reach the doorway at the top of the mountain."

"Is that all?"

"You are the final pieces in an ancient design," the Keeper explained. "Long ago, long before mankind ever set foot in your world, a race of creatures you now call 'the sentinels' passed judgment on all mankind. But they, Those Without Faces, did not *share* their judgment."

"What kind of judgment?" Albert demanded. "Who were the sentinels?"

Now the Keeper's face was upside-down, the flesh of its forehead hanging toward the ground, its black eyes staring at him. That hideous mass of wrinkled flesh lay against its left cheek. "The Faceless Ones were the last guardians of man."

"'Last guardians of man...'" repeated Albert. "What does that even mean?"

"The sentinels were the architects who made possible the survival of humanity beyond the expiration of their original world. They built the gateways and orchestrated the exoduses that allowed you all to be here today."

"We really came from another world?" asked Andrea.

"Humans have made *several* worlds their own over the ages. You have no idea how ancient your species is."

This was a lot to take in. Albert struggled to understand it all. Other worlds. Ancient races. Mysterious judgments. "So... We've outlived whole worlds?"

The little creature's head began rotating again, returning to its upright position. "That's correct."

"And the sentinels were the ones who moved us to new worlds each time ours died?"

"They were also the ones who decided if mankind should be *allowed* to survive."

Albert considered this. It was all starting to fall into place. A little. "Okay. So... Those fourteen women the Sentinel Queen told us about... They were sent through this temple from our last world?"

"Yes."

Emboldened by the fact that the creature did not seem to want to drink their blood, Andrea took a tentative step toward it, trying to see it better. It was the strangest thing she'd ever laid eyes on.

Startled, Olivia seized her by the arm and pulled her back.

"The *sentinels* sent those women here," said Albert.

"This was the doorway to the new world during the last exodus," confirmed the Keeper. "And also the next."

"The next?"

"This very mountain, this *temple*, that facilitated the journey of the mothers into the new world, is also the key that will ultimately open the way to the *next* world. Unless the judgment of the faceless ones deemed your race unworthy."

Albert stood silently, considering this. Salvation or doom, all depending on the whims of a race of long dead, faceless freaks. It wasn't entirely surprising. After all, he'd heard this argument already tonight. "The Sentinel Queen and that old man—"

"Yes," interrupted the Keeper. "The Mother and the Ancient One. They both had their roles to play in bringing you here. But it's not they who must decide. It's you."

It made sense now. The Sentinel Queen believed that humanity's only chance at salvation was the opening of the doorway. The old man, the one she claimed was the devil, believed opening the doorway would only bring doom. This was what they were talking about, this *judgment of the sentinels*. "So what are we supposed to do, exactly?"

The Keeper's face returned to its upright position and then continued rotating, its chin swiveling toward the sky in the opposite direction this time. "You are here to finish what the sentinels began. They passed their judgment on you long before you were ever born. Now you must pass your judgment on them long after they've died. You must decide for yourselves to open the door that awaits you atop this Temple of the Blind."

"And if we decide wrong?" Albert asked.

"Even I don't know that," the Keeper replied. "Many people have tried to walk the road that you've taken to get here, people from all over the world. At first they were following the stories handed down to them throughout history, from the mouths of the mothers themselves. Later, when the truth had faded into myth and was eventually forgotten altogether, only those with the old gifts were able to feel the pull of the doorway, people like Wendell Gilbert and Beverly Bridger." The creature's head was upside-down again. Its stare was dull, but piercing. "Many have come over the ages. And all of them have died. Until now."

Albert remembered the bones in the round room with the battered sentinels, the scattered remains of those who did not have the box to guide them.

"You are here…" the Keeper lifted one skinny hand and pointed up at the burning peak of the temple, its loose flesh dangling like the sleeves of an oversized shirt, "…to go there. Your entire world is balancing on the razor's edge of the actions you've taken and will take on this journey."

"No pressure…" grumbled Nicole.

"Your world could end today," said the Keeper, "or it could live on for thousands more years. But it *will* end. Humanity may die with it. Or it may live beyond it. It depends entirely upon the judgment the sentinels passed upon you. And it depends upon the judgment you will pass upon them."

"I don't understand," said Olivia.

"It doesn't matter." The Keeper turned its head ninety degrees and held it there, its ears pointing up and down. "You don't have to understand. You only have to choose."

Albert wanted to know more. He wanted the Keeper to explain these things that it had said to them, but it vanished before their eyes, withdrawing into the very rock behind it, as though sucked back into the darkness from which it came.

"Where did it go?" Andrea asked.

"I'm not the only one who found that whole thing weird, am I?" asked Olivia.

"What about that was weird?" quipped Nicole. "The freaky little Muppet thing just told us we have to choose the fate of the world."

"That's really messed up," said Andrea. She walked over to where the Keeper had been standing, trying to figure out how it had come and gone.

Albert looked around at his four lovely companions and sighed. "Well, everybody, Brandy might have a broken tailbone, Nicole's got a hole in her hand and I've got a broken arm. Who's up for some mountain climbing?"

Chapter 3

"We'll have to restock the first aid kit," Albert realized. "Maybe add extra aspirin and gauze."

"Here's a better idea," said Brandy as she applied a new bandage over the freshly cleaned bite mark on Olivia's shoulder. "Let's just stop trying to get ourselves killed in crazy adventures after this."

Albert chuckled a little and watched as Nicole finished fashioning a makeshift sling from a roll of gauze to hold his arm. She'd already bandaged the gash and secured his upper arm snuggly to his side.

"That should keep it from moving around too much."

"Thanks."

She met his eyes and gave him a tired smile. "You're welcome. But no more trying to get yourself killed."

"I'll do my best," he promised. But he wasn't sure what choice he would have in the end. None of them had asked to be hurt. Wayne didn't ask to die.

"You're all done, too," said Brandy to Olivia. As far as zombie bites went, the wound hadn't looked too bad, she didn't think. But the sight of it was nonetheless horrifying. It was a harsh reminder of the dangers that lurked out here in this awful place. Death here would be violent and agonizing if it found them.

"Sorry I couldn't be more helpful," said Albert. He'd managed to clean the hole in Nicole's hand and treat her burns, but with only one hand to work with—and his left hand, at that—he'd needed Andrea to wrap the injury.

Brandy kissed him on the cheek. "That's okay. You *really* didn't need to help bandage up the pretty naked girls."

Albert laughed. It wasn't even a thought that had crossed his mind. The pain from his arm had pretty much obliterated his libido, which was a good thing, considering he had suddenly and inexplicably found himself alone with four very attractive and very *naked* young women. "But it's *my* first aid kit," he joked.

"Not going to happen."

Nicole grinned. "I don't know. We don't know if we're ever going to get home from here and he's the only man we've got. If we get stranded, he's public property."

Brandy gave her an amused "how dare you?" look.

"Community boy toy," considered Andrea as she seated herself at the water's edge. "Nice."

"No way!" giggled Brandy. "He's *my* boyfriend! You bitches just back off!"

Nicole laughed. "I say we let Albert decide."

Grinning, Albert said, "I definitely think we should just see how this plays out."

Brandy tried to glare at him, but she couldn't quite keep a straight face. "If you weren't lame, I'd smack you."

"If I weren't lame, I'd let you."

Brandy kissed him.

Andrea turned away and peered into the shadowy water. She had only been joking, of course, but she found her thoughts lingering on the absurd idea of sharing Brandy's boyfriend. More specifically, she found her thoughts drawn to the singular idea of *having* him.

She even felt a twinge of jealousy at the sight of the two of them kissing.

Inevitably, she recalled those obscene statues in the sex room. Why did she look at them? Wayne warned her not to peek. He told her what might happen. But she didn't believe him. She didn't think it could really happen to her.

It felt so strange. Something seemed to be churning within her, filling her with unwanted heat. She told herself she did not want Albert Cross, but she was deceiving herself. For some reason, she felt drawn to him. She *desired* him.

She forced the unwanted thoughts away and concentrated on her thirst, instead. She was parched. And the water was cold. She dipped her hands beneath the surface and lifted it to her lips.

"How's the water," Olivia asked.

Andrea jumped a little and blushed, embarrassed, half-certain that everyone could see her shameful thoughts painted clearly across her face.

Fortunately, the water made for a decent distraction. She frowned down at the rippling surface, curious. "Tastes funny."

"Funny how?"

"I don't know, exactly."

Olivia knelt beside her and tasted the water. "Hmm."

Andrea took another sip, too. "Tastes funny, right?"

"It does. It's bitter…or something…"

Nicole appeared beside them and also tasted it. It *was* kind of bitter. It wasn't a good taste at all. "It's sort of… I don't know. *Mediciny.*"

"Minerals in the water?" Albert wondered. The tap water in Briar Hills had sulfur in it. It was exceptionally bad for some reason at the university dorms. He'd been unable to drink from the sink in his room when he lived in Lumey Hall unless it was ice cold, and even then it wasn't particularly good. His roommate, Derek, couldn't stand it. He kept soda and a pitcher of Kool-Aid in the little refrigerator they'd rented from the university. Albert didn't mind Kool-Aid, but it always made everything in the refrigerator taste fruity.

That was last year. Luckily, the water in the apartment he and Brandy shared now tasted much better.

"It's certainly not fluoride," Olivia remarked.

Nicole braved another drink so that she could swallow the aspirin Albert gave her. It didn't get any better a second time.

Brandy helped Albert to his feet and they joined the others at the water's edge.

Albert found the water at least as awful as the water on campus. He had to resist the urge to spit it back out. But it certainly wasn't sulfur. He wasn't sure what it was.

Brandy, on the other hand, did not resist the urge to spit. Repeatedly. Her face twisting into an expression of utter revulsion, she fought back a gag and groaned. "I know that taste…" It was extremely diluted, almost unrecognizably so, but there was no way she could forget that awful taste. "It's those...whatever they are. Those *squid* things."

"Oh gross!" squealed Nicole. She stood up and stepped away, as if afraid to be too close to it."

"This must flow straight from those reservoirs inside," Albert realized. Had all the water inside the temple tasted like this, he wondered. He didn't notice it when they were swimming, but then again, he hadn't been trying to drink it at the time. And it wasn't as strong as the chlorine in your average swimming pool. He wouldn't have necessarily noticed it.

Half-gagging, Brandy stood up and turned away. Those things had been swimming in that water. They'd squirted their filthy, foul-tasting excretions in there. And she'd put it in her mouth...

"That's just nasty," Andrea decided.

"What the *fuck*?" growled Brandy. "That little bastard let us *drink* that shit?"

"Well," said Albert, standing up, "He did, technically, only tell us it was safe to drink. He didn't say it was *clean*."

Brandy didn't care. It was disgusting. She swore again, her language growing even harsher, spouting several crude and rather creative remarks about the Keeper's stature and appearance.

Albert smiled and remained quiet. He didn't often see her get this angry this fast. It wasn't the water, he knew. She was angry about everything. She was angry about being trapped out here, about being afraid for so long. She was angry about Wayne and Beverly and those poor kids in Gilbert House. She was tired and hungry and thirsty. She wanted a cigarette and a shower. She wanted to go home. The water was nothing more than the final straw. She had no choice but to get angry or else she would probably break down and cry.

He let her vent her frustrations and gazed out over the water. Again, he wondered if all the water they'd encountered in the temple tasted like that. The Sentinel Queen told them it had a special quality that helped keep the hounds at bay. Could it be that whatever made that stuff so nasty also masked their scent? It didn't necessarily explain why they couldn't keep their clothes, since the clothes would have been drenched in the water, too, but it might explain why the hounds weren't drawn to them as soon as they wandered into their territory.

Perhaps the stuff was a natural repellent for the hounds, reason enough to include the spider-squid monstrosities in the temple's bizarre design.

Andrea stared into the water. It hadn't seemed all that bad. It was just a funny taste. She'd drunk from water fountains that tasted worse. But now that she knew what was in it, she didn't think she was quite thirsty enough to help herself to more.

Hopefully, they'd find cleaner water higher up the mountain.

She stood up and glanced timidly at Brandy, who looked as if she wanted very badly to hit something. Her eyes then drifted to Albert, who was surveying the rocks behind them and the path that led forward. Her eyes washed over his naked body and she forced herself to look away.

But something caught her attention and she looked again.

For just an instant there…

It was only her imagination. She was tired. That was all. But for just a second, she thought there had been someone else there with them, someone standing behind Albert, back in the shadows from which they'd come.

But there was no one there now. It was only the five of them. And no one else seemed to have noticed anything out of the ordinary.

Was it any wonder that she would imagine such a thing? After the startling appearance of that strange "Keeper" creature, of course she was going to be paranoid.

Still, she felt the hairs on the back of her neck stand up.

Albert walked along the path a short distance, just past the rocks that had been blocking his view of the landscape surrounding the temple. There was more water over here, more than enough to qualify as a lake. It was mostly still where the water met the land a few feet in front of him, but farther out, the surface was churning. There appeared to be a fairly strong current out there, breaking into long ribbons of dancing eddies wherever a large stone broke the surface.

There were also tall, chimney-like structures rising from the water and reaching high into the air. Each one of these spouted tall flames that illuminated the entire lake and an enormous, stone wall on the far side that looked like it might have been at least a thousand feet high.

At the very top of this wall, he could see the shadowy, skeletal shapes of dark, leafless trees.

The Wood.

Out there somewhere, Gilbert House stood silently, its dark hallways stained with blood.

Were there still zombies prowling the dormitory's yard? Or had the corpse monster Wayne described chased them all away.

It made no difference. Either way, the forest would be crawling with them. Wayne had described seeing dozens of them in his search for Olivia, very few of them the slow, shambling variety of old Hollywood movies. Many of them were quick and lithe in spite of their mummified and often broken forms.

And if a few flashlights could draw so many of them to Gilbert House, then how many would already be making their way to this enormous, burning mountain?

The very thought gave him a hard shiver.

Olivia appeared beside him and gazed up at the far wall. "Figures I'd end up back here again."

Albert looked at her. She was very pretty. Beautiful, in fact. Even with her hair a mess and her face dirty, she was a stunning young woman. But although she stood naked and uncovered before his eyes, it wasn't her sexuality that captured his attention. His eyes swam only over her pretty face. Her expression was incredibly haunting. She was clearly terrified. And she was very sad, of course. Although tears welled in her eyes, she held herself together with stony dignity. Looking back up at those distant trees, he said, "He's not here to rescue you this time."

"I know."

"You've got the four of us instead."

Olivia smiled. That was true. And she was truly grateful for their company. If she'd found herself alone beneath this black sky again, she was fairly sure she would have finally lost her mind.

Brandy appeared at Albert's side, apparently through with her tantrum about the Keeper and the dirty water, and gazed silently up at the distant wall with them.

It was difficult. Albert wanted to tell them all that it would be okay, that they could do this, but how could he make a promise like that? Two people had already died on this insane journey. He couldn't stop thinking of Wayne lying on the ground with that awful hole in his belly and Beverly in that gruesome pit, her blood pooling around her. Would they all end up like that? Dead and abandoned, alone forever in this unnatural darkness?

"Do you think that Keeper guy will watch over us?" Andrea asked as she stepped up behind them.

"I don't know," Albert confessed. He still had no idea what the Keeper's role in all this was.

"Or the Sentinel Queen? She didn't seem so bad. I didn't think."

Olivia turned her head and looked at Albert. He met her gaze. She knew. He could see it in her eyes. "She's dead, isn't she?" she asked.

Albert nodded. "She died before you guys caught up to us."

This surprised Andrea. "The Sentinel Queen? She's gone? But we just saw her."

Nicole was returning the first aid kit to Albert's backpack. Now she stopped and stared at them.

"She was already dying," Olivia said. "Her son…"

Albert recalled clearly the moment it happened. He didn't know what it was at the time. It was just a sudden and very profound feeling of loneliness, as if something that had been there the whole time was now gone.

And that was precisely what had happened. One moment she was there and the next…

"I remember," Brandy said. "I felt it too. We were suddenly alone."

"Her son was dying when we were there," Olivia recalled. "I saw him lying there. He must have died. And she must have died almost as soon as he was gone."

Albert felt a slight shiver as he remembered how the City of the

Blind had felt like an enormous tomb. Now that was precisely what it was.

Again, they all fell silent.

That far wall loomed over them. The trees looked so small up there.

"Will we ever be done?" Olivia wondered.

One way or another, was the answer that came to Albert's mind. Aloud, he merely said, "Eventually."

"How do you think it'll end?"

Albert and Brandy both looked at her. That was the question, after all. Would they ever make it home, back to their own lives? Or would they each fall like poor Wayne, one-by-one until none of them remained?

How would it all end?

"Well," decided Albert. "It'll end *well*."

Olivia met his gaze again. Her eyes remained as haunting as they were lovely. "I guess we'll see."

Chapter 4

Albert found that distant wall troubling. It appeared to encircle the temple, so that the mountain was standing in an enormous hole in the ground and he was at the very bottom, feeling very small.

Even after he turned away and focused his attention toward the path ahead, his eyes kept returning to those trees. They were so high up...

The Temple of the Blind had been one nightmare after another. Whatever lay waiting between them and the flaming summit was not likely to be any less terrifying. And his imagination, apparently growing more morbid with each horror he witnessed, was happy to feed him one gruesome suggestion after another about what might happen to them in this place. Perhaps the water would begin to rise, threatening to drown them if they weren't quick enough. Or maybe the mountain itself would crumble down upon them, burying them alive in burning rubble. Or perhaps they would simply be set upon by more blood-thirsty monsters.

He had to focus. There would be plenty of *real* horrors to think about soon enough, he was sure. And with his body broken, he couldn't afford to rely on his physical strength if and when things turned nasty. He needed to be able to think clearly.

He surveyed the path before him, studying it. It did not lead straight to the mountain, mercifully hastening their ascent. Instead, it followed a narrow strip of rocky land that separated the two bodies of water. The smaller pool stood between them and the massive temple on the left. The much larger bulk of the lake took up all the space between them and the looming wall on the right.

The advantage of this place was that he could see everything. Fire illuminated almost every surface of these temple grounds, lighting it up like a bustling city. The flashlights had therefore been returned to the backpack, within easy reach in case the flames suddenly burned out, leaving them stranded once more in the dark. At the very least, it would conserve the batteries until they needed them again.

Nicole now carried the backpack. Albert was no longer in any condition to wear it. And neither of them wanted Brandy to have to carry it on her bruised back (though she'd insisted that she was perfectly fine). It was the logical way to proceed, but he didn't like that he needed someone to carry his backpack for him. He didn't like that he needed *anything*. This was no place to be weak. He needed to be strong for these girls. How could he keep them safe if he wasn't strong? How could he keep them all from ending up like Wayne and Beverly if he couldn't even carry his own backpack?

But this was the way it was. Circumstances demanded flexibility.

He walked ahead of the girls, watching for anything that might prove dangerous. In particular, he kept his eyes on the water that crowded both sides of the narrow path. Unable to see what might be swimming below the surface, he half-expected something awful to lunge out at them. It wasn't even an illogical concern. If there were razor-armored hounds prowling the temple's corridors and a murderous monster guarding the labyrinth's exit, why wouldn't there be a ravenous sea monster lurking in the lake outside?

Behind him, the others followed close together, each of them anxious about what surprises must await them in this new place. Like Albert, Brandy kept her eyes on the water. She was nearly convinced that another hirsute cephalopod was lurking nearby, just waiting for the opportunity to squirt its nasty excretions in her face again.

She *really* hated those things.

Olivia was less concerned with the mysteries of the deep than with the known horrors of the forest that surrounded them. She kept scanning the top of the wall, watching for the zombies that would no doubt soon begin to swarm the ledge of that enormous wall.

And then there was the corpse monster... Nothing as insignificant as a thousand-foot wall would keep that thing from finishing what it started at Gilbert House. If it came, and she was sure it eventually would, would they stand any kind of chance?

Andrea, on the other hand, found herself looking back more than anywhere else. She couldn't convince herself that they were alone out here. She blamed the Keeper and his abrupt appearance. If it could pop up out of nowhere without warning, what else might be able to do the same? She kept expecting to look back and find that something awful had appeared from thin air and was charging after them.

Eager to break the uncomfortable silence that had fallen among them, Nicole glanced over at Olivia and asked, "Where do you get your nails done?"

Olivia looked down at her hands, distracted, and frowned at the one that broke when she was snatched into the Wood. "I usually go to a place back home. In Wilsing." Wilsing was about twenty-five miles north of Briar Hills. It was a small town, without so much as a Wal-Mart. It was almost entirely comprised of small, local businesses. Nicole had only ever been there when her parents dragged her to its antique malls, which Wilsing had in abundance for some reason. "But these came from the place at the mall. They're pretty good."

"I had mine done there for senior prom," Nicole recalled. "But the people there weren't very nice. I never went back."

"They were really nice to me," said Olivia, looking at her once beautiful nails. She'd scratched up the remaining nine crawling across the ground and clamoring over those fallen trees. Thinking about it now, it was surprising she'd only broken the one. "I'd go back again."

"Maybe I'll go with you next time you go." Nicole looked at her own nails, uneven and long overdue for a new coat of polish. She never obsessed over her nails. Sometimes she let herself become preoccupied with her hair and makeup. Also her clothes. And she *frequently* fretted about her weight. But never her nails for some reason. Suddenly, however, the idea of treating herself to a pretty set of French tips sounded like the most luxurious thing in the world.

After she ate, of course.

And showered.

And slept until noon.

Olivia smiled. "You're welcome to. I'm going to need a new set after this. It'll drive me nuts until I get them fixed."

"We'll call it our little reward for surviving this mess."

"That sounds good."

Nicole smiled. It *did* sound good. It sounded *wonderful*. But first they had a long, hard climb ahead of them. And who knew how many of them would actually reach the top?

Again, the silence came. Olivia didn't care for it. In the silence, she could only seem to think about Wayne. She looked at Nicole, searching for something else to talk about, and noticed the faint tan lines on her skin, the outline of a small bikini that no doubt had looked incredible on a body like hers. "Do you go somewhere to tan?" she asked.

Nicole shook her head. "I used to, for a while, but not anymore. I just sunbathe by the pool in the summer."

"Oh. I haven't been since I left Wilsing. I was hoping you knew of somewhere good in Briar Hills."

"Nope. Sorry. I might have some friends who would know a good place, though." Nicole looked at her, noticed the tone of her skin. "You don't have any tan lines."

Olivia shrugged, blushing a little. "I go naked."

It was odd. Olivia had been naked for hours now, right in front of him, but for some reason, the thought of her lying nude in a tanning bed was very distracting to Albert. A familiar twinge snaked through his gut and he suddenly found himself gazing up at those high, distant trees again, now quite content to imagine all the horrible things that must be prowling those strange woods.

"I never had the guts to take my suit off," admitted Nicole.

"That's how my sister does it and she took me my first time. I figure why not? I pay the same no matter how much of me gets tanned."

"That's true," Nicole agreed.

"I should do that," said Brandy. "Albert would probably like it."

Nicole laughed. "Ever since the two of you got caught in that sex room, you drive each other crazy *anyway*! You're going to kill the poor boy, you nympho!"

Brandy giggled.

Albert found it hard to worry about what was lurking in the forest with thoughts of his girlfriend sunning herself naked running through his head. She was right. He *would* like that. But he liked pretty much anything that had to do with her being naked.

Maybe the adrenaline was beginning to wear off. The pain no longer seemed to hold back these thoughts. He suddenly wanted to be alone with Brandy again. He had to get his mind off these things before something embarrassing happened.

Andrea glanced back again. She kept thinking she heard something. Was it just the wind? The echoes of their voices off that wall? The flames whooshing out from the cracks in the stone?

Chill out, she thought to herself. *Don't be stupid.*

"Maybe we can all go sometime," Olivia suggested. "When we get back. We could make a day of it." It seemed like such an impossible dream, talking about a girls' day out when they could all soon be as dead as poor Wayne, but it made her feel good to think of such things.

Brandy smiled back at her. "Yeah. That would be fun." It was good to have a plan for when they made it home. The last thing she wanted was for any of them to give up.

"What you should get," Nicole told Brandy, "is one of those." She pointed at Andrea's belly and the shiny, silver ring in her navel. "I *know* that'll drive Albert nuts."

Embarrassed, Andrea fingered the ring nervously and resisted the urge to cover herself. She always liked it when people noticed her jewelry, but she'd never before been naked at the time. She wondered vaguely what Albert thought about her piercings. Did he like them? Did he like *her*?

No. Why would she think such things?

The sex room. She never should have peeked. She chewed her lower lip and hoped she wasn't blushing enough for everyone to see.

"I've thought about it," Brandy admitted.

"You should," Nicole said. "I'd go with you."

Albert tried for a moment to imagine Brandy with a belly button ring, and then quickly pushed it from his thoughts. That *would* drive him crazy.

"I want to get my tongue done," Andrea said.

"Oh! Don't do that!" Olivia gasped. "Those freak me out!"

"I kind of like them," Nicole said, "but they look like they'd hurt."

Andrea shrugged.

Nicole looked at Brandy and grinned. "I dare you to get a *naughty* piercing."

Albert stared intensely up into those trees and tried really hard to imagine what a cross between a hound and a Caggo might look like.

"No," said Brandy bluntly.

Nicole laughed.

"I want a tattoo," Andrea announced.

"I don't think I would," said Olivia. "I'm a wimp."

"No," corrected Brandy, "you're the one who survived two days in Gilbert House and a zombie horde. I think that officially excludes you from wimp status for the rest of your life."

"Okay, but I still don't think I'd like to sit there and let someone needle a tattoo into my skin."

"Fair enough."

"I wouldn't mind getting one," said Nicole. "I just don't know what I'd want."

"You'd so get a tramp stamp," said Brandy.

Nicole laughed. "I probably would."

"I wouldn't mind getting something small," decided Brandy. "Somewhere out of sight."

Albert really wished they'd start talking about something else. He'd never really considered what Brandy would look like with a cute little tattoo. Now he was going to have a hard time getting it out of his head.

The pain in his arm had numbed. The combination of the aspirin and the bandages that kept it from moving around had helped. Now, he was less in pain than he was tired. It was so easy to let his mind wander as he walked. And it apparently wanted to wander right through every gutter it could find.

Andrea stopped and looked back the way they came. "Hey guys…?"

"What's wrong?" asked Nicole.

"I…" She shook her head. "I don't know. I keep thinking I'm hearing something. And just now I thought I saw something."

"In the water?" asked Brandy.

All of them were looking around now, searching for any sign of something out of place. The water's surface didn't appear to have been disturbed.

"No. On the path."

"The Keeper again?" suggested Olivia.

"Possible," agreed Albert.

"I don't know." Andrea searched the area, but there was nothing there. Everything was still and silent. "I'm probably just jumpy."

"Probably," said Nicole. "It's not like we don't have reason to be."

That was true. After all they'd been through, it'd be unnatural to not be at least a little paranoid.

Albert continued forward. Brandy, Nicole and Olivia followed. Andrea lingered only another moment and then turned and hurried after them.

Chapter 5

The narrow stretch of dry land on which the path was laid was nothing like the smooth, perfect surfaces inside the temple. The ground was rough and uneven beneath their tired feet. It rose and fell with the geography. Sometimes they were several feet above the waterline; sometimes they were almost even with it. And sometimes it grew too narrow for any of them to pass side-by-side, forcing them to proceed single file.

When they reached a long peninsula of land that jutted out from the mountain, the path did not turn and carry them closer to the temple, as Albert hoped. Instead, it led them through a gap between the tall, jagged rocks and back out over the water again. They seemed to be doing little more than circling the temple. And he doubted very much that they would find anything as convenient as a ski lift waiting for them on the far side.

He kept his eyes open for any sign of danger, convinced that something must be lurking out here, just waiting to strike, but they so far seemed to be alone. It was perfectly quiet but for the hissing of the rushing flames through the vents in the stone.

Behind him, Andrea kept glancing back. She was sure she kept hearing something. It sounded like murmuring, but the only voices out here should be their own. They were utterly alone.

Weren't they?

Her eyes swept over the water, across the face of the burning mountain, to the wall and those distant trees. There was nothing stirring, yet the hairs on the back of her neck were standing on end again.

Something was very odd about this place.

Yet no one else seemed to be noticing anything out of the ordinary.

"My feet are killing me," complained Nicole.

"I know," said Brandy. "I think mine are swollen."

Ahead of them was a small island. A tall rock formation jutted upward from one side of it, its highest tip pointed roughly toward the inferno blazing at the temple's apex. It was at least thirty feet tall, yet dwarfed by the size of the mountain. Another jagged hunk of rock stood on the other side of the island, sticking up out of the water at an angle that aimed its narrow end toward the lower half of the wall.

The stone out here was the same as that within the temple, but with the exception of that enormous wall and the flames that appeared to have been intimately threaded through the very landscape to light the way for them, this place looked like something only nature could have created. Even the path on which they walked seemed to be laid across a narrow ridge that rose just above the waterline. If the water were to suddenly drain away, they would no doubt see a complex landscape of hills and valleys rolling down toward the base of the wall. It was a far grander scale than the intricate corridors and chambers within.

The path wove through the tall rocks of the island, under a low ledge and back out over the water, where the uneven ground finally dipped all the way below the surface.

It was only about two inches deep at its worst, and less than ten feet across, but the cold water was an unwelcome discomfort.

Brandy and Nicole both swore bitterly as they made their way across. Andrea merely whimpered. Olivia managed to cross silently, with a respectable amount of grace. Like Albert, she was simply thankful to only have to get her feet wet. At least they didn't have to swim.

Yet.

Once she had reached the other side, Andrea went straight to the nearest flame to warm up.

"Be careful," Brandy pleaded. "Don't get too close to those."

"Don't worry about me," she replied. "My daddy's a fireman. It'd be really embarrassing to catch myself on fire."

"I'll bet it would be," laughed Albert.

Andrea tried to smile, but her teeth were chattering. The water here had a way of chilling right to the bone, even in small quantities. And this particular flame was narrow and focused. Most of its heat went straight up.

"I'll bet you hear a lot of horror stories, don't you?" wagered Nicole as she put her hand toward the flames.

Andrea nodded. "He's seen some pretty bad stuff, yeah."

"Keep them to yourself," said Brandy. "I don't want to know."

"My uncle's a police officer," Nicole recounted. "He sometimes talks about the shit he's seen. It's…" She shuddered. "I usually leave the room when he starts talking about it."

"Some of it's pretty sobering," agreed Andrea. She crossed her arms over her chest. "Daddy *makes* me listen to some of it. Makes sure I know what happens when you drive drunk and stuff."

"Makes sense," reasoned Brandy. "He doesn't want to get called to an accident and find you there."

Andrea looked up at the burning mountain and laughed nervously. "I don't think he'd approve of this place, much, either."

Brandy's eyes swept down her slim, naked figure. "I doubt it."

"I don't think any of our dads would approve of this outing," decided Olivia. She looked down at her exposed breasts and immediately covered them with her hands.

"What does *your* dad do?" asked Andrea.

"Computers," replied Olivia. "I couldn't tell you much more. Something to do with sales, I think. He does a lot of traveling. Most of it kind of goes over my head."

"My parents are both deans at the university," said Nicole.

"Wow," said Olivia. "No pressure there."

"I know, right?"

"My dad's blue collar," volunteered Brandy. "Construction."

Andrea gasped and stood up straight, her lean body abruptly tense, her blue eyes wide.

"What's wrong?" asked Nicole.

Andrea stared at her, then at Olivia. Both looked back at her, bewildered. "You guys seriously didn't hear that?"

Nicole and Olivia looked at each other, but neither had any idea what she was talking about.

"Hear what?" asked Brandy.

"That *voice.*"

"Voice?" Albert stepped up beside her and listened.

"I don't hear any voices," said Olivia.

"Like the one that told you about the blood and the tower?" asked Albert.

"No. That was different. This was a woman's voice, I think. None of you heard it? It sounded like it was right next to me."

"What did it say?"

"I don't know." She looked up at him. "Something weird. Like... 'Bike light' or something..."

"Bike light?" said Nicole. "What does that mean?"

"It probably wasn't 'bike light.' I couldn't understand it."

"Last time you heard a voice," recalled Albert, "the information turned out to be pretty vital."

Andrea considered this. "It wasn't the same voice. I'm sure of it."

"Maybe it was just an echo or something," hoped Brandy. "Nothing to worry about."

Albert nodded. There was no reason to waste time speculating. But he would not forget it. For all he knew, "bike light" might turn out to be the clue that saved their lives when they finally reached the top.

Andrea snapped her head back toward the island.

Olivia followed her gaze. "What?"

"Thought I saw something..."

"What kind of something?" asked Nicole.

"I don't know. Just...something moving back there."

"Following us?" wondered Brandy. Perhaps it was the Keeper again. Or something new.

"I don't know."

"Shadows from the fire," suggested Albert. "They play tricks on you." But he wasn't sure how much of it was really her imagination. This wasn't the park they were strolling through. The Temple of the Blind had shown them more than enough to warrant giving every paranoid thought at least a glimmer of consideration. It wasn't even *unlikely* that these things Andrea was seeing and hearing were real. "Let's keep moving."

Chapter 6

Another island loomed ahead. Again, the path snaked between large, jutting rocks and then carried them out over the water toward a cluster of protruding stones. Here, the path dropped again below the surface, forcing them to trudge through the cold water. It was only a little deeper than it was last time, but much farther. And Albert didn't like that it was too dark to see anything that might have been swimming near their toes.

But again, nothing attacked them.

It was these quiet moments that made him most nervous.

Flames belched from stone chimneys all around them, some barely protruding from the water, others reaching high into the air. Some flames rushed out with the force of a propane torch. Others flickered like great, lazy candles. No two made the same shadow. And as they made their way across the submerged path, the disturbed surface of the water became a chaotic gyration of light and shadow that preyed on their fear and gave unnatural life to every shape they glimpsed from the corners of their eyes.

They couldn't really be alone out here. There must be something lurking somewhere, waiting, watching.

The path rose above the water again and then continued to rise, carrying them along a tall ridge five feet above the water. Ten feet. Fifteen.

It was now that Albert finally discerned a change in the angle of the path. They were moving closer to the temple now, slowly approaching the mountain. At this rate, how long would it take them to climb all the way to the top?

The ridge widened, flattened. The land around them grew rockier. Huge rocks jutted upward on either side of the path. They had to weave around several massive boulders.

And there was something else here, too.

"What's that?" asked Brandy.

It stood behind a pair of large rock formations, backlit by a wide, dancing flame rising from a crack in the side of the mountain. Huge, naked branches stretched out over the water and across the path, a tangled spider's web of light and shadow.

"Night tree..." sighed Olivia.

Albert stared up at the tree as he approached it. It was as large as the full-grown oaks on his grandparents' farm. But it was no oak. Something was wrong about it. It glistened, for one thing. The firelight danced across its surface as if it were covered not in bark, but black, oily flesh. And the branches were strange, too. Some of them were twisted and coiled together, almost as if they were struggling with one another.

"Those trees from the Wood?" asked Brandy. "Aren't those

dangerous?"

"Wayne said he was told not to touch the roots when he was inside that tunnel," Albert recalled.

"And they get a little touchy-feely when they start to wake up," Olivia reminded him.

"That's weird," said Andrea.

It *was* weird. Albert continued to stare up into it. "How does it stay alive? There's no light out here."

"In the beginning, there was light in the Wood," Olivia reminded him, remembering Wayne's story. The old man told him that. He said that it had been a long time ago, longer than any of them could ever imagine, and she had no doubt that this was true. Time itself had no beginning. It never began, and yet always was. And she had a strange idea that this might be one of the first places that ever existed in that maddening eternity. "What do you think this place was like when there was light?"

"I don't know," said Albert. "This is all I've seen of it. This and what little I could see from Gilbert House's second and third floor windows."

"It's a lot of blackness," she told him. "It's just these trees and a lot of dirt and rocks. But I wonder if it was ever green."

"From what I've heard about those trees," Nicole said, "I can't imagine it being any better."

Olivia nodded. What would those trees have been like under a full sun? Would they have been more creature than plant, like writhing masses of coiling snakes, feeling and grasping and snatching at anything that moved? How could anything exist within a forest full of those things? What were they, exactly? Did they even have leaves? Were they carnivorous? Or were they only interested in light? After all, although it had been a little grabby, the tree she and Wayne climbed to get inside Gilbert House had not exactly tried to eat her. It seemed much more interested in the flashlight glowing in the window. Perhaps the trees followed the sun back then, swaying east in the morning, reaching for the rising sun, and then following it across the sky until it set.

She liked this image better. A world full of trees that worshiped the sun, gently swaying as they reached endlessly for that burning, life-giving globe in the sky, perhaps cradling nests of birds in their coiling branches, both living and giving life. In that light they were less monsters than sleeping guardians of a world long since dead.

But somehow, she didn't think that was ever the case.

"For that matter," said Albert as he gazed up into the black sky, "what is it that keeps this world warm? There's no sun, so how does it keep from freezing over? It should be an icy wasteland. We shouldn't be capable of even surviving here."

"Well it's not exactly warm out here," replied Nicole.

"Yeah. But it's a cool constant, like in a cave. What do you think? Maybe sixty degrees? Give or take?"

"Maybe we just can't see the sun," Andrea suggested. "Maybe it's always on the other side of the planet. Or maybe there's something between it and here, another planet or something, blocking it out."

"Maybe," Albert agreed. "Maybe wherever it is, the sun's close enough to keep it warm. Or maybe the atmosphere's thick enough to keep in the heat." He shook his head. "Or maybe it's getting its warmth from somewhere else. Maybe another world. Maybe even ours."

"Who knows," said Brandy. "Does it matter?"

"No," Albert replied. "It really doesn't."

He stepped beneath the tree's branches and stopped. It stood there, towering over him, motionless in the still darkness, the firelight still glimmering across its smooth surface. It did not snatch him up and eat him. Maybe it wasn't hungry.

More likely, it simply wasn't awake yet.

From here, he thought he could see things moving up in the branches. Subtle motion caught his eye. He didn't think there was anything living in the tree. It seemed to be the branches themselves twitching.

"Let's keep going," urged Brandy.

"Yes, please," agreed Olivia. "We don't know what it can do."

Andrea reached out and touched the strange trunk. It was smooth and cool, like flesh. "I don't know, but I'm pretty sure this one isn't trying to kill us."

"I don't care!" snapped Olivia. "Just get away from there before you wake it up."

"*Please!*" added Brandy.

Albert nodded, but he didn't begin moving. He was studying the tree. There was no earth here. The ground was entirely gray stone, yet it appeared to have burst from that stone as easily as from soft soil, lifting and cracking it. How deep did its roots have to run to find nutrients in this place?

He wondered if the tree had grown here naturally or if the sentinels had left it here for them to find. Either way, would there be more along the path as they made their way up? And would they become a real danger as they awoke to the glow of all these flames?

A shrill scream cut through the stillness as Nicole jumped back and swatted at the air in front of her face.

Everyone else turned to look at her, startled, and discovered a long, snaking branch dangling down where she'd been standing a moment before. It was twisting and coiling lazily, snake-like.

"Fucking thing touched me," explained Nicole, embarrassed. She rubbed at her shoulder, where the thing tickled her and gazed warily up, watching for more groping branches.

"Let's go," said Brandy firmly, giving Albert a hard nudge.

Albert turned and walked away. She was right. They needed to keep moving. If there was another one waiting for them up ahead, it would likely be more awake by the time they reached it. The longer they stood here, the more dangerous it would become. Next time, it might do more than just touch someone. It might snatch them screaming up into its murderous branches.

He had only gone a few short yards when he glimpsed the web-like shadows of another night tree growing between a pair of rocky hills at the base of the mountain. The path did not go over there, but it was a sure indication that there would be more trees. Possibly *many* more trees. If they were extremely lucky, they would not be found all the way up the path.

But Albert didn't feel all that lucky.

Chapter 7

As they slowly circled around the temple, a gap appeared in the surrounding wall, hidden until now by the mountain that stood between them and it. Almost as wide as it was tall, this gap appeared to be a channel allowing water to flow out from the lake.

It made sense. They'd already seen that water flowed through the temple, probably as life support for the hounds and the Sentinel Queen's people, as well as the Caggo, those things in the meadow and whatever other horrible creatures lurked unseen in the endless darkness. Therefore, it reasoned that it must flow *from* the temple. It had to come from somewhere and it had to *go* somewhere. Without some sort of outlet, this hole would eventually fill with water. A channel like this would prevent the temple from becoming submerged.

But then where did it empty out? Was there a river over there somewhere that carried the water away? A sea? Or would the water just eventually pour over the edge of the world and into some bottomless oblivion? He found himself remembering those old maps that he'd seen in books, the ones that assumed the world was flat and that the oceans eventually rolled off into hell. *Here there be monsters*, he thought, and shivered hard enough to send streaks of pain down his broken arm.

The flaming pillars reaching out of the water like giant candles had been designed in such a way as to illuminate the lake and the wall, but none of those towering stacks cast their light very far into the channel. Albert could only assume that a wide canyon stretched away from the temple there. He couldn't help but wonder what they might find if they were to sail down those waterways. What secrets must exist in a world like this?

He reminded himself to be careful what he wished for. The Temple of the Blind was wonder and horror enough for one outing.

They crossed another island and made their way around a cluster of tall rocks where the ground grew more uneven and the path dipped below the surface, wetting their feet again before rising into a wide, rocky hill.

Here, the path dispersed across the gentle slope among several fat boulders and Albert had to pause for a moment, uncertain of where he should go. But the flames steered him toward the mountain, past another drowsy night tree and around a small pool of still, dark water where the path narrowed and became more defined again.

He kept looking up at the towering temple. They'd still barely even begun to ascend toward the summit. At the rate they were going, it would take days to get to the top. And yet, if the path grew too steep, requiring them to actually climb, it might prove impossible for him in his condition.

And the path was by no means the only thing that concerned him.

"What was that?" Andrea asked, staring up into the sky.

Immediately, the other girls turned and followed her gaze, but Albert didn't need to look. He'd noticed it a while ago and had been watching it in silence, not wanting to alarm them. A shadow was moving through the air up there, circling the brilliant flame at the mountain's peak. It was difficult to see against the black sky, but it was far too big to be any bird he'd ever seen. And it flew in a strange, sporadic pattern that had none of the grace typical of a bird.

It seemed to be attracted to the fire, like a giant moth, but each time it approached the flames it twisted away, apparently changing course to avoid the intense heat.

"What is it?" asked Brandy.

Albert did not attempt to even speculate. He stared up at the shadow as it glided out over the water and then fluttered back around to circle the flames again, this time at a greater distance. He remembered the hounds, the Caggo, the sinewy thing that shot out of the temple and passed through Wayne's tragically mortal body. He remembered Wayne's story about the Wood, about the unearthly living dead and the thing that seemed to somehow be constructed entirely of their shattered carcasses. The throbbing pain in his arm told him he would not have the strength to face another monster. And now the damned things had taken flight.

"Will it come after us?" Andrea asked.

"Maybe it's more interested in the fire," Albert suggested, though he didn't think he sounded particularly confident.

"Maybe," Nicole agreed. "Those spider-squid things weren't really dangerous. Just disgusting."

"Nasty fucking things…" grumbled Brandy.

"You're not going to let that go, are you?" laughed Nicole.

"Never."

They pushed on, but their eyes kept returning to the black sky. Soon, they realized that there were at least two of them up there. Albert thought he could make out three, but it was difficult to tell for sure. They were black things against a black sky, dancing in random circles in the ever-changing light of the flames.

"Do you think they're like the hounds?" Brandy asked. "Do they have those scale-things all over them?"

The idea of a winged hound was terrifying beyond words. All that lethal viciousness entirely confined to those low tunnels was bad enough, but to have it swooping down out of the very sky…

"I doubt it," Albert replied. "The hounds weren't even able to jump. I can't imagine anything like them being able to fly. I think they'd be too heavy." He looked up at the mysterious gliding shape, saw it circle too close to the flames and then twist away. It was as much wishful thinking as sound logic. Perhaps these things were much more efficiently evolved, their bodies light and lean and every bit as voracious and deadly as their sturdier-built cousins. More likely, he thought, they were something completely new. Perhaps they were some kind of giant bug. Or maybe something more akin to a pterodactyl. Or maybe even a winged gargoyle. Anything was possible, it seemed. There was simply no way to know what horrors might call a place like the Wood home.

He'd begun to wonder how many worlds might be connected to the Wood besides their own. Wayne described several creatures that appeared to have once been very different beings, beings that could never have been human. Were those alien races from other worlds?

The old man Wayne met in that frightful tunnel told him that there were other worlds out there. And both the Sentinel Queen and the Keeper spoke of other worlds from which human beings apparently migrated.

Whatever lies any of them might have told, the empty sky above was proof enough that they had been telling the truth about the existence of at least one other world.

Andrea stopped, startled, and looked back the way they came.

"What?" asked Olivia.

"You guys didn't hear that, either?"

"Hear what?" Albert asked.

"I swear I heard something walking behind us."

"You're paranoid," Nicole assured her, though she knew no such thing.

Andrea didn't respond. She couldn't be imagining all this. Could she?

She wondered if it had something to do with the voice she heard back in the woods by Gilbert House. No one else heard that voice. Maybe this was somehow related.

Or maybe Nicole was right and she was merely on edge.

She tried to find something to justify her concern, but all she could see were shadows cast by the flickering flames.

The others moved on and she followed after them.

The path began to drift closer to the temple and led them across a wide, rocky shelf that protruded from the base of the mountain. From there, it took them up a steep hill and along a narrow ledge that ran between a steep cliff and a sheer, fifteen-foot drop to the water's surface.

Another narrow strip of land jutted outward from the mountain on the other side of this ledge, beyond which the high walls of the mountain met the water. Unable to continue forward, the path turned toward the lake again, leading them away from the temple once more before curving back along another ridge, past several more rock formations, up another steep incline and through a field of massive stones protruding from the ground.

Eventually, they emerged from the cramped rocks to find themselves facing an opening in a tall cliff face.

"More tunnels?" groaned Nicole. "I thought we were going to the top, not back inside."

But this wasn't like the other tunnels they'd encountered. It didn't lead inside. Albert could already see the far end. The entire passage was not as long as a football field. And although it was dark inside, the firelight illuminating both ends was bright enough that he saw no reason to retrieve the flashlights from the backpack.

Inside this passage, like inside the temple, the floor beneath them was smooth and level. Albert dragged his good hand down the wall. It was also smooth to the touch. Now and then he felt a tight seam between the large stones. He wondered how this place had been constructed. These seams indicated that the place was built from individual stones, but the outside looked like a perfect wonder of nature. If the sentinels had built the temple, they had done a magnificent job recreating a natural mountain…but why? What was the point in making it look like a mountain? Why not a castle or a tower? Why not just make a huge block of stone? Or could it be that the mountain *was* natural and they had merely carved the interior from the stone inside? If so, why were the interior surfaces comprised of these blocks? Shouldn't the surfaces all be smooth and utterly featureless?

He didn't understand it.

But then again, perhaps trying to make sense of the actions of an ancient race of faceless beings dedicated to ensuring the conditional survival of the human race was a lost cause from the start.

All five of them emerged from the tunnel without any surprises. They descended a shallow hill, waded across another low area in the path, and climbed another rising ridge that finally curved back toward the temple.

A shadow passed over them, low enough to draw their attention, but still too high to be seen with any clarity. There were at least a dozen of them now, all of them circling and fluttering in that curious, jerky motion.

Each of them gazed up as it swept out over the water, pumping its odd wings, rising high into the sky.

"I wish I knew what they were," said Albert.

"I don't care what they are," retorted Brandy. "I just hope they stay the fuck away from us." Yet her eyes continued to follow the creature as it flew, curious in spite of her trepidation.

Other creatures swept through the sky. Some circled the inferno atop the mountain. Others fluttered toward the flames and then jerked away. A few seemed to find the smaller flames more appealing and darted from one to another like hummingbirds flitting between blossoms in a flower garden.

As they watched, one sailed in from out over the water on outstretched wings, traveling much faster than the others.

It tried at the last second to pull back, shoving its wings forward in a vain attempt to halt its impressive momentum, but it was too late. Its body met the flames and merged with them as it erupted into a writhing fireball and dropped like a stone out of sight.

"Stupid thing, wasn't it?" Nicole said, hardly believing what she'd just seen.

"Not stupid," Albert corrected her. "Ignorant. How long has it been since this world's seen fire? It probably didn't know what it was."

"I don't care," Nicole argued. "It looked stupid to me."

"What about the Caggo?" Olivia asked. "Was it ignorant, too?"

"Nope," Albert replied. "It was stupid."

"It's almost funny," Brandy said. "How long do you suppose it lived down there? It must have avoided the hounds for ages. It *had* to know how to survive. And then we show up and it just jumps right down there with them."

Albert nodded. "It *is* funny. Stupidity is almost a human trait."

"I don't know," Nicole said. "Earl's mom had a dog I'm pretty sure was stupid. God I hated that thing." She realized after she said this that she was speaking of Earl in the past tense and something that was nearly glee rose up from somewhere within her. He was behind her now. Hopefully, that was where he would stay. In the past was where Earl Tannis belonged.

Albert smiled. He'd heard about that dog before. Earl's mom sometimes made him babysit the animal when she had errands to run or appointments to keep. It was apparently incapable of being left at home alone for even a few hours. According to Nicole, it was some psycho poodle from hell.

His eyes drifted across the lake to the wall. They were slowly passing the giant gap where the channel fed out. Was this the front of the tower, then? Or did this place even have such a concept as front and back?

He had no time to consider it. Suddenly, he became aware of a shadow moving across that high ledge.

It looked very small from this distance, but Albert was sure that it was the size of a man.

Scanning the trees now, he realized there were at least three or four of them.

Zombies.

The very idea gave him chills.

He glanced back at the others, saw that they were still watching the things in the sky, and moved on without pointing out these latest visitors. They were so far away. It didn't seem right to frighten them with news of more things they couldn't hope to control.

There were unknown flying creatures in the air and dangerous night trees along the path. Now they were being surrounded by hordes of zombies.

Things just kept getting better.

Chapter 8

Albert knew he wasn't the only one who would be looking for zombies in that tree line, and as he expected, Olivia caught sight of them only a moment later. The realization that they were there stirred an understandable anxiety through the group.

"Do you think they can get over here?" asked Olivia.

"I don't know," confessed Albert. He sure as hell hoped not. He wasn't exactly in zombie-fighting condition. But if they were as she and Wayne described them, he was sure they wouldn't hesitate to throw themselves over that ledge to reach them. And since zombies were already dead and therefore couldn't drown, they'd have all the time in the world to crawl across the bottom of that lake.

He hoped the current he saw was strong enough to sweep the reeking things down the river before they could make it across.

"They're really zombies?" asked Andrea, staring timidly up at those distant shadows. She could think of nothing more terrifying than having to flee from a horde of ravenous, flesh-eating corpses. Suddenly, she regretted every horror movie she'd ever watched.

"That old man told Wayne they weren't," Olivia replied. He'd recounted that the old man was adamant that the walking dead here were neither zombies nor vampires nor any other "Hollywood bullshit," as he put it. "But they looked like zombies to me." They'd made very convincing zombies, in fact, from the perspective of a potential meal.

"What's the difference?" wondered Nicole. "They're walking corpses. Isn't that a zombie?"

"The Sentinel Queen said they weren't infectious," remembered Andrea. "I think that's a prerequisite for a Hollywood zombie."

Albert considered it for a moment. He thought he recalled reading somewhere once that zombies were originally some sort of voodoo creation, or something similar. He couldn't recall exactly, but he thought he remembered a particularly frightening story involving drugging and burying a victim alive in order to inflict a particularly gruesome form of brain damage that turned him into a mindless slave. Or maybe he just saw that on television somewhere once.

"If they're not zombies," Nicole pressed, "then what?"

"Mummies, maybe," suggested Albert.

Olivia considered this. That sounded right, now that he mentioned it. They hadn't been gory, like Romero's monsters, but dry and dusty. Some of them had been quite brittle, allowing Wayne to hold them off for a short while with only his fists.

"We shouldn't assume we know anything about anything out here," Albert warned. "Hollywood's not an ideal instruction manual."

"So if we find a vampire, we shouldn't waste time looking for a cross?" joked Nicole.

"I wouldn't count on it," he replied. "But I'll bet the stake through the heart thing would be worth a try. Just seems like that would work on just about anything."

"Except probably on zombies and mummies," Andrea reminded him.

"True." He stared up at that wall. He wished he'd thought to bring a pair of binoculars. But perhaps it was better to not know what was up there.

He watched those distant figures as he continued forward.

The path had been carrying them both upward and closer to the temple for a while now. The terrain had grown steeper, the climb laborious. They were at least forty feet above the waterline now, with the mountain's cliff faces looming just to their left.

Albert gazed up at the burning summit high above them. Again, he wondered how long it would be before they reached it. And what horrors awaited them there?

They passed another night tree. This one seemed to be marginally more active than the first, many of its small branches twitching and coiling. It was disturbing to look upon, but at least it wasn't crowded over the path like the first one. It was far over by the water's edge, where its roots had broken through the stone and cascaded down the bank, into the lake.

Ahead of them, the terrain narrowed. The cliffs on the left crowded toward a ledge that dropped straight down to the water on the right. Albert could already see that the two would meet in a dead end, but the path curved purposely left, toward a shadowy crack in the cliff walls. As they approached, he saw that there was a sort of stairway there. Unevenly spaced stones provided foot- and handholds for a very steep and very narrow climb to the top of the cliff.

It didn't look like an easy ascent, and Albert dreaded attempting it with only one arm, but at the same time, he liked the idea of putting such a bottleneck between them and any flesh-starved corpses that beat the current and crawled up out of the lake.

"We'll have to go one at a time," Nicole observed. "I'll go first." She did not wait for a response. Taking hold of two stones, she began making her way upward.

Albert watched her climb, his eyes falling on her strong buttocks without thought or feeling. It was just the part of her that seemed to draw the eyes, like the way he tended to watch people's mouths when they spoke.

Olivia went second, followed closely by Andrea. Brandy urged him forward, and Albert reluctantly let her take the rear. He did not like the idea of her being behind him, vulnerable to anything that might appear from behind, but he could hardly argue with her. She was currently more capable of defending herself than he was. At least she could still use both of her arms.

He glanced up at Andrea, but quickly lowered his eyes again as he realized that all he could see of her was an awkward view of her sex as she climbed the protruding stone steps ahead of him.

He was reminded of the narrow tunnel back on the far side of the City of the Blind, where four of them had been forced to crawl on their hands and knees.

(That seemed so long ago now.)

He'd had a similar view of Nicole in there, and he still felt a twinge of guilt for having looked. It felt wrong, like he'd disrespected her, even though they'd each had to accept the fact that their bodies simply were not private in this place, and he didn't want to look at Andrea that way now. It wasn't right.

Also, he had no desire to give any fuel to that part of him that had been out of control ever since his first visit to that damned sex room. He had enough to worry about without his libido distracting him. Besides, if he reached the top of this stepping-stone-stairway sporting an embarrassing erection, he was certain that Nicole would never let him forget it.

Instead, he focused his full attention on the task of climbing and on the curious stairway itself. The mountain appeared as natural as any other, but the steps formed by the protruding stones in this crevice were too perfectly spaced to be here by chance. Although they looked like ordinary stones, it was obvious that there was a particular design in place here, one that he was willing to bet would remain apparent all the way to the summit.

He still wasn't sure why the Temple of the Blind looked like an ordinary mountain—except for the fire, obviously—but he couldn't complain. The convenience of these stones made it considerably easier for him to ascend one-handed than he'd originally anticipated.

One step at a time, he made his way steadily upward, keeping his eyes fixed on the stones at his hands and feet.

At the top of the steps was a narrow ledge that forced them to continue forward single file between a wall of stone and a sheer drop. Albert stepped out onto this path and looked around, taking in the length and width of the ledge as well as the distance to the ground. He also observed a few things about his companions. "You're afraid of heights," he said. It wasn't a question.

Olivia looked back at him, her eyes a little too wide. "Yeah," she confessed. "A little. I've been okay so far, but this is kind of scary."

"Yes, it is," he agreed, looking down. A seventy-foot drop to the hard, rocky ground awaited anyone who wasn't careful. "Don't worry about it. You'll be fine."

She gave him a timid smile. He had frightened her just a little, he realized, bringing attention to something she'd been doing a fairly good job at hiding.

"How could you tell?" Andrea asked. "Was it because you're psychic?"

"No. I just saw the way she was moving. Close to the wall. A little stiff. She was trying hard not to look down." He turned his head and looked at Brandy. She was a little uncomfortable with heights, too. He took her hand and squeezed it.

"Albert's good at stuff like that," Nicole said, keeping her eyes on the path ahead of her. "Puzzles. Mysteries. He's like Sherlock Holmes."

"But Andrea's right," Olivia said as she stared out at the high, surrounding wall, trying not to look down. "He's that way because he's psychic."

Albert looked at her, surprised. He hadn't considered that. "Maybe."

"I'll bet Brandy has something, too," she continued. It was good to talk. Talking helped keep her mind off the bone-shattering fall she desperately wanted to avoid. "Is she good at puzzles, too?"

"Hardly," Brandy replied for herself. She, too, made it a point to focus on that far wall. She was less afraid of heights than a lot of people she knew, but she didn't care at all for situations like this. It wasn't the height, really, but simply the possibility of falling. If there was a solid guard rail to hold onto, this might not have bothered her at all.

"But she's smart," Albert said.

"No, I'm not."

"Yes, you are. You get good grades, and you don't study that hard."

"She's always been like that," agreed Nicole.

"That's what it is," Olivia said. She glanced ahead and was relieved to see that Nicole was almost to the end of the ledge. "I'll bet if you didn't study at all you'd do just about as good. You probably just know some of the answers."

Brandy opened her mouth to argue, but realized she couldn't. There *had* been times when she felt as though she knew an answer not because she'd studied it, but just because she knew it. She'd always passed it off as something she'd learned somewhere and then forgot that she'd learned it, but maybe she just knew it. She'd even been known to do well on quizzes over material she'd missed.

The wall curved to the left and the path widened beneath their feet. On their right, a steep ridge rose sharply from the ground below and crowded over the ledge, creating a shadowy valley that curved around the mountain.

"What about you?" Nicole asked. "You're supposed to be psychic, too. Are you an A-student or are you good at puzzles?"

"Neither," replied Olivia as she stepped away from the scary ledge. Immediately, she felt herself relax a little. "I guess I've always been kind of lucky."

Andrea was intrigued. "Lucky?"

"I have a way of winning things. Sometimes I'll go into a convenience store to pay for some gas and I'll see some lottery tickets. The instant ones, you know. Scratch-offs. And I'll just have this urge to play, like I *feel* lucky. And I'll win. Every time."

"Must be nice!" Nicole exclaimed.

"Sometimes it's just creepy. I've also always seemed to be ready for pop quizzes in school. During the summers when I work, it's like I always know when the boss is watching, even when no one else does."

"I believe it," Albert said, gazing up at the rock walls that had closed in around them. "Anyone else would've died in Gilbert House."

Olivia's friends had always been amazed by her luck. It was the same way with games. She almost always won, which wasn't nearly as fun as it sounded. No one liked playing with her. And that mysterious luck never seemed to apply to anything truly meaningful, like relationships. There was nothing lucky about meeting Andy. Except maybe for meeting these people.

After talking to the Sentinel Queen—and while trying to find a distraction from the crippling fear of the endless darkness during her long trek through the labyrinth—she began to wonder if this luck might merely be a manifestation of her psychic abilities. And now that she had spoken to Albert and Brandy, it seemed perfectly plausible.

"Did you ever try the big lottery?" asked Andrea. "You'd never have to work again if you won Powerball."

Olivia shook her head. "I never won any of those. I always thought I was just lucky with the little things, nothing that really mattered. Now I think maybe it's because on a scratch-off, the prize is pre-determined. Whether or not you're going to win is printed right there, right under the silver stuff, even if you can't see it."

"Make's sense," Albert agreed. "I'll bet even Beverly couldn't have seen things like the Powerball numbers. I think they'd be too random."

"So how many of us are there?" Olivia asked.

"The Sentinel Queen acted like we were pretty rare," Albert replied. "Those of us with that perfect *goldilocks* kind of psychic, anyway. Some people are apparently *very* psychic, like Beverly and Wendell Gilbert, and she made it sound like *everyone* might be at least a little psychic. But she said we were special."

"Then how did three of us wind up here? If we're so rare, then how did we all turn up in this place? Was it meant to be this way? Did somebody arrange this?"

"Maybe," Albert said. "It seems like the Sentinel Queen meant for Brandy and me to come here. Maybe she meant for you to be here too." He looked up toward the flames at the top of the mountain, but the cliff was too high for him to see over it.

"I still can't believe she's gone," said Nicole.

Albert nodded. "I know."

"And Wayne's baby with her," Olivia recalled.

"God that's weird," said Brandy.

"It's so sad," said Andrea.

"I guess I can understand why she did it," Albert said. "She was watching the last of her children die. She was all alone. Her purpose in life was spent. I guess she thought that if she could make a new life she could steal a few more years, maybe survive at least long enough to see if we succeeded."

"I still think it's wrong," said Brandy. "She had no right."

That was true. He couldn't imagine how he'd feel if she'd seduced him instead of Wayne. It would have been his child, regardless of everything else, and to be told that she was taking it with her to the grave… It just wasn't right. The only thing sadder than the fact that

Wayne was gone was that that he managed to outlive his only child before he died.

The five of them fell silent. Albert looked out over the lake at those distant trees. The zombies on the horizon were rapidly growing in number. How long before one of them found its way across? Or a hundred of them? Or a million?

Ahead of them, the path grew steeper, but Albert found himself afraid that they would never reach the top in time.

Chapter 9

The shrill sound of Andrea's scream pierced the tense silence and echoed back and forth across the lake.

"Oh my god!" cried Brandy, her heart thudding violently in her breast.

Andrea clutched her arms over her chest and stared back at them. Standing there in everyone's gaze, she couldn't decide if she was more afraid or embarrassed.

"*What?*" demanded Nicole when she didn't volunteer the reason for her startling outburst.

In a small voice, she said, "Something grabbed my arm."

But a brief look at their surroundings revealed nothing that could have touched her. The path had dispersed itself into a wide, rocky field littered with a handful of large boulders jutting upward, but the nearest of these was a good twenty feet behind them. Nowhere else offered a place to hide.

"I didn't imagine it," she insisted, standing her ground.

"We don't think you did," Albert assured her. He had no idea if he spoke for everyone or not, but *he* believed her. He had no reason not to. This was the Temple of the Blind. Weird things happened here. "What did it feel like when it touched you?"

"It was just like a hand reached out and grabbed my arm. Just like if one of you did it. But no one was there."

"What could've done it?" asked Olivia.

"Something invisible?" suggested Brandy.

The idea made Andrea cringe. Was that possible? Could there be something out here in this darkness with the ability to hide itself? An invisible predator? A master of camouflage? What if they were surrounded by awful things but couldn't see them? How could they fight something like that?

Albert wasn't so sure they were dealing with some kind of cloaked enemy. For one thing, only Andrea had experienced these things so far. If there was something crawling over this mountain that didn't reveal itself to their eyes, it reasoned that they'd all have experienced something by now.

And if it was a predator of some sort, why hadn't it attacked them yet? Why was it toying with them?

Andrea gasped and stood straighter.

"What's wrong?" asked Olivia.

Andrea stared back at her. "You didn't hear that, either?"

Brandy and Olivia looked at each other, confused.

"I did," said Nicole.

Andrea turned to face her, surprised. "You did?"

"I heard *something*. I think. It sounded really far off, though."

"I swear it came from right next to me."

"Sweetie," said Brandy, "you're starting to freak me out a little."

"It's worth being concerned about," said Albert. "I really don't think she's just jumpy." To Andrea, he said, "What did it sound like?"

"Another voice."

"Bike light?"

"No. Something else. It didn't sound like words, really. It was just a yell."

"I couldn't tell you what it said," added Nicole. "It just sounded like a mumble off in the distance. It was just before she jumped."

Brandy turned away from Andrea and looked at Albert. "This is just like how we heard the Sentinel Queen's voice. You heard it, then me. Nikki and Wayne didn't hear it until later."

Albert nodded. That was true. This was remarkably similar, except for one major difference. "But according to her, we heard her voice first because we're psychic. Why is it that only the two of us who *aren't* supposed to be psychic are hearing things now?"

No one had an answer for this, of course. Like everything else they'd encountered out here, it was a mystery. And with the Sentinel Queen gone, it would likely never be answered.

A flicker of flames caught their attention and the five of them looked up at the sky as a fiery shape soared overhead and out toward the lake. Another of the strange, flying creatures had caught itself on fire.

Other, darker shapes gave chase, drawn by the flames that trailed from its burning body.

"God I hate those things," said Nicole as the pitiful creature winked out and dropped from sight.

Olivia hated them, too. She watched the jerking shadows heave themselves through the black sky, their massive wings beating against the air like the sails of a ship in a storm. "They look like bats."

Yes, they did. It was something in the way they moved, something about those great jerking motions, perhaps. But it wasn't precisely like a bat. A bat was graceful in its own way. These things made Albert think of rambunctious drunks attempting to dance. They did not fly so much as stagger through the air.

Andrea turned around and searched the barren landscape around them for any sign of whatever had touched her. She thought she glimpsed a shadow darting past the rocks behind them, but there were shadows everywhere. It was probably one of the things flying overhead. "I don't like it out here."

"I don't think any of us do," Olivia assured her. *She* sure as hell didn't. Her eyes kept drifting to those distant shadows pacing along the top of the wall.

"Let's just keep our eyes and ears open," suggested Albert.

They moved on.

As they approached the top of the hill, the path grew narrower. The steep walls of the mountain closed in on them, crowding them together. By the time they crossed the small depression on the other side and began climbing again, they were single-file. And still the stone pushed in at them.

Soon, the path before them became little more than a narrow crack, barely wide enough to squeeze through.

"This is going to be tight," said Nicole. She didn't look forward to this at all. It wasn't unlike the shrinking passage between the hate room and the spiraling stairs that led to the fear room, and *that* wasn't a pleasant experience. Claustrophobia had nearly gotten the best of all of them back there.

"It's not so bad," said Albert. But he wasn't sure he was convincing even to himself. It was going to be a very tight squeeze and he wasn't as limber as he was when he began this journey.

Nicole had to turn sideways and sidle between the rocks, her back pressed to the cold stone as she flattened herself against the wall. She couldn't tell yet how far back it went or how narrow it was going to get. Already, she found it difficult to breathe.

"This isn't even fair," moaned Olivia. Now it just felt like the mountain was making fun of her.

Brandy looked up. There was little to see but darkness and the odd shadow of a fluttering creature as it passed overhead. It was far too easy to imagine something scurrying into this narrow crack with them, stalking them, attacking while there was nowhere to run.

She closed her eyes and tried to force the idea away.

Albert's arm dragged across the stone and a twinge of pain thrummed from his broken bone. If this passage grew any narrower, he simply wouldn't be able to fit.

Nicole paused for a moment and tried to steady her nerves. She took a deep breath and felt the cold walls press against her bare body. She could feel a panic building within her and had to will it back. It wasn't that she couldn't breathe. She had plenty of room still to catch her breath. She simply didn't like it here. She had to keep telling herself it wasn't as bad as she was making it.

She looked ahead. The shadows were deep, but the light from a burning vent somewhere above them shined far enough down to allow her to see that the path continued on, curving slightly out of sight, but not closing. Not noticeably.

She tried to turn her head and found that she could do so. Olivia stood next to her, her eyes closed, breathing in quick, shallow breaths. Her body was bigger, her breasts mashed against the cold stone. She was clearly trying hard not to succumb to the crushing will of claustrophobia.

Nicole took her hand and squeezed. Her eyes opened. "You're doing great."

Olivia nodded. Immediately, she felt someone take her other hand. It was Albert.

"You survived a zombie horde," he told her. "Don't let a stupid crack beat you."

She smiled. "When you put it that way..."

"He has a knack for putting things in perspective, doesn't he?" said Brandy.

"He does," Olivia admitted. She was beginning to understand why Wayne was so determined to come back for them. They really were good people. They already felt like friends.

Still clinging to Olivia's hand, Nicole faced left again and continued inching along the path. "Maybe we should've put the smallest person up front. In case I need pulled out of here."

"I think that's Andrea," said Brandy. "She went last in case *I* need pulled out of here."

"Well that was selfish of you."

"I'm sure you'll be just fine."

"Right."

"You'd better be fine," said Olivia, "or my big butt is screwed."

"You'll fit just fine," insisted Nicole.

"The Keeper told us to follow this path," Albert reminded them.

"We have to be able to fit. Otherwise, what would be the point?"

"I don't see the point anyway," retorted Nicole. "It still doesn't make sense. Why do *we* have to decide whether to open this stupid door?"

"None of this has made any sense from the beginning," agreed Brandy.

Albert sighed. "I know."

Still clinging to Olivia's hand, Nicole slid between the rocks and around the narrow curve. A short distance beyond this, the walls withdrew a little, allowing them a small break from the gripping claustrophobia.

"Thank God," sighed Olivia.

"It's not over yet," warned Nicole. Ahead of them, the passage narrowed again. This time, the walls closed in even tighter. As she peered through this crevice between the rocks, she could see that the path beyond was open. They were almost through, but the last few feet were going to be brutal. It didn't look as if they could possibly fit all the way through.

A loud noise reached them from somewhere above, like a swift slap or the popping of a balloon. Each of them looked up into the narrow crack of sky that hung over their heads, but there was nothing to see but shadows and the occasional flutter of the mysterious flying creatures.

"What was that?" asked Andrea, but of course no one had an answer for her.

"Let's just keep moving," suggested Brandy.

Nicole fixed her eyes on the path before them again. It wasn't going to be pleasant, but they could do it. She was sure of it. Albert was right. The Keeper sent them this way. Surely the little bastard wasn't stupid enough to send them somewhere they couldn't physically go.

Right?

She turned to her side, as before, and slipped her arm into the crack. It took a few tries to find just the right angle, but inch by inch, she squeezed herself into the crack.

The largest obstacle here was a bulge in the wall at her front that pressed against her belly, making it difficult to catch her breath. She also kept bumping her head against the stone. It was angled so that the crevice became narrower as it rose, leaving little room to navigate.

When she'd passed about halfway to the freedom on the other side, she found a place where her head didn't seem to fit and her belly was so constricted by the stone that she couldn't breathe. Here, icy panic welled up from deep inside her, threatening to overwhelm her. Only by sheer force of will did she manage to maintain control and wriggle free.

Then, somehow, she was on the other side looking back.

Olivia peered out at her between the walls, her eyes filled with dread and doubt.

"You can do it," Nicole promised. "Just relax and don't let yourself panic."

Anywhere else and she wouldn't have done it. It was too narrow. And she was too big. She was sure she couldn't fit. But what other choice did she have? She turned and inserted herself between the crushing walls.

It was hell.

She couldn't breathe. She couldn't even cry. And the coarse stone bit her belly, her knees, her breasts, her thighs. As the walls pressed in on her, compressing her chest, it felt like sandpaper against the tender flesh of her nipples. But Nicole was right. Inch by inch, second by second, she made her way between the stone and through the crippling panic to the open freedom beyond.

Albert did the same after her, but his progress was hampered by his broken arm, which did not seem to want to fit between the rocks in its sling. Yet somehow he managed to make it through with only some minor adjustments and with only a small amount of agonizing protest from his broken bone.

Brandy slid through behind him, cursing bitterly when she struck the tender knot on the back of her head against the wall. She was considerably thinner than Olivia, much softer and lither than Albert and far less endowed than Nicole, and should have slipped through much easier than any of them, but the cold stone pressing against her bruised back made the task considerably more unpleasant. At one point, a protruding section of the wall at her back was located at the same unfortunate height as that tender spot where her tailbone ached. The agony of forcing herself through this crevice was enough to spill fresh tears down her face and inspire some truly creative vulgarities.

"That was scary," she declared when she was finally free of the crevice. "And painful."

"Very," agreed Olivia as she stood with her arms crossed over her tender breasts.

"Let's hope we don't have to do that again," said Nicole.

She received no arguments.

Each of them turned to check on Andrea, only to find her standing before them, already having squeezed herself through.

She looked back at each of them. "What?"

Brandy laughed.

"I just watched you guys all do it, so I knew I could fit. I just let the air out of my lungs and did it."

"Nice," giggled Olivia.

"That's how it's done, I suppose," laughed Albert.

Nicole turned and walked on. The path here was again wide enough for them to scatter out a little, and no night trees or monsters blocked their path.

Yet.

Albert gazed up at the creatures circling overhead. There were perhaps as many as a hundred of them in the sky now. It was impossible to keep any one in sight for long. They twisted through the air in great, jerking lunges, often changing directions with every beat of their enormous wings. Albert watched them for a moment, trying to grasp what they must look like up close. The only thing he could tell for sure as they fluttered against the black sky was that their wings were oddly formed. They seemed to grow wider as they stretched away from the body, giving them a strangely amusing bow tie shape.

As he watched, another one swept across one of the flaming vents and burst into flames. It bobbed twice in the air, still trying to escape, and then fell from sight as two of its companions set upon it, pursuing it to the cold ground.

There was something about these creatures that he could not quite put his finger on.

Wayne told them all about his frightening journey through the Wood and of the things he'd seen there. As far as he could understand, this was a land without hope, where life was swift to end but awareness was not. Here, even time was a curse, and anything that existed in this black hell would be desperate to get out.

But this wasn't the same somehow. These creatures were different from the lingering dead. He did not know how he knew this, but he did. Looking up at them now, he felt that he could almost touch them with his mind, as though there were something about them... something *significant*.

Chapter 10

A few hundred yards beyond the claustrophobic crevice, the high mountain rocks crowded the path again, this time funneling them into another tunnel. Although it was considerably longer than the last one, it was nothing like the endless darkness they had endured within the temple walls. And Albert, for one, found that he was relieved to be underground again for a short while. He didn't care to be walking beneath those unknown creatures in the sky. That bizarre *significance* he felt would not go away. It gnawed at him for some reason. And it was beginning to feel as though they were watching him.

Brandy took his hand and squeezed it. "So you think we'll make it to work today?"

Albert laughed. "There's no way in hell."

"I don't think we'll be home in time to even call in. Paula's going to shit when I don't show up."

"Let her shit. You can do better than putting up with her nonsense anyway."

"You're sweet."

"Where do you work?" asked Andrea.

"Old Navy."

"Oh. I have a friend who works there. Stacy Switcher."

"Yeah, I know Stacy. She's a sweet girl."

"She's an airhead."

Brandy laughed. Yes, she was. She was impossibly clueless. The girl couldn't seem to do anything by herself. She was utterly hopeless. But it wouldn't be very professional to say so. Instead, she said, "Small world."

Albert smiled at her. "Apparently not, as it turns out."

"That's true, I guess." In fact, the world had grown so much in the past few hours that it was nearly overwhelming. She thought about that queer, black sky and felt a chill creep through her.

Olivia turned and looked at Nicole. "What?"

Nicole looked back at her, confused. "What?"

"Did you say something?"

"No."

"You didn't just say my name?"

Nicole shook her head.

"I swear I heard someone say my name."

"Not me."

"I didn't hear anything," said Brandy.

Olivia faced forward again, frowning. She was sure she heard something.

Each of them remained silent, listening for voices in the darkness, but there was nothing.

Soon enough, the tunnel came to an end and the five of them

were again walking beneath that eerie, starless sky.

"My feet hurt so bad," complained Andrea.

"Ours, too," Brandy assured her.

"Should we rest again?" asked Nicole.

"I'm not sure we should stay in one place that long," worried Olivia.

It was a valid point. Their eyes drifted to the creeping shadows atop the high wall and those mysterious things flapping through the air overhead. It had so far been a mostly peaceful climb, but for how much longer? After all they'd been through, surely the temple had more in store for them than a difficult climb up an inconvenient path.

A noise, like the one they heard while navigating the narrow crevice between the rocks, echoed from somewhere above them. It was sort of like the sound of someone slamming a book down onto a tabletop, or the hard crack of a whip.

Olivia turned around, searching the rocks above them. "What is that?"

"Something really bad, I'm sure," replied Brandy.

Olivia glanced at her, then turned and looked at the others. She opened her mouth to say something else, but snapped it shut as she realized that there were more people here than there should have been. She turned in a circle, searching the area around her, trying to understand.

"What's wrong?" asked Albert.

She looked at him, confused, and then looked back at Brandy. Pointing over her shoulder, she said, "I swear there was someone standing over there just a second ago."

Brandy turned and looked in the direction Olivia indicated, but there was no one over there.

"Right by that ledge. I thought it was Albert. But Albert was behind me…"

"I didn't see anybody," said Albert.

"So weird…" Olivia stared at the ledge, trying to make sense of it.

Nicole turned and looked at Andrea.

"What?" asked Andrea.

"Did you just tap me on the shoulder?"

Andrea shook her head.

"Felt like somebody did…" But Andrea wasn't even standing close enough to have done it.

"What's going on?" asked Brandy.

"You guys," said Andrea, "I don't think we're alone up here."

"You think this mountain is haunted?" asked Nicole.

"Haunted?" Albert considered this. He wasn't sure he believed in ghosts. Not really. Though he'd always enjoyed a good ghost story, the *idea* of restless spirits and haunted houses, he'd always thought that there must be a rational explanation for every case. But so many fantastic things had revealed themselves to him in the long hours since he left the apartment… Why not ghosts? Was that really so much harder to believe than monsters? Other worlds? Keepers and Sentinel Queens?

"No way," whined Olivia. "I can't deal with ghosts. I'm still not over the zombies."

"I haven't even met a zombie yet," said Andrea, "and *I'm* not over them."

Nicole nodded. "Really not excited about meeting any more monsters of any kind."

"We haven't had to deal with anything so far," Albert reminded them. "Some chatty and touchy-feely ghosts. I think we can deal with that. If we…" He paused and looked at Andrea. "Did you hear that?"

Andrea nodded. "Voice."

"I didn't hear anything," reported Nicole.

Albert listened, but it didn't come again. "Sounded like a man…"

"I couldn't understand it," said Andrea.

"Wasn't English."

She nodded.

Albert considered this. "No reason a ghost would speak English here. I'll bet 'bike light' was something from another language, too. Maybe even a *dead* language no one's spoken in ages."

He had to admit, the idea of being the first person in centuries, maybe millennia, to hear words spoken in a long-dead tongue was a little bit exciting. He couldn't help but appreciate the significance of such an experience.

"Makes sense," agreed Andrea. "Maybe it means 'welcome.'"

"Or 'redrum,'" said Nicole.

"Way to stay positive," laughed Olivia.

Nicole shrugged.

"Could mean 'cow udders' for all we know," said Albert. "We have no idea what kind of people could be haunting a place like this, where they came from, what they were like." The more he thought about it, the more exhilarating he found it. And if the Sentinel Queen and the Keeper were telling the truth, these words could have last been spoken in an age and world he could not even begin to imagine.

If it was really true, if mankind really migrated to Earth like trans-dimensional nomads, what had those old worlds been like? What wonders might we have left behind?

"This trip just keeps getting weirder," groaned Brandy.

"Next time," decided Nicole, "we're just going to Vegas."

"Yes, please," said Olivia.

They moved on, each of them watching, anticipating the next unpleasant surprise. Nothing spoke to them as they climbed the next hill, nothing reached out to touch them. The spirits seemed to have stilled again.

Andrea wondered how many ghosts could possibly be out here. How many people had even seen this place? At first, it had seemed like the perfect location for a haunting, cold and dark and creepy, but the more she thought about it, the less it made sense. Didn't ghosts haunt places that were familiar to them? Meaningful places?

But what did she know? Perhaps this had been a busy place once upon a time, way back in ancient days, long before the world she knew had even been born from its primordial cosmic dust. Perhaps there had been a time when people flocked to this place by the millions.

But somehow, she didn't think so.

The five of them reached the top of the hill together and there they stopped. The path before them descended into a shallow valley to a fork in the road. One way continued down, deeper into the valley and around the next ridge, the other ascended a steep hill and appeared to continue out of sight along a high ledge.

"Which way do we go?" asked Nicole.

Albert studied both paths. Inside the temple, he'd relied on the box and its curious contents to guide him through places like these. But he'd used the last clue hours ago, before he even entered the City of the Blind. The labyrinth had been filled with forks and crossroads, but that was the point of a labyrinth, after all. You were supposed to make wrong turns. That's why there was more than one solution.

"We're supposed to be going up, right?" said Nicole. "So, the left one?"

That was the obvious choice. But Albert didn't trust the obvious choice. It seemed like a mistake to simply assume that the path that pointed them in the direction they wanted to go would actually get them there.

"What happens if we pick the wrong one?" asked Andrea.

"Bad things," was the reply on everyone's lips, but no one said it aloud.

Albert descended the hill toward the fork. Perhaps it made no difference which way they took. Perhaps they both led to the summit. But he didn't think so. This felt like an important decision. A mistake here could prove disastrous.

He searched the area, but found nothing that might indicate which way they were supposed to go. There were no signs, of course. And nothing stood out that might indicate a clue of some sort.

Olivia stood staring at the path that led up the hill. "No. Not left."

The others turned and looked at her.

"I don't like left."

Nicole looked up at the left path. There was nothing about it that struck her as ominous in any way. It was no different than the path on the right except that it promised to take them closer to their destination instead of farther from it. "You sure?"

"I get a really bad feeling about the left path."

"Right, then," decided Brandy.

"I vote right," agreed Andrea.

Albert nodded. "I'll go with the lucky girl on this one."

Olivia wasn't sure why she didn't like the left path. It was just a path. But every time she tried to imagine walking that way, she felt a strange dread creep into her. It almost made her feel sick.

"Psychic?" asked Andrea.

"I don't know. I just don't like it."

Albert didn't think he liked it now, either, but perhaps that was only because Olivia said she didn't like it. It was hard to tell. This psychic thing was still very new to him. Would he ever learn to use it for anything useful?

Nicole shrugged. "Right it is, then."

Each of them started down the path on the right. As soon as they had reached the bottom of the hill and circled around the ridge, the path began to rise steeply.

So far, so good.

"So where do you think that other path led, then?" asked Andrea.

Albert glanced back the way they came. A simple dead end would have been the most likely destination of a wrong turn, but if Olivia's gut feeling was any indication... He recalled the hate room and the deadly chamber that waited beyond it, the very chamber where Beverly Bridger's lifeless body still lay. If the architects of this place were capable of creating something like that, then there might be no limit to their cruelty. "We're probably better off not knowing."

Olivia hoped desperately that her luck didn't run out today.

Chapter 11

The path rose and fell and rose again as it wriggled its way across the crooked ridges and through the twisted valleys and gorges, slowly spiraling inward and upward, ever closer to the mysteries that awaited them high above.

They passed three more sleepy night trees along the path, and heard several more phantom voices on the wind, but still nothing attacked them. The zombies remained nothing more than pacing shadows atop the distant wall and the things in the sky remained preoccupied with the flames. When the path diverged a second time, Olivia again felt a profound aversion to one of them, resulting in a decision to avoid the open, rocky hillside in favor of a dark and narrow crevasse between two massive rock formations.

Still, nothing confronted them.

Eventually, the channel came into view again, emerging from behind the mountain, revealing that they'd completed their first lap around the temple. And yet, after all this time, they remained so very far from their destination.

And the landscape continued to punish them.

The steepest hill they had yet encountered stood before them. Its surface was a mosaic of uneven stones, like a funhouse stairway, tilting precariously in every direction. And not every stone was firmly set into the hillside. Many trembled and shifted beneath their weight, threatening to slip free and forcing them to choose their footing carefully or else risk a nasty fall.

"Oh my god, this is torture!" groaned Nicole as she lowered herself to her knees and propped her arms on the cool stone. Her legs and feet were on fire. The endless journey had been bad enough, but these awkwardly angled stones made her feel like she was trapped on a Stairmaster. And she was not yet halfway to the top.

Olivia stopped, too, seating herself carefully upon the stones, distributing her weight so that she could rest. "This sucks so bad," she agreed.

Andrea paused and looked around at her companions. Her body ached, too, but she'd been trying not to complain. She was the only one here still in high school. She didn't want to be the whiny child of the group. She looked back and saw that Albert was just below her, carefully picking his footing. Her eyes swept over his body before she could stop herself and she turned away, embarrassed. Why did she keep doing this? Why was she so distracted by him? Was it really those statues she'd peeked at? Had it really changed her? Or was it only in her head? He was attractive. And she wasn't exactly used to guys walking around naked in front of her. Perhaps the sex room had done nothing more than plant an idea in her head and the rest was only natural curiosity.

Or maybe she'd poisoned her mind by stupidly ignoring Wayne's warnings. Maybe this was the beginning of the shameless sex addict she was doomed to become.

The idea was far too scary to dismiss.

She pushed herself onward, distracted, and a stone slipped beneath her weight. She fell hard onto her hands and knees and slid gracelessly back down the steep slope with a startled shriek. Then she was lying sprawled across the steps, her arms and legs spread wide apart to catch a solid surface, her whole body enveloped in a sheet of sharp, stinging pain.

Vaguely, she realized that Albert was beside her. His hand was firmly clamped around her small arm, steadying her.

"Owie…" she squeaked.

"You okay?"

She blinked tears of pain from her eyes and peered up at him. "I'm all right…" she managed. "Sorry."

"It's okay. Did you hurt yourself?"

She did, a little. She was fairly sure she'd skinned both her knees. Her fingertips and the heels of her hands stung. Her toes hurt. Even her boobs were sore. But she merely shook her head. Realizing that her thighs were still wide open, she drew her legs back under her and sat up.

Satisfied that she was no longer in danger of sliding the rest of the way down the slope, Albert let go of her arm and stood up straight again. As he did so, Andrea found herself staring directly at his naked penis.

She felt her whole face burn with a furious blush and quickly turned away and began examining her stinging hands.

Did everybody see that? She couldn't help feeling certain that they had. She was so embarrassed…

"You need help?" asked Albert. Was he only pretending he hadn't noticed? He was such a nice guy.

She shook her head, still blushing. It felt like her whole body must have turned bright red. "I'm fine. Sorry."

"Don't be. I just want to be sure you're okay. That looked like a pretty hard fall."

"It looked really painful," agreed Brandy.

"A little, yeah."

"You sure you're okay?" Albert pressed.

Andrea nodded. "Just embarrassed."

"It's okay," Brandy assured her. "It was bound to happen to one of us."

Andrea seated herself carefully on the steps and examined herself. There were visible scrapes on her knees and hands, but they weren't so bad. The humiliation was much worse. And even now she couldn't seem to get the image of Albert's manhood out of her thoughts.

"We should take a break for a little while," decided Albert. "We all need a rest."

Another of those strange clapping noises rang out from somewhere behind them. Nicole lifted her head and looked back in the direction from which it came.

"This isn't the most comfortable place for a break," said Olivia.

Albert nodded. "When we get to the top."

"Sounds good to me," said Nicole. She stood and looked up at the top of the hill. Her legs and feet still hurt, but the idea of sitting down for a little while was empowering.

Again, that clapping noise, this time from somewhere in front of them.

"What is that?" asked Brandy.

No one offered a guess.

Albert began to climb again. It was a slow process. With only one arm, he couldn't afford to teeter off balance. He kept his good hand on the stones, constantly testing his footing, but his eyes drifted toward the temple's burning summit and those strange, flying creatures. There were so many of them now. They looked like a swarm of giant insects. Soon, they'd black out the sky. (Or they would if the sky wasn't already black.) He saw several of them swooping back and forth over the flames rising from a vent on a nearby ledge, close enough to hear the sound of their wings beating the wind.

As their numbers grew, more and more of them ignited in the temple's flames. Little balls of fire erupted from the darkness and winked back out again. It was like watching a bug zapper.

A strange voice drifted across the quiet slope and he paused.

"Did you guys hear that?" asked Brandy.

"I did," replied Nicole.

Olivia responded that she did, too.

In fact, everyone heard it this time.

"What did it say?"

"I didn't catch it," said Albert. Neither did Nicole or Olivia.

"It sounded muffled," reported Andrea. She was still blushing, but at least something had happened to take the attention off of her.

Brandy didn't like the idea of ghosts on the mountain. Why would anyone want to linger here? What did they want? She couldn't help but think that the presence of these apparent spirits were bad news.

A stone rocked beneath her foot and she forced herself to concentrate. There would be plenty of time to worry about ghosts after she reached the top, when there was no longer any danger of falling and breaking something.

They carried on, each of them listening for more phantom voices, but the dead had fallen as silent as the night tree that awaited them at the end of their long climb.

Chapter 12

It stood directly in front of them, growing out of the stone in the very middle of the path, its wide branches spread across the entirety of the space between the high walls on either side. There was no going around this one. The only way forward was beneath its twisting boughs.

Albert found himself doubting that it was here by chance. It seemed to him that this was as much a part of the temple's design as the emotion rooms and the hounds. It was meant as an obstacle for them to overcome.

And this one was much more awake than the others they'd seen. Its branches churned and convulsed in slow, purposeful rhythms, writhing like a nest of serpents. Against the backdrop of the black sky and the strange, flying creatures that fluttered overhead, the sight was like something from a science fiction movie, a horrific scene from a harsh, alien planet.

Long, slowly coiling tendrils, like the one that reached down and touched Nicole's shoulder from the branches of the first one they encountered, dangled down from the wide canopy, swaying as if stirred by the breeze…except that there was no breeze. To Albert, they looked like long, creeping feelers, waiting for unsuspecting prey to pass. There were dozens of them, blocking the way forward, some of them reaching nearly to the ground.

"You've got to be kidding me…" whispered Brandy.

"Can we get by this thing?" asked Nicole.

Olivia watched in silence. It was horrifying. The one she and Wayne climbed outside Gilbert House wasn't like this. It must have still been mostly asleep.

Albert was still standing on the crooked steps of the steep hill, watching intently, studying the thing. After a moment, he knelt and began to feel the stones around him, searching until he found a loose one, which he wrenched free. Standing up again, he took aim and tossed the stone onto the path beneath the tree. As he expected, it reacted. The coiling tendrils came to life at once, twitching and coiling, reaching for it, and the entire tree shook, as if agitated.

It made him think of a giant, black jellyfish.

But it wasn't much of a hunter. Its reaction to the tossed stone was slow. It came nowhere near snatching it out of the air. All things considered, it still looked pretty slow.

"The good news," he decided, "is it's still not completely awake."

"Oh good," exclaimed Brandy. "So they'll get worse. That's awesome."

"What do we do?" asked Andrea.

"I think all we can do is run for it."

Nicole watched the creepy tendrils as they searched lazily for the stone Albert threw. "You think we can?"

"I think it's the only option we've got." This was the only path, unless you counted the two forks, and he wasn't willing to gamble Olivia's gut feelings against a stupid tree. He'd relied on faith to get him this far, faith in the sentinel statues, faith in the Sentinel Queen, faith in the Keeper, trusting that if they wanted him to go where they sent him, then he must, therefore, be able to get there. It just made sense.

"If you say so. I guess…"

Albert glanced at Olivia. "You said the one outside Gilbert House grabbed you?"

"It wasn't nearly as awake as this one. It wasn't moving like that. It was just sort of bent over, reaching for the window, where the light was."

"But the branches were touching you?"

"They grabbed my hands and feet when I was climbing. But they weren't very strong. It was like Velcro, kind of. I pulled away easy enough. It was mostly just creepy. But like I said, it wasn't very active. This one looks…almost *mad*."

That was true enough. "But it's not like it *bit* you or anything."

"Oh. No. It was just grabby."

Albert nodded. "Then we probably don't have to worry about stinging thorns or anything."

"Unless it only does that when it's *mad*," Nicole added.

He stood up and began moving toward the tree. "Wait here."

"What are you doing?" asked Brandy, startled.

"Testing a theory."

"Don't!"

"It's okay. Just wait there."

There was no way to avoid all the tendrils. They seemed to be designed to detect anything passing beneath the tree. Therefore, it was safe to assume that none of them could pass here undetected. The question was, what happened if they touched one of the tendrils.

The other trees didn't have these. They must only descend when it was awake and hunting. His guess was that it would either seize him the moment he touched it, perhaps then attempting to drag him up into the tree, or it would bring the branches crashing down on top of him.

Suddenly, he found himself reminded of the whomping willow tree in the *Harry Potter* books. He doubted that these "night trees" would prove to be any less temperamental.

But he couldn't dismiss the idea that these things might possess other means of capturing and killing prey. Before he allowed anyone to simply rush beneath its branches, he wanted to make sure it wasn't going to suddenly sprout three-inch thorns and inject them with flesh-melting toxins or some other equally brutal thing.

He stepped toward the tree, his left hand outstretched, slowly approaching the nearest dangling tendril.

It looked like a thin, writhing eel with its glistening flesh and slow, serpent-like motions. But it was only a long, skinny branch.

"Be careful!" groaned Nicole.

"It's all right," he assured her. Although the fact remained that he was currently reaching out with his bare hand (the only hand currently of any use to him, in fact) to touch something they had every reason to believe was dangerous.

This was stupid.

But there was no way around this tree. It blocked the only path. They would have to pass beneath its branches to proceed. At least this way, they'd know what to expect. At the very worst, maybe they could bolt past while it was preoccupied with him.

When his hand had closed to within six inches of the serpentine branch, it seemed to sense him somehow. It twisted around, wriggling through the air, and snatched at his hand.

It missed.

Albert was far jumpier than the tree was quick. Yet, even without touching him, he seemed to have piqued its interest. Suddenly, all of those squirming branches were reaching toward him. Even the larger limbs above began to sag in his direction. More snake-like tendrils descended from the writhing, skeletal canopy above.

This might prove useful.

He reached out and seized the nearest one with his hand. Immediately, it wrapped itself around his fingers and squeezed. It had a firm grip. And that queer, clammy texture of its bark felt awful against the naked skin of his hand.

He could feel it pulling at him, trying to reel him in, but he put his weight against it and stood his ground. For a moment, he thought he was stuck in its grasp, it clung to him, not unlike the tentacle of an octopus, but with a little effort, he managed to wrench his hand free.

He remained unharmed. There were no ill effects from his contact with it. But it did suddenly seem more agitated. He moved to his right and the tree leaned subtly toward him, following him.

"Go left," he said. "While I have its attention."

Brandy looked to the left and saw that as the tree bent toward Albert, it left an opening between it and the rocks. They should be able to fit through. But... "What about you?"

"You guys get over there first. Then I'll back off and you can distract it."

"The man's got a plan," said Nicole. "Let's go."

One by one, the four of them darted toward the rocks on the left.

Brandy slipped under without trouble, as did Nicole. But as Olivia passed beneath the wriggling branches, one of those tendrils slipped down through the air and caught a small lock of her hair. She cried out, startled, and bolted for safety, leaving more than a few strands of curly brown hair behind. At the same time, the tree shifted. Something like a shudder passed through the branches and all those tendrils shifted their attention toward her.

But she and Andrea were already out of its reach by the time they swung around, leaving them grasping at nothing but thin air.

Now, only Albert remained.

He stepped back, but the tree didn't give up on him that easily. Those tendrils remained focused on him. They even seemed to be tracking him. They followed him as he moved from side to side.

"You need to draw its attention away from me."

Nicole looked at Brandy, saw the uncertainty on her face, and said, "I'll do it. You hold my hand so it doesn't drag me away or something."

Brandy nodded and firmly gripped her left hand.

Nicole had barely begun to reach out when the nearest tendril whipped toward her and wrapped itself around her hand. She cried out in surprise. It was stronger than she expected.

Albert began moving, but he stopped as he realized that the tree was still following him. This wouldn't work. He couldn't duck under if it wouldn't look away.

"What's happening?" Nicole asked.

"I think we woke it up a little more," guessed Albert. "It's acting like it knows what we're doing."

"It's a fucking *tree*!" exclaimed Brandy. "What does it know?"

"Apparently, it knows there's more than one of us," replied Nicole. She gritted her teeth as the branch twisted around her injured hand, squeezing and grinding against the blisters beneath the gauze.

Olivia stepped out and snatched one of the tendrils, too. She'd already dealt with these things once before, but she still had to bite back a scream when she felt it squirming against the palm of her hand.

This seemed to get the tree's attention. It began to lean toward them now, away from Albert. Perhaps it was motivated by the prospect of more prey to be had from the other side. But several of those tendrils remained fixated on Albert. Wherever he moved, they seemed to follow, watching him, waiting for the right opportunity.

It appeared that he wasn't going to get a better chance. Bracing himself, he ran for it.

The tree shuddered violently, a fast, quaking tremble that seemed to run all the way through it. Albert was sure that he had just jolted the thing a little more awake.

Olivia and Nicole cried out as they felt themselves jerked forward. Andrea and Brandy held tight to their other hands.

Albert felt something snatch at his bare back, his arm, his hair. He charged forward, trying to force his way to the other side. He lifted his hand in front of his face to guard his eyes and felt one of the coiling branches seize his wrist. With a hard yank, he jerked himself free, but not before he felt a sharp pain where it touched him.

Then he was safely on the other side.

Nicole and Olivia each wrenched their hands free and the five of them hurried away. Only when they reached the foot of the next rise did they finally turn and look back.

"That was really freaky," said Andrea.

Nicole laughed. "We just survived a fight with a *tree*. You realize that, right?"

"Nobody'd believe a word of this," said Olivia. "I know *I* wouldn't."

"If any of you say anything, I'll deny it," decided Brandy. "I'll tell everyone y'all are crazy."

"You would," laughed Nicole.

"That was really scary, though," said Olivia.

Albert had stopped several yards before the others and now stood watching the night tree, thinking. Its branches were writhing. From here, in the firelight, it looked like a mass of wriggling, pulsating tentacles, as if it were a monster right out of the pages of Lovecraft. It was horrifying, and yet he was sure he hadn't seen anything yet. "It wasn't fully awake."

The others turned and looked at him, curious.

"It's predatory. Those branches that hang down…like feelers… It's made to catch prey. But it's slow. We shouldn't have been able to escape that easily."

"But we did," Andrea reminded him.

"I know. But only because it's still waking up."

Nicole didn't care for this kind of talk. It made her uneasy. "You think we'd have been in trouble if we showed up much later?"

"I do. Also… I'm not sure how we're going to handle the next one."

The four of them exchanged startled looks.

Albert looked down at his wrist where the tendril grabbed him. A thin row of shallow cuts lay parallel to his watch band, beading with blood. They stung.

Apparently, when awake, night trees had teeth.

Chapter 13

"What do you know about the night trees?" asked Albert as he sat staring at the tree.

Olivia seated herself next to him and stared at the coiling branches. "Not a lot." She described her experiences in the Wood, beginning with her fall through the branches. The trees out there weren't moving. She didn't even know that there was anything different about them except for the bizarre feel of their fleshy bark. They were apparently in some kind of suspended animation as they waited for the sun to return. Even the one in the courtyard had only shown the slightest sign that it was anything more. It had leaned toward the light, not unlike many plants did, and only the smallest of its branches had been moving.

Nicole walked over and sat with them, listening. The night tree had burst several of her blisters when it seized her hand and it had begun to sting again.

Brandy chose to sit with her back against the wall, away from the others. She didn't care to talk about the stupid tree. She didn't want to look at it, either. She just wanted to close her eyes and rest for a while. For just a moment, she wanted to pretend there was nothing to be scared of.

Andrea saw that Brandy was alone and decided to take advantage of their momentary privacy. Sitting next to her, she said, "Can I ask you something?"

"Sure."

Her eyes drifted toward the others and lingered on Albert's bare back. "You and Albert saw the sex room, right?"

Brandy nodded.

"Is it true? Did you…?"

"Lose control and start screwing like animals? Yeah. We did."

Andrea blushed and bit her lip.

"It was terrifying. I barely even knew him."

"I'm sorry."

Brandy shrugged. "It happened. That's all there is to it."

"But you guys ended up together in the end."

"We did."

"What was it like? Afterwards, I mean."

She looked over at Albert, watched him as he watched the night tree and talked with Olivia and Nicole. "Everything was different after that."

"Oh." Andrea looked away, embarrassed. "Yeah. I guess it would be."

Brandy turned and looked at her, considering her. "How much of it did you see?"

She looked up suddenly, startled, and met her eyes.

But Brandy only smiled. It wasn't an accusing smile. Not in any way. It was warm. Kind.

Andrea giggled nervously and looked away. "Am I that obvious?"

"Not too much. Don't worry."

Andrea looked over at the others. "I just wanted a quick peek. I was..."

"Curious."

"Yeah. I didn't really believe it, you know?"

Brandy nodded. "It's *hard* to believe."

"Yeah."

"I know."

"I didn't think it could really happen to me. And... Well... I kind of thought... What if Wayne was lying? What if the room wasn't what he said it was?"

"A valid question."

"Yeah."

"But you didn't lose control." It wasn't a question. If Andrea had lost control, it would have caused quite a scene in that little chamber. At the very least, Wayne and Olivia would have had to constrain her. At most, they would have ended up in a freaky, involuntary three-way. Either way, she was sure there would have been a lot of tension in the air. And when their two groups met up in the labyrinth, there was nothing more than the expected awkwardness of their mutual nudity.

"No."

"So you didn't look very hard at it."

"No. I just saw a few statues. They were... Well... You know."

"I do." Brandy leaned back on her arms, stretching her aching legs out in front of her. She had to lean to one side because of her sore bottom. "They're pretty shocking."

"They are."

"They really get inside your head."

"Yeah."

"And now you're really horny for my boyfriend."

Andrea's eyes went shockingly wide. Her whole face flushed red in an instant. "No! I mean... I didn't... I'm..."

Brandy laughed. "It's okay. Relax."

The poor girl looked like she was ready to cry.

Leaning closer, whispering, Brandy said, "He's kind of the only guy here, and he's kind of butt naked."

Andrea said nothing. She stared at her own hands.

"Don't be embarrassed. I think I'd be insulted if you didn't want him. He's a cutie." She looked at Albert, watched him for a moment. "I mean, when I went in there, I was all over that."

Andrea giggled, but still she blushed.

Brandy smiled again. Then she sighed. "God, the things that place puts in your head."

"What was it like in there? For you? I mean, you guys saw it all, right?"

"We did. Every last freaky statue."

"What was it like for you guys?"

"It was the scariest thing I ever experienced," Brandy replied. "At least... It was at first. Now it doesn't seem so bad. Not looking back. I mean I still have him. But then... I mean, he was practically a stranger."

"I can't imagine."

"No. You can't. It's like you suddenly want something so bad you can hardly stand it. With all your being, like you'll actually *die* if you can't get it. It's like being hopelessly in love with someone you can't have, but much more intense. And then it's happening, and you want it so much, even while you're getting it, that you can't seem to realize that you already have it. It's like reality separates itself from the wanting and becomes sort of a dream."

"Wow."

"Yeah. Wow."

Andrea thought she could almost understand. She'd felt the beginnings of that, after all. That first tickling urge for something she'd never wanted so strongly before… Like an itch someplace she couldn't scratch. And that feeling hadn't gone away. It was still with her, gnawing at her from somewhere deep inside. "Did it change you?"

Brandy continued to stare at Albert. "I don't know, honestly. I say it did, but… In the end, I don't know. For a long time, I blamed the sex room because I felt like such a slut. The two of us… We started dating the next day. By the end of the week, I was practically begging him to take me somewhere and fuck me. It was like I couldn't get enough."

Andrea shifted her weight nervously and chewed her lip. She didn't like the sound of that.

"But over time…I had to admit to myself that… Well… I'm really not sure. It might not be the sex room at all. Maybe it's just *me*."

"But it all started there. You weren't like that before."

"Well, yeah. But… Me and Albert… *We* started there, too. That was where I started to fall in love with him. Maybe I was just using the sex room as an excuse."

Andrea considered this. It would be a relief to know that she wasn't necessarily doomed to turn into a sex-starved slut just because she peeked in the sex room. But she also didn't care for the idea that she was responsible for those lustful feelings about Albert...

"On one hand, it might just be that you've had your first real taste of a strong, sexual attraction and somewhere deep down you like it. Or it could be that something has actually planted those urges in your mind. Maybe it's all some kind of complicated illusion and Albert and I just keep feeding it to each other. If so... Maybe you'll just get over it."

"But what if I don't?"

Brandy turned and looked at her. "I think you'll be okay."

"How can you be sure?"

"I can't, I guess. But honestly, I think it gets into your head more than you realize. I mean I saw it all. I walked around in there. I saw every statue in that place and it's not like I have no control at all. I don't throw myself at every cute guy I pass on the street. I don't swoon over every guy who flirts with me in the bar. I'm not going to jump on Albert at my family reunion."

Andrea giggled. There was an embarrassing image.

"We're still completely in control. We just...want to have sex a lot more than we ever did before. That's all." She smiled. "Who knows? I was already crushing a little on Albert before he found that box. Maybe in a few weeks we would've gone on a date and ended up exactly the same way. Maybe we're actually just really awesome together in the sack."

Andrea giggled again. She realized she was fidgeting and made herself stop. It was an awkward conversation, but it was good. She needed to hear these things.

Still smiling, Brandy turned and looked at Albert again. He was staring at the tree, apparently lost in contemplation. Olivia and Nicole were talking about something, but she couldn't hear what they were saying.

She and Albert shared something special. She wouldn't change that even if she could. It didn't matter if it was natural or if some strange sex room gave it to them. They were stronger for it. They were happier for it.

"Well," said Andrea, "I *am* sorry about the whole…you know… your boyfriend thing."

Brandy laughed. "Yeah, well, he's the only one here. Just, promise me you'll crush on someone else when you get home."

"Definitely."

Brandy smiled. "Good."

Andrea felt relieved. Wayne had her believing that she'd poisoned herself in some way, that she'd never be the same, but he didn't know what it was really like. He didn't experience it. And she supposed he probably exaggerated what little he knew to scare her and Olivia into not being too tempted to peek. She certainly couldn't blame him for that. But there *was* a grain of truth to it. Perhaps the room's only power was suggestion. All it took sometimes was a single idea. Once momentum took over, the human mind was as unstoppable as any physical force of nature. "Thanks."

"No problem. I'm glad I could help. When it happened to me, I had Albert. We went through it together. I can't imagine going through it alone. So if you ever need to talk again, just let me know."

"I will."

"Try not to regret getting mixed up in this too much."

"I won't. In spite of it all… I'm glad I came. You guys are awesome."

Brandy sat up and smiled. "I'm glad you came, too."

"That's good. And I'm sorry I was spying on you guys at Gilbert House."

"Are you kidding? I'd have been spying on us, too! I mean, how weird were we being?"

Andrea giggled. "*So* weird! I didn't know what was going on."

"And it turned out to be even weirder than you imagined."

"*Yeah*, it did!"

Albert stood up and walked back to where they were sitting. "Feet feel any better?"

Brandy smiled up at him. "No."

"Mine either. What're you two giggling about?"

"My naked boyfriend."

"Nice. Just remember, it's cold out here."

"If you say so."

Andrea started giggling again. She was still blushing. She could feel it on her cheeks.

"Learn anything about the man-eating trees?"

"I honestly don't know what we'll do if we have to get past another one. Especially if it's even more aggressive than that one."

"Maybe there won't be any more," hoped Andrea.

Albert nodded. "I hope not." But hoping rarely made a difference in things.

Another of those loud, slapping noises came again. This one sounded like it came from somewhere below them.

"Seriously," said Nicole from where she sat, "what is that?"

"Maybe it's just rocks falling," guessed Brandy. "Maybe the explosion on the tower shook some stones free."

"Could be," agreed Andrea.

"We should keep moving," said Albert.

Brandy groaned. "Just another couple minutes?"

Albert sat down next to her. "Maybe just a couple.

Chapter 14

Olivia expected to find another night tree waiting for them nearby. They were, after all, in the middle of a vast forest filled with the disturbing things. And it was beginning to feel as if she were inescapably bound to the horrors of this dark world. But for the time being, at least, they continued up the mountain unimpeded.

They ascended a steep hill, crawled under a low ledge and crossed a narrow valley where the cracks in the stone were numerous and flames crowded uncomfortably close to the path. Managing somehow to pass unsinged, they then made their way up another steep slope and squeezed through a tight gap between two stone walls, eventually emerging onto a protruding shelf that overlooked the lake far below.

They were now standing approximately even with the surrounding forest and as they looked out across that empty distance, they could clearly see that those trees had changed. Awakening to the light of the burning temple, they leaned inward, stretching their branches toward the warm glow. The nearest of them were bent over the ledge, their tops reaching out over the churning lake. They looked like an army of great, tentacled beasts with their branches wriggling eerily in the firelight.

They weren't quite writhing like the one growing on the path behind them, though. Their greater distance from the flames seemed to be making them slower to awaken. But even wide awake, those trees would be of no concern to them. The only thing any of them found very unsettling about those far-off trees was that they now obscured the ground along the top of the wall, making it impossible to see what shadows were lurking over there.

And even that was perhaps not such a bad thing. Albert, for one, preferred the monsters over there to stay hidden. There was nothing they could do about the approaching horde, after all. If there was an army of undead creatures amassing in those trees, the less they could see of it, the better.

As he continued on up the mountain, Albert wondered if an awakened night tree would prey on those walking corpses as quickly as it would the living. If so, perhaps the eerie forest would do them a favor.

One could certainly hope.

A short time later, the path dipped into a shallow valley and twisted through a series of low bluffs that took them closer to the mountain and beyond the sight of the wall and its creepy army of tentacled trees. Meanwhile, those mysterious creatures overhead had grown more numerous and were passing over them closer and closer as the day wore on. Although that huge inferno at the very top was obviously the main attraction, every source of flame was an irresistible lure, including the vents along the path, and they now frequently passed within ten or fifteen feet of their heads.

This did allow Albert a slightly better view of the beasts, but they were still moving so fast that he remained at a loss as to exactly what they were. Their backward wings had a leathery look and sound as they beat against the air overhead. But their bodies were long, narrow and featureless. It reminded him somehow of a large moth, but he still couldn't tell if they were more bug, bat or reptile. Or any of the above.

The winding bluffs nestled themselves along the steep walls of the mountain and weaved back and forth, carrying them higher with each pass until they reached a narrow shelf, where another short tunnel led them to a small clearing surrounded by sheer walls.

Protruding from the wall to the left as they exited the tunnel were dozens of stones like those that had served as steps twice before. But these were not steps. Instead, these were arranged like the hand- and footholds of a climbing wall.

As soon as Albert looked at these, he very badly wanted to curse. "Good thing I didn't break my *leg*," he said.

"Can you make it up there?" asked Andrea.

"Of course he can," encouraged Nicole.

"I don't really have a choice," Albert reminded them. This was the only way forward. And turning back certainly wasn't an option. Unless he wanted to spend the rest of his life on this mountain, he was going to have to climb this wall. And at only about twenty feet high, it was hardly the face of Everest. What worried him was how he was going to keep his balance with only one arm. And of course, how much it was going to hurt if he fell.

"Are you going to be okay?" asked Brandy.

He nodded. "I'll just have to take it slow. What about you? You're not exactly a fan of these kinds of things."

Brandy shrugged. This was exactly the kind of situation she hated most. It was not really the actual height that she found intimidating. It was the idea of hanging precariously from such a height. She didn't even like standing on a four-foot ladder without someone holding it for her.

He glanced at Olivia. "And you too."

Olivia looked up at the wall and tried not to look nervous. "It's not so high," she said. But it was more than high enough to break an ankle if she fell.

"It's weird," said Andrea. "It looks so fake and natural at the same time."

Albert knew what she meant. It was the same as those steps. The mountainside, the walls, even the stones, themselves, all looked like natural formations, yet there was so much obvious intention. Did the sentinels design every last nook and cranny of this mountain?

Again, he wondered why? Why a mountain? Were they trying to disguise the temple? To hide it? That didn't seem right. It was a mountain inside a massive, walled hole in the ground, in the middle of a sprawling forest, in a world of eternal darkness. It was pretty obvious that it was unnatural.

He simply didn't understand it.

"Well, I'm not scared of it," declared Nicole. "I'll go up with Albert, in case he needs some help. You two go up first."

"I can stay with him, too," volunteered Andrea. As soon as the words were out of her mouth, she blushed and looked at Brandy. It wasn't that she wanted to stay with Albert. It was just that she wanted to be helpful.

But Brandy hadn't noticed. She was only looking nervously up at the climbing wall. "Maybe you should go up first," she suggested. "In case we need a hand at the top. I know that's going to be the hardest part for me."

Olivia nodded. Up there at the highest point… That was where she'd need a hand.

"Okay," Andrea replied. Immediately, she took hold of two of the stones and began to climb.

"Careful," cried Olivia.

"Make sure none of those are loose," Albert warned, remembering the steps that led up the hillside to the night tree.

"I will." She made her way up the wall quickly, making it look absurdly easy. In only a matter of seconds, she was sitting on the ground above, looking down at them.

"Should she have that much energy?" Brandy asked. "I don't feel like she should be that spry after all this walking."

"It doesn't seem quite normal," agreed Nicole.

Olivia nodded agreement. She was quite sure that she was going to look every bit as slow and clumsy going up as Andrea had been quick and graceful.

"It's easier than it looks," Andrea assured them.

"Let's get it over with," groaned Brandy. She took hold of the first stone and began to climb.

Next to her, Olivia followed her lead.

As predicted, both of them made much slower progress than Andrea. They were afraid of slipping and falling, even from the very start. And the higher they climbed, the more nervous they became about each move they made.

But Andrea was right. It wasn't as hard as they'd feared. The stones were perfectly sized for their purpose, allowing easy grips for their hands and plenty of surface for their feet. But the task was no less daunting when the fear of falling was like a cold weight crushing down on them.

Albert and Nicole called up to them, telling them that they were both doing great. Andrea watched and encouraged them from above.

Olivia paused now and then and closed her eyes, willing herself to remain calm. If she became too scared, she knew she would make a mistake. And if she made a mistake, she would fall.

"You can do it," Brandy told her as she clung to the stones.

"I know. I just need to take a second before I start rushing myself."

"You're doing great so far."

"Thanks." But she didn't feel like she was doing great. She felt like a fat girl clinging perilously to a stupid wall.

But little-by-little, she made her way to the top, where Andrea helped her and Brandy up over the ledge.

Now it was Albert's turn. He was not afraid of heights. He never had been. But he was attempting this feat with one arm literally tied. That meant that, while he could do the actual climbing with his feet, he would have to rely on his one hand to cling to the hand-holds. And each time he reached for a new stone, he'd have to let go for a moment, leaving himself balancing on his feet alone. If he should begin to tip backward at one of these crucial moments, he could topple over and plunge to the ground.

Nicole ascended with him, keeping pace, always ready with one hand to steady him.

Albert, for one, couldn't seem to make himself stop thinking about how much time this was taking. Every second they lingered was another second that a future night tree had to awaken. It was another second those zombies had to find a way across the lake. It was another second for those things in the sky to realize there was fresh prey on the mountain.

But he also could not afford to rush.

One step at a time. One foot. The other foot. His hand. And again.

Slowly, steadily, they both made their way to the top without trouble.

"Climbing gear," gasped Albert as he tried to catch his breath. "Add it to the list. Right after flares and binoculars."

"Right," said Brandy. "Or we could just not do this anymore."

"Or that."

Nicole gazed up at the burning summit above them. It still looked so far away. "How far do you think we've come now?"

"Not nearly as far as I'd like," replied Albert. He studied the path ahead. A wide shelf was spread out before them. They would be traveling downhill for a little while, at a shallow angle, toward the far corner. "Let's keep moving."

But within minutes Albert stopped as something on the ground caught his eye.

There was a certain, earthy grime covering the mountain terrain, but for the most part, there had been nothing more than stone beneath their feet since they left the clean, smooth surfaces of the labyrinth. But here, in front of him, was a splatter of black and greasy goop that he had seen nowhere else.

"What is it?" asked Brandy.

"Oh god…" groaned Nicole. "Please tell me that's not what I think it is."

Albert looked up into the sky. Those strange creatures had grown into a massive swarm. "Sorry to break it to you, but that would be the noise we keep hearing."

Olivia stared up at the flying creatures, horrified. "You mean they're…?"

"Living creatures with all the same disgusting bodily functions as every other living creature? Yeah."

Brandy swore loudly. This place just kept getting nastier.

Andrea simply said, "Gross."

"Thinking positively, they seem to be mostly focused on the big fire at the top of the temple, so fallout should be less common out this far."

Nicole stared up at them. "Goody."

"And when we get closer to the top?" asked Brandy.

"Probably best not to think about it too much," he replied.

"Wonderful."

Albert stared at them. He still felt that odd *significance*. There was something about them, something profound, but he couldn't even begin to grasp what that something was.

"I swear to God," growled Brandy. "If one of those things shits on me I'm going to totally lose it."

Albert had no doubt that she would. He pulled his eyes away from those strange creatures and continued walking. It was still a long way to the top of the mountain and he was sure there would be plenty more unpleasantness along the way. If all they had to deal with was some freakishly large bird droppings, he'd consider himself lucky.

Chapter 15

Brandy stopped walking. A shiver rushed all the way down her body. "Okay, did anybody else hear that?"

In fact, they all did. A voice rang out, as if from someone walking right there with them. It was the voice of a woman, sharp and desperate.

"What did it say?" asked Nicole.

"Sounded like, 'In a garden,'" said Olivia.

"I heard, 'Find the red one,'" said Brandy.

"Wasn't English." Albert turned and looked around, but there was nothing but shadows and stone to be seen. "Didn't sound like any language I've ever heard before."

Andrea turned to face him. "What do you think it means?"

It meant that this strange, black world had grown even more vast and mysterious. It meant that something unearthly was at work on this mountain. And it meant that he had one more damned thing to think about. Aloud, he merely said, "Can't say."

"Is it really ghosts?" Brandy wondered. The idea was actually less terrifying than it was intriguing, when she thought about it. She'd always liked supernatural things. Although she wasn't sure she wanted any ghostly encounters tonight.

"I always heard the tunnels under the city were haunted," Andrea said.

Nicole nodded. "Me too."

"I think everyone who grew up in Briar Hills probably did," said Brandy.

"I even heard about those tunnels a few times in Wilsing," said Olivia. But then again, most people from Wilsing commuted regularly to the Hill. Her family did all its grocery shopping there.

"But I never experienced anything in the tunnels," Andrea recalled.

"Us either," said Nicole.

Albert considered this. He wondered why it was that this activity was focused here and not throughout the temple. Had many people died here? He'd assumed that no one had been here in a very long time, perhaps not since the fourteen pregnant women passed through here, back at the very dawn of their world. (Assuming, of course, that the Sentinel Queen wasn't lying about that detail.) At the very least, he didn't think that so many people could have passed through here over the ages that there could be multiple restless spirits haunting the mountainside.

"I wonder if they're ghosts of people who died in the Wood," he said. "Maybe they gather here for some reason."

"But why here?" asked Andrea. "Why not Gilbert House?"

"I wouldn't haunt Gilbert House, either," decided Olivia. "That place really sucks."

Brandy, Nicole and Andrea all looked at her for a moment, and then all four of them broke into giggles. Albert watched them, smiling.

"Well, it's true."

"I know it is," said Nicole.

Albert gazed up at the burning summit above them. Was it possible that spirits could be drawn to this place? If so, what made it so special? Did it all have to do with the Sentinels' doorway? Their mysterious judgment?

The spirits, if that was in fact what they were, fell silent again and Albert led the way forward. As he continued along the path, he wondered if he'd ever find the answers he wanted. He wondered if there were *any* answers awaiting them at the top of this mountain.

The terrain grew rocky again and the cliffs crowded in on them, steering them to the left, beneath a stone archway. Here, where the path became narrow, a stone bridge crossed over a deep gorge.

Sweltering heat struck them as they approached, and they peered over the sides of the bridge to see that a long crack ran the length of the gorge's bottom. Flames spewed from the fissure, creating a wall of heat that they were now going to have to walk through.

"Well this is terrifying," said Nicole.

It certainly was. If any of them were to slip and fall while crossing, the hard rocks would be the very least of their worries. It would be like getting thrown into a furnace. Albert couldn't seem to stop his imagination from bringing the image to life in his mind. Falling, burning, unable to climb up. He tried to force it from his mind, but it was stubborn. Would it be quick, he wondered, a flash of excruciating pain and then peace? Or would the agony linger on and on?

Brandy glowered at the scene before her. "Just in case high places weren't terrifying enough, I guess."

"Can we even cross that?" asked Andrea. It certainly didn't look safe. A curtain of wavering heat separated them from the other side, parted only by the narrow stone bridge. How hot was the air there? She was surprised the stone wasn't glowing red-hot.

Albert stepped out onto the bridge. It was warm beneath his feet. Very warm. But it wasn't hot. Cautiously, he reached out over the edge. It was like the heat that escaped from the oven door when he checked on dinner, surprisingly hot, but not likely to burn them. "I think it's okay."

"Unless the whole fucking thing drops out from under us," snapped Brandy.

Clearly, her optimism was running low.

Albert ignored her and started across.

"Careful!" she pleaded.

"I'm okay." And he was. He felt the heat instantly. It was like entering a car on a hot parking lot in the middle of summer. It beat down on him, almost a physical thing.

And there was a wind. It rushed up from the fiery crevice below, stirring his hair.

As he inched his way cautiously across the bridge, he peered over the side and into the long, glowing crack beneath him. Again, the image of falling into those flames surfaced in his mind and gave him a hard shudder. Slow or fast, he was sure that would be a terrible way to die.

Spooked by the thought of roasting alive, he focused his attention on the path again, on the narrow, little bridge that was all that separated him from a thirty-five-foot drop to a fiery demise. It looked like an ordinary formation of the stone, but like the steps and the climbing wall before it, it served such a specific purpose that it could only have been here by design. He was sure, then, that it would not crumble beneath them.

But what was the purpose of such a thing? Why did this burning gorge exist? Did it serve any kind of purpose other than the twisted enjoyment of the sentinels who designed it? It didn't make any sense. It was like a needlessly drawn-out level in a bad video game.

A flash of light caught his attention as he crossed the midpoint of the bridge and he stopped to peer up at the sky. On a high ledge above them, a particularly large stream of fire was erupting from an unseen vent, casting light down onto him. One of the flying creatures had fluttered too close to it and was now spiraling down into the gorge, trailing smoke and flames behind it.

A second creature dived after it and nearly fell victim to the flames below before thrusting its wings and heaving itself back out of the heat.

In that light, he could almost see the creature. If it had not been the color of the deep shadows, he might have been able to see more detail, but against the dark backdrop of the stone, all that he could discern of it besides the odd shape of its wings was that there was something strange about its head, as well. It almost looked as if it didn't have one.

But he had no time to contemplate the beasts further. He could feel the sweat beading on his skin and the bridge was uncomfortably hot beneath his bare feet. He continued forward and stepped out of the heat without falling to his fiery doom.

When he turned around, he saw that Brandy was already making her way across behind him. She held her arms crossed against her chest, making herself as small as possible. He could tell by her wide, frightened eyes that she, too, had imagined the horrors of falling into that hellish crack.

But like him, she made her way across without incident. As did the other three, one by one. Andrea even took a moment to probe the rising heat with her hand, as Albert had done.

He liked Andrea. She had a marvelous sense of adventure.

Again, his eyes drifted to the sky. Those creatures were everywhere. They looked like a massive swarm of locusts. Several of them passed close overhead, great awkward things that still seemed to pay them absolutely no attention. Only the flames held their interest.

The cacophony of beating wings had become a constant drone upon the air. It covered the soft roar of all but the nearest flames. But another noise made it through the din: two more of those loud, clapping noises rang out from somewhere nearby as something foul fell from the airborne swarm and spattered upon the hard stone with a heavy slap.

Again, that bizarre feeling crept into him. It almost felt like they were looking back at him, although that was such a silly notion.

Somewhere on the other side of the mountain, another one caught itself on fire and fell out of the sky in a swirl of colorful flame.

The five of them moved on.

Ahead of them, Albert could see another tunnel, its black, yawning mouth waiting patiently to swallow them into the darkness again, and he, for one, was again eager to get out from beneath the queer gaze of that beastly swarm.

Chapter 16

Although this tunnel was considerably longer than the previous two, it was nothing compared to the endless passages of the labyrinth within. However, for the first time since emerging from that empty darkness into the firelight, they found themselves unable to see the path before them.

Albert, for one, hadn't felt the need to dig out the flashlights just yet. He wasn't sure they really needed them. The light had not even faded completely at their backs, after all. But Brandy retrieved them from the backpack before they had explored the first few yards and handed one each to Olivia and Andrea.

He didn't try to stop them. If the light gave them comfort, then he wanted them to have it, but he was concerned about attracting unwanted attention. It was, after all, the flashlights that originally drew the zombies to Gilbert House. Even with the entire mountain ablaze, he couldn't help being concerned about revealing their exact location.

He remained quiet, but also watchful.

Within a few short minutes, the lights revealed something both useful and dreadful waiting for them in the darkness of the tunnel: steps. These ascended well beyond the reach of the flashlights, up and up through the stone belly of the temple, promising to speed their climb considerably. But the price would be paid by their aching bodies.

They were so tired. The muscles of their legs burned. They had walked all night and all morning, from the university campus to the steam tunnels, all the way to the Temple of the Blind and through its endless labyrinths, the vast majority of that distance barefoot. Was it possible to do permanent damage to their feet with this kind of abuse?

Yet all of them began to climb without a word of protest.

What would they say, anyway? What choice did they have? The only option was to carry on and suffer whatever awaited them along this strange road.

Nicole, more than anybody was aware that the fun had worn off this adventure. She was so tired. Her feet hurt so much. And her heart was still broken for poor Wayne.

She'd been so excited to come. She remembered the first time Albert and Brandy told her the story of their trip to the temple. She'd listened so raptly to their amazing tale, taking in every incredible word, like a child enchanted by a particularly wonderful bedtime story. She'd wanted so much to go and see that place, to look with her own eyes upon what Albert had dubbed "the Temple of the Blind" with all its wonders. She'd since listened to their tale more times than she could recall, and she'd yearned each time to experience those fantastic marvels for herself.

Given the chance, she would have walked boldly into the sex room and looked with wide-eyed and satisfying greed at the vivid things within, just to *experience* it, just to know what it was like to be swallowed by that kind of lust. The very idea of that kind of sex—not love, Brandy had informed her adamantly, nothing at all like love, just hard, raw *fucking*—captivated her beyond describing. She'd made love before. She'd fucked before, too. Once or twice. But what they described was something altogether different. And a part of her *wanted* that.

There had even been a time or two, when she was alone in bed at night and feeling particularly exotic, that she fantasized about *Albert* taking her there and showing her what Brandy had once described as "lust like Armageddon." It was, of course, something she would never admit to either of them in a million years. They could never know. No one could know. Not ever. But it *had* crossed her mind.

It wasn't about Albert though. Not really. This was that same part of her that wanted to know what fantastic things lurked in the other emotion rooms. What amazing things had they *not* seen? What abominations of human hatred and terror did they simply stumble blindly past on their way through those other rooms? Her curiosity of such things was almost maddening. She'd lain awake so many nights wondering. She so badly wanted to be here, to experience all of it with her own eyes.

And now she was here. Now she'd seen for herself the Temple of the Blind in its endless shades of gray, and it had been far from the gothic fairy tale adventure she'd expected it to be. Sure, she felt some exhilaration when she first arrived—the wonder of that first room, of those first sentinels with their impossibly long fingers and toes and penises—but mostly she'd been cold and scared to death. Her two closest friends had almost died this morning and someone who could have been as dear a friend really was dead. The pain in her hand was endless. It ached and throbbed until she wanted to cry and there was nothing at all she could do to make it better. All she could do was walk, on and on, lost for all she knew, on feet that had gone beyond aching, that were almost numb.

The stairs seemed to go on for miles, although it was probably only a few stories before they reached the top. There, the passage curved sharply to the left and led them to still more steps, atop which could be seen the promising glow of firelight.

Andrea broke the silence by commenting that she couldn't believe it was already so late.

"I don't even want to think about it," growled Brandy. She couldn't believe she'd been gone so long that she was missing work. And she didn't look forward to trying to explain it to that bitch, Paula.

Albert was still of the mind that he simply didn't care. There was no reason to. It couldn't be undone now anyway. Besides, it wasn't like he was throwing away a once-in-a-lifetime career opportunity. It was just a stupid part-time job. There would be more.

Andrea wondered what her parents thought of her being gone. They would have been up for hours by now. She'd left them a note explaining that she'd gone to see a friend and didn't know when she'd be back, but she'd hoped to be home before they could find it. She'd never just up and left like that before. She always told them where she was going.

Would they be mad at her? She was eighteen, but just barely. She still lived in their house, under their rules. What would she even tell them when she returned home? She'd have to make up some kind of story. She could never tell them the truth. Her dad would have a heart attack if he knew she was parading around naked.

But at least she didn't have any injuries to account for. Not yet.

Olivia wasn't concerned with the time. She'd told her roommate not to worry about her. It would likely be days before Misty became worried enough to say anything to anybody.

Nicole wasn't worried, either. Her parents knew she was staying with Brandy. They trusted her. All she needed to worry about was reaching the top of these damned stairs.

She looked up toward the light above them and froze in mid-step. There, in the tunnel opening, something was waiting for them.

A tall, dark figure stood against the soft glow of the flames, an imposing silhouette. In the writhing light of the fire, it almost seemed to move, but that was only an illusion. It could not move.

Nicole continued on, feeling silly. It was only one of those freaky statues.

The sentinel beckoned them forward, one hand reaching out to them, the other pointing straight ahead, urging them across a flat, open area to another tunnel, where a second sentinel urged them onward still.

Straight ahead, folks, Albert could almost imagine them saying. *Single file now. No pushing.*

As they stepped into the open and gathered around the tall legs of the nearest sentinel, they saw that there were two more status. One stood on their right, at the top of another set of stone steps. It seemed to be beckoning to some other group of travelers, climbing unseen from the darkness below and urging them straight across, toward the fourth and final statue that stood on their left, which simultaneously beckoned those unseen travelers and motioned them on through an open doorway behind him.

The message was clear. These two spoke to them now, showing

them the way. The other two spoke to someone else, some other time. They were at a crossroads of some sort, and Albert felt suddenly and inexplicably humbled.

"What is this place?" Olivia asked, her voice hushed, as though she, too, could feel the importance of this spot.

"It's the real entrance to the Temple of the Blind." Albert replied as his eyes were drawn to the passage on his left. He was as sure of this as he had ever been of anything in his life. They had come through it backward, after all, beginning in the raw tunnel far beneath the city that had once been the temple's exit.

He'd seen this before, back on the other side of the labyrinth, before they'd even met the Keeper. It was a small room with two sentinels. The first beckoned them forward. The second seemed to be doing the same for someone coming the other way. He remembered realizing that the Sentinel Queen's fourteen mothers would have passed through that room and marveled at the idea of sharing that experience so many millennia after they had come and gone.

Far to the right, directly across from them, stood that wide gap in the wall. He was sure there was a river at the bottom of that canyon, carrying away all the water as it flowed in from whatever underground river fed the temple's many reservoirs. Those steps faced that river, and when he walked over to where the sentinel stood looking down, he saw in the firelight that they descended all the way to the surface of the lake.

It was so easy to imagine a ship lumbering between those high walls, struggling against the current while unimaginable horrors paced the ledges high above them, some perhaps hurling themselves off the wall and into the water in desperation. The idea of such a ship, its only cargo fourteen pregnant women and the future of all mankind, gave him a chill all the way down his back.

Andrea didn't understand. "But what about where we came out?"

"Just an escape hatch," Albert replied. "Our exit. I'll bet this entrance is sealed." And on the heels of that he thought, *Closed up by the only other people who ever survived the entire journey from one end of the temple to the other*, and a second shiver gripped him deep inside.

He looked again at the passage that waited for them. That path continued on around the mountain toward the top of the temple. That was where they had to go.

"How do you know all this?" Olivia asked.

Albert shook his head. He had no idea. "Just seems right is all."

"Psychic?" Nicole asked.

He shrugged. Maybe it was that he was psychic. Or maybe it was just good old fashioned intuition. Or maybe it was bullshit. He didn't know. But it felt absolutely right. If the Sentinel Queen and the Keeper hadn't lied to them about the fourteen mothers, and he had a strong feeling that at least some part of it was true, then directly behind him was the door by which those poor women had entered the temple all those ages ago.

If all this was true, then this was like stumbling onto the Garden of Eden and gazing upon the tree that bore the fruit that had ultimately ejected mankind from paradise.

"What's that?" Andrea pointed down the steps. A dark shape was there, about a third of the way down, lying motionless in the shadows against the wall.

Chapter 17

"Albert, what is it?" Brandy's voice was an anxious whisper in his ear.

The thing on the steps hadn't moved. Nor would it. Albert knew what it was the moment he saw it. He glanced up at the chaotic storm of creatures that circled above them. He'd watched several of them catch fire and fall from the sky. This was one of them.

Less afraid than curious, he descended the steps and knelt beside the odd carcass. It was difficult to see. It had come to rest behind a protrusion in the wall, a place where the shadows were deep, and its dark colors were friendly to the gloom.

Glancing up, he saw that the others were waiting for him at the top of the steps. Brandy, Olivia and Andrea were all still holding their flashlights. "Bring one of those over here," he said.

Andrea came to him without hesitation. Like Albert, she wanted to see it. She wanted to know what it was.

"Is it one of *them*?" Olivia asked. "Those things in the sky?" She started down the steps, too, also curious. Brandy and Nicole hesitantly descended behind her, not wanting to be the only ones left behind.

"It *was*." Albert leaned forward, fascinated. It was not quite like his first look at the hounds. Those had teased his curiosity for over a year with nothing but the enigmatic sound of their slashing scales to feed his imagination. Also, the first time he'd seen a hound close up it had still been alive. But the wonder of looking upon a brand new creature was exactly the same.

"It's repulsive," observed Nicole.

It was. Albert had earlier imagined these things as resembling giant bugs or pterodactyls or perhaps great, winged gargoyles, but this thing lying before them with small tendrils of smoke still rising from its blackened flesh was like none of those things. In fact, it was like nothing he'd ever imagined. It had no legs at all, only a short, fleshy tail protruding from a worm-like body as long as he was tall and as thick as his shoulders were wide. It had no hair or feathers, only naked flesh that was black even before it had charred itself in the inferno. Its wings made up the majority of its size, great folds of flesh stretched between long, bony appendages. They were now broken and torn like two mangled kites, but he could still see the basic structure. His earlier observation that these things did not have a head turned out to be correct. It had nothing that resembled a head at all, only two huge, black eyes protruding from the short, round stub of an otherwise useless neck. They were egg-shaped, he saw, and cooked into foggy stones by the flames that had engulfed it. Unlike the hounds, this thing appeared to have only one backbone.

It was lying on its side, propped up by one of its broken wings, and Albert knelt to get a closer look at its underside.

"Don't!" Brandy moaned.

"It's okay," he assured her, knowing damned well that he didn't really know if it was okay or not. But he couldn't walk away without examining it. He wanted a closer look at how this thing worked. "Shine it here."

Andrea aimed her flashlight where he pointed.

Its mouth was on its belly, a gaping gash, running lengthwise to the body. It was at least eighteen inches long and lined on either side with vicious-looking teeth. The biggest of these were an inch long, and each one serrated like a steak knife. Two limp tongues protruded from this horror of a mouth, one at each end, and there were two rows of four short, stubby limbs on either side. These were only four inches long but almost three inches in diameter. At the end of each one was a sharp, serrated spike.

"Come on," Brandy begged. "Get away from it."

But Albert didn't hear her. He was as fascinated as he was repulsed.

Farther down the belly was a swollen, fleshy orifice. A thick, yellowish substance was oozing from it. More was dried to the fleshy lips in a muddy crust. Protruding from this organ at the end nearest the tail was something long and fleshy. It hung limp and useless like a length of empty intestine. A slightly darker substance seeped from the end and dangled in a fine ribbon.

"So is it a boy or a girl?" asked Nicole. Her tone was sarcastic, of course, and beneath it he could clearly hear her disapproval of this close inspection.

"Uh… Sure. Let's go with one of those." He looked up at the creatures that were still circling overhead, wondering. Something wasn't

149

right here. Something didn't make sense. He stood again and gazed up at the sky, trying to see the things that flew up there. After a moment, he turned to Olivia. "What was it the old man told Wayne about the Wood? About those things going crazy when they sense something alive?"

Olivia remembered Wayne's story well. She'd heard it twice, after all. Once in the car with Andrea and once in the labyrinth after they'd caught up to the others. "Something about the smallest spark of life driving them into a frenzy? That stuff?"

Albert nodded. "Basically that the dead out here go crazy when anything alive enters their world, right?"

She nodded.

"So what?" asked Nicole.

Albert looked at her and then back at Olivia again. "I may be wrong, but I don't think these things are dead."

"This one is," Andrea assured him.

"Well, yeah. This one is. Now. But it wasn't."

"Then how do they keep away from the zombies?" Olivia asked. It was a good question, one for which Albert had no answer. He simply shook his head.

"Well, they *can* fly," said Brandy.

"I'm sure they can't *always* be flying," said Nicole.

Olivia stared at the carrion eater carcass. "If these things are alive, then their...life force, I guess...or whatever it is...should attract the zombies. It contradicts what that guy told Wayne."

"There's clearly a sustainable population of these things," Albert reasoned. "Meaning there's still plenty of *life* right here in the Wood."

"You think the old man was lying to Wayne?" Brandy asked.

"I don't know. Maybe they mask their life force or something. Or maybe they just keep out of reach. Like you said, it definitely doesn't hurt that they can fly."

"But how do they survive?" Brandy asked. "What do they eat?"

For this, Albert had an answer, maybe one that answered his last question too: "They're carrion eaters. They eat the dead. They eat the zombies."

For a moment, no one spoke as they digested this information, then Brandy asked the million dollar question: "Is that good or bad?"

Albert shook his head again. If they were lucky, these things weren't built for hunting, only for scavenging, but he found that unlikely. After all, when things died in the Wood they apparently got back up again. Hopefully these carrion eaters didn't have much of a taste for fresh meat.

From somewhere nearby came another of those slapping noises, followed immediately by either a second or a brief echo of the first bouncing off the high walls. The sound was easily as disturbing now as it was when they didn't know what was making it.

Albert gazed up at the crowded sky.

Nicole turned and saw that Andrea was now kneeling beside the dead creature, studying its gruesome underside. The sight for some reason startled her, as though she were reaching down to pick up a deadly snake. "You be careful!" She realized that the words had come out in almost a shriek and cringed a little when Andrea jumped. "I don't trust that thing," she explained in a softer tone.

Andrea had turned and looked at her. Albert could see the apprehension in her eyes but also her curiosity. He understood her completely. It was exactly the way he'd felt about the dead creature.

"Just stay away from it," Olivia pleaded. "I hate those things."

But she wouldn't. Albert could see it in those bright blue eyes. She looked at him instead. "Did you see its wings?" She was speaking directly to him, as though he were the expert on the Wood and all its insane creatures. "Does anything on earth have wings like that?"

Albert *had* noticed the wings. "I don't know. Some insects, maybe. I guess. I have no idea."

For the most part, an animal's wing, be it a chicken or a bat or a pterodactyl, consisted of a single limb, containing bones not unlike a human arm. Even whales, he remembered had bones in its fins that roughly resembled fingers. These things, however, had two limbs protruding from their bodies, with a tough webbing of flesh stretched between them like sails on a ship. There seemed to be a sort of elbow joint about ten feet from the shoulders, which seemed normal enough, but the overall shape of the wings remained backward. The farther they stretched from the body, the wider the wing became, giving them that bizarre bow tie shape.

Andrea turned her light back onto the creature. "Are those *hands?*"

Albert nodded. "Looks like it." At the end of each of the four bony limbs that made up those wings were long, four-fingered claws that looked eerily like monkey hands.

Brandy's curiosity overtook her. She walked over to where Andrea stood and bent to get her own look at the horrible thing.

"It's fascinating," Andrea said.

"It's *repulsive.*" The sight of those oozing gashes sent an icy quiver through her veins.

Andrea was staring at its mouth, that great, deadly gash. It was far too easy to imagine that thing perched atop a screaming victim clutched in its claws, its wings folded above it, slurping meat from bones. "Like a car wreck on the highway. The more awful the sight, the more mangled the vehicles, the more blood on the asphalt, the more you want to look."

Brandy shivered. That was a horrid analogy, but one she realized was absolutely true. Even now she couldn't stop staring at the horrible mouth on which Andrea's flashlight was aimed, wide enough to fit around her entire head.

Albert watched the two of them as they bent over the creature and suddenly he felt nervous. He could almost imagine it waking up and lunging at them, perhaps snatching off both their faces in one swift bite.

And for that matter, wasn't getting back up precisely what the dead tended to do in the Wood?

"Come on," he said, startled by this frightening realization. "I want to have a look at that doorway over there."

Chapter 18

The path that led through this doorway would have entered the temple through the labyrinth, Albert guessed. Those who passed through here would have to navigate those dark passages to the chamber with the forty-two sentinels and then continue onward to the City of the Blind.

Before she died, the Sentinel Queen told them of fourteen women who journeyed here. This had been ages ago, tens of thousands, if not *millions* of years. Where they came from was a mystery, but their destination was the world Albert called home, the only world he had ever known, the only world he thought *anyone* had ever known. It was a fantastic story, one that redefined the very origins of man. So much for Adam and Eve; it was more like Eve and her thirteen sisters. But then again, those women had come from somewhere. Maybe Adam and Eve were from their world. Or whatever world came first. Perhaps the journey of those fourteen mothers was just another version of Noah's Ark and God had decided for reasons beyond our comprehension to simply tear that page out and let us forget about it.

If the Sentinel Queen's story was true, then this was certainly the doorway those women—at least one of which would have been his own grandmother too great to count—used to enter the temple all those millennia ago. If this was all true, and he really had no way to know that it wasn't, then this was a very significant place.

Nicole took the flashlight from Brandy and stepped through the darkened doorway first, sweeping back the shadows and revealing no immediate dangers. But the temple was a haven for monsters. She'd seen them with her own eyes. She had no intention of assuming that a dark hole—especially one that opened onto the Wood of all places—would not be swarming with them. Just because she didn't see them didn't mean they weren't there.

The chamber was about forty feet across, round, with a four-foot-wide pillar of stone standing at its center. Like the rest of the temple's interior, every surface was dark, flawless stone. But there was a misplaced scattering of broken stones on the floor around the pillar.

Albert stood looking down at this debris. After a moment, he lifted his eyes to the pillar and then to the ceiling. Watching him, Nicole shined her light wherever his gaze fell. There was no sign of where the broken stones originated. It was like they had simply been carried here and scattered on the floor. She lowered her eyes and watched as Albert puzzled over it. She was learning from him, she realized. A day ago, she would have taken one look at those stones and simply dismissed them. But now, like Albert, she found herself looking for an explanation to everything. In this case, where did these stones come from and what were they doing here? For that matter, what was the purpose of such a large pillar that seemed to be holding up a room much smaller than many others that had needed no such support?

Andrea walked around the perimeter of the room, dragging her fingertips along the featureless gray walls. Olivia and Brandy followed her, avoiding the broken stones.

On the far side of the chamber was a narrow passage. A set of steps led up into the temple. "Did you say you thought this way was sealed?" asked Olivia as she looked at these steps.

Albert knelt over the scattered stones and picked one up. "Probably," he replied. He studied the stone for a moment and then dropped it and reached for another. "The place was sealed like a tomb. I don't think there'd be more than one way in or out at any given time." Although this was more of a gut feeling than solid deduction. It wasn't as if he really knew anything about this place.

He let the second stone fall from his hand and picked up a third. As he did, he lifted his eyes to the passage on the far side. Andrea had approached it and was now peering up into the darkness with her flashlight.

Olivia stood there for a moment, considering. "How can you be sure?"

Albert looked back down at the stone he'd picked up. "I'm not."

"Then how do you know it's sealed?"

Albert met Olivia's eyes and saw the question burning there. *I didn't see anybody*, he thought. They were Brandy's words, spoken thirteen months ago on the wrong side of the sex room. Hearing them again in his head, so suddenly and so vividly, almost made him shiver. Naked, shaken and scared, she had fixed him with a cold gaze very much like the one he saw now. *I didn't see anybody. I woke up and you were gone.*

Looking up at Olivia now, Albert could almost feel the same, numbing loneliness that he'd felt that night. Suddenly he found it hard to understand why Brandy didn't take the flashlight and run, leaving him to die in the darkness. Another woman probably would have.

He wondered what Olivia would have done.

"Because he's psychic," replied Andrea as she prodded the darkness atop the steps with her light. "Right?"

Albert glanced at Andrea and then back to Olivia. That mistrusting look was gone, replaced with simple curiosity. Her pretty face contained not a hint of ill thought. Was the accusation he saw ever really there, he wondered? Or had he only imagined it?

"I don't know," he replied. "Really. I just think there's probably a reason we didn't exit through here instead of where we did." He looked at the steps again. "Just a hunch."

"I'll bet being psychic doesn't hurt," added Nicole.

"If I really am, I guess." He turned his attention back to the stone he was holding. There were markings carved onto its surface, but nothing he could discern. Given time—*lots* of time—perhaps he could reassemble whatever these stones had once been—if they had been anything at all. But lingering here to do that would be as impractical as loading them into his backpack and carrying them up the mountain.

He let the stone fall back to the floor and stood up.

Their meaning wasn't important. He could feel it somehow. But there was something else here. Something that *was* important. It seemed almost to be calling out to him.

"Where do you think it goes?" Andrea asked as she leaned into the passage, trying to see to the top of the steps. "Anywhere?"

Albert turned toward her, toward the passage and those stairs, as his brain tiredly worked at these odd thoughts, and realized after a moment that he was staring at her naked bottom. Immediately, he closed his eyes and rubbed them. He was so tired. How could he possibly think straight in his condition? Could he trust himself to proceed logically?

And yet, he became more and more convinced that there was something important about this chamber. Was it really the psychic abilities the Sentinel Queen told him about? Did he have some kind of otherworldly connection to the world, something that other people didn't have? Or was it his own talent, his trained eye for detail, honed by years of mystery novels and brain teasers and puzzles? Or was it all just bullshit and dumb luck?

Then again, he'd also been told that psychic minds were susceptible to suggestion. Maybe it was nothing but some leftover message the Sentinel Queen buried in his subconscious before she died. Or maybe it was the Keeper. Or perhaps that old man Wayne met on his journey to rescue Olivia. If so, could he really trust these feelings? Was it intuition or intrusion?

He suddenly felt like screaming. Damn the Sentinel Queen for ever telling him these things. Now he was second guessing himself and he was sure that was a dangerous thing to do.

He forced these conflicting thoughts from his mind and focused on the steps. He *did* feel that he should go there. And so far his feelings hadn't steered him wrong. He was still breathing. And if he was right about it being sealed, what did it really hurt to go and see for himself?

"You okay?" Nicole asked.

He gave her a weary smile. "Just tired," he assured her.

"You sure?"

Albert nodded and turned toward the passage, but not before he saw the worry in Brandy's eyes.

Andrea had ascended the first few steps and was peering up at something. "What is that?" she asked.

Albert went to her and looked at what her light revealed. The steps didn't go far, but they didn't precisely end, either. At the top was a narrow recess with wide, rectangular grooves in the stone that were obviously ladder rungs. Albert climbed the steps and placed his hand on one of these rungs as Andrea shined the light up into the darkness above him.

The others crowded around the opening at the bottom of the steps and watched.

The ladder ran up the left side of the recess, climbing about twelve feet to a small opening. Staring up at this, he felt an odd prickling at the back of his neck. Something was up there. He was sure of it. Just standing here filled him with a profound sense of significance, even stronger than what he'd felt while looking up at the carrion eaters circling in the sky.

So strong was his certainty that something awaited him up there that he forgot his concerns about the origins of such feelings and began to examine the shaft itself. It was not very wide. If he braced his back against one side...

He turned and positioned himself appropriately.

"What are you doing?" Brandy asked in a tone of voice that was almost comically shocked.

"You're going to break your other arm!" snapped Nicole.

Albert didn't respond. Keeping his injured arm close to his body and his back against the wall behind him, he began to push himself upward with his feet.

"Let me go up instead," Andrea offered.

"Just wait there." It wasn't as easy as it had looked, but he was able enough for the task. Slowly, he made his way upward, steadying himself with his good arm and doing all the work with his legs. *This is stupid*, he thought. What did he think he was looking for? What exactly did he expect to find up here? It would serve him right to poke his head up and find a nest of something nasty ready to snatch out his eyes or rip out his throat. A lot of good he would be to everyone then. At the very least he would probably slip and re-injure his arm. Or do as Nicole predicted and break the other one.

He glanced down at the others as he neared the top. Andrea's flashlight was aimed directly at him, blinding him, but Olivia and Brandy had theirs aimed uselessly at the floor as they watched his strenuous ascent. "Give me all the light you can," he said, and when all three flashlights were aimed past him at the opening, he pushed himself up one more rung and lifted his eyes back to the hole, where a hideous black face was glaring down at him.

Chapter 19

Uttering a horrible belch of a cry, Albert jumped at the ghoulish sight and slipped. In the next instant, he was aware of falling, of a blinding pain in his right knee and screams that seemed to come simultaneously from below and above. But he was also aware of something else, something he'd seen alongside that horrible face: a glint of gold in the shadows.

Then he was swallowed in a firestorm of agony as his broken arm slammed against the cold stone.

The world swam away from him. He found himself adrift in a confusing sea of panic and fear and pain. He might have lost consciousness for a moment, but he couldn't recall for sure. His thoughts wouldn't focus. He couldn't seem to gain control of himself.

Somebody was lifting him. He was sitting up, but he couldn't seem to lift his head.

"What the fuck *was* it?"

"What happened?"

"*Albert?*"

"Is he all right?"

"Shit!"

"Get him out of here!"

"Oh god!"

"*Albert?*"

"He's bleeding!"

"Help me!"

"What the *fuck?*"

"What *was* it?"

Albert couldn't even tell who was speaking anymore. They were a spiraling crowd of voices circling his bleary head.

"Help me get him up." Nicole's voice. She sounded panicked.

He felt his arm lifted, a warm head against his chest, long hair, a hand reaching around his shoulders. She was trying to lift him to his feet, he realized. But he couldn't get up. His legs didn't seem to want to work. "I'm okay. Don't," he tried to say, but the words came out drunken so that it sounded like "'M'okay...Doan..."

"Albert?" Brandy's voice. She was right there, right next to his face. "Get up, baby. Come back to me."

"Never left," he assured her. "Just hurt like hell."

"What happened?" asked Nicole. She was still clinging to him, ready to lift him to his feet. Both of them were crowding over him.

Albert shook his head. "Nothing. Stupid." And it *was* stupid. He'd let himself be startled by the awful sight of that face. He hadn't expected it. But he should have been ready. He was embarrassed to have been frightened like that.

"Come on. Get up."

She and Brandy helped him to his feet and began guiding him back down the stairs. His knee felt like it was on fire. He must have banged it on one of those stone rungs on his way down.

"What happened up there?" asked Nicole.

"Stupid," he said again. "I was startled."

"What did you see?"

"Stupid corpse."

This alarmed Olivia. "*A zombie?*" She turned and aimed her light back up the stairs, half-expecting to see a mummified monstrosity chasing after them.

But Albert shook his head firmly. "No. *Not* a zombie. A *corpse*. A *cadaver*. Just a body. It wasn't dangerous. It just startled me."

"What the hell's a corpse doing up there?" wondered Brandy.

"I thought corpses turned to zombies in the Wood," said Andrea.

Olivia turned and looked at her, startled. A terrible thought suddenly occurred to her. What if *Wayne* had risen as a zombie? What if he was stalking them up the side of the mountain at that very moment? What would she do if she turned around and saw him there, his skin pale, his eyes glazed, the wound in his belly black and festering? The very idea was unspeakably awful.

It was like Andrea said. Wasn't that what the dead did in this world?

She couldn't think of a worse thing to endure than to encounter one of those things with the face of someone she'd loved, even if that love had been brief. The thought alone was agony. It felt as if a cold, dead hand had reached deep into her chest and tore a bloody gash in her heart.

"This one wasn't a zombie," Albert insisted. "It wasn't moving. It was just sitting there. It was wearing something. Some kind of medallion."

They crossed the room with the scattered stones and made their way through the open doorway.

"We need it," Albert said.

"Need what?" asked Brandy.

"That medallion."

Brandy and Nicole looked at each other, confused.

"I think maybe we should let the scary corpse keep its medallion," suggested Nicole.

"We can buy you some new bling when we get home," promised Brandy.

"I'm serious. I think we need it."

"Why do we need a medallion?" asked Nicole. The Keeper hadn't said anything about collecting a medallion from a corpse. The Keeper told them to follow the path.

"I don't know. We just do."

They carefully eased Albert to the ground, seating him at the feet of the nearest sentinel. He propped his back against its lean calves and stretched out his legs in front of him. There was a bloody gash in his right knee. The pain was both sharp and constant. But it could have been much worse.

Nicole knelt beside him. She removed the backpack and withdrew the first aid kit, then she bent over him and inspected his knee.

"I'll be fine," he assured her.

"I'll see for myself," she told him.

"What were you thinking?" asked Brandy as she, too, knelt beside him.

"Well, I wasn't thinking there was a dead guy up there. I know that."

Andrea giggled. The sound of it cleared some of the tension and made all of them smile a little.

"It doesn't look too bad," declared Nicole. "All things considered." She glanced at the sling that held his right arm. She wasn't there to see it when the Caggo did that to him, but it was still frightening how close he'd come to death. She also recalled his strange experience in the fear room, when he was convinced that he had been struck down by some unseen beast and that he was dying. It had been nothing more than a vivid hallucination, utterly imaginary, but it had been intense enough to even convince Brandy for a brief moment that he was dead. Counting the terrifying encounter with the monster in Gilbert House, this was the fourth time in less than a day that he'd scared the hell out of her and it was well past tiresome. She wasn't sure how much more of this her poor heart could stand.

"I mean it, though," said Albert. "About the medallion. Someone needs to get it."

"What do we need it for?" asked Andrea.

But Albert didn't know. It was just a very strong feeling he had.

It was *significant*.

The word kept coming to mind. He couldn't even begin to say why.

"I'm not going anywhere near a corpse," said Olivia. And she meant it. "Never again." She wasn't sure she'd ever even be able to attend a funeral again. She'd probably spend the whole time staring at the casket, just waiting for the person inside to sit up.

"I'll go when my knee stops hurting a little," Albert promised.

"The hell you will," snapped Brandy.

Albert looked up at her. He meant to argue with her, but he couldn't find the words when he saw the tears that shimmered in her eyes. He'd frightened her again.

God, he hated that.

"You're not going back up there," Nicole agreed. "I won't let you."

"But what if he's right?" asked Andrea. "He's supposed to be psychic. What if he's right and we need it?"

Nicole and Brandy exchanged a nervous look as Albert lay between them. They'd learned to trust Albert's feelings. If he said they needed it, then chances were good that they really needed it. But how did they go about getting it?

There was a loud sound, sharp and wet, like a beaver's tail striking the surface of a pond. Something black and foul crashed into the outstretched arm of the silent sentinel and splattered past it, spraying a thick, putrid mess across Nicole's naked chest and neck. Silence fell in an instant as she knelt there, stiff and wide-eyed, her mouth open in a frozen gasp of horror even as the stench began to rise around her. Her hands were half-raised; her fingers splayed as if she were loath to even touch her own soiled flesh. It was on her cheek. In her hair. On her nose. Thick dollops dripped from her breasts and oozed down her belly into her lap.

No one asked what the stuff was. They knew the instant they saw it, as did Nicole, whose utter revulsion could not have been more apparent in her huge, mortified eyes.

Somewhere above, the carrion eaters danced and jittered around the flames, almost as if in celebration of a perfect shot.

None of them made a sound, nor even breathed, as overwhelming pity fought with shameless amusement. Except Andrea, whose two simple words were perfectly adequate: "Oh, nasty!"

Nicole's eyes, still wide with shock, rolled right, then left, as if searching for some kind of escape. Then she looked down at herself, her mouth still open, her lips beginning to quiver in expectation of the retches she felt slithering up her throat.

Brandy stared at her best friend's soiled chest. "Nikki…"

Nicole jerked her head left, then right, her pretty eyes widening even further, bulging in a "*don't say anything!*" expression.

"Oh, Nikki…"

The stench was worse than she ever would have imagined. It was foul beyond words.

Albert reached up and took her hand, squeezed it. He had no idea what else to do. The gesture seemed to help because she snapped her gaping mouth shut and stared back at him, her expression changing from fury to misery to disgust and back again.

"I'm so sorry," said Olivia. "That's… That's just so wrong."

"It'll be funny as hell tomorrow?" tried Brandy.

But Nicole didn't think it would be funny tomorrow. She didn't think it would ever be funny. Not now. Not while she was covered in reeking carrion eater excrement. Perhaps after a long, hot shower she might see a time—somewhere far in the future—where this might be a *little* funny, but not now. Now she only glared at Brandy.

"I'll get the medallion," said Andrea, trying to take the attention off poor Nicole so that she could gather her wits.

But Nicole shook her head. "No. I'll do it."

"I can do it. Really."

"No. I want to."

"You sure?"

She nodded. Anything to try and scrub this experience from her mind as quickly as possible.

"Thank you," said Albert. "It's important. I don't know how I know it, but I do. I can feel it."

Again, Nicole nodded. For a moment she just sat there, trying to gather her thoughts, and then she looked down at herself, at the awfulness that had soiled her fair skin. Revulsion washed over her in slow, nauseous waves. She held her hands up, hesitated for a moment, loath to touch it with her hands even though it was already caked on her flesh, and then raked it from her neck and shoulder. Then she was looking at her hands, so pretty before, but now dripping with carrion eater dung. She made a sick retching noise in her throat and stood up, trying to shake it from her hands. When that didn't work, she wiped them on the sentinel.

"Medallion," she murmured as she wiped at her breasts and belly.

Brandy knelt over Albert. "Does she have to go?" she asked.

"Somebody does," Albert said.

"I'll get it," Nicole promised. Some of her composure was returning now. She continued to wipe her hands on the statue, hopelessly trying to rid herself of every sticky glob.

"Just be careful," Brandy begged.

"I will. Take care of his knee, okay?"

Albert had almost forgotten the pain in his knee. He looked down at it. The skin was peeled back. Blood oozed from it. It was such a little thing after all he'd been through, after all he'd seen, but somehow the sight of it made him feel weak.

"Of course," said Brandy.

Nicole turned and stalked away, grumbling under her breath.

Albert looked up at Brandy and met her worried eyes. "She'll be fine," he promised. And he hoped he was right about that.

Chapter 20

Nicole tried to wipe the foul, sticky filth from her breasts, but it was a stubborn mess. All she managed to do was scrape away the excess, leaving grimy trails across her skin and dirtying her hands. She smeared it on the wall as she passed through the doorway into the sealed temple entrance, but the effort was futile. She wasn't sure she'd ever feel clean again. "Nasty fucking things!" she growled. "I hate them!"

"That was really gross," Andrea agreed. Both she and Olivia had accompanied her back to this chamber. Andrea was curious about the medallion Albert wanted. Olivia was concerned about the corpse that was currently in possession of it.

Nicole was too pissed off to care that much about either.

"I don't like this," said Olivia. "I really don't want to disturb that corpse."

Andrea shined her light around the dark room. She was nervous. The very idea that there was a corpse nearby gave her a chill. "Albert said it was safe. Right?"

"I don't care what he said. I don't like it."

"What do you think?" Andrea asked, turning her eyes once more on Nicole.

"I don't know. But Albert wants it, so I'm going to get it for him." She tried to fling the filth from her fingers, but it stuck stubbornly to her skin. She kept trying not to think about what it was, but her mind insisted on whirling back to it, like a drug addict returning to her dealer. *Manure*, she thought. *Shit*. She shuddered with revulsion at the filthiness of the words, made worse by the unnatural feel of it on her skin, so thick and sticky, grimy and foul. She wiped her reeking hands on the column in the center of the room as she passed and then returned to the task of scraping gooey excrement from her naked bosom.

She could almost feel the germs swarming across her skin.

"You trust him a lot," said Olivia.

Nicole glanced at her, surprised. "Brandy and Albert are my best friends. I trust both of them with my life."

"But what if he's wrong about this?"

"He usually isn't wrong."

"But if he is?"

"Then he'll make it right." She looked up at the stairs as they approached. "I honestly don't believe any of us would've survived this long without him."

Olivia said nothing more. She watched the darkness melt away before them as they climbed, revealing the topmost steps and then the narrow recess with its stone rungs leading up to that mysterious hole.

"But what do we need a medallion for?" asked Andrea. "I don't get it. It doesn't make sense."

"None of this has made any sense. Why would anything suddenly make sense now?" Nicole stepped into the recess and peered up into those shadows. "Just keep the lights aimed at the opening, okay?"

"Whatever you want," Olivia agreed. "Be careful."

Nicole began to climb. She still felt filthy, but she tried to focus on where she was going rather than what had soiled her skin. Up here was a corpse that Albert said was harmless, but all that Olivia and Wayne went through outside of Gilbert House suggested that no corpse was necessarily harmless here in the Wood.

Why did they need this medallion? What purpose did it serve? She thought they were supposed to be going up the mountain, not lingering in long-ago sealed chambers. They had trusted the sentinels this far, and the sentinels outside this room told them to go forward. Only the sentinels facing the river beckoned anyone here, and those two had done their job long, long ago.

As she approached the top, she saw the corpse waiting for her. Immediately, she understood why Albert was so severely startled. It almost startled *her*, and she was expecting it. Like some tragic king, the wretched thing sat in the tiny chamber as if it were a makeshift throne, its body slumped forward, its face drooping with untold age. The mouth hung open, dislodged in a howling gape that drooped almost to the floor. It was little more than a petrified skeleton that had long ago sagged and settled upon itself.

"What do you see?" Andrea asked.

"Time" was the word that came to mind. She saw time. Infinite, unforgiving time. Ages upon ages had weighed down upon this tragic remnant of a human life.

She also saw the medallion. It rested on the floor, held up only partially by an ancient chain that hung around the drooping corpse's neck. This was what she'd come for. "The medallion's here," she called down. She lifted one leg up to brace herself, pressed her butt against the wall behind her, and balanced herself so that she could free both hands. Vaguely, she realized that the pose was probably very unflattering from below.

"Be careful," Olivia reminded her.

She would definitely be careful. She didn't even want to touch this thing. Looking at the corpse now, she realized that it had only one arm and wondered where and when that limb had been lost.

What a story this sad cadaver might have, she realized, if only there were a way to hear it.

She reached out and cautiously grasped the chain. She felt like a fairy tale hero trying to steal a key off a sleeping monster. Her heart pounded. She couldn't stop thinking about the story Wayne had told them of the corpses outside Gilbert House, slashing and gnawing at them, intending to tear them to pieces. It was far too easy to imagine that one gnarled hand shooting up and seizing her wrist, or that horrible, gaping mouth lunging forward, snapping closed on her face, the rotten teeth shredding her tender flesh.

She lifted the chain, wincing at the sound of the gold as it tinkled against the stone. It seemed as loud as a church bell to her ears, and a childish part of her insisted that the slightest sound would wake even this longest of dead. But the corpse didn't move. She had it in her hands. It was almost hers. She only had to pull the chain over the corpse's head.

But as she brought it toward her, the chain disturbed the fragile bones and the head slumped in a soft cloud of musty dust. Panic shot through her nerves like lightning. "Oh God," she sighed. It was not merely an exclamation. She'd actually meant the words as a prayer, a brief request for strength and courage, one that He must have received and understood, because she somehow managed to both maintain her balance and keep from screaming her head off. "Oh God," she breathed again, the same words now in gratitude.

"You okay?" Olivia asked.

"Yeah." She was surprised to hear that she actually had a voice.

"Hurry up."

"I'm coming." She pulled on the chain again, guiding it over the corpse's drooping head and forcing herself to believe that the motion she perceived was nothing more than old bones settling into dust.

And then it was in her hands. She lifted it before her eyes and stared at it. It wasn't really a medallion at all, she saw. It wasn't round, but oblong, much longer than it was wide. There was a strange symbol etched into one side. She'd never seen anything like it before.

"Hurry up," Olivia urged again.

Nicole's eyes drifted past the object that wasn't really a medallion to the corpse and a chill crept through her. She could almost imagine the thing rising up and trying to snatch back its treasure. She slipped it over her head and winced at the cold touch of the metal as it came to rest between her dirty breasts. The idea of it touching her skin after having been around the corpse's neck made her queasy.

She climbed back down, happy to feel the solid ground despite her aching feet, and then looked back up at where she'd been, half expecting the corpse to be staring down at her, accusing her with its empty sockets. "Well," she said, turning to face them, "I got it."

Andrea reached out and lifted the prize she'd taken from the corpse, gazing at its unusual markings. "Weird."

It was an odd sensation, Andrea's fingers brushing the skin of her bare breasts. It was in no way sexual. There was no part of her capable of feeling lust at that point, not after all the nastiness she'd just been through. It was merely surreal, somehow, a bit of tenderness amid ugliness, a bit of closeness within darkness, a bit of warm life in the aftermath of death.

"So simple," Olivia observed. "Some kind of medal? Or maybe a pendant?"

Nicole shook her head.

"What does it mean?" Andrea asked.

But of course no one knew.

"If we can believe all this stuff the Sentinel Queen and the Keeper have been telling us," Olivia considered, "then this could be from a language nobody remembers, wiped utterly out of existence."

"Like those voices we heard," Andrea recalled.

"Exactly."

"Why is it so important?" Andrea turned it over, but the back was only smooth metal. "Is it real gold?"

"I don't know," Nicole replied. She felt uncomfortable. It was awkward standing there while everyone stared at her naked chest.

"Let's go show Albert," Olivia said. "Maybe he'll know something."

"Yeah," Nicole agreed. "And maybe I can get crapped on again. That would be fun."

Andrea began to giggle again.

Chapter 21

"Are you sure she'll be okay?" Brandy asked.

In truth, Albert had no idea. He wondered if he'd done the right thing by sending her back in there. Did they really need the medallion? Was it really safe to send her up there with that corpse? It hadn't harmed him in that brief moment that he was up there with it, but that didn't mean that it was incapable of doing harm. What if it woke up when she tried to take the trinket? Yet he felt so strongly that they should have it. Even when he fell, when every other thought was washed away by the pain of his fall, he felt it. The *significance* of that medallion, of that brief glimpse of gold, was real. "Yeah. I am."

Brandy ran her fingers through his dirty hair. She didn't want to worry about Nicole. It was bad enough that she had to worry so much about Albert. How many close calls had he had now? How many times had he almost died? Her heart nearly stopped when he cried out at the sight of the corpse and fell to the floor like a broken doll. A part of her was sure that he'd broken his neck or caved in his skull, that this time, she'd finally lost him to cruel death. And here beneath the black and empty skies of the Wood, she found it hard to believe in any kind of heaven, hard even to believe in God.

It was troubling. She could not help but wonder how many people had been condemned to wheelchairs for less than what he'd survived so far with only a broken arm and a torn knee. It seemed like his life was riding on a set of invisible dice somewhere and the laws of probability were stacked against another miracle. What would happen next? Another fall? Another monster? Would one of the carrion eaters swoop down out of the sky and carry him off? Or would God, Himself, reach down from His mighty throne and wipe him away, weary of his unnatural resistance to death?

Tears flooded her vision, spilled over her lids, streamed down her face. How much more could she take? She wiped away the tears and reached for the first aid kit.

"Don't do that," Albert begged. He lifted his good arm and wiped a freshly spilled tear from her cheek.

"I'm fine. Does it hurt bad?"

"*This* does," he told her as he caught another tear.

She turned her head away and wiped at her leaking eyes. "I'm fine," she said again. "Can you bend your knee?"

He drew his leg toward him and winced at the pain. "Sore," he reported. "But not so bad. I'll be okay."

"Good."

He watched her as she wiped at her face again. She was avoiding his eyes. "I'm sorry," he said.

"Why?"

Because he'd upset her, of course. He'd frightened her. It broke his heart to know that he'd made her cry.

She sniffed back her tears and glanced over at the passageway through which their friends had disappeared. She could still see the faint glow of their flashlights inside. She was glad of that. It was comforting. "I hope they're okay."

Albert kept his gaze on Brandy, on those heartbreaking tears. "Nikki's strong," he assured her. "She can do this. I know she can." And he did. But he would still feel better once she and the others were back at his side.

Brandy wiped her eyes one last time and then bent and kissed him. There was no more time for tears. She'd allowed herself to be weak for too long. She could be strong now.

How many times now had she really been afraid for his life? She recalled Gilbert House. That monster. Its huge, mutant hand lifting him by his head, about to crush his skull. But it ran away before it could kill him. Then there was that bizarre incident in the fear room, when that "memory" from one of those hateful statues made him believe that something had sliced him virtually in half. But that was only an illusion. There were no real monsters down there. Not in that chamber. The only actual danger there was those wicked spikes. And the peril he'd faced only minutes ago was no less imaginary, when she considered it. He didn't even fall that far. His toes were only about seven feet above the floor when he lost his grip. The fall had been painful because he banged his knee and jarred his broken bone, but his life had honestly been in very little danger. Unlike when he faced the Caggo…

She was unconscious at the moment when that ugly beast threw him from the tower. And for that she was thankful. Had she been watching him at the moment he broke his arm, she might not have been able to weather the shock. She loved him so very much. It hurt like hell to see him hurt. To have watched him as his bone snapped, to have seen the agony wash over his handsome face, to have watched him struggling to get to his feet in the midst of all that pain, might have stopped her heart cold in her breast.

The more she thought about it, the more vulnerable she felt. Life was too fragile for all the close calls they'd had. Wayne had been proof enough of that. The human body was a durable thing, but it was not impenetrable. It took far less than an otherworldly curse to pierce flesh. It took far less than a hulking beast to break bones.

They were on their own out here.

Her thoughts drifted to the morning after their first visit to the Temple of the Blind. Despite having stayed out so late and being so exhausted, she'd been unable to sleep at all. She couldn't stop thinking about the temple, about the hound that had chased them—then still a maddening, nameless mystery to her. She thought about the mysterious man with no eyes, about the emotion rooms and the sentinel statues. But most of all, she thought about Albert. She thought about what they'd done together, first inside the sex room and then in the chamber's entrance on their way out. The thoughts were disturbing to her, like an unwanted obsession, an addiction…but it was a sweet addiction, and one that she soon realized she *wanted* to be at the mercy of.

When she closed her eyes, she saw him, could almost feel him pressed against her, slipping inside her, and the feeling was not creepy, but exhilarating, *intoxicating*. She found that she wanted him, that she couldn't wait to see him again, and before the sun had risen, she found herself wondering what he would say if she called him, if she asked him to meet her somewhere, somewhere quiet, somewhere private, because she needed him, because she *wanted* him. She almost *did* call him. She wanted him so much. She wanted to make love to him. She wanted to *fuck* him, just the way she'd done in the sex room! ...But it was not quite like that. It was nothing that ugly, nothing that vulgar. It was not that she was simply wet for him. That was not even close.

It was because he carried her out of the fear room, because he opened his eyes in there so that he could save her, because he risked his very life and sanity for her. It was because of that long goodnight kiss she'd shared with him before she climbed into her car and drove home.

It was because she had fallen in love with him.

The morning after, as she sat through her first two classes, she realized that of all the things she'd experienced in the prior twenty-four hours, the most terrifying was the nagging thought that perhaps Albert might have changed his mind about asking her out again, that after waiting all those hours, he would have realized for some reason that she was not the one for him, that he did not love her and never could.

But Albert hadn't changed his mind. He walked into lecture a few minutes after she did. He asked her how she slept. He told her that he slept terribly, that he'd been forever falling asleep with so many things on his mind. Then he told her she looked very pretty in the dress she was wearing and she thought that she must have looked completely stupid because she felt like she was beaming from the compliment. Then he finally asked her and she thought she might die of relief.

"I'd love to," she said. And then, without giving him time to ask, she said, "Tonight. Pick me up at six?" And he said he would.

But she couldn't wait for the date. When class was over and they had gathered their things, she leaned forward and surprised him with a kiss that had felt to her like every orgasm she'd ever experienced—or even *imagined*—all at once, but in slow motion, as though she had kissed him not with her lips but with the very fabric of her soul.

That night, he arrived a little early at her parents' house on Wilcox Street and her mother had commented on how handsome he was as she grabbed her coat. And he *was* handsome. He was the most handsome man she'd ever seen, and he grew only more handsome as the night went on.

They had dinner at Applebee's in a quiet booth under a light that had burned out so that it was shadowy and romantic, as though some playful cupid had arranged the ambiance just for them. Afterwards, they drove over to the movie theater, where they wound up spending more than an hour and a half just sitting in Albert's car in the parking lot beneath the glow of the street lamps and talking about things. All things. Everything. But nothing in particular. They decided not to see a movie and he took her back to Lumey Hall, where the two of them sat on a couch in the back of the same lounge where they first opened the box and talked about more things until at last their lips met and they kissed long into the night.

Albert was a gentleman, of course. He kissed her and he held her, but he never tried to take it any further and she was glad. It was their first date, after all, even if they had already shared each other's bodies.

But they met again the next day and they wound up back in her bedroom at her parents' house, and there they made real love for the first time. They did it twice, in fact, the first time hard and passionate, but full of tenderness, the second long and slow and romantic, and she knew without a doubt before they had finished the second time that there would never be another. She loved Albert Cross like she'd never loved anyone before and like she would never love anyone again.

She kissed him softly, lovingly. She was still fighting back the tears.

"How are you doing?" he asked her, when their lips parted. He reached up with his good arm and ran his hand over her tangled hair. At the back of her head he could feel the painful lump where her skull had struck the stone.

"Head hurts," she replied. "And I'm cold."

Albert kissed her again.

"I love you," Brandy whispered when their lips parted.

"I love you too."

"What are we going to do after all this is over?" she asked.

"We're going to go home," Albert replied softly. "*All* of us."

"Do you really think we can?"

"Of course we can."

"Wayne can't."

Albert stared back at her for a moment. She was right. Wayne could never go home again. He was beyond home. And who was he to promise that any of them wouldn't end up just like him?

"*We* will." He said these words firmly, a conviction so stern that he even surprised himself. "All of us. We're going to get through this. We'll do it *for* Wayne. Because of him we're going to all live very long lives. Especially us. We'll graduate college. We'll get married."

"Married?" Brandy's eyes were suddenly bright and alert. Had she heard him right?

Albert stared up at her, almost as surprised as she was. The words had left him almost without thinking. But it was the truth, wasn't it? Wasn't that where they were eventually headed? "Yeah. Married."

182

"You want to marry me?"

"Of course I do."

"Are you proposing to me?"

"No," he replied. "Not now. Not the same day Wayne died. Not on the same day I broke my arm. Not on the same day I almost lost you. But I will. Maybe tomorrow. Or the next day."

Another tear slipped down her cheek and she smiled. It was wonderful to see that smile.

"I will," he said. "I promise."

"I'll say yes," she replied. "I promise."

Albert smiled. "I love you so much."

"I love you, too."

The doorway to the sealed entrance grew brighter. Their friends were returning. They were still safe.

All was well.

Chapter 22

Albert traced the strange symbol with his thumb. Like Nicole, he immediately realized that it was not a medallion, as he'd been calling it. Was it a medal? A badge? A pendant? Did it serve a practical purpose or was it merely for decoration? He didn't know and probably never would. Looking at it, he continued to feel that strange significance, though he had no clue what it meant or what purpose it might serve.

What was it about that word? Why did so many things feel "significant" suddenly? It was just a word, yet it was the only way he could think to describe the things he kept feeling.

Maybe it was nothing more than his mind's strange way of trying to process the idea that he might really be psychic.

Frustrated by his lack of answers, he closed his hand around the mysterious object and looked around.

All of them had crowded into the doorway to take shelter against any more horrors that might fall from the sky.

Nicole sat beside him, trying to rake the filth from her tangled hair. He could smell her. The stench of the carrion eater excrement was even worse than the putrid reek of the mud chamber. Her anger had finally begun to subside, but what replaced it was a growing misery that welled in her pretty eyes and quivered subtly at the corners of her mouth. He hated to see her like this. His heart ached at the sight.

But it was only shit. As nasty as it was, as disgusted and degraded as she must feel, at least she wasn't hurt. At least she hadn't died. Unlike poor Beverly. Unlike Wayne.

Olivia sat a few feet away. She had unwrapped the bandage around her arm and was inspecting the wound beneath it. It would probably leave a faint scar, but otherwise the injury was superficial. Worse would be the one on her shoulder. She wondered what she would tell people when this was all over. She certainly couldn't say that she was bitten by the living dead, but what else could she say? Although the scar might not necessarily look like teeth marks, not with the poor dental hygiene of her assailant, it would always be vividly clear to her what had left the mark. And what if someone else saw it, too? What if her mother saw it? Her doctor? What would they think? How would she explain it?

Albert realized as he watched her that this was the first time he'd really looked at her. He'd seen her in Gilbert House, of course, had gotten a good look at her pretty face, but when he saw her again in the labyrinth, she'd been bashful, hiding as much of her naked body as she could with just her two arms and a twist of her thigh. Furthermore, he'd been too embarrassed to give her more than a glance. After that there was the Caggo and his damned broken arm. And then what happened to Wayne, of course. Always that. He simply hadn't taken any time to really observe his companions.

Not that he intended to dedicate their naked bodies to memory. He had simply grown accustomed to their nudity. Their bodies were now familiar. It wasn't in any way sexual. It was different. It was special, somehow. They felt like sisters. Except of course for Brandy, who was and always would be his only lover.

Looking at Olivia now, he did not feel like he was looking at a sexy, naked woman, but as if he were admiring a pretty outfit. For the first time, he noticed *how* she was beautiful. She was blessed with neither Brandy's girlish features nor Nicole's shapely figure, but instead with a soft, curvy voluptuousness that was in its own way just as magnificent. There were smudges on her skin that had not been washed away in the temple's pools and more cuts and scrapes and bruises than he could count in the dancing shadows, but these only accented her otherwise flawless body. Her breasts, at least as large as Nicole's, but softer and slightly more affected by gravity, were fully visible to him. He could see her plump nipples standing firm against the chilly air. He could see the soft gleam of her necklace as it lay against her skin above those breasts as well as the metallic flash from her watch as she began to wrap her arm again. He watched her pretty hands work the gauze, observed her slender fingers and those delicate pink nails that had grown scratched and chipped.

She glanced up and caught Albert looking at her. He smiled half-heartedly and then turned away from her, a little embarrassed to be caught watching. He turned his face the other way, toward the tunnel's entrance and the ushering sentinel beyond. Andrea was standing there, just outside the door, gazing up at the creatures that fluttered through the sky above.

Like Olivia, Andrea had been bashful when he first saw her

without her clothes and he hadn't gotten a good look at her. Now he found himself gazing at those glittering rings in her ears. All those piercings did something for her, he realized. They simultaneously confirmed and contradicted her sweet, girlish appearance. It was the same with her pigtails, tied much higher and farther forward than he usually saw on women who were bold enough to wear them. The style was usually more suited to a girl whose age was in the single digits, but he liked it on her. The result, he had to admit, was nice. It was cute and also a little sexy. She was beautiful in ways that a lot of people weren't. She was much skinnier than the others were, smaller even than Brandy, with a kind of precious, little girl charm. Her skin was fair, and he spied a pair of moles on the left side of her lower back. He wondered for the first time just how old she was. He hoped she was at least eighteen. He had no interest in dating her, of course, but he certainly didn't like the idea of running around with a naked minor.

"Can I get you anything?" Brandy asked, drawing his attention.

Albert smiled. "Martini."

Brandy giggled. "I'll see what I can do."

Nicole laughed. "While you're at it, get me a margarita the size of my head."

"Ooh, I'll take one of those," said Olivia.

There was a soft rustle of laughter. It was genuine, but it was also weak. *They're tired*, Albert thought. *And unhappy.* And why shouldn't they be? Hadn't they all suffered? Hadn't they seen enough horror to wipe away any joy that could possibly be found in a place such as this?

Albert lowered his eyes again to the golden medal and the mysterious symbol carved onto its surface.

Significance. The word kept entering his mind. It was the perfect word to describe every impulse he'd had. The box had been significant. The wall that had looked like a dead end between the raw tunnel and the first chamber of the Temple of the Blind had been significant. The scratches on the floor. The darkness that had concealed the tower. All the things that had been important on this journey had encouraged his closer inspection by simply projecting a perceived *significance*. And now here was this medal with that same significance. But what did it mean?

Nicole groaned as she wiped her hands on the floor. "I need a shower so bad."

Albert felt terrible for her. She'd been through so much.

Andrea watched one of the flaming carrion eaters fall from the sky and then turned around to face them. She leaned against the wall, her feet crossed, relaxed, stark naked and hiding nothing. With the clearing at her back lit by the inferno, Albert thought she looked like the subject of a piece of pinup art, perhaps the most treasured piece in an artist's collection.

"We should go," he said. "We're already in trouble if we find another night tree."

"Are you sure you can?" Brandy asked.

"I'll be fine," he assured her. They'd lingered far too long already. He didn't like the idea of remaining in one place in a world he had no way of understanding. Carefully, he rose to his feet. Brandy and Nicole both tried to help him. In her haste, Nicole bumped his arm and drew a startled gasp of pain.

"I'm sorry!"

"It's okay," he assured her. "I'm fine." And he was. As soon as he was on his feet, he found that his knee hurt less than he expected it to. He still had a bit of a limp, but he thought that would go away as he loosened up along the path. Even if it didn't, the pain in his knee was nothing remotely like the one in his arm.

Andrea peered up at the carrion eaters again. There were so many. They were everywhere. And they were dropping their cargo more and more frequently. She'd heard those telltale slapping noises several times while lingering in the doorway.

She really didn't want to get pooped on. But they obviously could not stay here forever.

"I really hate those things," growled Nicole.

"We know, you do, sweetie," said Brandy.

"We really don't blame you," said Olivia.

"Look at the bright side," added Brandy. "At least you didn't take it in the face."

"True," agreed Nicole and then said no more. She knew that Brandy was referring to that hairy squid-like thing in the reservoir that shot its gross fluid into her face. She was the first to admit that it had been horrid. But if given the chance, she wasn't sure she'd choose getting crapped on over getting sprayed in the face with rancid spider-squid juice.

The five of them walked past the soiled sentinel, each of them careful not to step in something foul. Now that they were out in the open, they could hear the beating of wings above them again, even louder than before. There were so many of them. And they seemed to be swooping lower and lower as the day dragged on.

Another one caught fire and spiraled out of the sky. Albert watched it fall until it was gone from sight and then gazed toward the nearby steps where they'd found the charred carcass. Suddenly, he wondered why the carrion eaters didn't get up after they died like the things in the Wood. Did it take a while? Or were these things somehow immune to whatever it was that caused the dead to remain animated in their perverse imitation of life?

Again, he gazed up into the chaos of that unearthly swarm. There was so much mystery out here, so much he'd never understand, even in an entire lifetime.

His eyes drifted to the sentinel that pointed the way forward. A tunnel opening waited to take them back into the darkness and once again Albert looked forward to it. He didn't want to walk beneath these creatures.

But Olivia was walking toward the steps that led down to the lake.

"Hey guys…"

"What's wrong?" asked Brandy.

Olivia stopped at the top of the stairs and stood there, motionless, gazing out across the lake. "Do you see that?"

"See what?" asked Andrea.

But Albert saw it. As soon as he looked past her, he glimpsed it. Still limping, he walked to where Olivia stood.

The others joined them, too.

"What are we looking at?" asked Brandy. But then she saw it. A small, dark shadow streaking across the surface of that wall, glimpsed for only an instant in the dancing firelight. And then another. And another.

Nicole felt a hot weight of fear form in her belly. "Is that…?"

Albert nodded. "It is." It was like rain. One after another, dark shapes fell, plunging down the face of the wall. He could even see the occasional glint of white as they splashed into the water below.

"Oh my god…" sighed Brandy. "How many are there?"

"Countless," replied Olivia.

Andrea could not even speak. It was the most terrifying thing she'd ever seen.

Zombies drizzled like rain over the wall, undead lemmings throwing themselves over the ledge, coming for them, surrounding them, *swarming*. And there was nothing between them but the lake and a set of steps. How long before they were shambling after them, their corpse hands outstretched, their jaws snapping?

"I've officially never been this scared in my life..." said Nicole.

Still unable to find any words, Andrea merely nodded her agreement.

"I have," whispered Olivia.

"We've got to go," said Brandy. She seized Albert's hand, then Nicole's and pulled them both toward the tunnel leading on up the mountain.

Olivia shook her head. Would it really do any good to run? Did they even stand a chance? "So many..."

"Come on," said Andrea.

"Let's go!" cried Brandy. "Hurry!"

Still numb with fright, Olivia turned and followed after them. Wayne wouldn't want her to lose it now. Wayne would want her to be strong. He'd want her to survive. And he'd want her to take care of the others.

But she couldn't take her eyes off those raining corpses.

"What are we going to do?" asked Andrea.

"We pray," replied Olivia.

Chapter 23

The tunnel leading away from the four sentinels was much longer than the others they'd encountered since leaving the labyrinth. The darkness within was much deeper, and was both a blessing and a curse. It hid from view the horrors that poured over the wall, horrors that had left them all considerably rattled, yet none of them wanted to be in the dark confines of another tunnel if those horrors caught up with them.

It was far too easy to imagine their lights suddenly falling on a dripping corpse in the darkness, finding themselves trapped as the rotting horde closed in from both directions, overwhelming them and then...

Olivia hugged herself tightly, clenching herself against the terror that was quickly rising within her, filling her, threatening to drown her. The zombies were coming for her. They were an unstoppable force, determined to finish what they started at Gilbert House. Why did she ever think she could escape them?

"Are you okay?" asked Andrea.

Olivia looked at her, her dark eyes wide with dread. "I don't know," she confessed. "I'm just...really scared right now."

"Us too," Brandy assured her.

"Fucking zombies..." said Nicole. "I can't believe there are *zombies*."

"My friend Mindy is a huge horror movie fan," said Andrea. "I wonder how she'd do out here."

"I don't think there was ever a movie made that would prepare anyone for this," said Albert.

"I guess not."

"Horror movies are supposed to be fun," agreed Nicole. "When blood starts flying in the real world, the fun kind of goes out the window."

"*Way* out the window," said Olivia. In her mind, she saw Andy's friend, Nick, his head dashed against the wall of Gilbert House's third floor hallway, the bright crimson on the pale, yellow brick.

Andrea nodded. "Mindy could probably tell us everything that was ever written about zombies."

"Almost all of which is probably wrong," said Albert. "It's like vampires. If there really were vampires out there somewhere—"

"Dear God, please no," sighed Brandy.

Nicole laughed. "Definitely not. I think we've got enough shit to worry about for one day."

"I agree," said Albert. "But if there *were* vampires out there, which vampires would they be? Every incarnation is different. Some can go out during the day. Some have reflections. Some have no reaction to crosses or garlic. Some can't cross running water or enter a house uninvited."

"The stupid ones sparkle," added Nicole.

"Says the girl who's watched every one of those movies," challenged Brandy.

"So? I watch a lot of stupid stuff."

Andrea giggled.

"I'm just saying," continued Albert, "that being a horror movie expert wouldn't necessarily be an advantage out here. You might be better off not knowing anything."

"That's true," said Andrea. "I just wonder if she'd be braver if she were here than I am."

"You're braver than most people already," Olivia said.

Andrea smiled, but she didn't feel very brave. She felt almost sick with fear.

"I guess it would depend on the person," Albert decided. "Mindy might have been desensitized by enough violence and gore to take all this in stride. Or she might find that every scary movie she ever watched comes back to her all at once and she's utterly paralyzed by the terrible realization that all those nightmarish things are actually real."

Andrea nodded. Both scenarios were believable.

"Shouldn't those trees be eating the zombies?" asked Nicole. "They try to eat everything else."

Andrea looked up at her. "Hey, that's right."

Albert shrugged. "Either those trees over there aren't fully awake or...more likely..."

"There's just too many," finished Nicole.

"Right."

"Can we talk about something else?" asked Olivia. "Please?"

"Of course," said Brandy. She was thrilled by the opportunity to change the subject. "What about you? You're a student at Briar Hills, right?"

Olivia nodded. "It's my first semester."

"That's cool."

"I came to the Temple of the Blind my first semester, too," said Albert. "That's some tough curriculum we picked."

Olivia gave him a small laugh. "It is, isn't it? My mom wanted me to make new friends. I don't think this was quite what she had in mind."

Albert laughed. If it was in any way possible to get past the fact that they were naked and probably in mortal danger, he had a feeling that Olivia's mother would probably be profoundly proud of her. "What are you studying?"

"Nursing."

"Really? That's cool." Albert remembered suddenly that Wayne was an art major and he felt surprisingly depressed.

"What about you?"

"Computer science."

"Is that pretty tough?"

"Yeah, but it's not so bad. It's mathematical problem-solving, so it's kind of just right for me. Every computer program is kind of like a big puzzle, when you get down to it."

Looking at Brandy and Nicole, she asked, "You guys in computers, too?"

"Hardly," replied Nicole. "Special Education."

"History," said Brandy.

"Oh." Gesturing at Albert, she asked, "Did you two meet at the Hill?"

"We did," said Albert. "In Chemistry, actually. But it was the box that brought us together. It was this place."

"We were kind of thrown together," said Brandy, blushing a little.

Olivia considered this for a moment. Was that such a good thing? This place was bad. It was evil. This place had broken Albert and killed Wayne. It might end up killing them all. Yet it had brought two lovers together… If they survived, they might someday have children together. Then this place would be responsible for beginning life as well as ending it.

Perhaps it was all about balance. Good and evil. Life and death. Pain and pleasure. Or perhaps it had no structure at all. Perhaps the Temple of the Blind was only about chaos and randomness.

Andrea stopped and looked around.

"I heard it, too," said Albert. It was another voice. A man, he thought, though he wasn't entirely sure. It still seemed to be speaking that unknown language.

"Yeah," said Nicole. "Did it just say 'gold digger?'"

"It wasn't talking to me!" said Andrea, giggling.

Olivia threw her arms up. "That was totally just a phase, okay! I'm not like that anymore!"

Everyone laughed. It was brief, but it felt good. For that moment, it didn't feel like there was a horde of flesh-eating zombies closing in on them. For that moment, it didn't feel like they were missing a friend. For that moment, there was no fear. There was only the laughter.

But it was only a moment.

And then the silence returned as the humor succumbed to all-encompassing fear again.

The tunnel curved as they followed it. Albert had a feeling they were circling just within the perimeter of the mountain, though he couldn't be certain. There was a subtle slope to it. They were gradually climbing, but it was far too slow. For all he knew, the dead could be swarming the sides of the temple right now. They needed to climb faster. They needed to reach the top as quickly as possible. He didn't know how much longer they had.

But they were at the mercy of the road. It wouldn't change to suit them. It would take as long as the sentinels wanted it to take.

"So you guys really didn't know each other before you came down here the first time?" asked Andrea, breaking the heavy silence that had fallen around them.

"We were lab partners," said Albert. "We'd talked during class. That was about all."

"That's a pretty crazy way to meet."

Brandy smiled. "It was."

"What about you," Andrea asked Nicole.

"Brandy and I've been best friends since kindergarten."

"Oh. So you're the only two that didn't meet because of this place."

"That's right."

Albert nodded. "We met a few weeks after Brandy and me started dating."

Andrea grinned. "And *we* met when the weird girl with all the piercings showed up at your door with a strange envelope."

Albert laughed. "That's right. I'd almost forgotten about that." It seemed so weird to think about now. That was such a strange encounter. That odd girl with the envelope at his door… Looking back now, it almost didn't seem like the same person.

"So what about you?" Albert asked. "Do you go to the Hill?"

"Me? No. I'm still in high school."

Albert felt his stomach roll over. "How old are you?"

"Eighteen."

"Oh good."

Andrea smiled. "Don't worry, I'm legal."

"I was a little worried," Albert admitted.

"Understandable. Me all naked and stuff."

"Definitely problematic if you were a minor."

"Really awkward," agreed Nicole.

"I always get that. People think I look younger."

"It's the pigtails," Brandy said. "They take years off you."

"But they're so cute!" said Olivia.

"I like them," said Albert, looking at them. "Kind of cute and sexy all wrapped up together."

Andrea smiled shyly and blushed again. "Thanks."

Albert reflected on how pretty they all were. It didn't seem quite right, now that he was thinking about it. Hadn't he himself often scoffed at how in novels and movies all the women are beautiful and all the men are either handsome or comically unattractive? Most of the time only the villains were truly ugly. But all four of his companions were actually very beautiful. And what were the odds of that? Shouldn't one of them have been at least a little plain? The world was full of unattractive people, after all.

Or maybe they were all just perfectly ordinary people and he had just grown biased, perceiving them as angelically beautiful simply because they shared this grand adventure with him and he had grown to care about them all.

Ahead of them, a set of steps appeared.

This was good. This would take them much more quickly up the mountain. But it would come at painful cost. Albert's injured knee would make this a very unpleasant climb.

Chapter 24

Albert thought he did a fairly good job of hiding his pain, yet it seemed impossible to hide anything from Brandy's watchful gaze. By the time he reached the top of the steps, she'd taken it upon herself to help carry his weight and would not take no for an answer.

The others all offered to help as well, but Brandy was nothing if not stubborn. He was her boyfriend. The least she could do in this world was let him lean on her.

Albert, meanwhile, felt embarrassed and useless. It seemed that he'd fallen all the way from brave leader to burdensome cripple. It was unfair and infuriating.

At the top of the steps, the tunnel ended and they emerged into an open clearing with a high wall on the left and a sheer drop several yards to the right.

Above them, the carrion eaters continued their chaotic dance. And on the other side of the lake, the zombies continued to rain endlessly from the black forest.

Looking around, Nicole immediately saw a black splattering of carrion eater dung clinging to the wall. "Nice," she groaned. She could still feel the nastiness of that stuff dried to her chest.

Olivia glanced at the mess, wrinkling her nose at it. Now that she had seen it, she could smell it, a rank, pungent odor that wasn't like anything you'd smell in the barns at the state fair. This stuff had its own unique stench, one that lingered in the nostrils long after the source of the smell was gone.

Albert walked up to the ledge and peered down at the rocky ground below. It was a long ways down, meaning they'd made considerable progress. Even better, he saw no sign of the forest's dead crawling out of the water down there, although they'd been throwing themselves over that wall for a while now. Was it the current? He'd hoped it was strong enough to keep them away, but he couldn't be sure. There *was* a current. He'd seen it. And it was clear that *something* was obviously keeping them from crossing. And if their rotten bodies were brittle, they might be breaking on impact, making them even easier to wash down the river.

Whatever the reason, he was thankful that the mountain was not already being overrun by the shambling dead. Time remained on their side.

Olivia cried out as one of the carrion eaters swept over her head, close enough to feel the wind from its wings.

"God, I hate those things," sighed Brandy.

"There's another dead one up here," said Andrea, who had wandered ahead.

It was lying in the middle of the path, smoke rising from its charred body. There was less of this one than there had been of the last one. It had burned itself almost to a crisp.

Olivia covered her mouth and nose as she approached it. "Smells awful."

It was little more than a misshapen black lump in the dancing shadows. Albert looked up at the others above them just in time to see another one ignite itself on a column of jutting flames spewing from a high ledge. He watched as it dropped from view. As their numbers grew, so did these occurrences of spontaneous combustion. Most dropped immediately out of sight, like the one he'd just seen, but some soared out into the darkness toward the lake, trailing fire and smoke behind them. They were starting to resemble falling stars.

And still the creatures showed no interest in them at all. It seemed that they were completely subdued by the flames. But what would happen, he wondered, if that inferno suddenly died out, its mysterious fuel spent? Would they come swarming down on them like a living tornado?

Deciding that such things were better left unconsidered, he walked around the dead carrion eater and continued forward. Without thinking about it, he reached up with his good hand and stroked the golden trinket Nicole retrieved from the corpse at the temple's entrance. He'd hung it around his neck when they left that chamber. There was something compelling about the symbol that was carved into it, but he couldn't quite put his finger on it.

As they rounded the next curve, another night tree came into view. This one was growing out of a crevice about twenty feet above them, those long, snaking tendrils dangling down the side of the wall from its coiling branches.

It was easy enough to avoid it. The path was wide here. But it was easy to believe that the tree might be smart enough to reach them anyway. It was more awake than the last one, and those strange tendrils seemed to follow them as they circled around it as close as they dared get to the ledge behind them.

It was creepy to look at, with its branches twisting and wringing and writhing. In the firelight, Albert thought that it resembled a black, pulsing brain. He had no idea what they would do if they came to another place where the path was blocked by one of those things.

"What do you think it'd do if it caught us?" asked Andrea.

"Eat us, I'm sure," said Nicole.

"How? Does it have teeth?"

"Don't know," said Brandy. "Don't care. Just keep it away from me."

Andrea turned and looked at Albert, as if he could offer her an answer. "What does it do once it catches its prey?"

"Something horrifying, probably," said Albert and left it at that. He didn't speak of the cuts the other one left on his wrist. He didn't want to talk about those dreadful possibilities. His mind, however, was apparently more than happy to offer up some suggestions. Perhaps it would split open, revealing a great, slimy gullet lined with awful, grinding teeth. Or perhaps it would simply crush them to death and absorb the juices that oozed out of them into its creepy, black flesh. Or maybe those tendrils would burrow into their bodies and devour them from the inside out. The list went on and on.

"I just wonder how they work. That's all."

"I don't want to know how things work out here," said Olivia. "I just want it to be over."

Leaving the night tree behind, they continued along the path, their eyes drifting from the swooping carrion eaters above them to the countless corpses raining from the surrounding wall.

Albert was beginning to wonder which of the mountain's horrors would end up killing him.

They walked for a while in silence before the path led them to another tunnel. This one cut straight through the heart of the mountain and up a steep staircase. Flames illuminated the far side, revealing exactly where they were going. The last set of steps allowed them to climb four or five stories. These steps looked like they might carry them fifteen. While Albert's knee was not particularly happy about it, this was exactly what they needed to speed their ascent. A few more of these and they'd be at the top in no time.

"That's a lot of steps," groaned Nicole.

"But there're no trees," noted Olivia.

"Or birds," added Brandy.

Nicole nodded. That was true.

And since the tunnel was as straight as an arrow, with flames burning at both ends, they wouldn't even need the flashlights Andrea, Brandy and Olivia still carried.

Albert liked the idea of conserving the batteries. Until they were safely at home, there was always the possibility of being caught in the dark again. With each horror he witnessed, the idea became more and more unpleasant.

"Are you going to be okay?" Brandy asked.

Blushing just a little, and despising himself for it, Albert replied that he would be fine, knowing full well that she wouldn't let him suffer these steps on his own. It didn't bother him that she wanted to help him. Not in the least. He loved her. And he loved that she cared so much about him.

He simply wanted to be stronger than this.

Chapter 25

As soon as they entered the tunnel, they could hear the muffled roar of flames racing up through unseen vents in the walls. Albert placed his hand against the stone and could feel the subtle vibrations. The temple was truly marvelous. It was only stone, yet just beyond these smooth surfaces were any number of chimneys and exhaust vents designed to carry flames from whatever massive furnaces burned deep in the bowels of the mountain to the surface, feeding all the fires that burned outside, including the inferno that blazed at the summit.

Now both water and fire flowed through the temple's veins, sharing it in spite of their opposing natures. It was not unlike the two labyrinths, one for them, another for the hounds, everything working together and coexisting in curious harmony, perfectly executed, even after all this time.

How long had the temple been sitting here in this dark land? How many tens of thousands of years, patiently waiting for this day? And everything had come together just as the sentinels knew it would.

It was humbling.

"What do you think it is?" Nicole asked, speaking to no one in particular. "Ninety degrees in here?"

Albert nodded. "Maybe." He thought it was probably closer to eighty, but the exertion of climbing all these steps made it feel much hotter.

"I like it," Olivia said. "I've been cold for three days."

"I'll bet you have," said Brandy.

"It feels sweltering to me," complained Nicole.

They moved on, their legs burning, their feet nearly numb. The temperature grew hotter as they went, well after they had passed the midpoint of the tunnel and were nearing the exit, the heat rising with the incline.

Andrea paused and drew a deep breath. "Can't hardly breathe in here."

"It's fucking hot," Nicole sighed.

Albert stopped, winded. He could feel his armpits growing slick. He could feel it between his thighs too, way up by his crotch. He looked at Brandy and watched a single bead of sweat roll down her forehead.

Olivia, who had been saying how much she enjoyed the warmth, was now damp with perspiration. It glistened upon her neck and chest in the faint firelight.

"I wonder how hot it'll get," said Albert as he pressed his hand against the warm stone again. Even the floor was warm against the soles of his feet.

"I don't care," said Nicole. "Let's just keep moving." But she stopped as she lifted her eyes to the tunnel opening above them, startled.

Someone was standing there, looking down at them.

"Who's that?" asked Andrea.

"Hello?" called Albert.

It looked like the figure of a man. He stood in the mouth of the tunnel, silhouetted against the flames behind him. He didn't speak. He merely turned and walked away. As he did this, he seemed to shimmer a little, as if he were nothing more than a mirage.

Albert glanced around and saw from everyone's expression that he was not the only one to see this. "Come on," he urged, pushing himself to climb faster in spite of his sore knee.

From there forward, the tunnel did not seem to grow any hotter, but neither did it become any cooler. The heat pushed against them as they climbed, dragging them down like a weight, until they stepped out into the open and felt the breeze blowing cold against their skin.

Andrea was the first to emerge and she immediately searched the area outside the tunnel. "Where did he go?" There was nowhere to hide. The temple walls out here were steep, and the path leading up the mountain was wide and open. Unless the stranger had been unnaturally fast, it didn't seem possible that he could have fled.

"Who was that?" asked Brandy.

No one had an answer, of course.

"Could it have been somebody sent by the Keeper?" asked Nicole. It wasn't the Keeper himself, unless that strange creature was only a clever disguise of some sort, because whoever had stood at the top of those steps had clearly been human. Or at least far more human than the Keeper.

Albert thought it was more likely related to those mysterious, disembodied voices they'd been hearing.

Andrea came to the same conclusion. "A ghost?"

"That's so weird," sighed Olivia.

But none of them could dismiss that queer shimmering. They'd all seen it. Although the shadow seemed to turn and walk away, they were all quite certain that it vanished before it walked entirely out of view.

Albert gazed up at the carrion eaters above them and then out over the lake at the raining zombies. The swarm hovered overhead and the horde surrounded them. Deadly night trees grew along the path and, apparently, ghosts haunted here as well.

It just kept getting stranger.

"I didn't notice the wind before," said Brandy, shivering a little in spite of the sweat on her body.

"It's subtle," explained Albert as he turned and glanced up at the flying things again. "I think the fire's probably stirring it up."

"At least it's not raining," offered Olivia.

That was definitely true. This would be a miserable climb to make soaking wet and muddy.

When he looked back out over the lake again, he thought he saw something odd in the darkness just above those distant, undulating trees, but it was gone in the time it took him to blink. It was likely nothing more than the imaginings of a weary mind, but if there was one thing this odd journey had taught him, it was to never dismiss even the slightest of possibilities.

But he wouldn't have time to ponder it further. As he stepped up to the ledge and looked down at the lake far below, he spied a lone figure stumbling across the stone. A closer look revealed several more prowling in the shadows.

Zombies.

They'd finally begun to surface from the lake.

"Oh god…" sighed Brandy as she stepped beside him and peered down. This brought the others rushing to look as well. Olivia paled noticeably when she saw them.

"There's not very many," said Albert, trying to remain positive. "Not many at all, considering how many are out there."

"There'll be more," Olivia promised.

Albert had no doubt there would be. Now that they'd begun to make land, they'd continue to crawl up from the depths, slowly swarming up the mountain. But for the moment there remained fewer prowling cadavers by far than were casting themselves over the ledge. And he felt fairly confident that it would remain that way. "Most of them won't make it across. That's a strong current or they'd have been here long before now. The vast majority of them are being swept out of the lake and down the river."

"But not all of them," said Nicole.

Albert turned and met her eyes. "Not all of them. But most. That's much better than none."

She didn't reply. Though she supposed that was true, it didn't make her feel much better. Even one was far too many.

"We'll take what we can get," decided Brandy.

Albert nodded. Exactly. Those that were making it across were likely the strongest, meaning that if they did catch up, they'd have to deal with only the meanest of the monsters. But at least they weren't outnumbered by the millions.

Olivia turned and hurried back to the path. "We should really keep moving."

The others followed her.

Would the zombies be able to catch up? Would they be smart enough to follow the path? The night trees might claim more than a few of them. And if they were attracted to the flames like the carrion eaters, they might incinerate themselves long before catching up.

That's it, he thought. *Just keep up that optimism.*

They hurried on, going the other way now, with the mountain looming over them on their right, while the ledge receded to the left, gradually replacing the sheer drop with a steep incline that dropped off rapidly beyond the edge of the path. One of the steep ridges ran along the bottom of that slope, blocking their view of whatever might me moving around at the water's edge below, which was good, Albert thought. Because if he could see the zombies, then they could probably see him as well, and he wasn't sure that incline was steep enough to stop something so desperately motivated.

Overhead, a particularly bright flame burned from a protruding ledge. It had attracted a number of swooping carrion eaters and they could hear their leathery wings beating through the air well before they passed beneath them. It had also already claimed two of the unwary creatures and they lay in smoking heaps sprawled upon the slope below them.

Again, Albert wondered what it was that made these things different from the zombies. Why didn't they get back up? And how did they coexist? If Wayne had recounted the old man's words correctly, the dead in the Wood were drawn not by the promise of warm flesh, but by their very life energy. But these creatures were a contradiction to that. They were clearly alive. These had *died*, after all. And there was obviously no shortage of these creatures. What was the difference between his life and that of one of these carrion eaters?

Ahead of them, another tunnel waited. Within it were more steps, promising to lead them ever higher, ever closer to that mysterious doorway and ever farther from the voracious dead.

Albert recalled being in the fear room, his heart racing, expecting to find something awful waiting with each step he took. This was a lot like that. The only difference was that he could see this time. But he wasn't sure yet if that was a good thing.

Chapter 26

This passage was even hotter than the previous one. Albert could hear the roar of the flames echoing from within well before he reached the opening and he felt an instant sheen of sweat upon his skin as he entered.

Again, he could see the end of the tunnel at the top of the steps, although this time those distant flames wavered behind a curtain of rippling heat.

This was going to be unpleasant.

Nicole and Olivia both started up the stairs without hesitating and both of them gasped at the heat that met them. Nicole cursed it. Olivia, as always, bore it with silent dignity.

As Albert began to climb, Brandy slipped beneath his arm, determined to help ease his ascent, and he could feel the perspiration on her skin as well.

He hoped he wasn't beginning to stink of sweat. Then he recalled that he already reeked of the mud chamber and supposed it wouldn't matter much if he did.

"It's miserable in here," said Brandy. And it was. By the time they'd climbed the equivalent of two stories, the temperature must have reached at least a hundred degrees.

Nicole groaned. "I feel like I'm going to get sick."

"You should let me do this on my own," Albert said, pulling his arm from around Brandy.

"Let me take a turn," offered Nicole. "You'll give yourself heatstroke or something."

"Or me," volunteered Olivia.

"I'm okay," insisted Albert, embarrassed by the attention. "I can do this. It doesn't even hurt that bad."

"There's no reason to push yourself too hard," Nicole told him.

But he was already climbing the steps. His knee hurt. The effort of climbing step after step was hard on his injury, but it wasn't unbearable. He could take it. He didn't need help. It wasn't about being macho. He simply needed to be strong. He needed to know that he wouldn't be a burden if things suddenly turned nasty.

When, he thought, remembering the shambling figures that had crawled from the lake. *When* things turned nasty.

But Brandy was right there beside him. He felt her warm hand on his damp back and became suddenly aware of a bead of sweat trickling down his spine. Looking at her, he saw that she was dripping wet. Her hair clung to her face. A fat drop of sweat hung from the rim of her glasses.

Ahead of them, Albert could see the sweat running down Olivia's and Nicole's bodies. Even their hair seemed to droop with the heat as it stuck to their sweaty backs.

"Oh my god!" sighed Brandy.

Albert could feel the heat when he held his hand against the wall. That roar of flames was getting louder again. The last tunnel had passed by several of the main vents that ran up from whatever furnace burned far below them, but this tunnel seemed to pass beside considerably more of them.

Were these passages designed this way intentionally? He was sure they were. They'd been tested with freezing water and darkness, why not flames and sweltering heat?

He was beginning to grow weary of the sentinels and all their bizarre bullshit.

"This really sucks, you guys," said Andrea from behind them.

Albert chuckled. "I agree. It certainly does."

"I'm going to be really pissed," said Olivia, "if I get home and find I haven't lost any weight."

"Me too!" said both Brandy and Nicole at once, then giggled in spite of the heat.

Albert thought it would be a shame if any of them lost so much as a pound. They were all so lovely just as they were. But he didn't have the energy to argue about such things.

He looked up at Nicole and Olivia again. Their bodies glistened with sweat in the faint firelight. He could see it beading on their skin, dripping down their backs, emphasizing every curve of their bodies. Then he looked at Brandy, saw the glistening droplets clinging to her pert breasts, and found himself reminded of another day when he saw her naked and gleaming with sweat.

It was back in August, when they were still getting ready to move into their new apartment. They were at her parents' house, up in the attic. Her closet was too small to fit her entire wardrobe, so some of her winter clothes had been stored up there for the summer. In order to pack them, she'd had to find them and bring them downstairs.

It had been hot up there, naturally. Almost as hot as this. They'd become sweaty. She'd knotted her tee shirt between her breasts, exposing her glistening belly in hopes of catching what little air circulated up there. Between that and her short denim shorts, she'd looked incredible. He hadn't been able to take his eyes off her.

They found the bins and moved them to the top of the steps. Then he kissed her. And like they often did when they found themselves alone together in those days (and still did, for that matter) they made love up there in that breathless heat.

It was amazing. The heat and the exhilaration of the sex had been intense, one building on the other until they were both dripping with sweat and gasping for breath. He could still remember the way she looked lying there, her body wet and shining, her breasts heaving with every breath she took.

"What?" Brandy was looking at him, puzzled by the expression on his face.

Albert shook his head. "Nothing. I'll tell you later." He turned his attention to the steps themselves. The memory of the two of them in that stifling attic, their sweaty bodies sliding together to the rhythm of their lovemaking, was too much to think about right now. He would have to wait until he had pants on again if he didn't want to embarrass himself.

Behind him, Andrea groaned. "Those sentinel people were seriously messed up!"

"They were a bunch of psychos!" snapped Nicole.

Albert chuckled. That seemed to be putting it mildly. All that they had gone through... The emotion rooms. The labyrinth. Gilbert House. The Caggo. The hounds. The endless darkness. What was it all for? What did it all accomplish? Was it really necessary?

Would there ever be any real answers?

As he tried to catch his breath, he wondered what was going on inside the temple. Had the fire spread throughout the labyrinth? Were those narrow passageways growing hot, the hounds struggling in the heat? How would they ever get home if the temple was burning inside?

There was no sense in thinking too much about it right now. He had other things to worry about. Like his knee, which had begun to scream at him, making him limp in spite of his efforts to hide his discomfort. And as he expected, Brandy took it upon herself to help him again in spite of her own obvious exhaustion.

He loved her so much, but he feared he would be the death of the poor girl at this rate.

"How many steps have we climbed now?" gasped Andrea.

"Ballpark figure?" Albert looked back down the steps. They were so far. That other opening looked so tiny from here. Between this and the last tunnel... "Maybe thirty stories."

"No shit?" panted Nicole.

"Maybe more."

Brandy groaned. "Feels more like a hundred."

"That's because you insist on carrying your boyfriend's dead weight," he reminded her.

"He's not dead weight," she replied, jabbing him gently with her elbow.

The gesture raised a grin on Albert's face.

Andrea sat down on the steps behind them. "I feel like I'm going to throw up."

"It's not far now," he promised. The equivalent of just a few flights remained.

Groaning, she stood up again, then she turned and glanced back down the steps, blinking away the sweat in her eyes. She thought she'd heard another voice, expected there to be someone standing down there, like the figure they saw waiting at the top of the last tunnel, but there was no one.

Looking back up at the others, it didn't appear that anyone else heard it. And she didn't bother telling them. She barely had the energy to speak the words anyway, and was sure they didn't have the energy to be concerned by it.

It was odd. She couldn't even say for sure what the voice sounded like, whether it was a man or a woman, certainly not whatever foreign words were likely uttered, but she couldn't seem to shake the feeling that the voice had been encouraging her.

It was probably the heat and the exhaustion. Next she'd be seeing ghosts fanning her and offering her lemonade.

Up and up they climbed, all of them falling silent as the heat slowly drained their strength. Their legs ached. Sweat ran down their bodies. And each of them began to wonder if they would reach the top before it all became too much for them.

But each of them knew by now that they were stronger than they knew.

Eventually, they reached the top of the steps and emerged from the tunnel into the welcome relief of a cool, steady breeze.

"Thank God," Nicole sighed, practically staggering into the

firelight. "I was starting to feel dizzy." Her body was ringing wet. Her ponytail clung to her back. When she leaned against the wall and hung her head, trying to catch her breath, Albert could see the sweat dripping from her nose and chin.

"We should probably rest for a while," Olivia suggested. "Before one of us gets sick up here." She had already dropped to her knees and now sat there in the middle of the path, her shoulders slumped, her damp, heavy breasts heaving between her arms, her hair plastered to the sides of her wet face.

Andrea walked over to the edge of the path and gazed out over the lake. Sweat dripped the length of her lean body. Her pigtails felt like lead weights pulling down her head.

She looked down at the rocky valley below and felt a wave of vertigo wash gently over her, prompting her to step quickly away from the ledge, lest she suddenly take a much closer look at the ground far below.

Turning around, she saw that Albert had seated himself on the ground near Olivia and that Brandy was kneeling next to him, fanning him gently.

"Don't do that," he told her, chuckling a little. "I'm fine. Check on them."

Brandy sat up and looked around, concerned.

"I'm fine," said Olivia as she stretched her legs out in front of her and lay flat on her back on the cool stone. She spread her arms out over her head, her eyes closed. Albert stared at her for a moment, surprised by how lovely her body looked like that. The sweat highlighted her muscle tone. Her legs were strong and lean, her belly soft but lightly toned. Her ample breasts settled across her chest, accenting her curves.

He rubbed his eyes tiredly and tried to push the image away. He felt as if he'd been leering, but he hadn't meant to. She was just pretty. She had a very nice body.

Wow, he needed some rest.

"Shit it was hot in there," gasped Nicole, her words not so much spoken as belched between panting breaths. "Fucking miserable."

Brandy stood up and went to her side. "You okay?"

Nicole nodded.

"Stand out in the open where you can feel the wind. If you're lucky, maybe you'll get pissed on this time."

Nicole turned and scrunched her face up at her. She wasn't amused.

At the same time, Olivia's eyes snapped open and she stared up at the carrion eaters fluttering through the sky above her. With a startled squeal she sat up, covering herself. When she saw everyone looking at her, she whimpered, "Forgot about those stupid things…"

Once again, everyone began to laugh. Once again, it felt good. But once again, it couldn't last.

Albert looked up at the flames that awaited them atop the mountain. They were closer now, much closer than they were before all those steps, maybe even as much as two thirds of the way to the top. More if there were more steps. Less if the path decided to torture them for a while longer and take its sweet time leading them there.

But those steps came at a steep price. If there *were* more steps like the ones they just climbed, if there *were* more tunnels, it would likely only get worse. As the mountain grew smaller and the heat rose, and as the inferno burned longer, the higher tunnels would only get hotter.

Nicole spat onto the ground, trying to rid herself of the salty taste of sweat on her lips.

"That was lovely," Brandy told her.

Nicole began to giggle. "I'm not exactly out here hoping to hook up with someone, you know."

"Better not be. I've got dibs on the only man-candy out here."

"I'm not an object," Albert called to them.

"Just be quiet and look pretty," Nicole told him.

He shook his head. "That's just not right."

Andrea began giggling again.

Soon, Olivia had joined her. "Oh god, I'm so tired," she panted.

"We all are," Albert assured her.

Again, they fell silent.

Nicole stepped away from the wall and seated herself near Albert and Olivia, where the breeze washed over her whole body.

Brandy sat next to Albert, who looked from her to Nicole, to Andrea. He hoped so much that he would prove strong enough to bring them all home.

When his eyes turned to Olivia, he found her staring back at him, her dark eyes piercing.

"Can we really do this?" she asked him. "Do we really have any kind of chance of making it home?"

Now all of them were looking at him. It was, after all, the only question that mattered at this point.

He sighed. "I don't know. Honestly. I mean, on one hand there's a swarm of...winged...*monsters*...flying around above our heads. For all we know, they could strip us to skeletons in an instant if they wanted. There's an apparently endless *horde* of flesh-eating zombies surrounding us, probably making their way up the mountain already. Night trees.

Heat stroke from those blast furnace tunnels. *Ghosts.* Let's not forget about them. Oh, and if we do this wrong we might bring about the end of the world, although it's still a little sketchy on that point."

"Wow," said Nicole. "You really suck at pep talks. You know that?"

A small grin touched Albert's lips. "On the other hand… We've come this far and those…" He glanced up at the sky. "Whatever those are… Haven't shown any interest in us yet. Maybe they won't. Those zombies might never catch up. It looks like most of them can't even get past the lake current."

"You think maybe we're not really in any danger?" asked Andrea.

"No, we're probably in danger. But I don't think we're *doomed.* I mean, we've survived a lot so far. We survived Gilbert House. We survived the temple. The labyrinth. I don't know who…or *what* the Keeper is… But I don't think he's trying to kill us. He's already had plenty of creative chances to do that."

Olivia nodded. "Okay, then."

Albert reached out with his good arm and took her hand. "I think we just have to stay strong a little while longer."

Andrea reached out and took Olivia's other hand. "You guys rock way too much to not make it through this."

Olivia smiled. Then her smile faded a little. "Wayne wouldn't let us give up."

"No, he wouldn't," agreed Albert.

Nicole reached out and took both their hands in hers. "No more talking about our chances. We're all going home and we're going to shower and eat and sleep and then we're all going to get our nails done and we're all going out drinking."

"Awesome!" exclaimed Andrea.

"Except the high school girl."

"Boo."

"I'm a minor, too," said Olivia.

Nicole rolled her eyes. "*Brandy and me* are going out drinking, then. And you're all going to like it!"

Olivia smiled. "We've all got each other," she said. "That's way more than I had in Gilbert House."

"You had us there, too," Albert assured her. "We were just late showing up."

"Totally," agreed Andrea.

Olivia smiled. Maybe they *would* make it after all.

Just maybe.

Chapter 27

Another stifling tunnel did not await them around the next corner, nor the next. Instead, the mountainous terrain closed in around them, shutting them into a narrow canyon between forty-foot-high walls of rough, gray stone. Bathed in deep shadow, far below the glow of the flames, they were forced to again rely on the remaining three flashlights.

This darkness was far more unsettling than the gloom of the tunnels, where they had been able to see the light at both ends the entire time. Here, they could see nothing more than the narrow crack of black, carrion eater-infested sky above them. The crooked, winding path refused them a glimpse of either end as it wove deeper and deeper into the mountainside.

For almost an hour, the five of them traveled with their three lights, nervously scanning every crack and crevice for any sign of danger, until at last they came to a split in the road.

Left or right. There didn't appear to be any difference between the two. Both were narrow and dark and equally ominous. With no sign, no clues, nothing to tell them which way to go, all of them turned and looked at Olivia.

But this one was tricky... She looked left, then right. Left again. "Are we sure we should be trusting my feelings? I'm not sure about this one."

"It's all we've got," Albert replied. "You've done fantastic so far."

Right. Left. Olivia puzzled over them. This one wasn't like the others. Those were obvious. The very idea of turning down one of the paths gave her a strange and profound sense of utter dread. But this time... "It's like I don't want to take either of them."

Albert looked around. These were the only paths. What else were they supposed to do? "*I* don't feel anything," he observed. That odd *significance* was still there when he looked up at the darting shadows of the carrion eaters. He also felt it when he stroked the gold surface of the medal that hung from the chain around his neck, but he felt nothing when considering the two paths before them. Nor had he felt anything at any fork that came before this one.

"I don't either," said Brandy.

"Me either," said Andrea. "But I guess I'm not supposed to, so..."

"I wouldn't turn down anybody's feeling at this point," said Albert.

Left. Right. Olivia chewed her lower lip. She didn't like this. She didn't like being responsible for choosing the safe path. She didn't like that her feelings might be all that stood between them and a bad end. Where had those other paths gone? The ones she'd so desperately wanted to avoid. If she hadn't felt that odd urge to avoid one path, where would it have taken them? After all she'd seen, she shuddered at the thought of a fate so terrible that it filled that newly-discovered psychic part of her mind with such alarm.

But more importantly, why wasn't that obvious feeling working for her here? Why did neither of these paths seem right to her?

She tried to picture going left and felt a twinge of that dread. But when she tried to picture going right, she felt the same thing. What was the difference?

"What do we do if she can't figure it out?" asked Brandy.

"We'll find a way," Albert replied, but he had no idea where to even begin. All he could think to do was reach for the box, but he didn't think that would help them. The box had spit up one last clue for him when he needed it most, back before the City of the Blind, directing them through that awful mud chamber, but it had remained spent ever since and he didn't expect it to help him now.

But then what were they supposed to do? Sensing the path up the mountain had seemed to be Olivia's job. But now, suddenly, she had come up blank. Why? It didn't make any sense. There was no logic in it.

But then again, there was nothing logical about letting Olivia "feel" her way up the mountain. Logic had pretty well failed him the moment he first began to unravel the clues carved into the sides of the box, when the Sentinel Queen reached into his mind and steered him toward the solution, urging him to see the answers he might have otherwise missed.

Psychic powers. Monsters. Ghosts. Sunless worlds filled with murderous trees and ravenous zombies. Logic simply did not serve him as well as it used to.

Olivia began to walk toward the path on the right.

"That way?" asked Andrea.

"Just wait," Olivia said. "Let me try something." She closed her eyes and walked forward. Just as she entered the crevice on the right, she felt strongly repelled. Something was up there. Something bad. She was sure of it.

She backed up, reluctant to take her eyes off the path, and then turned left. "I think... Maybe this way." Still watching the path on the right, as if she expected something to jump out at her, she entered the left path and felt a moment of relief. Whatever was on that other path, she'd be safe from it as long as she went this way. "Yeah. This one."

She started forward.

The others immediately started after her.

But then Olivia stopped. She gasped. "Oh god!"

Brandy grabbed her arm. "What's wrong?"

"What is it?" asked Albert.

Andrea and Brandy shined their flashlights around, searching the tall stone for any sign of danger.

"Not this one!" cried Olivia. "Oh god! Not this one!" She turned and fled, pushing through them, desperate to be away from this path.

"What is it?" Albert asked. "What do you feel?"

"*Wrong*," Olivia gasped. She stood outside the passage, looking back at the tunnel, her hands clamped together against her bosom. "It's just...*wrong*... I can't really explain it."

Albert nodded. "Okay. Good to know. So we go the other way."

Olivia shook her head. Her eyes shimmered with frightened tears. "They're both bad."

Albert looked at Brandy and then Nicole, confused. "They're *both* bad? How can they *both* be bad?"

She shook her head again. "I don't know. They just are."

Albert licked his lips. His mouth had been dry for a while. He hadn't had anything to drink since that sip of foul lake water near where they spoke to the Keeper.

"I just don't know…" Tears welled up in Olivia's eyes. She was afraid. She didn't like this at all. Why was this happening? Why couldn't they just reach the top and go home?

He walked over to where she stood and clasped his free hand over both of hers. "It's okay," he promised. "There must be some way through here."

"I don't know what to do."

"It's okay," he said again. Letting go of her hands, he turned and looked back at the two paths. He scanned the high walls around them. There seemed to be no way out but back the way they came. But that wasn't an option. There was nothing waiting for them in that direction but zombies.

He felt a hand on his shoulder. It was Olivia. "I'm sorry," she said.

"Nothing to be sorry about," he assured her. "There's a reason for this. I'm sure of it. We just have to find it."

He looked back at the tunnels, thinking. Why would both tunnels feel bad?

Olivia peered over his shoulder, her body lightly pressed against him. She was troubled by this turn of events. He could tell. And so could Brandy. She appeared at her side and slipped an arm around her.

"You guys can figure this out," Brandy told them. "I'm sure of it."

Albert nodded. "So am I."

"The one on the left felt a lot worse," Olivia recalled. "It was a lot more intense. But I didn't go as far into the other one."

"Then maybe we should try the one on the right. See if it feels better or worse. If they don't feel exactly the same…maybe that would mean something."

Olivia nodded. She closed her eyes and took a deep breath. Then she stood up straighter. "I'll try."

"We'll go with you," Brandy offered.

"No. I can do it on my own."

"You don't have to," Albert said.

"I know. But I want to. This is kind of my job. I guess it's probably the whole reason I'm here, huh?"

Albert considered it. It made sense. Perhaps this gift of hers was the only thing that would allow them to reach their destination. Maybe that was the whole reason for Gilbert House. Maybe the whole purpose of that place was to bring her to them so she could light the way to the top.

…But that was a terrible thing to think. Four people were dead because of that place. That was a dreadful price just to ensure that Olivia joined their party. The thought that he could be the cause of so much tragedy, even unwillingly, was more than he could bear.

No. He had to believe that those deaths were not inevitably linked to his purpose on this mountain. He had to believe that they didn't have to die for him to be here now. Maybe it was the Sentinel Queen and that old man. Maybe *they'd* killed those people. They were clearly in disagreement about opening the sentinels' door. And they were both obviously more than willing to use people to meet their ends.

He'd never met the old man, but the Sentinel Queen gave him the distinct impression that she commanded an impressive amount of control over all that had happened.

Another thought occurred to him now: If they really needed Olivia to reach the summit, then he and Brandy were never meant to reach the doorway the previous year. She wasn't even in Briar Hills the night he found the box. She would have been in Wilsing, still a high school senior. If they couldn't make this journey without her, then the Sentinel Queen must've known that they would fail in the fear room and turn around. She must've planned it all, every detail.

It was a little overwhelming to think about.

Olivia slowly started forward. She was terrified. Not since she and Wayne escaped the Wood had she felt this uncertain.

"Be careful," Andrea begged.

Slowly, cautiously, she stepped into the passageway on the right. Her eyes drifted up to the towering walls overhead. She could feel something deep inside her telling her to get out.

But step after step that feeling grew no stronger.

"This one's better," she decided. She turned and looked at Albert. "This one's not as bad as the other one."

Albert nodded. "Then that's the way we go."

"But why does it still feel bad?" Andrea asked.

Albert had a theory, but Olivia beat him to it.

"I think there's something bad here, too," she said. "It feels dangerous. But not as dangerous as the other way. I'm not sure what it is, but I think we're supposed to go this way. We just have to be careful."

Albert squeezed her shoulder as he passed. "Good job," he said. "I'll lead. Maybe I can spot whatever's wrong with this passage before we get there. You keep that extra sense of yours wide open."

"I'll try."

He continued forward, his four companions close behind him, his eyes open for any sign of danger.

But nothing waited in the shadows ahead. In fact, they followed the cramped canyon for several hundred yards without incident, until at last the stone withdrew and they entered a small clearing between the high walls. A pool of water covered the left half of the ground here, its surface rippling gently.

Olivia eyed the water, but she sensed nothing odd about it. Yet something was here somewhere. That strange aversion she'd felt when she entered this passage had not subsided, nor had it grown. It was strange.

A set of crooked, narrow steps led up through a winding crevice in the wall in front of them, reaching up to a short tunnel. Firelight shined from the other side, where carrion eaters fluttered through the air, enthralled by the flames.

Albert thought he caught a whiff of burnt flesh, but that might have been his imagination. Or maybe not. It didn't matter.

Nicole looked up into the black sky and began to walk toward the steps, but Albert reached out and halted her. For a moment, she was confused. She clutched his outstretched arm against her chest and looked at him, wide-eyed and expectant. "What's wrong?"

He looked back at her and smiled. "Nothing. Just watch where you step."

She looked down and saw that she was one more step from planting her bare toes in a huge spattering of carrion eater dung. Instantly, she backed away, repulsed, and cursed loudly. "Thanks," she said when she'd regained her composure.

"There's lots of it," Andrea realized.

There was. This area had taken a considerable pounding from the airborne menaces. There was crap splattered everywhere. Albert looked up, wary of any foul, aerial assaults, and recalled how big the carrion eaters were. It was no wonder they made such a mess.

"Let's not hang out here," Brandy decided.

Agreeing emphatically, Nicole set off across the clearing toward the steps, careful to avoid the filth that littered the ground along the way.

Olivia hurried after her, calling for her to wait up.

Andrea and Brandy followed them and Albert took a moment to look back the way they came. He still saw nothing that concerned him, but he had no doubt that Olivia was right about it being dangerous.

At the base of the steps, Olivia turned and waited for Albert as Nicole and Andrea started up the steps. "This still feels wrong," she told him. "I don't know what it is, but it's not right."

He nodded. "Keep your eyes open."

The steps here were steeper than those in the tunnel, and a little bit crooked, too. Albert had to take care to keep his balance.

Ahead of him, Olivia and Brandy walked together. Ahead of them, Nicole and Andrea were already approaching the top of the steps. Andrea was a few steps ahead.

"This feels wrong," Olivia said again.

Andrea stopped and looked back at Nicole. "Did you just…"

Nicole stared up at her, confused. "Did I just what?"

But she couldn't have. "I was going to ask if you tugged on my hair. But you weren't close enough…"

"Wasn't me," she said, and continued past her up the steps.

Andrea reached up and caressed her dirty pigtail. It felt just like someone grabbed hold of it. But there was no one there. She looked back down the steps and realized that there was someone standing at the bottom, looking back up at her. It was hard to see for the shadows, but she thought it was a man. Squinting, she descended a few steps and tried to see who was there.

"You okay?" asked Nicole from above her.

"What's wrong?" asked Brandy as she and Olivia approached from below.

Andrea glanced at them and when she looked back, the person was gone, vanished in that brief moment when she'd taken her eyes off him. "Nothing," she said.

Could she just be getting tired? Was that it? It was so hard to be sure.

Olivia followed her gaze, but there was nothing to see down there but shadows. "You're creeping me out," she told her.

"Sorry." Andrea turned and continued up the steps.

Olivia looked at her, and then looked up at Nicole, who had just reached the top of the steps and entered the tunnel. Seeing her there sent a fierce stutter through her heart and she suddenly cried out her name.

But it was already too late. Nicole emerged from the far side of the tunnel and turned to see what the fuss was about. The next second, something reached down from above and seized her by the hair.

Her screams filled the darkness and sent the nearby carrion eaters into frenzied flight.

Chapter 28

Nicole shrieked first in surprise and then in pain as she was lifted up off the ground. Her feet flailing, she reached up and seized her assailant, expecting to find a hand or claw buried in her matted ponytail. Instead, she felt the cold flesh of something long and sinewy.

Almost immediately, two more of these things snaked around her wrists. Another slithered around her neck. Others wriggled around the backpack. One slid slowly and purposefully down her naked spine. Wherever these strange tentacles gripped her, sharp needles of fiery pain pierced her flesh.

She screamed and kicked, struggling desperately against the iron grip of her strange captor, but the thing was incredibly strong. She arched her back, pulling against it with all her strength, and peered up. Through a blur of tears, she glimpsed a massive canopy of twisting, coiling branches.

It was a night tree. And it had her firmly in its grasp.

Andrea rushed through the tunnel and quickly seized one of

Nicole's thrashing legs. An instant later, Brandy was beside her, clutching the straps of Albert's backpack and pulling down with all her weight. Though Andrea still clung to her flashlight, Brandy's was gone, dropped, though she couldn't quite remember when. Nor did she care. The only thing that mattered was tearing her best friend from the clutches of this murdering tree. Even when one of those tentacle-like branches coiled itself around her wrist and burned against her flesh, wrenching from her an agonized scream, she did not let go. Her feet came off the ground, all her weight pulling down on those two canvas straps, yet the night tree did not give an inch. It clung firmly to its prey, utterly unyielding.

Olivia felt as if she were seeing every detail of the horror that was playing out before her eyes. The branches of the tree were slowly descending, preparing to envelop them all, like the jaws of a great and complex Venus flytrap. More and more of those serpentine branches were descending, twisting through Nicole's hair, tightening around her throat, threatening to strangle her and silence her terrified cries. Tears streaked down her face. The muscles in her body as she struggled were so tight they looked like they would snap at any moment. She even saw the spittle that flew from her lips as she screamed for help.

And during all of this, she was racing toward that horrid scene, moving almost without realizing what she was doing, determined to prevent this gruesome tragedy from passing. She tossed away the flashlight, unconcerned about something as trivial as the light. She didn't need it anyway. She could see just fine at the moment and the future was a far off place she had no business thinking about right now. She gripped one strap of the backpack and put all of her weight into it alongside Brandy, determined to pull Nicole down.

This was what she'd been afraid of. This was why she didn't want to come down this path. The other one had probably led to certain death. Some horrible, inescapable trap awaited them that way, an unthinkable fate far worse than what fell on Wayne and Beverly, perhaps even worse than the long suffering of poor Trish at the hands of that awful monster in Gilbert House. But on this path, *this* was waiting.

She'd known it somehow. She'd foreseen it.

No wonder she'd always been lucky. Apparently, she had the ability to see the outcome of things. To a degree. Was this how it was for Albert and Brandy, too? Or did their abilities work in entirely different ways?

Somehow, all these things went through her mind as she desperately pulled on the strap of the backpack, praying to God for the strength to pull her friend to the ground, safe and unharmed.

Brandy was crying, screaming Nicole's name. More of those strange tendrils were snaking around her wrists. Each one stung her flesh as it gripped her.

Andrea released Nicole's leg and reached for one of the straps as well, thinking that she'd be of more use by adding her weight to Brandy's and Olivia's. But as soon as she stood up, she felt something sting the tender flesh of her exposed back. When she cried out and turned, her arm was instantly entangled in two, fleshy tendrils. She screamed in revulsion first, then in pain as her flesh began to burn at their touch.

Then she was tackled hard and ripped from the tree's biting grip. She struck the ground with a shriek and found herself in Albert's rough embrace.

"Stay here!" he shouted, speaking through clenched teeth as he bore the pain of his freshly jolted arm. The last one on the steps, he'd been the last one to arrive and so he stood for a few brief seconds in the tunnel, forcing himself to observe the situation in spite of his horror, making himself think clearly before charging in. When he saw that the tree had begun to entangle Andrea, he did all he could think of, which was to knock her bodily out of its grasp.

"You have to save her!" shrieked Andrea.

"I know!" He stood up and turned around. The same strategy wasn't going to work with Nicole. She was firmly entangled in those eely branches. The tree wasn't going to give her up easily. Soon she would be entirely ensnared. Soon all *three* of them would be hopelessly bound by the mighty branches. It already had a firm grip on Brandy's arms and now one of them had Olivia's hair.

All the branches had begun to curl downward, closing on them like the walls of a giant cage. Countless more tendrils were wriggling out from them, dancing expectantly through the air. Time was running out. Soon the predator would have its prey.

Albert rushed forward and jumped, hooking his arm around Brandy's shoulders and using his weight and momentum to pull her down. Her hands slipped from the strap of the backpack and she fell, tearing her hands free of the tendrils that held her.

Both of them struck the ground and Albert saw the world double as a thunderbolt of pain tore through his broken bone for the second time in only a handful of seconds.

As he staggered to his feet, the tree shook violently, its branches shuddering and thundering together, and then it began to reel Nicole up higher, dragging Olivia up with her.

Nicole felt the tendril around her neck begin to close. Her screams cut off as she gasped for breath. All over her, the creepy, fleshy things slithered like cold serpents, biting her, stinging her. They were everywhere. Her arms and legs were on fire. Her neck burned. Ribbons of pain encircled her body, down her belly, even between her thighs.

With a loud rip, the straps on the backpack gave way and Olivia dropped, her arms tearing free of the tendrils, a lock of her hair tearing free of her scalp.

Brandy stared up at her best friend, saw the blood that trickled from under the fleshy tentacles that held her, and felt icy terror well up inside her.

It was killing her!

Albert jumped up and pried one of the tendrils off of her leg, revealing a series of long, bloody gashes where it had stuck to her. As soon as it was off of her, it twisted itself around his hand and bit into his flesh.

Andrea sat on the cold ground, her hands pressed to her face, too terrified to move. Everything seemed to be happening in slow motion. She could see tendrils reaching down, grabbing Albert's arm as he struggled to pull his hand free, lifting him up off the ground. She could see Nicole struggling for breath, her eyes wide and afraid, beads of blood oozing out from beneath the snake-like coil that was strangling her. She could see Brandy standing up, desperately trying to rescue the people she loved.

Olivia was still on her knees, staring up at the tree, tears streaming down her face. Those tendrils were everywhere. They looked like tentacles, as if the tree were really one of Lovecraft's monsters in disguise. They reached toward her, all around her, unavoidable. She was going to die here. They were *all* going to die here. And she couldn't do a damn thing to stop it. She stared up at those twisting, stretching branches as her heart thundered in her chest.

Albert struggled to free himself as he rose up into the closing branches and screamed at Brandy to let go of him, to get away and save herself, but already the night tree had her in its grasp, was already pulling on her arm.

Nicole's face was turning purple. Her eyes bulged. Blood dripped down her body in long, shiny streamers.

She had only a moment longer before cold death closed in on her.

And then a voice whispered in Andrea's ear: "Fire. The bag."

Blinking away the tears, she turned and looked over her shoulder. Flames were belching from a vent on the far side of the path. She could feel the heat radiating off it.

Fire.

She did not consider whose voice it might have been or why the spirits were suddenly speaking English. The only thought in her brain was that she had just one shot at this.

She stood up and ran beneath the tree, dodging several snatching tendrils, and grabbed Albert's backpack off the ground. Twirling around, she batted the snaking branches away and screamed at Olivia to move. Then she was fleeing from the tree's grasp, running as hard as she could go back to the vent.

She plunged Albert's bag into the spewing flames. It caught quickly enough, and when she turned around with it, its fabric burned like a torch. Immediately, before it could go out, she turned, spilling the box and the first aid kit onto the ground, and rushed back to the tree.

She ducked under the descending canopy and shoved the burning bag up into the branches between Nicole and Albert.

The tree seized the backpack greedily and hauled the light load up into its branches. Seconds later, it gave another violent shudder and dropped the burning bag…and everything else, too.

Nicole fell hard to the ground, coughing and gagging and weeping.

"Help me!" Andrea cried as she tried to lift her to her feet. She didn't think she'd be able to do it, but then Olivia was at her side, finally snapped out of her terrified paralysis.

Brandy and Albert helped each other up and the five of them fled the ambushing night tree.

Albert stopped long enough to gather up the two remaining flashlights, which had somehow been kicked clear of the tree's reach in all the commotion, as well as the first aid kit and the box. The remaining sidewalk chalk and the batteries, as well as one of the flashlights, were lost with the smoldering remains of his backpack beneath the thrashing limbs of the night tree. He felt a twinge of regret to have lost it. It was more than a convenient bag for carrying his gear. It was a piece of the amazing adventure that brought him and Brandy together in the first place. But he wouldn't have traded that old pack for anyone's life in a million years.

The path thinned into a narrow pass between a steep incline rising to meet the high walls of the temple and a sheer drop into a low valley far below. They made their way past this, well beyond the sight of the violent night tree, and took their rest on a wide ledge overlooking a watery inlet. Here, they gathered themselves and immediately began tending to Nicole, who managed in spite of all that had happened, and even in spite of her own sobbing, to insist that she was fine.

"You're not fine," Brandy told her, her voice wavering. "You're bleeding."

A ring of shallow gashes circled her neck where bruises had already begun to gather. Blood trickled down her chest.

"You're lucky it didn't open your jugular," said Olivia.

Nicole wiped her eyes and looked down at her arms. Long chains of these gashes circled them from her hands to her shoulders. More ran down and around both legs. Others crisscrossed her belly. One had reached around her ribcage and bit into the underside of her right breast. She felt plenty more in places she couldn't see. Her back. Her bottom. The backs of her legs. "Stings."

"We know," Albert assured her. They'd all been bitten by those strange branches. He could feel them down his arm as well as on his back and chest. It reminded him of the stubborn sting of a well-aimed cat scratch.

He knelt beside her and opened the first aid kit. One end of the plastic container had melted, but the contents seemed fine. There would be enough to clean her up. But again he wasn't much help with his one useless arm, so he passed it to Brandy, who began to clean those small, but horrid-looking wounds in her throat with a motherly tenderness.

"Do you think it could've poisoned us?" asked Andrea.

Albert considered it, but shook his head. "I doubt it. What would be the point? It's a tree. I think we've already seen how it defends itself. Any kind of toxin would just be redundant." Not that it mattered whether he was right or wrong. If the night tree had poisoned them, there was nothing they could do about it at this point. They would either live or die. It was out of their hands.

"That was some quick thinking," Olivia said. "Using the backpack to torch the tree."

"It wasn't really my idea," Andrea confessed. "A ghost told me to do it."

"A ghost?" asked Albert.

She shrugged. "Another voice."

"I'm not complaining," decided Brandy. "I don't care if Barney the dinosaur told you to do it. Thank God for whatever help we got back there. That was too close."

Olivia had to agree with that. For a moment there, she'd thought it was over for all of them. She'd practically given up.

"I don't usually think that hearing voices is a good thing," Nicole said, sniffing back her tears and frowning at the scratchiness of her throat. "But I'm making an exception for you."

"She and her voices have been really useful," agreed Albert.

Andrea blushed. "Sorry about your backpack."

Albert smiled. "Small price to pay." He picked up the box and examined it. One corner of it was burned black, but otherwise it remained unharmed. Setting it back on the ground beside him, he handed Brandy the two flashlights and then stood up and looked out over the lake. They were well above the top of the wall now. He could see the tops of those distant and suddenly far more frightening trees swaying rhythmically at the edge of the firelight.

The zombies continued their lemmings run over the ledge and into the depths of the lake.

How long had that been going on now? How many hours? It was amazing that the entire ground down there wasn't crawling with undead corpses. Instead, he could make out only a few tiny shapes lurking in the dancing firelight far below.

Stepping closer to the ledge, he spied a rocky slope just beneath him, leading down to a narrow pool of shallow water, part of a bigger inlet separated from the lake by one of the ridges they'd crossed when they first set out for the Keeper's mysterious doorway. These were the tallest cliffs on the mountain. The view looking down made him feel a little dizzy, so he turned his back to it.

"We got really lucky back there," said Olivia.

"Don't feel particularly lucky," coughed Nicole.

"But you *feel*," Brandy pointed out as she tenderly dabbed at the cuts on her neck.

"True."

Andrea stepped up beside Albert and looked out over the lake as he had done. She didn't like the zombies. She hoped he was right about there being a current that swept the vast majority of them out to sea.

"I should've seen that coming," fretted Olivia. "I mean I *did* see it coming. Sort of. But I didn't. I knew something was wrong with that path…"

Nicole shook her head. "I should've been paying more attention."

"Doesn't matter," said Albert. He walked over to where Nicole sat and knelt beside her again. "We're all still here. That's all that matters."

He looked up at Andrea as she turned to face him.

She smiled.

That's when Albert heard it, a subtle sound against the ever-present rush of flames. He looked up into the sky and saw it coming.

It all happened so quickly. He tried to open his mouth, to warn her, to warn them all. He wanted to jump up and do something, but all he could do was sit there like an idiot and watch.

It came down from the top of the mountain, slicing vertically through the air like the blade of a guillotine, and then curved at the last instant, a perfect ninety-degree turn, its leathery wings spread wide to catch the air.

It went straight for her, as though it had only been waiting for this chance.

Andrea didn't even scream until the last second, aware of the danger she was in only after it was too late. Brandy screamed, too. Olivia leapt to her feet, her eyes wide with terror.

And then Andrea was knocked backward by the carrion eater, over the precarious ledge.

Albert saw her for a moment as he scrambled to his feet, and then she was falling. Her screams followed her all the way down.

And then she was just gone.

"Oh God!" Nicole gasped.

"No…" breathed Brandy.

Olivia seemed unable to find her voice at all.

Albert could not even seem to think.

Chapter 29

Albert stared down at the dark water far below. He kept hoping that it was deeper than he thought, that she'd somehow survived the fall. But Andrea was gone. He could not even see her body. The only sign of her was the churning of the waves against the rocks.

He never should have let his guard down. He never should have stopped watching those damned creatures. They'd left them alone for so long, ignored them entirely this whole time…until he'd begun to believe that, like moths, they were only interested in the flames. He'd actually begun to believe that they were harmless.

He felt like an idiot.

"We have to go down there," Olivia said, her voice barely audible. "She might be okay. We can't leave her there."

But Albert knew that there was no way she could still be alive. It simply wasn't possible. It was so far down, much farther than Brandy had fallen when the Caggo threw her off the tower, much farther than he had fallen when he broke his arm. He'd heard her scream. It followed her all the way down and then… And then it just ended.

He wanted so badly to be wrong. He prayed, pleaded for one more miracle, to hear her small voice from the bottom of the temple, frightened, perhaps even hurting, but still somehow alive. He listened, but she did not call out.

"We have to at least try!" Olivia pleaded. Her voice was louder now, almost shrill.

"She's right," Nicole said. She was still sitting on the ground, her back against the stone face of the cliff. Her eyes were wide with shock and shimmered with welling tears. She couldn't rise to her feet if she wanted to. Her legs felt like jelly. "We can't just leave her down there. What if she's still alive? What if she's in pain? We have to try and find her."

Albert turned, his face empty of all expression. When he shook his head, a slow, heartbreaking gesture, Olivia burst into tears.

Brandy went to her, wrapped her arms around her as tears spilled down her own face. She couldn't believe that Andrea was really gone, didn't *want* to believe it. It happened so fast. She was just here with them. She was smiling. And in the blink of an eye…

It seemed so unfair. So *cruel.*

Albert couldn't bear to see them like this. He looked at the ground, instead. Even if she wasn't dead, even if she'd somehow managed to remain miraculously alive after such a fall, there was nothing they could do for her. She'd be at the mercy of those zombies. He'd even seen them scrambling toward the water where her body splashed down. They'd have her in pieces before they could ever get to her. *If* they could ever get to her. There were two awakened night trees between here and there. Probably more than a few eager zombies as well. And how long would it take to retrace the miles of mountain path they'd already climbed.

She was lost.

He walked past Brandy and Olivia without looking at them, without looking at anything but the gray stone of the path beneath his feet. He no longer felt the pain in his knee. He didn't even feel the pain in his arm. He didn't seem to feel anything. His whole body was numb. He sat down next to Nicole and stared out at the darkness that hung over that distant, crawling forest.

Why couldn't it have been him? Why couldn't he have taken her place and plunged through that darkness? Why wasn't it *his* body that was dashed on the stone at the bottom of that shallow pool? He wasn't much use to anybody anyway with his broken arm and swollen knee. He couldn't fight. He couldn't protect anyone. Even if it was possible to go down there and find Andrea, he couldn't pick her up and carry her up the mountain. It wasn't fair.

Nicole stretched her aching body out and lay down, resting her head on his thigh. She closed her eyes and let go of the tears. They spilled down the sides of her face. First Beverly, then Wayne. Now poor, sweet Andrea.

The Temple of the Blind was a merciless place.

Albert lay his good hand on her belly. It made no difference that they were naked. It meant nothing that his blood was now smeared on her skin, nor that hers now stained his. All they had up here was each other. Only the four of them now...

Brandy wiped her tears and looked back at Albert and Nicole. She met his sad gaze and saw the depth of his pain. It mirrored her own.

She went to him.

Olivia didn't want to come. The energy was gone from her. The weight of this pain was so much to bear. But neither did she have the strength to refuse. And Brandy was determined. She led her by the hand, refusing to let her stay. Far away from that ledge was where they all needed to be, as close to the wall as possible, where no one else could be lost like that again.

Why was she standing there in the first place? Why did she have to be so damned adventurous?

They sat down together next to Albert. None of them spoke. There was nothing to say.

Olivia lay her head against Brandy's shoulder and stared up at that dark sky filled with those awful creatures, watching them as she wept.

Brandy never let go of her hand.

Albert sat there, staring out toward the black horizon. He no longer cared about hurrying. What were they hurrying toward, anyway? More tragedy? He didn't want to go any farther, didn't want to see who would die next. He just wanted to stay here, where he could see the three of them, where he could hear them breathing, where he knew they were all still alive.

He looked at Brandy, then down at Nicole. His lover and his best friend. His feelings for them were already as strong as he thought any bond could be and those feelings had only grown by leaps and bounds as they journeyed these strange roads together. He turned his eyes on Olivia. He'd only met her less than a day ago. For much of that time, he thought her dead. For much more of that time, he thought that maybe she was alive, but he never expected to see her again. Yet as he gazed over at her pretty features, he realized that she'd become as familiar to him as his own sister. Perhaps even more so, because hadn't Becky

Cross drifted away from him as they grew older, as they moved on toward their own separate lives?

He closed his eyes. *Please,* he thought. *Please don't let me lose anyone else.*

Chapter 30

Olivia stared up at the swarm of killer carrion eaters. She despised those things. It filled her with a dark glee each time she saw one of them catch fire. It was such an odd feeling, hating something so much. She never knew she had it in her. But she did. She had it in abundance for these things. For what they did to poor Andrea.

She still couldn't believe that Andrea and Wayne were both dead. She'd traveled so far with them, from Gilbert House to the Temple of the Blind with all its horrible secrets to the maddening depths of the labyrinth. Why did they have to leave her? Why? What did their deaths accomplish?

Wayne died making sure that the rest of them made it safely out of the labyrinth. Perhaps that was his whole purpose in life. Perhaps that was the very reason he was born. It was sad, but at least it was noble. At least he died feeling like he'd done something for someone. But why did Andrea have to die? Was her only goal in life to bring them the message about the blood atop the tower? That seemed wrong. Why even bother with Andrea? Why not give the message to any of the rest of them? Why not Wayne? Why not Albert? Why not her?

She remembered Wayne asking them to keep quiet about what happened to him, to not bring any trouble upon themselves by trying to make people believe the truth. Were they supposed to do the same for Andrea?

She suddenly realized that Andrea was different. They would eventually find Andrea's car. When they did, hers and Wayne's fingerprints would be all over it. Probably traces of their blood, too, given the state they were in when Andrea drove them to the campus. The police would connect her to both missing persons and it wouldn't take long for them to realize that she had been dating Andy, connecting her to three more missing persons. They would make her tell them what happened. When they did, the truth was all she would be able to tell them, and what would they say then? Would they believe her? Would they even bother checking to see if her story could be proven?

She might as well have gone over that ledge with her.

The tears began to fall again, as much for herself as for those she had lost, and for the selfishness of the very tears she shed.

She lowered her eyes and looked around at the others.

Albert, Brandy and Nicole. Her sole remaining companions for this bizarre journey. She understood now why Wayne was so determined to come to their rescue. They really were remarkable people, brave, strong, caring... But now that he and Andrea were gone, she felt like the stranger in the group again.

Perhaps it was silly, but having Andrea around made her feel less like a stranger. They had been strangers together, and that had somehow added up so that neither of them was really alone.

But now it was just she and they and right now that seemed very profound, even if it didn't really make much sense, especially while they sat huddled together like this, a bloody pile of quietly weeping, naked flesh.

If not for the pain in her heart, she could almost have laughed. If anyone she knew could see her now... No one would ever believe that proper, prissy, reserved Olivia Shadey was stark naked, sweaty, filthy, bruised and bloody, and sitting here with three naked strangers in a place like this. Never mind that they were in another world, that they were on an artificial, flaming mountain, that monsters surrounded them. Even without all those things, no one would believe that she could be here. She didn't even believe that she could be here.

Another carrion eater burst into flames and streaked across the sky briefly before being struck down by its own murderous flock.

She closed her eyes and tried to think of a happy place. But all she could see were Andrea and Wayne.

"What are we going to do now?" asked Nicole, breaking the heavy silence.

For a moment no one answered. Nothing, was the word that came immediately into Albert's mind. He didn't want to do anything. He wanted to sit here and feel the warmth of Nicole's head on his lap, of Brandy's shoulder pressed against his, and not risk losing another of them to the cruelty of the temple. But that wasn't an option. They couldn't stay here forever. Eventually they would have to get up and start moving. And since they could never go back the way they came...

"We keep going," he said at last. "We don't have a choice."

"We need to patch everyone up first," said Brandy. She rose to her knees and picked up the first aid kit, frowning at it. They'd already used so much. They didn't have enough bandaging left to care for all the wounds inflicted by the night tree. They had no choice but to patch up only the deepest and direst of cuts and simply bear the rest.

Olivia lifted both her arms and held them out in front of her, examining them. Fortunately, the biting tendrils of the night tree had very small teeth. Almost all of the cuts had already clotted closed.

But they still stung.

Next to her, Albert lifted his good arm and examined his own injuries. Like Olivia, he was no longer bleeding, but the pain remained.

She stared at him for a moment. Though they were both naked, she didn't feel awkward sitting here with him at all. Perhaps they weren't the strangers she thought they were.

A thought crossed her mind at that moment, one that didn't exactly ease her heartache, for that was profound, but gave her just a little something to warm her poor, broken heart: Maybe they were never strangers. Maybe they'd always been friends and they just hadn't met yet.

Albert met her eyes. He tried to smile for her, but he couldn't quite pull it off.

She tried to smile back and was sure hers looked just as false.

Chapter 31

"That should do it," said Brandy as she secured the last of the gauze around Nicole's neck and dropped her hands wearily into her lap.

Nicole felt the wrapping, tested its snugness, and then straightened her necklace. It was a wonder she hadn't lost it. Thinking about it now, she realized that if it hadn't been around her neck where she left it, she wouldn't have been able to say whether she still had it before the night tree grabbed her and slipped its fleshy, biting tendrils around her. The last time she recalled checking to see if it was still there was after they escaped the mud chamber.

What was missing was her bracelet. That was probably lying beneath the tree with the remains of Albert's bag. The necklace she might have considered going back to look for—she'd had it for a long time—but the bracelet was nothing special. It was merely a pretty thing she'd found cheap at the mall. She could get another one easily enough.

She lifted her arms and examined them. The tendrils had done a number on her wrists, and Brandy used up the rest of the gauze and an entire box of Band-Aids treating as many of the deeper cuts as possible.

"How do you feel?"

"Like a mummy."

"Welcome to the club," said Albert.

"Still sting?" asked Brandy.

Nicole nodded. Her neck and wrists were on fire. Several ropes of pain circled her torso and upper thighs. Even her right breast was stinging. "I'll be all right now. Thank you."

Brandy gave her hand a squeeze and then turned and looked at Albert and Olivia, who still remained sitting against the wall. Olivia was staring up at the monster-infested sky with tears shimmering in her eyes.

She'd known Andrea better than any of them, after all. Wayne, too. To have lost both of them so abruptly...

"We should take a look at you guys, too," she said.

"I'm fine," said Olivia without taking her eyes off that sky.

"Should we be sure?"

"It only got my arms. And my hair."

"She looks okay," Albert assured her. "She's not bleeding anymore. I think she'll be fine. Physically. Emotionally, I think we'll all need some time."

Olivia blinked away the tears and wiped her wet face with the heel of her hand. With lots of time, maybe. But she wasn't sure anymore how much they were going to get. Soon they could all be dead as well.

Brandy sat next to her again and wiped a tear from her face. "It'll be okay," she promised.

But it wouldn't be okay. They all knew that everything was far from okay. An eighteen-year-old girl was dead. Her body was lying in a pool of water at the bottom of this mountain. Her remains would probably end up mutilated and half-devoured by the monsters lurking down there, never to be recovered.

Brandy forced these terrible thoughts from her mind and turned her eyes on Albert. "What about you?"

"Didn't get me too bad," he replied. "Mostly my arm. Stings, but I'll be fine."

"Sure?"

"Positive."

Brandy nodded and then began examining the wounds on her own arms. If they'd had more supplies in the first aid kit, she might have insisted on mending every last cut, but the fact was that they'd almost exhausted it. Little more than an ice pack, some useless bug bite cream and a couple packets of burn gel remained. She'd chosen to use most of it on Nicole, since she was the one most likely to bleed to death.

That tree really did a number on her.

Albert stared out over the ledge, watching the steady drizzle of zombies hurling themselves off that high wall.

It was so absurd to see a sight like that, yet it had practically grown mundane before his eyes. It was so hard to fathom the enormous reality that he was in another world, so hard to grasp the fact that everything he'd ever known was somewhere else entirely, and yet the fact was that he was here. He was sitting on the side of a great, burning mountain, watching zombies throw themselves over a ledge, his body broken and battered by monsters. This was real. He saw it, felt it, tasted it, smelled it… And so he sat here, accepting all these things without a shred of doubt. Because it was all right there.

It was real.

Maybe he'd gone crazy and was really locked up inside a mental institution somewhere.

But even if that were true, it was still real to him. So what did it matter in the end?

On the far right side of what he could see of that wall, the zombies throwing themselves from the cliff suddenly stopped falling. It was like a curtain opening up, drawing slowly across the face of the wall from right to left. All at once, there was nothing there. But only on the far right. Elsewhere, they continued raining down to the water's surface uninterrupted.

Were they coming to an end? Had they finally exhausted their endless numbers?

He stared out at the wall, trying to contemplate the strangeness of this new thing that was happening before him.

Then a great black hump rose up from the churning night trees and settled back into them again.

All at once, his blood chilled. Fear clasped its icy hands around him and squeezed the breath from him.

"Oh hell…" he breathed.

Olivia sat up straight, alarmed. Brandy and Nicole snapped their heads toward him, their eyes wide with startled concern. Then all three of them followed his gaze to the far wall.

At first, nothing moved out there. For a moment, none of them saw anything.

But then that great shadow reared up again, lunging to the left.

"Oh god…" breathed Olivia. "It's here…"

"What is it?" asked Nicole. "What's here?"

"We have to go. Now."

"What?" Nicole asked again, rising shakily to her feet.

"It's the corpse monster," replied Albert.

Olivia nodded weakly. The corpse monster. The very creature that chased her and Wayne from the Wood, the monstrosity that pursued them even through the empty hallways of Gilbert House.

Or perhaps it wasn't the same one. Perhaps there was more than one. It didn't matter. It was here, in the forest around the temple, drawn by the zombies who were drawn by the flames, and if it found its way across the water, it would add the pieces of their broken bodies to its own nightmare form.

It made sense, really. Albert was ashamed of himself for not thinking of it before. The undead had been swarming the mountain, drawn from miles and miles around by the lure of the flames that towered over the forest. It had taken only four flashlights probing the darkness of Gilbert House to bring them running to it like cattle at feeding time. A burning mountain would draw them in droves. And where prey gathered, predators would soon follow.

"It's probably been there the whole time," he said as he rose to his feet, "just out of sight, feeding, eating the things that were drawn to the fire, getting bigger and bigger."

Olivia rose to her feet, too, but her knees felt too weak to hold her up. She reached out for Albert's hand, but found only air. That arm was bound in a sling. Instead, she leaned back against the wall.

"What does it want?" Nicole asked.

"To kill us," replied Olivia.

"Don't say that!" Brandy cried, frightened.

"It will!" Olivia shouted. She felt sick with dread. It was an awful thing. She'd seen it with her own eyes. It had almost killed her. It would have killed her and Wayne both had they been any slower escaping Gilbert House.

Was this the way it would end for her? After surviving Gilbert House and the Wood and even the deepest corridors of the Temple of the Blind, was she going to die here on this mountain, torn limb from limb in a reeking storm of broken corpses? It was as though fate was toying with her.

She shouldn't have come back with Wayne. It was a mistake. She'd already survived Gilbert House and the Wood. She never should have pressed her luck again.

"Let's go," said Brandy. She collected the box and the last two remaining flashlights and clutched them against her belly.

Nicole bent and snatched up the first aid kit. After a quick inspection, she took only the burn gel packets and tossed away the rest. She doubted any of that other stuff would come in handy, but the mountain was on fire, after all. She tucked the packets into the gauze on the back of her hand and led the way forward.

The path was narrow ahead. In several places, the ground dropped away only inches from their feet and the crowding wall threatened to push them over, ending them as swiftly and brutally as poor Andrea.

Watching the sky for more murdering carrion eaters, the last four travelers continued on in silence, their thoughts haunted by the dead.

Poor Andrea, thought Albert. His heart ached with regret. He hadn't known her for long, but it was long enough to know that she was a sweet girl. Any world would be a colder place without her in it.

Wherever she was, he hoped that she was at peace.

Chapter 32

Andrea sat up with a breathless gasp. She was lying on the ground in half an inch of freezing water, her small body shivering violently against the unrelenting cold.

Although she had opened her eyes, she could not see. She no longer had a flashlight and the world around her was utterly black. Even the inferno that blazed atop the temple was gone. She reached out around her, searching for something to tell her where she might be, but there was nothing. She seemed to be completely alone. Covering her small breasts as though she expected the whole world to be staring at them, she called out, "Hello?"

No answer came back to her. The silence was overwhelming.

For a moment she tried to peer through the blackness, still trying to understand what had happened to her. She recalled standing on the ledge, looking back at Albert. Then one of those flying creatures dropped from the sky, as though out of nowhere, and swept across the ledge, right over his head.

The wind was knocked from her and she was shoved backward, out over that empty space, the hot flesh of the disgusting creature pressed against her. She had enough time to realize that she was beyond the ledge, enough time to realize how much the creature reeked of death and rot, enough time to realize that she was going to die…and then the creature wrenched itself away. She couldn't hold on…

And then she was falling. The ground raced up to meet her. She remembered panicking, throwing her hands out in front of her as if that could save her from being dashed to death against the stone. It was all so fast.

She couldn't remember landing. Not really. But she thought she recalled the water being close enough to reach out and touch.

And then she woke up here.

Carefully, for her legs were still weak and trembling from the fright of her fall, she stood up and began to feel her way around in the darkness. Soon enough, she discovered that there was a wall on two sides of her. Her fingers brushed a low ceiling when she reached up.

She was in a tunnel of some kind, but not one of the tunnels from the temple. The stone here was not smooth, but coarse and damp, like the dank walls of a natural cave.

It was so cold in here, at least twenty degrees cooler than it had been inside the temple. She thought she would be able to see her breath if only she could see.

"Hello?" she called again.

Her voice died away almost as quickly as it left her mouth. Wherever she was, it was eerily silent, and even her echo had no voice. It was as though this tunnel went on forever in either direction.

"Anybody?"

A tremble came over her, starting from deep within her chest and rising up her throat until it exploded from her lips in a violent sob. She was all alone here, without even a light to see by. "*Anybody?*"

"Don't be afraid." The voice came from not one direction, but every, and she recognized it immediately. It was the same one that had spoken to her outside Gilbert House the previous evening. "You're not in any danger. Not now."

There was no reason why this voice should fill her with relief. She still had no idea where this voice came from or what it wanted of her, yet she felt a vast wave of relief nonetheless. "Where am I?"

"This place has no name, really. It's not even a place. It's a place between places. A gap. A road."

"A road to where?"

"Not where. That is not a place either. Not as you would know it."

"I don't understand." She began feeling her way along the wall. "How can a road go somewhere that isn't a place? You're not making any sense."

"It has been called many things over the ages and in many languages. It has inspired many legends. It was the River Styx, Bifrost, even the Tunnel of Light."

"Well *that's* a stupid name for it." Her eyes were wide open, straining to see something in this inky blackness, but she could see nothing at all. Could there really exist somewhere this black, or had she been struck blind in her fall?

"At one time it was called by a name that meant 'Journey of the Dead.' You stand now on the very path that all living things travel when they leave the mortal worlds."

"Journey of the Dead?" Andrea's frightened eyes searched the darkness around her. She touched herself, feeling the smoothness of her naked flesh, wet and cold, covered with gooseflesh, but seemingly intact. "Am *I* dead?"

"No. Not at all. I brought you here."

"You did?"

"Yes. Or more specifically, I helped you bring yourself here."

"Huh?"

But the voice did not elaborate. Instead, it said, "I must apologize for frightening you, but you were never in any danger. The creature that attacked you was only a tool I used to take advantage of the moment and bring you here. I controlled it."

Andrea started walking, her hands out in front of her, trying to locate the source of the voice. But it didn't seem to be coming from any direction. Like the first time she heard it, in the forest outside Gilbert House, it seemed to be coming from inside her own head. "Why?"

"Because your friends need you."

"My friends?"

"Listen very carefully to me. If they open the door atop the Temple of the Blind, they will all die."

Andrea stopped walking and stood silently, her eyes still open wide.

"Only you can save them."

"How?"

"By using your special power."

"What power?"

"The very power that brought you here."

"I thought *you* brought me here."

"I helped you bring yourself here," said the voice, reiterating its earlier cryptic statement. "I merely gave you a gentle push."

Andrea recalled the carrion eater, how it slammed into her, knocking the breath out of her. "That was supposed to be gentle?"

But the voice went on: "You don't realize yet what is inside you, what gift you possess, but you will. It is much greater than the powers your friends have. Theirs are merely powers of the mind, and the mind is only a part of the body. Your power is one of the *soul.*"

"I don't understand."

"I know. But you will. Can you feel them?"

"Feel what?"

"The dead."

Andrea did not understand. Was this voice referring to the ghosts she'd encountered along the path up the mountain? She'd felt *them.* She'd heard them, too. She'd even seen some of them.

"Try. Relax and try to feel them."

She closed her eyes, still not understanding and reached out into the darkness. There was nothing there.

"Try," the voice said again.

Andrea shook her head. "I don't feel anything." But she did. Even as the words left her mouth she felt something whistle past her, something faint, something almost insignificant, but bristling with something like electricity. She opened her eyes, but could still see only darkness. Something seemed to caress her leg, but only briefly, as though it had only been there for a fraction of a second.

"They are the dead undertaking their final journey."

Andrea shivered. The dead. The very idea intensified her trembling.

"They will not harm you. They have no way to. Nor do they have any reason to."

Something whispered past her, slower than the others, and Andrea thought that it circled her once, passing around her thigh, caressing her intimately before moving on again, but so quickly. It made her flesh bristle, but not in the way that she would have expected. It was almost sensual.

"You are connected to them," the voice explained. "You are like a bridge between worlds, connected to both the living and the dead. It is this connection that gives you your power."

She stood there, feeling the dead all around her, marveling at the realization of what they were, of what they meant. They were the *dead*. They were the *souls* of the dead.

She hadn't thought much about it when she experienced those things on the mountain. She hadn't been sure exactly what she was experiencing, but it struck her now how utterly profound this was. It was proof that souls existed. It was proof that there was an afterlife, that death was not the end.

It was almost proof of the existence of God Himself.

"What do I do?" she asked through her astonishment.

"You will know when the time comes."

"I will?"

"In the meantime, follow the one who is lost."

"'The one who is lost'? What does that mean?"

But the voice was gone, and Andrea was alone with the dead.

"Hello?" She turned and listened. Another something rushed past her face, caressing her cheek as it passed. They were moving so fast down this tunnel, rushing through the darkness toward whatever final destination awaited them.

The tunnel of light… That was one of the things the voice called this place. Was this what people claimed to see when they were near death? The tunnel with the brilliant light at the end of it? There was no light at either end, no light at all, in fact, but perhaps she could not see the light. Maybe because she was not dead. Perhaps it was not a light at all but merely a thing, a presence, a goal to which the dead were drawn, something merely *perceived* as a light by those who've seen it and returned. Or perhaps this tunnel *was* light to those who had left their mortal shells behind.

Follow the one who is lost. What did that mean? Who was lost? Who, that was, besides herself? She stepped forward and began to walk in the direction she was facing. Another tiny something spent the barest of instances caressing her bare stomach before moving on around her and she realized that she was going against the traffic. They were all moving the other way. She turned and gazed in this direction. If she followed it on and on, would she eventually find heaven? She thought that she would probably simply walk herself to death and never find anything but darkness and cold.

She stood there, feeling the tiny touches of the dead. It reminded her of small fish pecking at her flesh, as if she were standing not in an open tunnel, but submerged in a calm stream.

"Hello?" she called through the darkness. "I don't know what I'm doing."

But as she stood there listening for the reply, she realized that something was there. It was not something she saw or heard or even really felt, as though her body were slowly gaining another sense, one that required no part of her body. It was in front of her, a fair distance away, and high above her.

She remembered the fall from the temple, how she had plummeted toward the water that surrounded the mountain. Why hadn't that fall killed her? Looking back it seemed as though the water had given beneath her, as though it had actually tried to part for her.

Follow the one who is lost. Her friends were lost. They were moving closer and closer to their deaths, higher and higher, toward the very top of the mountain, and she realized that she could see one of them now. Was it Albert? Or maybe Nicole. They seemed to be the two who were leading, but it could be Brandy or Olivia, too. They were all very strong people, perhaps more than capable of catching this new eye of hers.

Either way, that was where she had to go. Somehow, even though she was somewhere else, somewhere different from them, in a strange place that apparently wasn't a place at all (whatever that meant) she had to go to them.

"Okay," she said, bracing herself. She was all alone down here, like Wayne had been in that other tunnel, the one where all the scary things were imaginary only as long as he did not prove them otherwise.

Hopefully this journey would not be nearly as frightening.

The idea of being alone terrified her. The idea of being responsible for the lives of her friends terrified her even more. But she could do this. Wayne had done far scarier things and she could do it for him. She *would* do it, or she would die trying. "I'm coming guys," she said into the silence, and was surprised by the calmness of her own voice. Then she added, "Please don't do anything stupid until I get there."

Chapter 33

The narrow path eventually opened onto a wide shelf that degraded into a teasing series of rolling hills, rising and falling beneath the shadow of the temple's highest peak. It was more up than down, truthfully, ultimately carrying them closer to the summit and their goal, but to Albert the very notion of going downhill when they desperately needed to be traveling up was torturous.

All four of them kept glancing between the scavengers in the sky and the forest beyond the lake. The carrion eaters swept through the sky, some of them low enough to almost look them in their strange, bulging eyes as they passed. The path here was littered with their waste, forcing them to further divide their attention to the ground to keep from stepping in something deeply unpleasant.

The thing in the forest had apparently moved on out of sight. The zombies rained down without interruption.

They traveled mostly in silence, afraid and weary and emotionally drained. Brandy held the wooden box clutched against her bare chest.

Besides the two flashlights, which Nicole and Olivia carried, it was the last remaining remnant of Albert's backpack. She probably should just leave it behind as well, but she had no idea if it might yet come in handy. For all she knew, it might have one last secret to give up. Also, there was a certain sentimentality to the box. This was what brought her and Albert together in the first place. She couldn't bear to leave it behind. Especially after all they'd lost.

None of them could stop thinking about Andrea, least of all Olivia. What if she had survived the fall? What if she was lying at the bottom of the mountain right now, broken and battered, but still miraculously alive? What if she was in pain? What if the zombies found her?

What if her suffering had only just begun?

In her mind, she could still hear Trish screaming inside Gilbert House, on and on and on…

She tried to take solace in the idea that such a fall should have killed her instantly, her life over almost before she knew the end was upon her, extinguished with the quickness of a candle on a birthday cake. That was much better than lingering on and on in agony when there was no chance, no hope of ever being free of the pain. And would it have been any better to have actually seen her body with her own eyes, shattered, broken, smashed? So far she'd been lucky. With the exception of Beverly, who'd been nothing more to her than the evil witch behind all the horrors of Gilbert House, she'd been spared the sight of the dead she was leaving behind. The cold facts of their deaths might haunt her dreams, but the memory of their broken corpses never would.

Still, she wished she knew for sure. It was the uncertainty that made it all so hard to let go.

At the top of the next hill, the path turned and climbed a steep rise to another wide clearing. Here, two tunnels awaited them. Olivia was relieved to find that she immediately felt a clear aversion to the one on the left. They would not be forced into a night tree horror by this decision.

She hoped.

The tunnel was noticeably shorter than the other two, perhaps only ten stories this time, but the heat was even more intense. It took their breath away from the very start, promising a miserable climb. And after the first few steps, the salt from their sweat found the shallow wounds left by the night tree, stinging them, burning. But they dared not linger. Every moment they wasted was another moment that the corpse monster might decide to turn its vile attention on the mountain.

So they climbed. Sweat dripping off of their bodies, gasping for every smothering breath, they ascended the steps through the continuous roar of flames that rushed by just beyond the hot walls, turning the passage into an oven.

Brandy felt the sting of sweat in her eyes and tried to blink it away. Her glasses were fogging up. Her body was drenched. Never in her life had she ever felt so hot. She knew they couldn't go on long like this. Especially in their increasingly exhausted state, one of them would eventually collapse from this heat.

She looked up at Albert, who was climbing ahead of her, where she could see him and therefore help him if he needed it. The gauze that held his broken arm was soaked through. His hair was plastered to his head. His naked bottom gleamed with a shining sheen of sweat.

About a third of the way up, Nicole slumped to her knees and hung her head.

Startled, Albert and Brandy both knelt beside her.

"I'm okay," she assured them. "Just... Trying to catch my breath." It was like trying to breathe in a plastic bag. "Fucking hot..." Her body was flushed. Sweat fell in fat drops onto the steps beneath her, where it quickly evaporated.

Brandy tried fanning her with the hand not holding the box, but it did no good. The air she stirred remained hot.

"Feels like this tunnel passes through a furnace," said Albert. "We can't stay here long."

Nicole nodded and stood up, fumbling with her flashlight a little. Her cheeks were bright red. Drops of sweat dangled from her eyelashes. One hung from the tip of her nose. She looked weary.

Albert slipped his good arm around her and together they continued climbing. He could feel their sweat mingling where their bodies touched.

"I'm okay," she insisted, yet she did not try to pull away.

"We'll do it together," he said. "We can help each other."

She nodded. She didn't have the energy to argue. "How are you doing? How's the knee?"

"Not nearly as bad as it was." Perhaps that was simply because he was too exhausted to care about the pain, but he didn't say this aloud.

"That's good."

"What about you? How do you feel?"

"Sweat burns."

"I know. Mine too." The stinging wounds inflicted by the night tree felt as if they had caught fire, but his wounds only stretched the length of his arm. She, on the other hand, had been bitten all over her body. He couldn't imagine how much more miserable she must feel right now.

"I'm scared," she confessed.

"I know. Me too."

She shook her head. "You're never scared. You're our hero."

Albert smiled. "I'm scared all the time. Scared of losing people I care about. You and Brandy. Olivia. …Andrea and Wayne."

"Wasn't your fault. Nobody's fault."

But Albert wasn't so sure of that. It was his box. He brought Brandy and Nicole into this world. If not for him… He closed his eyes. The heat was draining him, dragging him down. So was the loss. The failure. He felt as though he could just sit down on these hot steps and sleep, perhaps even die. But he couldn't let himself do that.

Wayne asked him to take care of the girls. It was one of his final requests. But now Andrea was gone and that promise broken.

"You're awesome," Nicole told him. "I know you'll save us."

He hoped she was right.

With all his heart, he hoped it.

As they neared the midpoint in the tunnel, they found a small landing. The steps continued up in front of them, but there were also two other sets of steps leading up, one on the left and one on the right.

Olivia was the first to reach it, as she'd been leading the way the whole time, content to keep the others at her back so they didn't have to see the tears she couldn't seem to stop shedding. She didn't need to examine the tunnels. Only the one on the left didn't repel her with that queer sense of impending dread. Without a word, she turned and led them up the safe steps and continued her silent weeping.

"Are you wishing you'd stayed home, yet?" Brandy asked Nicole.

"No," she replied without having to think about it. "I don't. I'm glad I came."

"But it's been so hard," said Albert.

"But I got to help. I got to find the way out of the labyrinth and I got to see everything. I never would've forgiven myself if I'd stayed home."

Albert smiled. "I just hope you don't get hurt any worse. I feel like that hole in your hand should've been mine."

"Albert, Sweetie, you couldn't solve the secret of escaping the labyrinth. You were too busy killing the Caggo. You can't do it all yourself. It's just not fair to the rest of us."

Albert laughed. It was little more than an exhausted huff of air.

Brandy smiled a little in spite of the heat. She couldn't say yet whether she was glad she came. She was still terrified that she was going to lose somebody she loved. She'd already lost poor Andrea, who she'd grown quite fond of in the short hours she'd known her. But she *was* glad she didn't let Albert come here alone. And since she was sure that *he* would not have stayed away from all this for anything, she supposed the choice was always obvious.

But she prayed no one else would have to die here today.

Chapter 34

Olivia stepped from the tunnel's opening and managed several shaky steps before dropping to her hands and knees. She heaved twice, and had there been any food in her stomach to lose, she was sure she would have vomited right there on the ground.

Nicole and Albert shuffled from the tunnel and sank to the ground as if melting.

Brandy stumbled out behind them, dizzy, disoriented and gasping for breath. When she saw Olivia struggling to keep from getting sick through the haze of fog on her glasses, she went to her. She knelt next to her, setting the box aside, and lifted the hair from her friend's face.

Olivia smiled weakly up at her.

Nicole flopped onto her back and lay with her face to the sky, welcoming the cool breeze. It blew stiffer up here than it had below.

Albert leaned back against the wall and looked up at the cloud of carrion eaters. He could hear the roar of the flames from that main inferno burning at the top. They were close now. Each set of steps, for all the pain and discomfort they caused, brought them much higher much faster than any path, shaving many hours from their travel time. And as they rose, the circumference of the mountain shrank. Even at a shallow incline, the path moving forward would take them to the top in far less time than it had taken them to make those first wide circles around the base of the temple.

But there were more carrion eaters this high up. They soared just overhead, zipping by as they furiously circled the burning flames. The ground and walls here were spattered with their reeking droppings. The stench did nothing to soothe the hot ball of nausea that filled their weary bellies.

And yet, the foul creatures continued to ignore them as if they had no interest at all in anything other than the flames.

Why then did that one attack Andrea? It had seemed so purposeful. It was as if it had precisely intended to harm her, as if it had actually wanted to murder her. Why? What provoked it? Had she simply looked extra vulnerable, standing there on that ledge?

He hated those things. He wished they would all just fly into the flames and burn to ash.

As if in response to this, one of them did exactly that. It burst into flames and then danced crazily on the air for a moment before another one sliced down and swept it out of sight.

That strange significance remained. He still couldn't put his finger on it, but there was something about them... He just couldn't seem to grasp it. Even as he looked up at them, they seemed to change. Their flight appeared more chaotic. More of them brushed the flames and caught fire. It almost seemed as if they were showing off for him. But that was ridiculous. He was merely tired.

Tearing his eyes from those loathsome creatures, he looked down at his watch for the first time in a very long time. It was well past dinner time now. He couldn't decide if he was astonished by how late it was or how early. It felt impossible that he could have been here for so long already. Yet at the same time it felt as if he'd been here forever.

Vaguely, he wondered what had happened at work. How many people had he angered? He didn't look forward to apologizing for his unexcused absence (assuming he ever made it home at all) but at least he had legitimate injuries to report. He'd only have to make up some excuse for how he came by them all.

Olivia spat onto the ground, but her mouth was so dry that very little saliva left her lips. She still felt as though she might vomit, but by now it was clear that she wasn't going to, so she sat up. "Thank you," she sighed as she gazed out over the black forest, searching for the terrible thing that she knew was out there.

"You're welcome," Brandy assured her. "Feel better?"

Olivia nodded, but she still felt awful. She was both physically and emotionally drained. She was beginning to believe that they would all die out here. If that was the case, if that was the hand fate dealt for her, she prayed she wouldn't be the last one standing. She did not want to be left here in this place where zombies tried to tear the flesh from your bones and great, shapeless monsters built their evil forms from your carcass even as you were dying. She did not want to stay here, even if she was dead. She was not like Wayne. She could not die peacefully knowing that her body would just rot here, never to be found, never to be mourned over.

She could not help but think that Andrea would have felt the same.

Brandy looked up at the carrion eaters and then turned to Albert. "We're almost there, aren't we?"

He nodded. "Almost." He couldn't see the top from here, but he didn't think it could be more than a few hundred feet at most, maybe as little as a few stories higher.

"Those things," Olivia said, and Albert realized at once that she meant the scavengers. "Are they going to attack us when we get closer?"

He answered honestly: "I don't know."

"How close do you think we'll get to them?" asked Nicole.

But Albert didn't know that either.

Another one soared out into the emptiness in a cloak of flames. And somewhere close by another pile of droppings spattered loudly against the stone.

Let's just keep going," said Brandy, collecting the box from the ground and clutching it to her breasts again. "Before something worse catches up with us."

Albert nodded. As Olivia and Nicole rose to their feet, flashlights in hand, he turned and looked out over the Wood. He instantly felt the blood drain from his face. It was there, rising from the trees, a great, black mass like nothing he'd ever seen before.

"Oh fuck!" gasped Nicole from behind him.

"That's it!" Olivia cried. "That's what chased me and Wayne through Gilbert House!"

The thing slid to the ledge, enveloping night trees as it went, a great mass of disembodied and decaying corpses that looked more fluid than solid, and poured itself over the edge. From that distance, it looked like crude oil running down the wall. And it seemed to go on and on. Albert wondered just how far it stretched into those trees. He could almost imagine a grotesque sea of broken corpses reaching to the horizon behind it and the thought made him shiver all the way to his soul.

"*It's coming!*" Olivia cried. She was already backing away, terrified. "We have to go!"

Albert nodded, but for a moment he couldn't move. He was staring at the great mass of darkness that was oozing down the far wall, as fascinated as he was terrified. It occurred to him suddenly that until now he had never really believed that such a thing could exist. Somewhere in his mind he had always clung to the idea that it simply couldn't be, that whatever was out there must be something else, something that actually made sense. But there it was, stretching out like a great black blob, plunging into the mysterious darkness below. Soon it would reach the bottom and from there it would probably cross the lake as if it were nothing more than a narrow stream.

Without thinking about it, his hand went to the golden medal that hung at his heart.

Brandy seized his good arm and yanked. The terror in her eyes, more fierce and absolute than anything he'd ever seen in her before, set him in motion and he began to move as close as his broken body would allow to a run.

Chapter 35

Andrea traveled the mysterious black tunnel at a brisk jog in spite of her sore feet. Walking was too slow. It felt like she was going nowhere. It *still* felt like she was going nowhere. But at least jogging kept her warm. She was freezing. The water beneath her toes was numbing.

Why was there water here, anyway? Wasn't this a pathway for the dead? What did the dead need with water?

She looked up into the darkness at the presence she was following. (She was not really able to see it with her eyes—she found that she could "see" that far-off presence no matter which way she was facing—but she found herself using her eyes as a tool with which to aim and focus whatever it was that she saw it with.) It was closer now, but it was so very high up. It had to be her friends. Only they would be way up there, as though atop a high mountain.

She hoped she could get to them in time. They were depending on her. And she was beginning to get the feeling that they were all running dangerously low on time.

If she could have perceived whatever she was looking at as a color, she might have thought that it darkened a few shades. Something was going on up there, she realized, something bad. The realization made her want to go faster, to run as hard as she could all the way there, but her legs were too weary to carry her much faster. The icy water eased her tender feet a little, but merely keeping up this jogging pace was mild torture.

How many miles had she walked since she left Gilbert House the day before?

She could still feel the dead at her back. They felt like faint little raindrops pelting her. She wondered what they saw as they made their journey toward whatever awaited them. Did they see her? A girl with dirty pigtails, naked and jogging, splashing through this endless shallow stream? Or was she something else to them?

Another thought crossed her mind. Had Wayne been down this path? Had he passed by here recently?

And then another thought: What if one of the others passed by here? Olivia? Albert or Brandy? Nicole? What if something happened to them? Would she know them as they passed? Would they know her? Or would they travel this spirit road at some other place, missing her entirely?

She shook the thought away. They wouldn't die. They couldn't. She was going to save them. It was her job. It was what she came here to do.

She hoped.

In spite of her aching feet, she pushed herself a little harder.

Chapter 36

One last set of stairs leading straight to the top of the mountain would have been the fastest way to the top and away from the nightmare monster of shattered corpses, but Albert wasn't sure they could all suffer another climb through one of those furnaces without passing out on the steps. The part of him that was exhausted was pleased when the path circled to the left at a steady incline. The part of him that was terrified of what would soon be slithering up the side of the mountain was less ecstatic. How many times would they have to circle? How long would it take? How long did they have?

Dead carrion eaters littered the path, most of them badly charred, a few of them still smoking. They weaved around the unfortunate beasts, sometimes stepping over an outstretched wing.

There was also a vast amount of spattered droppings. This was harder to avoid. Something about this area, perhaps the shorter cliffs or the lack of surrounding peaks resulting in some difference in the wind, or simply the fact that the ground had risen closer to the horrid creatures, resulted in much more of the disgusting stuff hitting the path. Sometimes it was impossible to step over or around it. Sometimes all they could do was bear it and curse about it on the fly.

Worse still, this reeking filth had begun to fall down around them like vile rain. Wet, steaming droplets found them as they ran. They felt it upon their naked skin.

It was amazing what a person could tolerate while fleeing in terror.

Albert ran along the outside of the path, peering down over the ledge as often as he dared take his eyes off the treacherous ground, watching for any sign of the monster. But he had lost sight of it.

Somewhere down there, he had no doubt it was making its way up and he didn't think it would waste any time following the path. Given its almost fluid composition, he wondered why it didn't simply stretch itself all the way to the summit.

Using the canyon as a marker for what he considered to be the front of the temple, he was able to count how many times they circled the mountain as they spiraled upward. He was also able to keep track of where he last saw the monster. The third time he came around, he glimpsed a darkling shape rising above a ridge down there, urging him to move faster.

"How much farther?" cried Brandy.

Albert looked up. He could now see the flames of that inferno. They weren't that far away. A few more laps around and they should be there. But he was starting to wonder if he was strong enough for this. He was out of breath, struggling to keep up his speed. It had been too long, too far. He hadn't slept or eaten. He simply couldn't keep running.

Neither could the others. He could see it. They struggled with every step. If this journey didn't end soon, it just might kill them, even if the monsters didn't.

About halfway around again, he spied another hump rising and falling beneath them and was freshly alarmed. Either the thing was circling the mountain beneath them, or it had encompassed its entire base. Either way, they would not be able to avoid it if it arrived before they reached the top. It would crash down on them from every angle.

"I can't do this much longer!" gasped Olivia.

"Yes you can!" Albert insisted. "We're almost there!"

"I'm really scared!"

"We all are," Brandy assured her.

Albert opened his mouth to say something encouraging, but the words never left his lips. A massive arm of churning gray flesh reached up into the air and crashed down onto the path in front of them, disintegrating into a landslide of broken body parts as it did.

All of them screamed as heads and arms, hands and feet and all manner of rotten bits and pieces spilled across the ground at their feet. It was as gruesome a sight as any Albert had seen on this long and crazy journey, but it grew considerably worse as he quickly realized that among these horrid remnants of lives long ago extinguished, some of the dismembered zombies still lived.

A head still attached to a shoulder and arm with only two fingers remaining on its mutilated hand reached out for him, snatching at his leg and snapping its dead jaws.

The experience was so absurdly terrifying that he could do nothing more than back away, his wide eyes fixed on the gruesome thing.

At the same time, a headless torso was dragging itself toward Nicole and Olivia on stumps that were all that remained of its arms. Both of them staggered back from it, crying out in horror and revulsion.

Brandy stood frozen with fright, the box still clutched to her chest, screaming like a terrified child at a mostly smashed head that was still attempting to work its shattered jaw as if it very badly wanted to snack on her ankles. It was attached to a wriggling spine and nothing more.

Other abominations crawled from the morbid wreckage, including one that was nearly whole from the chest up. Albert managed enough rational thought to make a mental note to stay clear of that one if at all possible.

"We have to keep going!" he shouted, forcing himself to remember that it was not the zombies they should be fearing but the thing that had ground them into this moldy mess. "Hurry!"

He grabbed Brandy's hand and pulled her forward, toward the pile of rotting corpse pieces. He meant to go around the vast majority of them, but like the carrion eater droppings, they would not be able to avoid them all. They were going to have to tiptoe through the carnage.

Something reached up and grabbed Brandy's ankle. A fresh scream on her lips, she yanked her hand free of Albert's gasp and began beating the thing with the box. Later, she would recall that the hand was attached to little more than an arm and realize that it could not have possibly done much to harm her. She also would realize that bludgeoning a zombie was as pointless as trying to drown a fish, but for now she was blindly determined to bash it into dust.

Again, Albert grabbed her and pulled her forward. He called out to Nicole and Olivia again and then paused to kick one of the snapping heads from his path, wary of its rotten teeth.

Nicole managed to compose herself enough to take Olivia by the hand and hurry after Albert, although not quite enough to stop screaming. She couldn't make herself stop. It was as if her voice had suddenly begun working independently of the rest of her.

Behind them, another of those strange arms rose up and crashed onto the path, scattering shattered corpses across the mountain like jigsaw puzzle pieces dumped onto a table.

It was more than enough encouragement to make the four of them run through the littered zombie parts without hesitation.

Why was it playing with them like this? Why not just climb up and take them? Albert didn't understand it. Surely it knew they were here. Why else would it reach up and dump those zombie pieces on them?

Unless it didn't know exactly where they were.

Maybe it was just swatting blindly.

But that still didn't explain why the thing didn't just stretch itself as high as it could go and jump straight to the summit.

But again, he thought he understood. The way it fell apart when it struck the ground… Maybe being made of brittle flesh and bone made it fragile. Maybe it couldn't hold its own weight. Maybe that was why it fell apart like that.

Or maybe he was just thinking too hard. Where was all this coming from? If the Sentinel Queen was still alive, he'd wonder if she was messing with his head again, answering his questions without him realizing she was there. But she was long gone.

Unless someone else was doing it.

He was pulled from his thoughts when another of those odd arms stretched up into the sky and fell onto the path in front of him. This time, the spilled carnage produced a mostly intact zombie, and a terrifying one at that.

Wayne had told them that not all the zombies were entirely human and this was a prime example of what he'd been talking about. It was a hulking creature with a caveman-like forehead, a too-pronounced chin and six fat fingers on each of its large hands. It tumbled from the pile as if with a purpose and knocked Albert to the ground, its powerful jaws snapping at his face even as he cried out against the pain in his arm.

Brandy tried to run to him, the box lifted, ready to beat the creature as she'd beaten the groping arm, but something crashed into her and she fell. The box left her hands and bounced away. When she sat up, she found a creature that looked more like a dog than a man, reaching out with strangely-shaped, skeletal hands. Its lower jaw was missing, torn from its body along with most of its neck, but it was still apparently determined to sink its remaining fangs into her flesh.

Then Nicole stepped up beside the creature and swung what looked like a large stick, knocking it off of her and sending it rolling away. That done, she immediately threw aside the stick (which Brandy realized was not a stick at all but a dry, dismembered leg) and wiped her hands on her bare thighs with a shudder of disgust before helping her to her feet.

Olivia found herself with her back against the temple wall, staring wide-eyed at a scrawny corpse that was dragging itself toward her on broken limbs. It was so badly mangled that it was difficult to see what it might once have been, but it was only the size of a child.

Albert cried out again as he struggled to free himself, but even with both its legs sheared off, the creature was too heavy to toss aside, especially with only one hand at his disposal.

Clutching the reeking thing's throat with his good hand, he managed to shove it back far enough to keep it from taking bites out of his face, but it was clear he had the strength to do this only for a moment longer.

Fortunately, that was all the time it took for Brandy to retrieve the box and rush to his aid. A few well-aimed strikes and the thing's brittle neck snapped all the way back and lay against its shoulder blades. A few more and the thing no longer had a face with which to bite.

Then Nicole was there, too, and together they were able to pull the still-struggling monstrosity off of him.

Brandy embraced him, crying.

Once again, he had frightened her. But now was no time to dwell on regrets. Now was the time to run for their lives. Still holding onto her, he rose to his feet and looked around. The scene was horrific. Dismembered bodies lay everywhere, yet not a drop of blood was to be seen. Everything here was long dead and dried and brittle. The vast majority of it was not alive even by living dead standards. It was simply dead. Yet there remained scattered throughout this carnage a few that remained somehow animated. The large creature that had nearly bitten off his face was flopping around, lifting itself onto its large arms, intending to come again. Nearby, something much smaller and reduced to little more than a skeleton was reaching up from under a pair of rotten limbs, groping with two gnarled fingers. The dog-like thing that had attacked Brandy was crawling toward them again.

He could only imagine what it must have been like for Wayne and Olivia alone out there in the Wood, surrounded by hundreds of these things that remained mostly whole, most of them still able to walk and even run.

Nicole kicked aside Olivia's scrawny pursuer and grabbed her hand. "Snap out of it!"

Olivia nodded weakly. But it was hard to make herself move on her own. She was surrounded by them again. They were reaching for her, trying to eat her. She didn't want to end like that. She didn't want to be eaten alive, but she was so afraid. And she was so tired.

Somewhere behind them, another arm reached up. The sound it made was almost wet as the pieces of the undead slammed against the stone.

Albert led Brandy through the pile of bodies, kicking aside a severed head that split open at his touch like an overripe melon. Below them, a dark tide was rising around the mountain.

It was almost upon them.

"Don't stop!" he shouted as he waded through the cold, dead flesh that had once roamed this world as walking corpses.

It crossed Albert's mind that if he made it home and was not stark raving mad, perhaps he should consider the possibility that he was not entirely mentally healthy to begin with.

Chapter 37

Andrea abruptly stopped, her eyes wide and alert in the darkness.

The entire time she'd been trying to catch up with her friends, the tiny, electric-like things had been flying past her, giving her little fish-kisses on her back and legs, batting at her pigtails, pausing occasionally to circle her, but now one was coming the other way.

She could not see it, but she knew it was there, a thing without a body but somehow possessing a presence. She could feel it moving against the current, pushing through all the other spirits.

It stopped when she did, as if it was as surprised by her as she was by it. And why shouldn't it be surprised to find her here? It wasn't as if she belonged on this road. This was a place for those no longer bound by mortal flesh.

For a moment the two of them stood that way, each regarding the other, two completely different things and yet somehow exactly the same.

"Hi," Andrea said at last, surprising herself. "What's your name?"

But the presence did not speak. It moved closer to her instead. She did not shrink away. It was not hostile. She could tell. It was pure.

She reached out to it.

It was then that something incredible happened. They touched, and all at once it was as though their souls had entwined within her body. It took her breath away and filled her with warmth. Everything blossomed around her and she was no longer standing in a dark, wet tunnel. Time seemed to slow almost to a halt. Suddenly she could see the spirits around her. They looked like raindrops falling horizontally. They were long and silvery, glistening, gossamer things. The tunnel walls gleamed with silver light. It stretched out before her and she could see forever.

The ghost passed through her body, sending warm shivers through her, and several of the horizontal raindrops bent around her, orbiting her, caressing her tingling skin, filling her with an electric energy like she'd never experienced before.

She turned, reaching out to the phantom, preserving the wonderful moment for as long as possible.

She could almost see it, a wispy, delicate shape pushing through the cool air, the fair features of a handsome young man, wondrous eyes gazing back at her.

Then the presence was gone, vanished back down the tunnel, back to wherever it had been going when it met her. Time sped up again. The little raindrops twirled around her and rocketed away.

Andrea stared into the darkness after it, and she realized that she'd just been a witness to something very special. That one had been going the other way, not toward whatever destiny the others seemed hell bent on finding, but back the way it had come, back home.

Somewhere out there in the enormous world, a young man would be waking up soon...with a second chance at life.

She turned, energized, a feeling of profound happiness radiating deep within her heart, and began to move again, a little faster now.

Chapter 38

Above them, the flames were much bigger than they had looked from the bottom of the mountain, reaching several hundred feet into the air. Already able to feel the heat, Albert worried about approaching that inferno. How close would they have to get? A terrible image surfaced in his mind of the doorway they sought surrounded by blistering flames. What if they were forced to choose between being torn apart by the corpse monster or burning themselves alive?

He buried this awful thought with all the others, deep inside his mind, and pushed on. When this was all over, those imaginings would probably turn into nightmares. They'd go well with the ones about all the *real* horrors he'd witnessed here.

Dodging dead carrion eaters and reeking piles of filth, the four remaining travelers fled the gruesome heaps of broken zombies and made their way up the path to the far side of the mountain. There, another tunnel and another set of steps awaited them. It was not nearly as long as the tunnels that came before it. It did not pass all the way through the temple. Instead, it was aimed steeply up at the burning summit so that the brilliant flames blinded them as they ascended.

Albert motioned the girls ahead of him and then glanced back over the side of the mountain. There, he saw the creature, if it was a creature at all. Massive beyond words, oozing across the stone like liquid shadows, it looked more like a force of nature, a supernatural storm the likes of which could only have risen from the foul atmosphere of hell.

A great mound of writhing flesh rose up as he watched it, taking a form that was almost human in shape. A long, slithery arm protruded from the mass and reached toward him. Fingers of brutalized corpses spread wide and danced through the air like oily smoke.

Albert dared not linger any longer. He turned his back on that great, shifting form and hurried up the steps after the others. But what he saw remained in his mind, a nightmare shape, fluid and unstoppable, a great, festering blob coming at them with all the deadly power of a tsunami, promising to obliterate them on contact.

Nicole was in the lead. She raced up the steps, shielding her eyes against the glare of the flames ahead of her. The opening at the other end was horizontal. They were going to emerge right onto the mountaintop. Their climb was almost over.

She could see the darting shadows of carrion eaters soaring overhead. One had fallen onto the steps, dead and reeking of burnt flesh. It took up most of the passage with its bulk and she had to pause to shove one of its heavy wings out of the way before she could continue.

The topmost steps were almost completely covered in foul droppings. As she rushed through it, she could feel it beneath her feet, cold and sticky between her toes, and somewhere deep inside she was both revolted and furious. But here on the surface, here where she needed to be, with an unthinkable monster at her back and the end of this impossible journey waiting right before her, it was little more than a distant distraction.

Albert looked back over his shoulder, half expecting the thing to be right behind him, already reaching for him, but so far the passage behind him was still empty. Only their own shadows, dancing in the swimming firelight of the inferno, could be seen.

Olivia fumbled past the dead scavenger, dropping her flashlight as she tried to push the fleshy wing out of her way while avoiding its charred and oozing flesh. A part of her wanted to leave it, to just run away, but she had no way of knowing if she might yet need it, and the fear of being left in the dark again was strong enough to make her take the time to pick it up.

Brandy kept looking back at Albert, making sure he was still with her. She didn't like that he was behind her, where that thing could snatch him away while she wasn't looking, but she knew he would have refused to go ahead of her.

Nicole paused at the top of the steps and stood there for a moment, her senses overwhelmed. The mountain was flat here, a great stone plateau, littered with the smoldering remains of those creatures that had flown too close to the flames. Just above her head, those that still lived rushed by, creating great gusts of hot, foul-smelling wind as they passed. There were thousands of them, perhaps tens of thousands. Had there actually been anything but blackness in the sky, she was sure that they would have blotted it out entirely. Some of them came within just a few feet, making her duck away, ready to guard herself, but even now they seemed to have no interest in her. Some of the creatures had landed, she saw, and many of these were perched atop the dead, feasting on their own. Others were simply resting, perhaps overheated, or perhaps utterly exhausted and dehydrated. A slow, scattered rain of excrements continued to drizzle down around her, virtually coating the hot, stone floor. She felt it sprinkling onto her shoulders. Something hot and wet splattered against her leg. Something else struck the back of her head and clung to her dirty hair. Just a few, short hours ago, this would have been impossible for her to endure. But not now. Now the only thing that mattered was what awaited them here on the summit.

At the very center of this plateau stood a huge, round structure that was nearly as big as the university stadium. Like the interior of the temple, it was made entirely of smooth, gray stone, featureless, windowless. It was atop this structure that the inferno blazed. The heat was intense. The smell was worse. Both sent tears streaming down her face.

Between her and this structure waited another sentinel. It stood straight and tall, the featureless plane of its face staring back at her. Its long, bony hands were outstretched to her, its palms lifted to the sky. Carrion eater droppings dripped from them. The entire statue was covered with it.

Olivia stepped up beside her, surveying the area and covering her mouth and nose against the stench. "Where do we go?" she asked, screaming to be heard over the roar of the flames and the chaos of flapping wings. She ducked instinctively as one of the creatures sailed too close for comfort.

Nicole pointed straight ahead, past the sentinel to the structure. There was a place there, an arch that looked like it might be a door.

"There!"

Olivia shouted at her to keep moving and rushed ahead, hurrying across the smoking landscape.

"*Olivia! Wait!*" But her voice was lost in the chaos. Turning back, she saw that Brandy and Albert were emerging from the steps behind her. "*Come on!*" But the words were barely out of her mouth when she saw the thing rushing up the tunnel behind them, a wall of dead flesh and bones.

Albert glanced back and saw it, too. It was almost upon them, and if it caught them… He shouted at them both to go, even gave Brandy a hard push as they rushed after Olivia. "*Run!*" he screamed. "*Don't look back for anything! Just go!*"

They ran as fast as the vile, slippery surface beneath their feet allowed, oblivious of the foul rain that spattered their faces.

A great wave of broken carcasses reached up out of the hole behind them and slammed against the ground at their heels. Brittle bones and hardened meat shattered against the stone and a great, nauseating wind rushed past them, reminding them of the death that would become them if they were too slow.

Brandy screamed, terrified, and Albert nudged her forward through the whirlwind of heat and wings and reeking wind, ignoring the pain in his screaming knee and arm.

Nicole sprinted forward ahead of them, running after Olivia, who had already crossed more than half the distance to the final door. She ran right through the filth, unconcerned about the feel of it on her bare toes and unable to do anything about it anyway. It was unavoidable. And since the revolting thought of it touching her skin was nothing compared to the sheer terror she felt at the idea of being caught by that awful monster, she did not even notice it. Neither did she notice when something hot and wet struck her right thigh and ran down her bare leg in thick, sticky clumps.

Albert looked back over his shoulder at the creature. It was spewing from the hole, building upon itself, growing out of the ground like a vile tumor. Never in his life had he seen anything so simultaneously awesome and terrifying. He could see flashes of pale bone glinting in the glow of the fire. Black and gray flesh swam among these bones and he found himself reminded of a trout hatchery he had visited once with his family. The movement of those dead body parts made him remember the way the fish had swarmed over the food when he threw it in, practically boiling up out of the water in the throes of their furious hunger.

"*Hurry!*" Brandy urged, tugging at his good arm, and he turned away from the creature, but he could still see it. It was there, behind them, growing and growing. In another second it would start after them, and he had a feeling they would not be able to run fast enough to escape it.

Nicole saw one of the flying creatures soaring low. It came at her from her right and she threw her arms up in defense. Its left wing crashed into her shoulder with the force of a well-aimed slap and both she and the creature stumbled. She screamed and dropped to her knees, her right hand mashing into a crusted pile of warm dung as the carrion eater crashed to the ground, scattering two others that had been feeding on the corpse of a third

Brandy saw all of this and cried out for her friend.

But Nicole was fine. She looked up, rubbing at the place where the creature had collided with her, and saw that it was already forcing itself back into the air again, completely uninterested in her. She stood up and looked back, saw the thing that was growing behind Albert and Brandy, and cried out to them to hurry.

Meanwhile, Olivia had reached the door and was examining it. She recognized it immediately from Wayne's story. It was a huge, half-disk of stone, covered with ancient markings. On the left side was a single circle with nothing inside it. Had Wayne not traveled that terrifying tunnel and told them his amazing story, would any of them have known where to place their hand to make the door open?

She looked back at the others, frightened. Was this the door they were supposed to reach? Was this where they were supposed to stop and judge the sentinels? If so, it was not much of a decision. Either they opened the door and hoped to escape or they left it closed and let the corpse monster tear them apart and add them to its gruesome form.

The idea was too terrifying to even consider. Unwilling to waste time waiting for the others, she placed her hand against the circle on the stone and watched with wonder as it slid effortlessly forward. Another dark passage waited beyond.

She stood inside the newly opened doorway, feeling the heat that was rolling out of it, and looked back. Nicole was almost there, but Brandy and Albert were still dangerously far behind. Albert was still limping and the thing that had nearly killed her and Wayne at Gilbert House was stretching up into the sky, swallowing the flying creatures that could not get out of its way. "*Hurry!*"

Nicole stepped into the doorway with her and looked back. The creature was moving now, sliding toward them like a great black blob. Its fluidness was almost hypnotizing. It struck the sentinel and enveloped it. She caught only a glimpse of it tipping backward before it was lost from sight. It was a grim preview of what would happen to them if they didn't hurry. "*Come on!*"

"*Go!*" Albert screamed. "*Don't wait!*"

The thing lunged forward, its body arcing and curling into something that resembled a massive wave.

Olivia and Nicole backed away from the door, giving them room.

Albert could feel the thing behind him, closing in. Around him, the bird-like things were rushing past them, disorientating him. It had been so calm most of the way up the mountain, but up here it was like a storm. Up here, he could almost believe that the world was coming to an end.

Brandy reached the door and turned back to see Albert just a few yards behind her. The monster wasn't as close as she'd feared. He was going to make it.

"*Hurry!*" Olivia cried. She was still backing away, her flashlight switched on, ready to rush deeper into the sweltering passage as soon as she was sure that everyone was safe.

As Albert ran through the doorway, he spotted the circle that Wayne had described and threw his weight into it, turning the door on its axis. He almost stumbled because it moved so easily. "*Go!*" he screamed again, and the girls turned and fled down the hot corridor.

Albert pushed the door around until it was closed and then kept pushing, opening it up again. He went completely around, like a child playing with a revolving door, and then paused and looked in. The girls were hurrying down the hall, still thinking that he was behind them. "*Brandy!*" he screamed and she turned and looked at him. Her eyes shimmered behind her glasses, wide and alert, trying to understand what was going on, what he was doing. "I love you!" he said, and he slammed the door between them.

"ALBERT!" Brandy dropped the box and rushed back to the door. She shoved at it, but there was no circle on this side, no way to open it. *"ALBERT!"* She beat on the hard stone, desperate, but it would not budge. It was solid stone. Beside her, Nicole had appeared and was also trying to force the door open, but there was simply no hope.

They both screamed his name.

Olivia stood precisely where she had been when she saw the door close and stared back at them with wide, terrified eyes.

Albert... What had he done?

Chapter 39

Albert heard Brandy's screams even through the dense stone.

His heart broke.

Closing the door between them was the hardest thing he'd ever done. The look on her face... The anguish in her voice... She was the most wonderful woman he'd ever known, so lovely, so strong, but not without that certain need for him. He felt like the luckiest man in the world every time he looked at her. She was perfection in his eyes. She was the first to ever love him that way, his first of so many things...the first he ever fell in love with...and she would be the last. He would never see her again.

It killed him inside to think that he had hurt her so much, but at least he got to tell her one last time that he loved her.

It was the way it had to be. She wouldn't have understood that. She would have fought him with every ounce of her being, would have thrown her own life away to prevent it...but he had to do this.

He had no choice.

He turned and faced the creature that was sliding toward him, that great swirling mass of death, and prepared for the end.

Chapter 40

Andrea stopped suddenly as a strange sensation overcame her. Somewhere high above, those presences that she'd been moving toward changed. She couldn't say exactly how they changed. It was an odd thing to perceive. It was as if they simultaneously expanded and diminished, flared and faded. It was difficult to describe but impossible to ignore.

She didn't know how she knew, but she was sure that something awful had just happened up there.

Had one of them died? She prayed to God it wasn't that.

She was supposed to save them. All of them. It was what she was here to do. Wasn't that what the voice told her? Or had it not specifically said that. Now that she thought about it, she couldn't quite remember.

What if she wasn't here to save all of them?

She closed her eyes and tried to feel those presences. They had grown stronger as she traveled. Or perhaps she had grown stronger.

She wasn't sure which. But she could tell now that there was more than one. In fact, there were more than four. There appeared to be lots of presences on that mountain. Some were very faint. Others were very strong.

Those others must have been the ghosts she glimpsed haunting the path before she was sent here to this odd place.

Why were the ghosts over there so different from those in this tunnel?

Or were they? She supposed these were simply busy moving on to wherever it was they were meant to go while those over there lingered for some reason. After all, she hadn't known to look for them until the voice told her to do so.

Another thought crossed her mind. How was she supposed to tell the living from the dead? Would she know if one that was alive suddenly became...not?

That one presence still remained, whichever one that was. Was it Albert? He seemed the type. That presence, that soul was a strong one. It dwarfed the others in its brilliance and it was that one to which she was drawn.

Albert. Brandy. Olivia. Nicole. They felt like family to her. What would she do if she finally reached them and only three returned? Or two? Or only one? For that matter, what if she couldn't save any of them? What if she failed them all?

She began moving again. Now she was running. As fast as she could go, she ran, holding her arms in front of her in case the tunnel curved or in case she began to drift. Her heart pounded in her chest. She felt cold all over.

"Please..." she breathed. "Please let them be all right."

Chapter 41

"I know who you are," said Albert. Although his voice was utterly lost in the chaotic cacophony, he was sure he'd been heard.

The towering mass of death stopped. For a moment it was still, except for the shifting carcasses within its queer skin of broken corpses. It hovered above him, seeming to stare at him.

"I know who you are and I know what you've done." In his hand he gripped the medal that Nicole had robbed off the corpse in the temple's old entrance. The chain was wrapped around his wrist. He couldn't remember exactly when he'd taken it from around his neck.

The creature shifted again, its body rippling. It was a blur of sliding and rolling corpses, moving too fast to see any single detail. To try and perceive it was like trying to read the text on a microfilm machine at full speed. It was impossible. It moved toward him, quickly, fluidly, and for a moment he thought that the end had come, that he was already dead, but it sailed around him instead, circling him in a whirlwind of reeking flesh and bone.

Albert stood there, watching the death-blur whirl past, his body straight and tall, unflinching.

The monster did not touch him. He didn't think it would. Not yet. "Come out so we can talk," he said into the festering storm…and a moment later it withdrew, rippling and reshaping itself. It reached up into the hot sky, stretching up into the carrion eaters, swallowing those that were unable to avoid it, tearing them to pieces before his eyes.

Then it fell apart. Dead legs, arms, heads, hands, toes, fingers and torsos scattered across the ground in a sea of leathery flesh and brittle bone and from within stepped a man Albert had never seen before. But he knew him well enough.

He was an old man with a kindly face and pale blue eyes. His hair was white. He was naked.

He was just the way Wayne had described him.

"So you're the devil?"

"That's what they say," said the old man. His voice, like Albert's, never made it past his lips in the noise, but somehow he made himself heard as if they were standing in a silent room. It was the same psychic connection the Sentinel Queen used. Although they spoke normally, the conversation was actually taking place inside their heads. "You're a sharp one, I'll give you that."

"So are you," Albert replied, still gripping the piece of gold in his good hand. The symbol on it meant DEVIL. He knew this now just as surely as he had known any other truth about this twisted place. "You had me fooled for a while. You certainly had Olivia and Wayne fooled back at Gilbert House. They really thought they were in danger."

"Oh they *were* in danger. If the Mother had had it her way, the dead would have eaten them alive. She did her best to stop me, you know." He reached up and tapped his temple. "Tried to confuse me."

"The Sentinel Queen."

"'The Sentinel Queen?'" The old man repeated the words with unmistakable scorn. His eyes blazed. Between them, one of the corpses still wriggled on the ground, but neither of them acknowledged its presence. It couldn't harm them anyway. It was nothing more than a broken torso with half a head. "She was no *queen*, Albert, just a senile old whore. She carried on like she was a modern day Moses, leading all mankind to some great promised land. But she was just the Mother. That's all she ever was. Her only purpose was to be *pregnant*. And that purpose ran out more than four hundred years ago when she stopped laying like an old used-up hen. And you just stood there staring at her with your dick getting stiff and believing every word she said like some lovesick fool."

Albert laughed, and the old man's expression actually faltered a little.

"What's so funny?"

"So you're the expert on all this, then? You know everything there is to know?"

The old man's eyes grew even harder. "I know what's going to happen if those bitches throw open that door in there. Do you really think they'll survive? Do you really think any of you will get off this mountain alive?"

One of the corpses was crawling toward them. Albert saw it in the corner of his eye, a broken shape dragging itself through the carnage. The old man waved a dismissive hand and swept it over the ledge.

Telekinesis. He controlled things with his mind. That's how he created the corpse monster. It was both remarkable and remarkably simple. It was no different than the way he communicated without his voice being heard.

"You're the reason Beverly was afraid of me, weren't you?"

The old man's expression fell again. "What?"

"You let her see me and Brandy when we came here the first time. You *made* her see us, and subconsciously, you made her believe that I was going to bring about the end of the world. You were going to make her kill me, weren't you?"

The old man smiled a little. "Don't try to play mind games with me, Albert. I know you're a clever boy. I never said you weren't."

"You were going to kill me one way or another. You used Beverly to get me into Gilbert House and if I survived that, you were going to have her finish me herself. She wouldn't have been able to help herself. You would've driven her insane. But what I can't figure out is why you used Andrea? Why did you send *her* the envelope instead of sending it straight to me?"

The old man gave him a bitter smile. It was actually much more chilling than the scowl he'd been wearing when he emerged from his corpse monster disguise. "You're wasting your time, you know."

"Am I?"

"You think you can distract me long enough for your friends to reach the doorway. But as I'm sure you already know, I'm much more talented than you are. I don't have to be *inside* the doorway chamber to hold the gates closed. I can trap them in there until they suffocate from the heat. Or, if I get impatient, I can just reach inside them and crush their lungs."

Albert did not doubt him. The girls were in mortal danger. He already knew that. It was why he was here. He had one chance to save them. He had to play this out right. So instead of getting angry, instead of demanding that he let them go, which he knew was something the old man would never do anyway, he simply said, "Then we have time to talk, don't we?"

Chapter 42

"Come on," Nicole said at last, hardly able to even find her voice. "We have to go."

Brandy shook her head. "Why?" she sobbed. "Why would he do that?" For a while, she'd been incapable of doing more than screaming his name, and then she could not even do that. She'd merely wailed at the heartless stone that stood between her and the man she loved. But she was too hot and exhausted to even do that for very long. "Why?"

It was a question Nicole had no answer for.

Olivia stared at the two girls as Brandy slid down the smooth stone door and into a heap of quivering flesh on the floor. She was sobbing, and she had every right to weep. She'd barely known Wayne and Andrea, and losing them had broken her heart. What must it be like for Brandy, having lost her own boyfriend, the man she loved? It was nothing like her losing Andy. That had been a non-relationship if ever there was such a thing. She was truly sorry that he was dead, but she never loved him. She couldn't imagine the pain that Brandy must be in right now. And to not even know what was going on behind that door... He must be dead by now. Or dying. But as long as that door remained closed, and she doubted it would ever open again, there would always be that maddening shred of doubt.

"Come on," Nicole said again. She took Brandy's arm and pulled, but she didn't move. She only sat there, slumped over, sobbing. "Please..." Her voice cracked as she spoke. "I can't go on without you. Not without you *and* Albert."

But Brandy still did not move and Nicole fell to her knees beside her and cried.

It couldn't end this way. He said he would ask her to marry him. He promised. Albert always kept his promises. So it couldn't end this way. It just couldn't...

Albert was her hero, her love. In her eyes, he was everything. But even he, who had taken on the Caggo and won, who had challenged the insanity of the fear room for her and walked away, could not survive the horror that stood on the other side of that door. It was not possible. He was only a man. He was only flesh and blood, standing against a mountain of death.

That thing was the Grim Reaper, she realized, Death himself. He was not a dark figure with skeletal hands and a shadowy hood wielding a scythe. The harbinger of death was also the robber of bodies, cloaked in his own grotesque spoils. And now its festering claws were at her Albert's throat and she would never see him again.

Why, Olivia wondered. *Why?* What could he possibly have to gain from committing suicide like that? Did he know something they didn't? A part of her wanted to think that he could come back through that door, just swing it open and stand there like David having slain Goliath.

But he told Brandy he loved her before he closed that door, and so she knew that he meant not to come back.

She walked over to where Nicole and Brandy lay in a heap and took hold of Brandy's arm. "Help me," she said to Nicole. "We've got to keep moving or we'll suffocate in here." Her voice was soft, but even, as though tears weren't running down her face.

Nicole wiped at her eyes and nodded. She was right. They couldn't remain here, bawling like children. She took two deep, shuddering breaths and rose shakily from the floor.

Together, the two of them lifted Brandy to her feet. They could feel the sweat and the filth on her skin, but they were well beyond caring about such insignificant discomforts. They were more than friends now. They were sisters. And they needed each other now more than ever.

"Let's just walk," Nicole whispered. "Just walk, okay?"

Brandy nodded and let them lead her toward the final tunnel of the Temple of the Blind.

Olivia took the time to collect the box. Albert's box. The item that began it all thirteen months ago, more than a year before she ever knew them, before she even knew there were monsters in the world. It was burned and beaten now, much like the three of them.

As they walked away, Nicole looked back over her shoulder at the door that her friend had closed between them, separating them forever, and she realized that he had broken her heart worse than any man she ever could have dated. She could not fathom his reason for remaining out there, but she knew in her heart that he had done it for them.

Au revoir, mon ami, she thought, and fresh tears spilled down her sweaty cheeks.

Chapter 43

"Then we have time to talk, don't we?" said Albert.

"I'll decide how much time we have," returned the old man.

A control freak. That was good. He could use that. "Why Andrea?" he asked again.

"I said don't toy with me," he growled. "You already know the answer to that."

"You didn't send it to Andrea," Albert replied without hesitating. "Your messenger fucked up." He looked down at the ground and scratched at his chin, making a show out of thinking. When he looked back up he said, "But you don't make mistakes. You know *everything*."

The old man smiled. "You've got balls, boy, taunting the devil."

"You're not the devil."

"Oh?"

"You might be close. I'm sure a lot of people have believed you were him. But you're not. In the end, you just don't measure up."

The old man inhaled a long, slow breath through his nose, as though trying to contain his growing rage. Then he surprised Albert by smiling. "Well, you can't blame me. The word does have a certain power all its own, doesn't it? *Devil.* It scares the hell out of people, makes them do all sorts of things. After all, what do you think 'caggo' means? It's just another word for devil in a dozen or so long-dead languages."

Something hot and wet struck his shoulder and oozed down his back, but he kept his eyes fixed on the old man. "Fascinating."

"Isn't it? But the word isn't the only thing frightening about me, boy."

"Oh, I know. You're terrifying." He wasn't being sarcastic. This man scared the hell out of him. "But I've already figured you out."

"Have you now?"

"I have." He stared at the old man, directly into his pale eyes, but he was not actually looking at him. His attention was focused *over* him, at the sky. "You used Wayne and Olivia and Beverly. You even used Olivia's friends. It wasn't Beverly who got them killed, it was you. *You* fueled her obsession with Gilbert House and she died thinking she was a murderer when she was just another of your victims."

Above them, the movements of the carrion eaters began to change. A greater chaos was forming from within the swarm. Several strayed too close to the flames and ignited, but the old man didn't seem to notice. He didn't even react when a large, black glob of dung struck his cheek. He was concentrating. A part of him was inside with the girls, Albert realized, watching them, plotting, holding closed the gates he mentioned.

That was good, too.

"The Sentinel Queen told us that the psychic part of the mind was susceptible to suggestion. She used that to help guide me to her, even made me leave my car unlocked so her messenger could deliver the box. That's how you used Beverly. Psychic manipulation. You can do it just like she could."

"It's not that hard, really. Anyone can learn to do it, given a few centuries to practice."

"Which, of course, most of us don't have," Albert said, stating the obvious. "And you're very good at it. You even coached Wayne and Olivia through those zombies. In their panic, they thought they were running from a monster. And they were so lucky that monster *just happened* to collide with all those zombies that stood between them and the exit, providing them a chance to escape." He barely heard the words that he spoke. His thoughts remained focused on the sky. "In reality, you weren't chasing them at all. By pursuing them, you shepherded them toward Gilbert House and made sure the zombies fled instead of attacking them. You even made sure Wayne perceived every detail exactly as you wanted him to. He didn't see a monster suddenly backing off, giving him time to find the night tree and climb to safety. He saw a monster that ate the zombies to maintain its mass and marveled at his luck that he led it to a feast just in the nick of time. He saw all that even though he was scared out of his mind...and even though it was dark as hell out there."

He understood now. He'd wondered why such a creature would snatch Olivia into the Wood only to drop her. It never made sense before. But now he saw that it was all little more than a convoluted scheme.

"I don't have time for this," the old man sneered. "Yes, I got into their heads. I used them like puppets. I arranged everything.

Congratulations. You figured out my part of the game. I'm the big bad monster. You win the prize. If you get out of my way, maybe I'll let you live to try and find your way home."

But Albert didn't move. With his eyes fixed firmly on the old man's and his thoughts following the storm of the carrion eaters above, he said, "Of course, the Sentinel Queen lied too, didn't she?"

The old man raised an eyebrow. "She did."

"She lied to me about not knowing why Beverly was afraid of me. Right to my face she told me she didn't know the reason, but she did."

"She knew lots of things," the old man agreed.

She *had* known lots of things. And she must have known, too that he'd see through her lies eventually. So why lie to him? What difference would it have made if she'd told him the truth? "And she didn't bother telling me that you were the monster outside Gilbert House, even though she clearly knew. She gave Wayne some bullshit about protecting them from the monster, instead. She took credit for their escape when she had nothing to do with it."

"She did try to stop me," the old man said. "She distracted me, just like she claimed, made me stumble, but not to protect them. She was hoping to make me tip my hand, reveal my lies to him. It was a dangerous move. She could've gotten them both killed out there."

That was true. She'd claimed that she was protecting them the whole time, but she'd put them all in danger. Whatever game she was playing, it seemed she was not above letting people die. "She lied about a lot of things," Albert said. He recalled how she told Wayne she had something to give him and then seduced him, taking a child from him that she later took with her into death.

"She was always good at lying," said the old man.

"But a lie is just a lie. It's not like murder."

"True. But don't think she never had blood on her hands."

The chaos had grown above them. Dozens of those creatures ignited in the flames and sailed away like comets. But amid all the chaos was some order. It grew from within, slowly taking over.

"There was plenty of blood on her hands," Albert agreed. "She didn't lift a finger to save poor Beverly. She just let her walk into that room and die. She could have warned her. She could have warned *me*. She'd made me do all sorts of tricks already." She'd pushed him along the whole time, steering him toward her city, bringing him to her, but she hadn't done a thing to make him realize that Beverly was in danger.

The old man was smiling knowingly. It pleased him that Albert knew the evils the Sentinel Queen had done him. It was clear that they had been enemies for a very long time.

"But none of that matters now, does it? She's dead, right?"

"I'm tired of this pointless talk," said the old man, and at his feet, the broken corpses began to stir as though something had breathed life into them again.

"One thing I really don't understand, though," said Albert, pretending not to notice the threatening limbs. "If you wanted to stop us from reaching the doorway, why did you spare Olivia? Without her special psychic abilities, we never would have made it past the traps here on the mountain."

The old man glared at him. His eyes were suddenly burning with fury.

"Oh..." said Albert. "I see. You didn't know. Well, that must be embarrassing... I guess the Sentinel Queen got the last laugh after all."

"*Enough!*" growled the old man. "We're *done*. I'm not going to let

317

them open that door. I'll gut them all and wear their corpses like a coat!"

Albert grinned a little, and the old man's temper flared. *"What's so fucking amusing?"*

"You don't know so much, do you?"

The old man glared at him, and Albert caught a glimpse of something in his eyes, something deadly dangerous. Time was running out.

"You killed the Sentinel Queen," Albert said, and the old man's face twisted a little, almost as though he'd been wounded. "You murdered her son. Poisoned him somehow."

"I didn't give you enough credit. You're really learning to use that sixth sense of yours, aren't you?"

Above them, order had gained control. The creatures were circling together now in neat rows, collecting, preparing. Albert focused on them, concentrated, and found that he could see each and every one of them as clearly as if they were standing still. That queer significance had blossomed into understanding. This was what he'd been feeling all along. He could control these things the way the Sentinel Queen and this old man controlled people. It was psychic suggestion, except that these things were susceptible to much more than mere suggestion. He could *control* them. *All* of them.

He also understood one other thing: this old man wasn't going to let him live.

"You murdered her by murdering her last son," he said. "You knew she'd die once he was gone. And the really amazing thing is that she could do nothing more to you. You killed her just for spite, just because she beat you."

"She did not beat me!" the old man growled. Around him the scattered corpses were moving across the ground, spinning around him, getting ready to collect again. He was going to kill Albert, tear him apart for daring to challenge him. He would make his bloody, severed limbs a part of that festering monstrosity and then use that, use *him*, to murder the girls.

"Oh, she beat you," Albert pushed. "What, did you not have the balls to admit defeat? Did she wound your pride?" He smiled, his dark eyes gleaming. "Or was it something else? She had a way of getting people aroused. Let me guess…you could never get it up for her?"

He could have gone on. He could have mentioned that the Sentinel Queen had helped him and Brandy to reach the temple even after he'd done everything in his power to bury it beneath Briar Hills, miles and miles of tunnels whose only purpose was to hide the *real* tunnel, the ancient, rock-lined passage that led back to the temple. He could almost have named the men he'd controlled over the centuries to accomplish it, but in the next instant, the storm that had been going on around them became a hurricane. The old man roared, making a sound that he'd never heard a human being make before, and the disembodied corpses came to life, leaping into the air and enveloping him.

At the same instant, the creatures in the sky changed course, twisting and rolling away and then circling back again.

Albert saw it coming for him, and in a moment when time seemed to have paused, he found himself thinking of Brandy. He was sorry he didn't get to keep his promise to her. He really did want to marry her. But this was the thing he'd had to do. This was what he'd been born for. He realized now that the Sentinel Queen had not picked him because he was mildly psychic. She picked him because he could talk to the things in the sky. She picked him because she knew, somehow, in all her infinite wisdom, that he could face this man, this monster who imitated the devil, and challenge him.

The thing rose up, swirling and pulsing.

The sky ignited into a sea of fire.

Albert whispered one last "I love you" to Brandy as a dark sea of death struck him.

Chapter 44

There were no mazes inside the topmost level of the Temple of the Blind, only a single corridor leading to the center of the structure.

The temperature was sweltering. The flames that burned above them were fed through ducts built into the stone of these very walls and it had grown dangerously warm. Even the floor was hot beneath their naked feet as Olivia and Nicole guided Brandy toward their final destination.

Brandy tried. She really did. She did not want to stay here. It was too hot, so hot she could hardly breathe, but she could not make herself think, much less walk on her own. Albert was gone. She had loved him so much and now he was gone. How could anything else in the world matter?

A pair of narrow, stone columns stood at the end of the corridor, blocking the way. They approached these columns and shined their light into the chamber on the other side.

The room was about sixty feet across, utterly dark except for the lights Nicole and Olivia carried. There were no statues, no obstacles, only a single square pillar standing at the very center of the room. It was this pillar that drew their eyes. About six feet wide, it was covered in markings like those on the door that led into this structure, the door that Albert sealed between them. And on the side facing them, right at eye level, was a single, perfect circle.

"That's it," Nicole said. "That's the door."

"It doesn't look like a door," said Olivia.

"Doesn't matter what it looks like," Nicole replied. "That's it. It has to be."

Olivia shined her light on the columns in front of them. "But how do we get to it?"

Nicole didn't know. She looked back over her shoulder. Albert had sealed them in when he turned to do whatever it was he meant to do out there. They had no way back. They were trapped in here if they couldn't figure out how to enter that room. And if the sweat dripping from her body was any indication, they didn't have much time to discuss it.

"Nobody said anything about this."

Nicole shook her head. "I don't get it."

"We're supposed to decide whether to open the door, right? How can we make that decision if we can't even get to the door?"

It wasn't much of a choice. But then again, it wasn't much of a choice anyway. Even if they could get to the door, they either opened it or they waited for the heat to kill them.

"The Keeper said we were supposed to judge the sentinels. We were supposed to decide for ourselves whether to open the door or not."

"If we open that door, and the judgment is wrong," said Brandy, her voice distant, "if the *Sentinel Queen* was wrong...the world ends at that very moment." Nicole and Olivia looked at her. She had sunk to the floor again. She could still feel the lingering pain of her broken tailbone, but like everything else, it seemed so distant. "If we don't open it, then no matter what the judgment was, we all die eventually anyway, maybe when the sun explodes or when some asteroid finally arrives."

"Then why risk it?" Olivia asked.

"Because maybe there's something good for us if we do," replied Brandy. She did not know how she knew these things, but she knew them anyway. It was like the way Albert knew to push down the wall at the end of the ancient tunnel, first opening the way to this strange, new world and all the wonder and horror that came with it. "And maybe because the world might end tomorrow."

"So what if we're not supposed to open it?" Nicole asked. "Do we just stay here and cook?"

Brandy said nothing. Perhaps it was their duty to die here rather than to open that door. Perhaps it was their destiny. Behind them, the way had probably been sealed when they lit the fire inside the tower. Perhaps that was all they were ever meant to do. Perhaps they were only here to make sure no one ever opened this door.

Nicole stared at the pillar as drops of sweat rolled down her face and dripped off her chin. What kind of a decision was this? It was like jumping off a building and then trying to decide whether to shoot yourself. Except that this decision did not just affect the three of them.

"None of that matters anyway," said Olivia, "if we can't figure out how to get to it."

Brandy stared past the two columns. Nothing mattered, anyway. She already felt dead.

Chapter 45

Even as darkness closed around him and the cold flesh of the dead snatched him off his feet, Albert saw the carrion eaters ignite. They came through the fire in a great wave, their bodies catching like paper. As though it were their only purpose in life, they plowed into the great mass of corpses, injecting themselves into the churning storm and setting it aflame.

Suddenly, the old man was not inside a swirling mass of disembodied corpses, but a tornado of fire. He screamed as his hair and flesh burned, as much in surprise as in pain, and the monster he had created came apart around him.

Albert was lifted off the ground. The dead mass contracted around him. A thunderbolt of pain rushed through his broken arm and then another through his right thigh. He cried out into the darkness that had swallowed him, a roar of pain and self-pity, but also of satisfaction and accomplishment, of fear and sorrow, but of triumph. The darkness was joined by flames, and he felt the heat against his flesh, burning his belly and shoulders and singeing his hair. Then the darkness and flames fell apart and he struck the filthy ground with a hard thump that sent pain exploding throughout his body.

The old man shrieked as the flaming scavengers plowed into him. His body was burning. He stumbled and fell and still the fiery birds kept coming, piling onto him, burying him under the flames.

By now the top of the Temple of the Blind resembled a war zone. The dead lay everywhere, burning and smoldering, some still twitching. The last sentinel lay upon its back, broken, its long, open hands reaching for the empty, black sky.

Albert lay motionless in the wreckage, slowly sinking into a sea of darkness.

Chapter 46

The two columns blocking the way into the doorway chamber abruptly dropped into the floor, as if whatever force had been holding them up had vanished. In the blink of an eye, the way to the temple's doorway was open to them.

"That was easy," said Olivia. "What did we do?"

Nicole shrugged. It didn't matter. She stepped forward and shined the flashlight around the room, wary for any more surprises. On one hand, it seemed far too simple. The doorway was right there, waiting for them. There wasn't even a monster guarding it. But then again, it was never going to be as simple as merely reaching it. Now came the part where they had to make a decision that could determine the entire future of the human race.

It was funny. Saving the world had become such a tired cliché in the movies. Yet standing in this place now, considering the possible consequences of the actions she was about to take, it struck her how utterly profound the idea really was. She wiped the sweat from her dripping face and stared at the pillar in the middle of the room. Never had an object looked so ominous.

Brandy rose slowly to her feet and stepped into the chamber behind Olivia. She, too, stared at the circle carved into the pillar. She wondered how it worked. When Olivia and Albert touched the circle on the door leading into this structure, the stone slab rotated as though it were made of hollow plastic instead of solid stone. And after that door was closed again, and the circle on the other side and out of their reach, no amount of pushing would budge that great slab. Did something about the circle magnify a person's strength? Or was it simply a trick of balance and pressure? It could have been magic, for all she knew. It wouldn't surprise her at all after all she'd seen and done.

Olivia, too, wondered what would happen if she placed her hand on it? There was not any door to open. It was like finding a doorknob set into a solid wall. Could she simply not see the door? Was it hidden somehow? Would it swing open and reveal some new place no one had ever seen before, someplace even more distant and wondrous than the Wood? Someplace even more terrifying?

"What would Albert have done?" Nicole asked, and to Brandy the words stung like a slap. They were already talking about him in the past tense. For all they knew, he could still be alive out there. "I wish he was here."

"We can't just stay here," Olivia said, shifting her feet on the hot floor. "We'll cook."

"Do we open it?" Nicole asked. "Just do it? Hope?"

Brandy shook her head. "We do what Albert would do."

Nicole and Olivia looked at her.

"Albert would have thought about the whole picture, everything

328

we've been through." She began to walk toward the pillar, her eyes fixed on that mysterious circle. "We're supposed to be judging the sentinels."

"But how do we judge someone we don't know?" asked Olivia.

Again, Brandy shook her head. "But we *do* know the sentinels. They've been here the whole time. They've pointed the way. They've warned us of danger."

"The statues," said Nicole. She was beginning to understand. Brandy was right, the sentinels had been speaking to them this whole time.

"It was the sentinels who put this place here, and they put themselves inside it, their likenesses. Remember the messages they gave us. They wanted us to trust them, to have faith. We got through the temple because we had faith in them. We're alive now because we trusted them." She remembered all the sentinel statues, from the five in the very first chamber to the final one that stood alone on the mountain top with its hands outstretched to them. There had even been one in the fear room, watching over them in the deepest and darkest of places. "So much depended on that trust," she continued. "We had to trust them this whole time…and *they* had to trust *us*… And now we all have to trust each other one last time." She never took her teary eyes off the circle. She was standing right in front of it now, close enough to reach out and touch it…

Nicole nodded. It made sense to her. As much as anything had made sense in this place. She recalled that final sentinel, just outside, with its upturned palms dripping with carrion eater droppings. Before the monster knocked it down, it had been reaching out to her, offering her its trust, asking for her faith. The answer was clear. "Okay."

Olivia looked at Nicole, then at Brandy. She was still clutching the box against her bosom with one hand. It was strangely comforting. "I guess so."

Brandy lifted her hand. Her fingers brushed the warm surface of the stone.

Olivia held her breath.

Nicole closed her free hand around Olivia's.

All three of them mouthed a silent prayer.

Chapter 47

The stone circle shattered beneath her touch and the pillar broke with a resounding crack. Now free, the lower half of it fell like lead, vanishing into the floor and leaving only a square hole and a littering of broken stone.

The pillar whistled down the narrow shaft like a great dart, all the way to the very bowls of the mountain, where it cut through the vast, burning sea that Nicole's blood had ignited. There, at the bottom of that boiling liquid, it crashed into another circle, this one carved onto a great, stone slab in the temple's very foundation.

The door shattered like glass beneath the weight of the falling pillar. And the judgment of the sentinels was complete.

As Brandy stared down into the hole, trying to understand what had happened, fire belched up from it and she stumbled back with a shrill cry. The heat and flames rushed out in a bright, billowing ball, expanding like a great, yellow balloon, threatening to incinerate all of them.

But then the flames were gone, swallowed back into the very hole from which they'd come, followed by a great whistling of air.

The mountain rumbled around them, trembling, and the roar of the inferno began to soften. Far below, the liquid flames swirled down into a great, spiraling abyss.

"What's going on?" screamed Olivia.

Brandy stared at the hole. It felt as though all the air were being pulled into there. Had she been wrong? Had she thrown open the door to the apocalypse after all?

A great crack appeared in the wall, shooting up like a bolt of black lightning. Somewhere far below there was a noise, like a long thunderclap.

Deep in the bowels of the temple, the remains of the tower on which Nicole had ignited the inferno collapsed into a black abyss that swallowed stone and flame alike. Elsewhere, a sentinel statue cracked at its ankle and tumbled forward, shattering both of its arms. Throughout the narrow passageways of the labyrinths, shrieking hounds fled through the darkness, their razor-like scales slashing at the air around them, desperately trying to escape what they instinctively knew would be their doom. The reservoirs broke open and drained, flooding the corridors below them in an instant. Other chambers, chambers no human had ever seen—nor would ever be seen—quaked and cracked, soon to be buried forever.

The City of the Blind, once a gateway of hope for humanity, now an empty, lifeless hole, cracked and crumbled beneath a rain of stone and water. Even two or three centuries ago there could have been heard amid that roar of approaching doom the cries of a frightened, dying people, but now the city was dying in deathly silence.

Brandy, Nicole and Olivia stood there for a moment, staring at the hole in the floor, feeling the heat vanish into it. The temple was coming apart beneath their feet…and they had nowhere to go. They were trapped here with no way out.

"What do we do?" Olivia asked.

But there was no time to answer. With a great crash, the hole in the floor disappeared into a bigger hole and the whistling became a roar.

"Run!" screamed Nicole and fled toward the passage through which they'd come.

Olivia turned to follow, but paused as she realized that Brandy had not moved. "Come on!" she shouted.

But Brandy stood there, staring at the hole she'd made. There was nowhere to go. They were sealed in. They were all going to die. Just like Beverly and Wayne and Andrea. Just like her poor Albert. What was the point in trying?

Nicole looked back and stopped. Brandy had not moved and Olivia was rushing back to her, trying to pull her away. She screamed at them to run, but her voice was lost in the roar around her.

As she stood looking back, her heart filled with terror, another large portion of the floor fell away. Olivia and Brandy, her last two companions on this strange journey, fell, swallowed whole and screaming into the darkness that opened beneath their feet.

Chapter 48

Albert's body was a maelstrom of pain. His right arm felt freshly broken while his left lay beneath a hunk of burning carcass that blistered the flesh of his forearm before he could fully struggle his way back from the edge of consciousness and brush it aside. His head pounding, gagging on the heavy stench of scorched and rotting flesh, he forced himself to sit up. Then he was staring at the black and gnarled hand that protruded from his right thigh.

In the insanity of all that had happened, in all that was *still* happening, he could hardly comprehend this hand. It was missing the little finger and most of the ring finger, and the remaining three digits were curled so that it would almost have been flipping him off had it not been turned away from him. With his good hand he wrapped his fingers around the wrist of the dead limb and pulled. That thunderbolt of pain came again and he howled as he pulled the long, jagged bone from his bloody thigh. Then he threw the appendage aside with a cry that was part revulsion and part amusement. The obscurity of it all was actually quite funny.

Or perhaps he was merely hysterical. It was difficult to tell for sure.

The old man lay beneath a pile of burning bodies and Albert thought he could still hear him screaming under there, shrieking in pain and rage. He never knew what power he was up against any more than Albert did.

But he had no time to contemplate his victory or the miraculous fact that he was somehow still alive.

The mountain trembled beneath him.

Above him, the inferno suddenly died away, sinking back into the shafts through which it had risen as though it had simply tired of burning. All around him, the flames that had illuminated the mountainside extinguished and the light faded, swallowing the mountain into the darkness that had blanketed it for untold eons before they set it ablaze.

Somewhere far below, a great crack rattled the very foundation of the temple.

He scrambled to his feet, screaming at the pain in his knee and thigh, and limped through the burning sea of festering flesh to the door behind which he had sealed away his friends. The pain did not matter. He had to reach them. Guiding himself now by the light of the burning dead, he pushed open the door and staggered down the final tunnel as the Temple of the Blind came apart beneath him.

Chapter 49

Nicole watched in horror as the floor broke away, spilling Brandy and Olivia into the darkness. They were there for just a moment, their feet slipping, their faces contorting into expressions of surprise and terror. And then they were gone, sucked down into the blackness below.

She stood there, too shocked to do anything more than stare into that great black hole. This was the way it would end. This was how she was going to die. It didn't seem fair.

There was another great crack and suddenly the floor was moving beneath her. She turned and lunged for the passage, trying to save herself, but it was too late. Her flashlight dropped from her hand and she began to fall.

But then something unexpected happened. Someone had her hand. Her body hung there in the darkness, dangling over the black abyss.

"*Hold on!*" Albert shouted.

But Nicole was slipping. She stared up into the darkness above her, unable to see. "Albert?" she asked, her voice impossible to hear.

"*Hold on!*" he said again.

"*Don't let go!*"

But her hand was slick with sweat and his with blood.

Albert tried to free his injured arm from the sling, determined to use it no matter the pain. He knew it was useless. He was only delaying the inevitable. But he needed to do something. He needed to help her.

But then her weight was gone and all that remained was her receding screams.

"No!"

His whole life had just gone down that hole. He wouldn't have it taken from him that way. With nowhere else to go, with no other option left to him but to sit here in the darkness and wait to die, he jumped to his feet and leapt into the abyss.

And so the journey was ended. Albert felt the hot wind rushing past him as he fell, pulling him downward into a great darkness. The Temple of the Blind, like Gilbert House, was only a place for the dead. He remembered Andrea and Wayne and Beverly, and wished that he could apologize to them. He wished he could apologize to Brandy and Olivia and Nicole, too. He had brought them all here. It was he who translated the box, who found the first chambers far beneath the earth.

It was his fault they were all dead.

It wasn't fair at all. Such an adventure should have a happy ending. But perhaps it was all for the better. Perhaps the sentinels knew better than they. Perhaps, in the end, death was simply the better way.

Far below him, a great ball of fire appeared and began to rise. Soon, it would all be over.

Soon the pain would finally end.

Chapter 50

Andrea was right below them now. She stood and stared up into the perfect darkness, seeing without seeing the distant form that seemed to be calling out to her. Something was happening. Something bad. She could feel it in her soul.

But what was she supposed to do?

The voice told her that she would know, but she didn't. She was nowhere near them. She couldn't get up there where they were. Even if the tunnel rose beyond this point and carried her straight to them, she'd run out of time.

"Hello?" she called into the darkness. "Are you there? I don't know what to do."

But the voice was no longer with her.

She stared up at the presence. It seemed somehow to be pleading with her, begging her. But she still didn't understand. How was she supposed to use her power if she didn't know what that power was?

Suddenly she realized that the presence was approaching,

plunging straight toward her. Would it come to her? Would it come and find her? Would it show her what to do?

No. It was falling. They were falling. Her friends were falling and she had to do something!

She closed her eyes, but she could still see it. They were all going to die and it was going to be her fault because she didn't know what to do.

"HELP ME!" she screamed into the echoless tunnel. But the voice remained silent. She was on her own.

She sobbed once, terrified, a sick, wet sound, loud in the silence of this endless darkness.

And then it happened. Without thinking, she turned and faced forward, toward the destination of the dead, and planted her feet apart as though to guard against a strong wind. She threw her hands out in front of her and focused all her attention on that mysterious presence.

Although she could not see what happened next, she felt it. The tunnel seemed to snap apart around her. It jerked her upward and around, whirling with her until she was standing not on the floor but on the wall, with her hands stretched up into the darkness through which her friends were falling. The water at her feet fell away, back into the tunnel that was now both behind her and below her. The air changed, becoming a hot wind, and her dirty pigtails whipped about her face as she stared both forward and straight up into the air.

A light was coming toward her, and so was a sound, a scream. No. Two screams.

The light sailed past her. It was a flashlight. And then Brandy and Olivia were speeding toward her, falling through this bizarre, crumbling world.

So this was how she survived her fall from the temple. This was what the mysterious voice meant when it told her that it helped her bring herself to this place. At the final, crucial moment of her fall, she must have panicked and instinctively triggered this…was it a gift? She opened some kind of doorway between that world and this tunnel, saving herself from certain death. And just now, in her moment of deepest desperation, fueled by her fear for her friends' lives, she panicked again. This time, however, she opened the tunnel not for herself, but for them.

Brandy and Olivia fell past her, into the tunnel she'd shared with only the dead until now. It was too dark to see them clearly, but she knew it was them. She recognized their voices. And although she had no time to contemplate it, she found that she recognized their spirits, too.

Andrea had only a moment to worry whether they could land safely at the speed they were traveling before a piece of stone struck her belly hard enough to bruise. A second sailed past her left temple. Debris rained down around her. A piece roughly the size of a small car flew past beneath her feet, just missing her tunnel and plunging into the unknown below.

It was getting brighter. A soft glow was illuminating the chaos around her. She could see dust and smoke and crumbling stone falling all around her.

The sound was deafening after the complete silence she'd been wrapped in since she first awoke on this highway of the dead.

Was this the temple? What had they done?

Another flashlight fell, close enough for her to feel the kiss of a breeze as it sailed past her left knee. Another piece of stone struck her right breast hard enough to make her clench her teeth against the pain. A chunk slightly larger than a basketball passed over her head and her concentration wavered. If she was struck by something like that, she could be killed.

But the thought had barely entered her mind when she saw Nicole. She was hurtling toward her, her eyes wide and terrified in the blossoming light. For a moment they were staring at each other. She could actually see the terror and bewilderment in her eyes. And then Nicole was behind her, tumbling into Andrea's tunnel.

Only one more.

She watched as he fell toward her, his body stiff and flat, as though he believed that he would soon grow wings and learn to fly. And then she realized just how well she could see him. Yellow light was quickly filling the crumbling shaft around her, illuminating everything, growing brighter and brighter at an alarming rate.

It was coming up from below them, she realized, from the belly of the temple, a fireball that would probably blow what remained of the mountain to pieces. And it would be here any second.

In this light, she could see everything clearly, could see the great chunks of stone that were falling around him, any one of which could kill her in an instant. Fear gripped her heart. Her concentration slipped. A strange sort of quiver passed through the tunnel beneath her feet and she had to force herself to concentrate. She couldn't lose it now. If she lost her grip, Albert would die. She couldn't afford to be afraid.

She focused all her attention on him and only him...and then it occurred to her that he was coming straight at her.

He hit her squarely and hard enough to knock the breath from her lungs. Their chests collided first and then their bellies and hips, knocking her backward, which was also down, and as they fell, the black tunnel was lit with a great yellow explosion of fire for just an instant before everything snapped back like a bent bow, uncoiling and returning to its former, horizontal existence. There was a sudden silence, as though she had been struck deaf by the impact, and gravity, for a moment, was chaos. The two of them clung to each other, their naked bodies pressed together as down became up and then down again, and then they were falling sideways. Then Albert's back struck cold stone and they were sliding across the wet floor of the tunnel.

At last, the two of them came to a halt and the chaos became only silence. In this silence, the water came rushing back, cold and crisp, surrounding Albert and splashing up onto Andrea as though it had yearned to touch her again.

Still gasping for breath, Andrea lifted her face and looked down at him. Nearby, the last two flashlights still miraculously shined and she saw in the reflected glow that he was real, that he was awake. His face was twisted into an expression of pain, but it was good. Pain was good. The absence of pain was an absence of life and therefore nothing but cold death. He was alive. Albert was alive and she had saved him.

She grabbed his face and held it between her hands. He was warm, despite the cold wetness of the tunnel. She was laughing. Giggling, actually. She pressed her lips to his, still giggling, and held them for a moment. When she drew back, he was looking at her, his deep, dark eyes like gleaming blackness in the shadows.

"Andrea?"

Andrea laughed. She kissed him again on his lips, then his cheek, then just hugged him. "I did it!" she cried and her voice was like a child's, full of bursting joy.

"I don't believe it," Albert sighed, still dazed. What happened? Why was he still alive? Did Andrea just kiss him? He closed his eyes and lay still beneath her. God, he was tired.

"Andrea?"

She lifted her head and looked around. Nicole was rising to her feet just a few yards away, her eyes big and shocked and glistening with the promise of tears. She was trembling so badly she could hardly walk.

"Is that really you?" The words felt lame, but she could not believe it. She started toward the girl she'd thought dead and Andrea sat up to meet her arms.

Beyond where Nicole had landed, Brandy and Olivia were sitting up. They had landed together, clinging to one another in the darkness, still half-waiting to die. Suddenly both the heat and the noise of the Temple of the Blind were gone and they were once more cold and wet. They were not dead, and the fall they had expected to kill them was simply gone in a moment of wildly shifting gravity.

"Andrea..." Olivia sighed. "And Albert...?" Was this real? Was she really seeing this? Were they really alive?

...Or were they all dead now?

Brandy straightened her glasses and stared, not yet wanting to believe, not yet willing to risk being wrong, but he was there, lying in the cold and shallow water as Andrea—who should also have been dead—sat atop him, straddling him in a way that was not very unlike she, herself, had often done in bed. Nicole was kneeling beside them both, her arms wrapped around Andrea, her small, white bottom glowing in the flashlights' reflected beams.

Andrea peered over Nicole's shoulder and saw that Olivia and

Brandy were rising to their feet. Tears began to spill down her cheeks. "I did it!" she cried. "You're all safe!"

"How in the world are you still alive?" Nicole wanted to know. But before Andrea could answer she was wrapped in Olivia's arms so quickly that she was shoved back, off of Albert and into the cold water with a squeal of laughter, taking both Olivia and Nicole with her.

And then Brandy was there, scooping Albert's aching head into her arms with a sob. She wanted to hit him, to beat him with both her fists and scream at him for what he did to her, but she could only hold him and cry.

Nicole sat up and wiped at her eyes. This was too much. They had both come back. Somehow, and against all odds, these two wonderful people had survived and made it back to them. But how? She'd watched Andrea fall from the mountain with her own eyes. And Albert... She turned and looked at him, lying there in Brandy's arms, freshly bruised and beaten, freshly bloodied. Like a hero sent by God, he'd been there in that last room when she fell. She hadn't seen him, she'd lost her flashlight by then and it was far too dark, but she felt his hand, she heard his voice. He caught her arm, tried to pull her up, but the grip was slippery. She could still feel his fingernail marks in her wrist where he'd tried to hold on. She'd begged him not to let her fall, but he couldn't help it. Besides, what would they have done if he had pulled her up? The temple was falling. It was like the whole world was swallowing itself.

"Oh, God!" Brandy gasped between hitching breaths. "You're hurt!"

"I'll live," Albert said softly. He did not open his eyes. He lay there, motionless, letting Brandy hold him, relishing the feel of her skin, the warmth of her body. He had actually believed that he would never see her again.

"What did you do this time?" Nicole demanded, but the ever-present strictness in her voice was lost beneath the sobs that burst from her throat.

Albert actually laughed, his voice soft, weak. It was the image of the hand, protruding from his bloody thigh and flipping him the bird. He didn't even know where to begin.

She lifted her fists, threatening to hit him, but she hugged him instead.

"Are you in pain?" Brandy asked.

Albert opened his eyes now and gazed up at her. "Yeah," he admitted. "But it's not so bad." And it wasn't. Not while she still held him.

"I don't understand," said Olivia. "Where are we? How are you both still alive?" She looked at Andrea. "I watched you fall."

Andrea smiled at her. "It's complicated."

Chapter 51

"I swear you're just *trying* to get yourself killed," growled Nicole. She'd taken the gauze from his makeshift sling and repurposed it to wrap the fresh wound on his thigh, which needed it far more. His entire leg was covered in blood. Even the water beneath him had turned red.

"I had to do it," Albert explained. He'd unwrapped the chain from his wrist and was holding the strange piece of gold in front of his eyes, examining it. DEVIL, that symbol said. He knew it without a doubt. "He never would have let us open that door. He would've killed us all first. Closing the seal behind us wouldn't have stopped him."

Olivia shivered at the thought of Albert standing up to that thing. She'd seen it with her own eyes, had been chased by it. It didn't matter that there was an occasionally kindly-looking old man beneath all those carcasses because that didn't make it—*him*—any less capable of doing what it did to those zombies to any one of them, to *all* of them. Never in her life would she have been capable of facing it, especially not all alone like that. She couldn't imagine the amount of courage it must have taken for Albert to have stood there and called that thing out.

"Maybe he was right," Brandy said. "The temple fell apart when I opened it. I judged the sentinels wrong."

Albert shook his head. "I don't know. Not necessarily. Remember that somebody went to a lot of trouble to make sure we got out safely. What would be the point in that if we made a mess out of everything? Maybe you did exactly what you were supposed to do. It's what *I* would've done if I'd been there. I trusted the sentinels, too."

"I wish I knew for sure," said Nicole. "If we did it wrong, I can't help but wonder what might've happened back home. The Sentinel Queen and the old man couldn't agree on much, but they both seemed pretty sure that the wrong decision would mean the end of the world."

"You don't think there's any real chance that the world could've ended while we were here, do you?" asked Andrea.

Albert shook his head. "It's hard to imagine, but then again so is everything else I've seen since I left home yesterday."

Andrea shivered at the very thought of climbing out of the service tunnel only to find everything they'd ever known reduced to ash. What would they do? How would they live? How would they go on knowing that they had something to do with the loss of everyone they loved? She forced the thought out of her mind. She did not want to think about those things, the very thought of finding her home gone and her parents dead made her sick.

Nicole finished wrapping Albert's thigh and withdrew the burn gel packets from the gauze on the back of her hand. She remembered thinking that they might come in handy. After all, the mountain *was* spewing flames practically everywhere they looked. It never hurt to think ahead.

"I don't think we did it wrong," Albert decided after thinking about it for a moment. "In fact, after hearing Andrea's story, I can't help but wonder if someone might have meant for all this to happen just this way."

"Yeah, but who?" said Brandy. "The Sentinel Queen? You said she was lying to us."

"She was," replied Albert. "About a lot of things."

Olivia felt violated. She remembered the Sentinel Queen standing before her, a strangely arousing monster in the darkness, telling her how she'd been with her inside Gilbert House, whispering assurances, promising her that all would be well. Had that been a lie? Was she just trying to win her trust?

"We'll probably never know," continued Albert. "She's dead. The door's open, just like she wanted. It's over."

"And the Keeper?" asked Brandy. "Did he lie to us, too?"

Albert considered this. The Keeper never took a side. It merely pointed them forward and told them about ancient sentinels and mythical judgments. It warned them of dangers, but unlike the others, it made them find their own way, both through the labyrinth and atop the mountain. If it told them any lies, he didn't see how it would have made a difference in the end.

"Doesn't matter right now," said Olivia. "What we need to do is find our way out of this place."

"You're right," agreed Albert. He watched as Nicole gently applied some gel to his forearm. It felt good on his blistered flesh, nice and cool. Then he looked up at Andrea and asked, "Do you know where we're supposed to go from here?"

Andrea looked first in one direction, then the other. The voice never told her what to do after she rescued everybody, but she quickly realized that she knew. It was there, in the opposite direction from which she'd come, the same presence she'd felt before. "There," she said, pointing into the darkness. "We go that way."

"How can you tell?" asked Nicole.

"I just can…" Andrea replied. She was staring at this presence, suddenly distracted. It was still there, yet her friends were all here. But how? That would mean that the presence guiding her all this time was someone else. But who?

"Then let's get moving," said Albert as Nicole finished wrapping his leg. "We won't get anywhere sitting here."

Chapter 52

"I can't believe you guys can't feel them," Andrea marveled. They were invisible to her eyes, even with the help of the flashlights, but she could still sense them. She could still feel them.

But nobody else could. As they stood there in the darkness, the dead zipped past them all, kissing their naked bodies, caressing them as they sped by on their way to whatever awaited them all at the end of the tunnel, but no one could see or hear them. Except Andrea. She alone seemed to have that ability.

"It's creepy," said Olivia.

"Not really," Andrea corrected. "It's kind of cool."

"It's so weird," Brandy marveled. "It's like absolute proof of an afterlife." It was different from the ghostly activity they'd experienced on the mountain path. That was so mysterious, so fleeting. They could never be entirely sure that what they were experiencing was really ghosts. Not with so many other unanswered questions out there. This place, if Andrea was right, was something far more substantial.

"I know," said Andrea. "Makes you feel a little less vulnerable in the world, doesn't it?"

"It really does," agreed Albert. And it did. Even though he couldn't see or feel it, he found himself believing her. Why not? How would a highway of souls be any less believable than a forest filled with man-eating trees and voracious zombies?

He smiled to himself as he realized that once one experienced the Temple of the Blind, Gilbert House and the Wood, it wasn't so difficult to believe in anything, really. If she'd told him that Santa Claus brought her here in his sleigh, he'd have had a hard time dismissing it.

"How much farther is it?" asked Nicole.

"Not far." Andrea could tell the presence was getting closer, but they were not quite there yet.

"Good," said Brandy. "Because I'm ready to go home." She looked down at the box as she cradled it against her chest. Its charred corner had left a sooty smear against the side of her breast, but she didn't dare let go of it. It was starting to feel like a good luck charm of sorts.

She thought she'd lost it when the temple fell apart and she fell through the floor into that vast shaft of hot wind and darkness. But it was lying on the tunnel floor with the rest of the litter that came here with them when they gathered up the flashlights.

Once upon a time, before she was the woman she was now, she looked upon this box and thought it was creepy. She remembered wanting to throw it away. She told Albert to do just that.

That felt like so very long ago.

Olivia turned and looked back the way they'd come and Nicole followed her gaze. "What is it?" she asked.

Olivia stared into the shadows. "I'm not sure. Something just feels…*wrong*."

"I get that, too," said Albert. "I don't think we're alone in here."

"What?" Andrea turned and looked into the endless darkness at their backs. She didn't sense anything back there, except the same spirits she'd been feeling since she arrived in this place.

"What is it?" Nicole asked.

Albert shook his head. "I don't know." Whatever it was, he didn't think it was close. It might have been miles away, maybe even light years considering the supernatural qualities of this tunnel, but he felt certain that something was moving toward them quickly and purposefully. "Let's just keep moving."

The five of them pushed on, a little faster than before.

Andrea did not understand. If there was something in the tunnel with her, why hadn't the voice warned her of it? She kept looking back now, but still she felt nothing. The only presences were those next to her and the mysterious one waiting for them up ahead.

"Do you think we'll make it home?" Brandy asked Albert.

He smiled at her. "Yeah. I do."

She smiled back at him. "Soon?"

"I hope so."

"Me too," said Nicole. "I'm ready to be home. I'm *starving!*"

They all were. But they weren't done yet. They still had to find a way out of this tunnel.

Olivia walked on quietly. That feeling of wrongness only grew. This tunnel was starting to feel like the ones she'd avoided back on the mountain path. A deep dread was taking root in her belly.

Chapter 53

"Here." Andrea stopped and put one hand on the cold wall of the tunnel. The presence she'd been following was right there, just on the other side. "There's another tunnel over there," she realized.

"Okay," said Albert. "How do we get over there?"

"Can you do your trick again?" asked Nicole.

Andrea stared at the wall, *through* it, to the presence beyond. Who was it? She kept wondering this. Was there something familiar about it, or was that merely her imagination? "I don't know," she replied. "I guess I probably can." She turned and looked at them, a little embarrassed. "But I really don't know how I did it the first time."

"Try," Brandy urged. "It's all we've got."

Andrea nodded. "Okay." She walked a few steps ahead and stopped. She tried to remember what it was she'd done before. She planted her feet apart, just like before, and lifted her hands in front of her, but the only thing this did was make her feel silly. "Um…"

"I saw you when you were doing it the first time," Nicole said.

"You looked really cool. It was like something out of a comic book or something."

Andrea looked back at her, blushing a little. "I don't really know what it was I did. I kind of just panicked."

Albert turned and looked back into the darkness behind them. The thing was closer now. Much closer. Whatever it was, it was rushing toward them at an unimaginable speed. If they didn't figure out how to get into that other tunnel very soon... "I hate to rush," he said, "but it may be a good idea to panic a little."

Olivia nodded. She could feel it, too. That sense of dread was growing rapidly, threatening to smother her.

"Just relax," suggested Brandy. "What did you do last time?"

Andrea closed her eyes and tried to remember. It'd all happened so fast. She hadn't really known what to do last time. She got scared and it just sort of happened.

Albert stared into the darkness behind him. It was like he could almost see it. It was moving much faster than he first realized. It was not upon them, by any means, but it would be within the next few minutes. Maybe sooner.

"I don't like this," breathed Olivia.

Brandy stared into the same darkness, squinting to see past the shadows.

"Can you feel it?" Albert asked her.

"I don't..." she looked up at him, her eyes fearful. "I don't know." She looked back, tried to focus on the darkness. "I feel something...maybe...but I don't know what."

"I'm getting more sensitive," Albert said. "I'm learning, I think." Whatever it was, it was covering an enormous distance very quickly. At that speed, it would need neither claws nor teeth to kill them all. It would simply run them all down in a single, bloody instant.

In his mind he pictured a great phantom train rushing toward them on invisible tracks, but a living thing, seeking them out, *wanting* to kill them. But that was only his imagination. The real threat, he was sure, would be much more terrifying.

"A guardian," he said, and Brandy looked at him. "It's a guardian. Like the blind people were the guardians of the temple. Whatever it is, it's the guardian of this tunnel."

Brandy turned and looked back into that darkness as her flesh began to prickle with goose bumps. He was right. She knew it as soon as he said it. This was a road for the dead. It was no place for the living. They were trespassers here and that thing, whatever it was, its job was to set that right.

Andrea realized suddenly that she did not even know what had become of the ghostly horizontal rain when she split the tunnel the first time. Did they stop and wait? Did they just keep on moving, seemingly unaffected by the merging of the two worlds? Or had she spilled them out into that other world where they might be lost for all eternity? She hoped not. The very idea of such a grim possibility gave her chills. She didn't want to be responsible for something like that.

"What if she can't do it again?" Olivia asked. She turned and looked at Nicole. "Then what?"

Nicole looked at Albert, who was still studying the tunnel behind them with that hard expression of thought that meant that something was concerning him. "It might be better not to think about it," she replied.

Andrea's heart was beginning to pound. If she couldn't do it again, they were all in a lot of trouble. She closed her eyes and tried to focus, tried to think. She could still "see" the presence. It lingered over there, beyond the wall in that other unreachable tunnel, calling to her.

She took a deep breath, tried to calm herself, and felt for the right mindset, the right *feeling*. It was an emotional thing, she realized. Something she did with neither her body nor her mind, but with her heart, with her *soul*.

She shifted her feet a little, and realized that it felt right. She lifted her face, eyes closed, to the ceiling, but that wasn't right. She faced forward instead, and there it was. It was almost a physical thing, like a magnetic attraction between her and the presence. She threw her hands out, straight into the flow of the ghostly traffic, and opened her eyes. After that, she wasn't sure if what happened was because of her or because of the mysterious presence she was reaching out to. It felt as if they met in the middle.

The tunnel snapped apart and rolled through a blur of stone and darkness and then she was staring into the *other* tunnel.

The shift took the others by surprise. Nicole and Olivia fell to their hands and knees with nearly identical shrieks. Albert fell against the tunnel wall, still holding onto Brandy, and somehow they managed to stay on their feet. The water that had been on the floor now ran down the wall in places and dripped from the ceiling in others. Andrea felt the water splash up her legs and over her body as if she had suddenly been twirled upside down.

"What happened?" Brandy asked.

"She twisted space," Albert replied as he watched Nicole stand shakily to her feet. Though they all still appeared to be upright, the displacement of the water suggested that the tunnel itself no longer lay as it had. The watermarks actually spiraled over Nicole and Olivia's heads.

The path forward was empty. The presence she'd felt a moment before had receded. She could barely feel it now. It was still there somewhere, but she could not tell exactly where.

"Go on," she urged. "I don't know how long I can hold it."

Nicole took a step toward her and stumbled. Gravity was suddenly strange. As she got closer to Andrea, she felt her weight shift, as though she were trying to walk up one side of the tunnel. She had to pause repeatedly to reorient herself.

Behind her, Olivia was groping along the walls for balance. "So *weird*," she marveled.

Nicole paused next to Andrea and shined the light into the new tunnel. It was dark and dry, of old coarse stone and bare earth, completely different from both the clean, smooth textures of the Temple of the Blind and the wet monotony of the one behind them.

Albert and Brandy were slowly making their way toward them, trying hard not to hurt Albert's leg or arm as they fought the spiraling gravity.

"Is it an illusion?" Albert wondered. He thought it was. It seemed to him that Andrea had twisted the tunnel and they only appeared to be walking in a straight line when they were in fact walking up one wall, across the ceiling and down the other.

"Hurry," Andrea urged. She could feel herself tiring.

Nicole stepped into the next tunnel slowly, half expecting to fall to the ceiling or something. When nothing like that happened, she turned and offered Olivia her hand.

Albert and Brandy stepped into the next tunnel and then Brandy turned and held a hand out to Andrea. For a moment the two of them stood there looking at each other. "Come on," she urged.

"She can't," Albert realized. He stared at her, into her frightened eyes. "If she lets go, the tunnel snaps back and she's stuck there."

"No way!" snapped Nicole. "She's not stuck over there!"

Albert's eyes drifted past her to the dark tunnel behind her. He could still feel it coming, moving ever closer, barreling toward them at unfathomable speed. If she was trapped over there when it arrived...

"She can't be stuck!" insisted Brandy. "She got herself *into* that tunnel. She can get herself out."

That was true. The first time she opened this strange portal she was in freefall, a split second before she struck the water and the hard stone that lay just beneath the surface. But that happened so fast. She didn't know how she did it. She couldn't even remember it clearly. All she knew how to do was hold it open.

And they were rapidly running out of time.

"What do we do?" Olivia asked.

But Albert didn't know. None of them knew.

Albert stared into the darkness of the tunnel behind Andrea. What would happen if it came while Andrea was holding the tunnel open like that? Would it enter this world? What would happen then? He remembered the old man telling him that the world was going to end if the girls opened the door and he shuddered as he recalled the biblical tales of Revelations and the beast that would rise from the bottomless pit in the world's final days.

"It's okay," said Andrea. "I did my part. I did good, right?"

"You did great," Albert assured her. "Now just shush and let me think. We're going to get you out of there."

"No you're not." She stared at him, her eyes soft, afraid, but also confident.

"Don't say that," Olivia insisted.

But Andrea understood the situation. "I was the only one who could do this. I was the only one who could pull you out of the temple and the only one who could get you home. There's only one of me and four of you. It makes sense, really."

"No, it doesn't!" snapped Nicole. "That doesn't make any sense at all. Now hush!"

Albert considered her words for a moment. Was she saying that she'd brought them home? Were they back on earth? If so then where were they?

"It's okay," Andrea assured them and smiled again. Then, remembering something Wayne had said, she added, "I think I ended good enough."

The words struck the others like a slap.

"No," said Albert. "Don't even think about it."

"If you're not coming over here, then neither am I, Olivia insisted. She was already moving toward her.

But Andrea was not going to let her. She took a deep breath, preparing herself, and then closed her eyes and let go.

Chapter 54

It was in that brief instant of time between closing her eyes and letting go that Andrea saw the presence. It came from among her friends, stepping through them like a familiar face in a crowd, reaching out for her. It moved faster than the snap of the separating worlds and reached out to her, taking her hand. It was then that she finally understood what it was.

Who it was.

It was the same presence that spoke to her on the path, telling her to use the fire to save the others from the night tree. It was also the same presence that tugged her pigtail before that, giving her pause so that it was Nicole, not her, who was ensnared by the night tree, leaving her free so that she would be able to receive the message about the fire.

He'd been there the whole time, watching over them, protecting them.

She felt Gravity shifting, turning, twisting, and then she was in the air. A second later, it was over and she struck the ground with a sharp cry.

She might have remained there, her eyes closed, waiting for the thing in the tunnel to catch her so that she could join the horizontal raindrops on their long journey into oblivion, but she realized two things. First, that she was lying on hard earth instead of in cold water. And second, that she was not alone.

When she opened her eyes she found neither eternal darkness nor some grotesque thing barreling toward her, but Albert staring down into her face. "What happened?" she asked.

"You scared the shit out of us," snapped Nicole. "*That's* what happened!"

Ignoring her, Albert said, "You let go and the tunnel disappeared, but you were still here."

Andrea sat up and looked around. All four of them were there, staring at her. "I don't get it," she said, but then she did. She turned and looked around, searching. That presence…

"You were wrong," Brandy said, as if in awe. She was smiling now. All of them were, except Andrea.

"No," she said. "I wasn't. He grabbed me before it could close. He pulled me out."

"Who did?" Albert asked.

Andrea looked at him, her eyes large and pleading.

"Who?" he repeated. "We didn't see anyone. Who pulled you out?"

"*Wayne*," Andrea said, and the others stared at her. "It was *Wayne*. I know it was. He was the one who was lost. He was up there with you on the temple, calling out to me so I could find you. And he was here in this tunnel before. He was showing me where to go."

Albert and Brandy looked at each other. Was it possible?

"Could that be right?" Olivia wondered.

But before they could discuss it any further, Nicole shattered the quiet of the tunnel with a terrible scream.

It came out of the darkness on stiff legs, its flesh black and charred, glaring blindly at them through eyes that looked like curdled milk. Andrea scrambled to her feet and backed away. Brandy grabbed Albert's arm and clung to him. Olivia made a sound that was not unlike a wounded animal. After all they'd been through, why wouldn't the horrors just end?

But Albert was not afraid. At the sight of the burnt figure, he instead grew angry. He actually took a step toward it. "*The fuck do you want?*" he snapped.

The old man stopped walking and merely stood there for a moment, his flesh naked and cooked. He seemed to be looking at all of them at once, but not at any of them at all. His cloudy, boiled eyes did not even rotate in their sockets. He did not speak, but at last lifted one cracked and blackened hand toward them. The flesh had split over several of the knuckles and Albert could see the scorched bones beneath.

"It's over," Albert said. "You're too late. The door's been opened. You lost. Deal with it."

But the old man did not lower his hand and Albert realized that he was not pointing at him.

"Me?" Brandy asked. She shrank behind Albert, fearful of the dead thing that stood before them. Her heart pounded in her chest. It had been she who actually opened the door, she who physically did what he set out to prevent. Was he here to punish her for that? Was he going to kill her?

"Over my dead body," Albert snarled.

The old man began to shuffle forward again, still holding its hand out, and Albert realized as he and Brandy stepped back that it was not pointing at her, either.

Olivia, Andrea and Nicole backed against the walls of the tunnel, their eyes wide with terror, but the old man walked between them, seemingly uninterested.

Then a single word was uttered, a question, weak and cracked from his singed throat. "How…?"

Albert turned and looked in the direction the old man was facing, where they'd had their backs turned as the old man approached, and saw the other figure standing there, shrouded in shadows.

"Shouldn't you already know?" replied the Keeper. "Aren't you familiar enough with deceit and lies to figure it out for yourself?"

The old man dropped his arm at last and stood there. He was so badly burned that he was incapable of facial expressions, but Albert could tell even by looking at his charred back that he was furious. "I don't like…being used…" he growled, his words wet and forced, bubbling out of his throat like blood from a gushing wound.

"You never had any say in the matter," replied the Keeper. "Now leave."

Infuriated, the old man turned and glared with soupy eyes at Albert. He shouldn't have been alive, much less able to speak, but somehow he was still forming words. Like before, Albert realized they were mostly inside their heads. "Do you think…you can face… oblivion?"

"What?"

"Leave," repeated the Keeper.

"If we ever...cross paths again..." gargled the old man, but before he could finish his threat, he was gone, seemingly sucked away by some phantom force unseen and unfelt by any of them.

The five of them looked around, confused, trying to understand where he had gone, but they all knew well enough that the explanation was out of their reach.

Albert turned and looked at the Keeper. "It was you," he said. "You did all of this, didn't you?"

"Yes," replied the Keeper.

"You played all of us, even the old man and the Sentinel Queen."

"That's correct."

"But what did we do, exactly?" Brandy asked.

"You opened the doors on the judgment of those without faces."

"But what did it *do*?" she pressed.

"It did many things. You've begun a great chain of events, one that will forever change the fate of all that is alive and dead."

"Was it good or bad?" Albert asked.

"Yes," replied the Keeper. "No. I have no idea. The full scope of your actions is far beyond my ability to see. But there will be good and there will be bad. By opening the door, you've brought about the end of an entire world, but perhaps the birth of another. You've altered the natural course of fate in ways that will not be fully realized for billions of millennia."

"Did we blow up our world?" Andrea asked.

"No. It is undisturbed, but things will happen there. Miracles. Curses. Small things in between."

"So we didn't save the world, either, did we?" Albert asked.

"Not directly. But much is yet to be seen."

"So what were we?" Nicole asked. "Just pawns in all this? Your puppets?"

"In a sense," replied the Keeper. "You were my tools."

"Were you in my head?" asked Albert. "After the Sentinel Queen died? Did you…guide my hand?"

"I may have given you an occasional nudge in the right direction," admitted the Keeper.

Albert recalled referring to the structure at the end of the labyrinth as a "tower" even though he'd only seen the base, which had looked more like a pyramid. Using that word had reminded Andrea to pass along his message, confirming that they were in the correct chamber. At the time, he thought the Sentinel Queen had planted the word in his mind, and didn't realize why it bothered him. Since then, he'd come to understand that she was already dead by then. He just hadn't realized it yet.

"Are you God?" asked Olivia, and the others looked at her, surprised.

"No. God is…something else. I'm just the Keeper."

"And the sentinels?" asked Albert.

"They were just the sentinels."

"So is someone pulling *your* strings?" asked Albert.

"Perhaps. It is not my place to ask such things."

"The voice was yours, wasn't it?" Andrea said suddenly, changing the topic.

"Yes," replied the Keeper, although its voice was not quite like the voice she'd heard in her head, perhaps because there was a difference between hearing a voice with your ears and hearing it with your mind, especially when the voice was as harsh and alien as this strange creature's. "And you did very well."

"And the one who was lost?" Andrea pushed. "It was Wayne, wasn't it?"

"Yes." The Keeper turned and lifted one arm, pointing into the darkness behind him, the flesh dangling from its wrist. "You should go to him."

"What?" Olivia stepped forward and shined her light into the darkness.

"Is he still here?" Andrea asked, her eyes searching the air around her, trying to feel the presence she had felt before, but it was no longer with her. Wayne seemed to have vanished back into the mysteriousness from which he came.

Olivia walked past the Keeper and a form appeared in the glow of her flashlight. "Oh my god..." she sighed. It was Wayne's body, lying motionless on the cold floor of the tunnel. She ran to him and knelt beside him. His glasses were still on his face and his hands were resting on his belly, as though he had just lain down for a quick nap. He wore a thick, gray wrapping around his torso where the thing that came out of the labyrinth passed through him, and when she touched his face, he was still warm.

"He will be fine," assured the Keeper. "He will need rest, and he will be in pain for a while, but he will not need medical attention."

"You mean he's alive?" stammered Nicole.

"But I just saw his ghost..." said Andrea. This was confusing.

They gathered around Wayne, amazed that he could possibly still be alive.

"But how?" Albert asked. He turned and saw that the Keeper was rotating its head again, twisting it until its face was nearly upside down, revealing its dull, black eyes to him.

"I realize you're tired, Albert, but you know the answer to that."

Albert didn't understand at first, but then he realized that the Keeper was right. "The zombies," he said. "The undead. You can't die in the Wood."

"That is correct. There is nowhere to go. There is no exit for the dead out there, no road to the next world. A weak soul will cling to its body and fester with it, eventually becoming the death in which it is trapped, but a strong soul like Wayne's can wander freely. Wayne was with you all the whole time, right by your side as you climbed the mountain. And he remained with Andrea from afar as she made her journey with the dead, guiding her to where she needed to be. When you faced your adversary atop the temple, he added his spirit to yours, increasing your strength. It was he who helped you do the things you did. It was he who made it possible for Andrea to rescue you. And now he has returned to his shell."

"And his body is okay?"

"It was not difficult to fix him. I patched his wounds. I kept his heart beating, his lungs breathing, and I brought him here to wait for you."

"I see," said Albert, but he wasn't entirely sure if he did. It was all so much.

"I gave him back his body. It was my decision to make. I am the Keeper."

"The Keeper of the Dead," Albert guessed.

"Of lots of things."

"I see."

"Is there anything else before I go?"

"Lots of things," replied Albert.

"There will always be."

He turned and looked at Wayne, still lying there. Olivia and Andrea knelt over him while Brandy and Nicole sat nearby, looking back at him and listening to his conversation with the Keeper. Beyond Wayne, just visible within the light, he could see a broken wall. He recognized that wall. They were back in the tunnels beneath Briar Hills. Beyond that wall was a tunnel they'd have to crawl through. Beyond it, the next led to the one that was flooded. Behind him was the fork in the path and beyond it, on the left, was the entrance to the Temple of the Blind. But the temple wasn't there anymore. He turned and looked at the Keeper. Its face was upright again. "Why did the temple collapse when Brandy opened the door?"

"The temple *was* the door," replied the Keeper.

"I see."

"You are safe now. Rest. Let Wayne rest. And then you can all return to the surface.

The Keeper did not vanish, as the old man had, but simply turned and walked away. Albert watched the frail figure for a moment, and then asked one more question.

"Will we ever see you again?"

The Keeper did not turn back. "No," it said. "Never."

Albert watched until it was gone and then turned and walked over to where Wayne lay.

Olivia was still bent over him, gently stroking his head. Andrea was holding his hand. Behind them, Albert saw for the first time the bundle that was lying on the tunnel floor. "Are those our clothes?" he asked.

"I think so," replied Nicole. She stood up and went to them, digging through them. They were all there, everything except what the blind man had taken from them. She turned and looked at Albert, her expression noticeably sad, even in the shadows. "All except Beverly's."

Albert turned and looked back toward the temple. Those the Keeper had left down there, lost along with her body, never to be seen again.

Also among their belongings was Brandy's backpack, which she'd left behind when they disrobed. She'd completely forgotten about it. Inside were the three jackets and the three swimsuits she'd packed, along with the bare basics of her purse, which included her cigarettes and lighter, some makeup and a tube of lip-gloss. Her driver's license and keys were also in there. Now that she remembered bringing them, she was very thankful they weren't lost when the temple self-destructed.

Wayne opened his eyes and looked up at Olivia, who smiled down at him. "Hey there," she said, her eyes filling with tears.

"I told you to go on," he said.

Olivia looked up at Albert, then down at Wayne again. "What?"

He looked up at Albert, and then around at the others, trying to focus his eyes. "Take the light and go."

Olivia smiled down at him. "Silly," she said. "We're done now. You're fine."

He stared up at her, not comprehending. "What?"

Albert knelt beside him. "Don't you remember anything?"

Wayne looked up at him. He didn't understand.

"It's been hours since we left you in that tunnel," Albert explained. "Don't you remember any of it?"

Wayne looked at Olivia and then up at Brandy, as if for confirmation. "I don't..." He closed his eyes and tried to focus his thoughts. "I had a dream...that's all. Somebody was talking to me..." He shook his head. "But I can't remember what the voice said." He opened his eyes and looked up at Albert. "Something about you and Andrea and... What happened?" He felt something wet on his chest and realized that Olivia was crying again. He reached up and touched her cheek. "I...felt like there was something very important I was supposed to do." He looked up at Albert again. "But it was just a dream..."

"Relax," Albert said, smiling. "Rest for a little while. We'll tell you everything."

Chapter 55

Scattered about his bare feet were the stones that once concealed the entrance to the great labyrinths of the Temple of the Blind, stones he'd twice tumbled with his bare hand to reveal the first wonders of that ancient place that now was not even a tomb. It was nothing. Before him stood a wall of cracked stone, not gray and smooth like the walls of the temple, but coarse, pale bedrock.

"Albert?" Brandy stepped out of the shadows behind him, dressed now, except for the items the blind man had taken. Behind her, just out of sight around the next turn, the others sat around Wayne with one flashlight. Albert had taken the other when he went to see what had become of his Temple of the Blind. "I brought your clothes."

"It's gone," he said without turning. "There's nothing left. Not even a hole."

"Would it matter if there was?"

Albert didn't respond. He wasn't sure if it would or not. He wasn't sure if *anything* mattered.

"Wayne's okay. Says he hurts, but he managed to sit up okay."

"That's good."

"It's like a miracle."

"Like he never died," Albert said, almost too softly to be heard. "Pretty soon it'll be like it never happened, like he was never down here...like none of us were ever down here."

"Like there never *was* a here?" She was beginning to understand what was going through his head.

"It was all fake. Wayne never died. There was never any end of the world. The whole thing was a bunch of lies."

"Not all of it."

Albert sighed. "I know. But too much of it was."

"Not the part where I fell in love with you."

He turned and faced her now. "I know." He kissed her soft lips, held them, savored them. She was right. That was all that should have mattered. But there were so many things he still didn't know, things he would probably never know.

When he pulled away, Brandy sighed lovingly and smiled. "I love you so much."

"I love you, too."

She held his shirt and pants out to him. "Put some clothes on, stud, you're making me horny."

Albert smiled. "Yes, Ma'am." As she helped him into his jeans, his thoughts returned again to the lies they'd all been told. "How much of what we did was really us?" he asked. The question was like a poison, eating away at his thoughts. "How much was us and how much was someone else inside our heads?"

"Maybe we'll never know."

"Did I really solve the clues on the box or did someone solve it for me? Did I really know to knock down the wall that used to be here or did someone tell me to do it? Was it really *us* down here?"

Brandy gazed up at him, her blue eyes soft and pretty. "I don't know. Maybe it wasn't us at all. Maybe the only reason I survived my fall from the tower is because someone told me just what to do, just how to fall, just how to land. Maybe that's the better way. Don't think so much about it. It doesn't matter. We're going home."

He shook his head. "I don't know if I can."

"Why not?"

"Because something's not right."

"What's not right?"

Again he shook his head. "I don't know. Just...something."

"Come on." When his shirt was on and his broken arm tucked warmly inside, she took his good arm and pulled him away from the wall of stone that had once been the doorway to the impossible. "I don't want to think about it for a while."

Albert nodded, but as they walked away, his eyes drifted back to the place where the Temple of the Blind had once been.

Chapter 56

Wayne drew himself slowly to his full height as he stepped into a taller tunnel. The pain was dull, but relentlessly constant. There was a burning sensation in the muscles where the dark thing entered and exited his body and a general aching inside him, making every step he took feel like an exhausting feat of impossible strength.

But he was still alive!

He couldn't understand how... He'd been run through. The thing in the labyrinth, the dark thing they'd somehow let loose by igniting the inferno beneath the temple and opening the door into the Wood, had chased him down and speared him like a fish. He never even saw it, save for some brief hint of movement in that hellish wall of darkness, some unthinkably black thing in a complete and oily blackness that defied all laws of both nature and God.

But he was still alive.

Albert said that it was the Keeper who brought him back to the world of the living, or else someone or something by his instruction.

And yet Wayne had never even seen the creature with his own eyes.

What was it he'd done while he was in that darkness of death? It felt like a distant dream now, a permanent haze. Andrea claimed to have seen him...or felt him...or something... She claimed that he'd called out to her, guiding her along that strange, dark tunnel. She told him that he'd been purposeful, that he'd saved her life and everyone else's as well. Yet he remembered nothing but brief, distant flickers of things, memories of dreams submerged in his subconscious mind, never floating fully to the surface so that he could examine them.

Albert had wondered aloud if perhaps his inability to remember the things from his time among the dead had to do with being separated from his human body and therefore his human brain and its biological memory banks. Perhaps he was right. That sounded logical, after all. But he had no idea.

"How are you holding up?" Olivia asked him. It was a question she'd been asking almost constantly since they first started moving nearly an hour ago.

He looked down at her, into her beautiful face, and wondered how he could ever have asked her to leave him. Right now he never wanted to be away from her again. "I'm okay," he assured her, although he felt like someone had repeatedly struck him in the belly with a sledgehammer.

"We're almost there," Albert promised.

Olivia's dark eyes lingered on him for a moment before turning forward again, and in that moment Wayne found himself distracted in a way he hadn't been in several years.

He watched her for a moment longer and then lowered his eyes to the floor. He thought about all that he'd been through and wondered, not for the first time, if he would ever be the same.

Laura Swiff's advances seemed like an eternity ago. He felt as though he hadn't been inside his apartment in months. Even the Sentinel Queen's horror tunnel, her "Road Beneath the Wood," seemed like a distant memory to him.

But of all the things he'd seen and felt, from his mixed disgust and desire for Laura to the unthinkable nightmares of Gilbert House and the Wood to his struggle with the murderous Caggo, what suddenly lingered in his thoughts were the Sentinel Queen and her unborn child. *His* unborn child.

What would such a child have looked like, fathered by a man and mothered by a being like the Sentinel Queen. Would it have been a hairless, faceless freak, but possessing a voluptuousness that would have been irresistible to either sex? Would it have been human? Or would it have been something in between?

He did not know how to feel. On one hand, he never asked for a child. He never wanted to father a child that way. He had been seduced, even raped, after all, by a woman only half human. But on the other hand, the child was his. It was his genes. It was his blood. It was a part of him, and the Sentinel Queen had no more right to take it with her to her grave than she'd had the right to take the seed from his body. Now, walking home with the friends he'd made in the course of the longest night of his life, he didn't know whether to feel relieved or to grieve.

Olivia took his hand and squeezed it and he gave her a smile. "It's over now," she said. "It feels weird. I guess I'd started to think it wouldn't ever end."

"Tell me about it," sighed Nicole. "I can't wait to be home. I'm going to take a long, hot bath."

"Mm. That sounds good," Brandy said in a voice that was almost a purr.

Wayne looked around at them, happy to still be alive and surrounded by these new friends, but his eyes fell on Albert and remained there. *He* didn't look happy to be done. He was staring at the floor at his feet, his right sleeve dangling beside him. His broken arm was tucked inside his shirt. It must have been torture to travel so far and do so much with a fractured bone. But it wasn't pain he saw in Albert's dark eyes. It was concern.

"What's up?"

Albert looked up at him, a little startled, and then shook his head. "Nothing," he replied, and he even managed a smile for him. "Just daydreaming, I guess."

Wayne thought about calling him a liar, but decided not to. What did it matter, really? They were going home. There would be no more danger now. He looked back at Olivia, caught her gleaming brown eyes gazing up at him again, and decided he didn't really care to know.

Chapter 57

Olivia helped Wayne into the back seat of Andrea's car. It felt strange being in the sun again. It had been days since she last saw it. But it felt even stranger, oddly enough, to be in her clothes. She couldn't believe how accustomed she'd become to being naked. "You okay?" she asked.

Wayne nodded. "Yes. Thank you."

"I'll drop you guys off and then I've got to go home," Andrea said. "My mom and dad are probably going to be pissed."

"Just tell them what we discussed," Albert reminded her.

Andrea nodded. The story they'd agreed on was that there was a little get-together over at Hilltop Park. There were hiking trails over there, and Albert planned to tell the people at the emergency room that he got a little too adventurous and fell down a steep hill and over a bluff. (He still didn't know what he was going to tell them about the burns he and Nicole had suffered.) "If they're not too mad, I'll try and come see you guys."

Albert eased into the passenger's seat of his own car. Brandy would have to drive him and Nicole to the emergency room. Between his broken arm and the hole in his leg, he had no choice. But first she'd have to take them all back to the apartment to clean up. It was going to be hard enough to explain these injuries without smelling of rotting muck and excrement. And they were also going to have to grab a bite to eat. (She simply couldn't wait any longer.)

Once the stench was washed off of them, Albert thought he could explain his injuries to a doctor. A sharp, broken branch, a jutting rock. Even the gash on his knee and the cuts on his left arm were easily enough explained by a clumsy tumble down a rough embankment. Nicole could probably get by without having anything looked at, but as long as they were taking Albert, she might as well let a doctor look at her hand. She'd tell them that she punctured it rushing down the hill to help him. But she wouldn't show them all the cuts and bruises the night tree left on her.

Brandy, at least, wouldn't need any medical attention. The worst she had was a broken tailbone, and they couldn't do much for that.

Albert looked over at Wayne as Olivia climbed into the seat next to him and a grin touched his face. He was getting around pretty good for a dead guy.

They'd somehow managed to get out of the steam tunnels without being seen. Albert thought it was a minor miracle, even for a Saturday evening, considering how many people lived and worked on campus. Another miracle was the fact that there had been few people to see them hobbling to the parking lot like they'd just lost a brawl.

"Give me a call later," Wayne called over to them. "Let me know everyone's okay."

"Give us your number," Brandy said, tossing away her cigarette. She took a pen from the glove box and wrote it on the palm of her hand as Wayne told it to her. "And Andrea?" She wrote this number and then Olivia's beneath Wayne's. "Okay. Cool."

Olivia turned and looked at Wayne, her eyes still a little red from crying. "Is it okay if I stay at your place for a little while?" she asked. "I'm not ready to go back to my room yet."

Wayne smiled. "That would be nice. I'd like the company."

Nicole tossed Brandy's backpack into the back seat of Albert's car and then stood in the open door, finishing her cigarette. The wooden box, now considerably more battered (and a little more charred) than it was when it left his apartment, was stowed safely inside the backpack with the swimwear and the three jackets.

Albert stared out the window, tired. It was hard to believe they were home. For a while, it didn't seem like they'd ever make it back.

"Nothing's going to be the same after this, is it?" asked Andrea.

He smiled. "No. It won't. But that's not necessarily a bad thing."

She returned the smile. "I know it's not."

Nicole finished smoking and slid into the back seat. "You guys take care of yourselves," she called to the other car before settling in.

"You too," replied Olivia.

Andrea almost didn't want to go home. After all they'd been through, she felt closer to these five people than she'd ever been to anyone else in her life, and she was afraid that if they said goodbye now, she might begin to lose that even as they drove away.

"We're all still going to get our nails done, right?" Nicole asked.

Olivia smiled. "Of course." She held her hand up with the broken nail for Nicole to see. "I can't walk around like this."

Nicole smiled. "Good. I'm holding you to that."

Brandy and Andrea sat behind the wheels of their respective vehicles and closed the doors. Albert watched the other half of their party drive away and felt the same sort of sadness that Andrea had felt, that all of them were feeling. It was all over now.

After all that time, after all that wonder, he could hardly believe that it was done. Not only had they conquered the Temple of the Blind, they had brought it down. Never again would they be able to go inside, even if they wanted to.

"How you feeling?" Brandy asked, and Albert turned to look at her.

"I'm okay," he replied. "You?"

"I'm okay."

"*I'm* exhausted," announced Nicole as she leaned forward between the front seats. "I'm sweaty. I'm filthy. I *reek*. And I'm not wearing any panties. You guys throw the *coolest* parties. Did you know that?"

Epilogue

Brandy lay with her head on Albert's chest, listening to the sound of his beating heart, which had finally slowed to its usual, comforting rhythm. Hers too had finally calmed from the love they'd just made. Lying here now, with his strong arm around her, it was hard to believe how close she'd come to losing him.

It had been more than three weeks since they thrust open the door and pierced the heart of the ancient Temple of the Blind. And it was hard to believe that the world still turned exactly as it always had, swaddled in blissful ignorance of all that had unfolded so far beneath the ground.

"No one will ever know, will they?" Brandy had asked as she drove Albert and Nicole through the Saturday evening bustle of Briar Hills, mud still in their hair and their feet still aching.

Albert had gazed through his window at an SUV that was sitting beside them at the light. The woman at the wheel was talking on a cell phone while two young girls sat in the back seat. The younger of the girls looked down at him with large, brown eyes. "Not in this life," he replied.

Brandy ran her hand up Albert's belly, lightly dragging her new nails across his skin. She felt him shudder lightly beneath her and smiled. Olivia kept her promise to take her and Andrea to get their nails done. Nicole declined the invitation because she wanted her hand to heal first—she was tired of explaining to everyone how she'd hurt herself—but promised to go next time. So far she was thrilled with them. They were very pretty and it didn't take long to realize that Albert really liked them, which was good since she wanted nothing more than to find ways to distract him from the pain of his healing arm. It wasn't easy, after all, when she had to be so gentle with him and with the full-arm cast that made it difficult for him to do so many of his everyday tasks.

In the emergency room, a tall and rather gangly-looking doctor named Jude Ponchey had taken care of both Albert and Nicole. Naturally, he had been curious as to how they had sustained such injuries, and Albert gave him the story they'd all agreed on. According to this story, which was the one he would later use to explain his injuries to anyone who asked, including his and Brandy's families, he had wandered off a hiking trail, slipped and went tumbling down a hillside where he probably collided with a rock or a tree (he really couldn't remember). Nicole had gotten the hole in her hand while rushing down the hill after him, but none of them were really sure what had jabbed her. Brandy thought that making the more complicated details relatively vague seemed realistic to her and prevented too much contradiction in their stories. Nevertheless, she could tell that Dr. Ponchey wasn't entirely fooled.

"So what," Albert had said on the way home from the hospital. "He can't possibly suspect the truth." And that had pretty well ended it. The worst Dr. Ponchey could do was suspect that they'd gotten injured doing something illegal and he was a physician, not a detective. Their medical history was private and he would have to honor their confidentiality.

There were plenty of messages waiting for them on their machine when they arrived home, and Albert deleted them all without listening to them. The following morning, they both arose much earlier than they cared to and drove to their respective places of business to set things right. The guys at Staples were predictably cool. The moment he walked through the door with his arm in a cast and limping, the only thing any of them cared about was hearing what the hell happened to him. His boss, Dave, told him not to worry himself over it, telling him he knew it must've been a real emergency for him not to call in and to take as much time to heal as he needed.

After that, they drove to Old Navy. Brandy walked in the door with her keys in her hand, ready to throw them in that bitch Paula's face when she yelled at her. To her surprise, the woman rushed forward as soon as she saw them and seized her in a huge hug, proclaiming that she'd been worried sick all night long!

"As if she ever gave a shit about me before," Brandy grumbled when she slid behind the wheel of her car afterwards, looking utterly perplexed.

But Albert had only smiled. He never thought Paula would be angry. Brandy was too reliable. She'd proven herself a good employee. People worried when reliable people didn't show up when they were supposed to. Even the ones you didn't know cared.

Olivia called that evening to ask how Albert and Nicole were. She'd returned to Wayne's apartment with him and nursed him through the night, leaving him the following morning only long enough to return to her dorm room for a fresh change of clothes and an overnight bag. Wayne suffered some nausea and fever and quite a few aches, not all of which were necessarily related to the same injury, but by the middle of the following week, his seemingly mortal wound had healed almost completely. All that remained were two ugly scabs where the thing entered and left his body. They were only even slightly painful to the touch.

His shredded shin from his encounter with the hound gave him considerably more grief.

Albert's parents came to visit on Sunday. Having been alerted to their son's broken arm the day before because it was their insurance he was still living under, they came to visit and to hear exactly how he had managed to break his arm and stab a hole into his leg. Albert's sister, Rebecca, had been unable to come, which suited Brandy just fine. Julie and Rick Cross treated her as if she were their own and she had grown very fond of them, but she had the distinct feeling that Becky didn't care much for her. She didn't know why. Becky never openly admitted any dislike for her, but it was there. She could feel it.

Since then, their apartment had become a busy place. Hardly a day went by that they didn't see Nicole or Andrea. And Olivia and Wayne dropped by almost as often. This past weekend was Halloween, and they'd all gotten together as though they'd known each other since they were kids.

It didn't take anyone long to realize that there was something going on between Wayne and Olivia, and Brandy certainly thought it was wonderful. After all they'd been through, they deserved each other. And after all the bad things that had happened, it was nice to see that they brought back something good as well.

Nicole had also expressed her happiness over their new relationship, but Brandy detected something a little sad about her lately. Perhaps a part of it was that she was still single while her friends had found love, but she wondered if her friend hadn't fallen a little for Wayne during their time in the temple.

On the other hand, she'd erased Earl Tannis from her life completely and that was certainly a good thing.

Meanwhile, Andrea was trying to convince them all to go and get a tattoo with her, but Brandy remained reluctant. That needle looked painful, after all. And it was so *permanent.*

But she *was* starting to consider it…

Brandy was still looking at her hand, but her eyes had drifted away from her nails to the small, golden engagement ring on her finger. Albert had kept his promise to propose to her. The first opportunity he had, he went out and spent all he could afford on it. It wasn't much, just a small, quarter-karat solitaire, but it was everything she'd ever wanted.

The only person more excited than Brandy was Nicole, who'd been bouncing off the walls ever since she heard the news. Naturally, she would be the maid of honor, but that was the only thing they'd planned thus far. They didn't even have a date. They'd both agreed that since the engagement came so quickly, after only thirteen months of dating, they would have a long engagement.

She turned her hand a little and watched the light twinkle off the diamond. Never in her life had she felt so completely happy.

Albert stared up at the ceiling, his thoughts somewhat less cheerful than his fiancée's. Ever since that last conversation with the Keeper, he'd felt a little uneasy. He'd taken to reading the paper and watching the news every day, searching for some sign of the things of which the Keeper had spoken. "There will be good and there will be bad," it had said. "Things will happen there. Miracles. Curses. Small things in between." But how was he supposed to separate the things they had caused from the ordinary day-to-day goings-on of the world?

The first few days following their return from the temple, Albert had discovered a number of reports of small seismic activity. Some people had gone as far as to say that the New Madrid fault line was getting ready to let loose the "big one." But Albert knew that the only thing the seismologists had detected was the distant collapse of the Temple of the Blind, whose debris he himself had nearly ridden into hell.

Far more disturbing was the news of several grisly murders in the small, nearby town of Amicson—which, he realized with great horror, was only two or three miles north of Gilbert House. And he was not the only one to grasp the connection.

"We did that," Wayne said soon after the news began to spread. "We let that thing out of Gilbert House and now it's killing people."

"You and Olivia never would have gotten out of there if we'd stopped to seal that door on our way out," Albert reminded him. "You'd both probably be dead now. For that matter, we all probably would be. I don't think we'd have made it out of there alive if it wasn't for you."

But Wayne wasn't convinced and Albert could hardly blame him. An elderly couple, a middle-aged man and two young women were now dead, mutilated almost beyond recognition, and Albert had seen first-hand what that thing's victims looked like. He couldn't imagine the horror those poor people must have suffered in the last moments of their lives, much less the grief their families must still be enduring.

Also in the news were three missing college students. Andy Lanott, Nick Shrewd and Patricia Strep (poor Trish) had finally made it into the paper. So far, no one had approached Olivia with questions about them, but both Albert and Wayne had encouraged her to tell anyone who connected her to them that she broke up with him that Wednesday afternoon and to say nothing of Gilbert House. It was painful to think that their bodies might lie there in the darkness forever, but the Sentinel Queen said something terrible still lived on the fourth floor, and anybody who went there looking for them would probably wind up dead.

"The police will search that whole place," Albert had told her. "They'll have to. And they'll probably all die."

Olivia hadn't been convinced that keeping quiet was the right thing to do, but she understood their reasons. She'd watched enough "CSI" to have a good idea of how a crime scene was handled. It was all too easy to imagine a group of officers storming into the building, fanning out to clear the scene, climbing higher and closer to their deaths. And when the first of them met the terror that waited on the fourth floor, something so terrible she could not imagine it even after all she'd seen, the others would rush to help, each of them in turn dying a gruesome death. However reluctant she was to allow those poor people to become just three more mysterious missing persons, it was truly better to leave the dead where they lay than to lead more to their doom.

Beverly Bridger took longer to surface. It was a week and a half before her disappearance reached the news, and even then it was hardly front page material. Albert had read the article several times, hardly believing what he was reading. When she didn't return after her vacation, the hospital where she worked—the very one that had fixed Albert's arm and Nicole's hand—left a message on her machine telling her that she was fired. When she didn't show up to pick up her last paycheck for a whole week, someone finally became concerned.

"She was a nurse?" Brandy had asked, stunned.

"Looks that way," replied Albert. It really was hard to imagine. She certainly didn't seem to have the mindset to be a registered nurse. But as he thought about it, he supposed that Beverly's obsession with Gilbert House might actually have encouraged her to stay in school long enough to acquire any number of degrees, perhaps even a doctorate or two.

He'd stared at the article for a while. There was no picture, as there had been of Olivia's ex-boyfriend and his friends. No one had missed her. It had taken her not showing up for her paycheck before anyone realized something might be wrong. He felt a renewed surge of pity for the woman.

"She was only thirty-six!" Brandy marveled. She'd appeared so much older than that.

He still read the paper every day, front to back, and scanned the national and world headlines on the Internet, searching for something, anything, that might connect back to their actions in the Temple of the Blind. So far, the only other news in those three weeks that stood out from the ordinary and mundane was something about an accident at a factory in Wisconsin. Thirty-seven people were reported dead under "unusual circumstances" at some manufacturing facility owned by Vertical Industries.

And he remained frustrated by all the things he still didn't understand. Neither the Keeper nor the Sentinel Queen had answered all of their questions. He still didn't understand how Wendell Gilbert built Gilbert House, or why their nakedness was supposed to fool the hounds, or why the old man had been misled to believe that the doorway atop the temple would send the world crashing into ruin.

He also didn't understand why, when they finally returned home, all their watches were wrong. It seemed that they had each lost some time during the night. Was it the Wood? Did that dark forest exist in a different flow of time from this word?

Brandy told him to relax. It was over. They did what they were sent to do. But he could not. They *had* done what they were sent to do, but there was something else. There was that strangeness he'd felt from the Keeper's last words. It had bothered him for days, but now he'd come to understand what that oddness was. The Keeper *lied* to him. Albert asked if they would ever meet again, and the Keeper said no. It said *never*. But the Keeper lied.

And how many other lies might they have been told?

He was drawn from his thoughts as he felt Brandy's nails sliding softly back down his naked belly. He looked down and found her gazing back at him with her lovely blue eyes.

"What are you thinking about?" she asked.

"You," he replied, and it was the truth. When she looked at him like that, when she *touched* him like that, it was hard to think of anything else.

"I love you."

Albert smiled at her. Somehow, after all they went through, they were still here, still together. "I love you too."

In the top of the closet was the box that had brought them together. It was unlocked, the key resting inside with Beverly's envelope and the golden medal with the cryptic symbol that meant DEVIL and all the rest of the clues that allowed them to make their unforgettable journey and still be alive to make love. So many mysteries there, so many questions left unanswered. But so much more as well.

Perhaps they would never know what kinds of things they'd set into motion by throwing open the sentinels' door. Perhaps they'd never understand the meaning of all they had seen and heard. It didn't really matter. He had Brandy. They were together. They were happy. And they'd made great friends along the way.

He closed his eyes and briefly thought of the Temple of the Blind. The sentinels. The labyrinth. Gilbert House. So many wondrous places. He thought of the Sentinel Queen and her sightless son. The Keeper. The Caggo. The old man who pretended to be a devil. He thought of Nicole. Of Olivia and Wayne. Of Andrea with her childlike eyes. But he thought mostly of Brandy, whose soft skin was pressed against him, warming him, whose lips brushed his chest and sent shivers through his body, who would one day be his bride. So much he'd found there in the driver's seat of his car that night. So very much.

And it was just a stupid wooden box.

Turn the page for a preview of the first book in this
author's other horror-adventure series:

Rushed

by Brian Harmon

Available now!

Chapter One

Eric Fortrell lived a perfectly unremarkable life until he happened to have a very extraordinary dream. It wasn't that it was an especially meaningful dream. In fact, he could remember nothing about the dream except that there was something about a bird, and even that vague detail was so far lost to his waking mind that only the word itself remained. "Bird." It was not any particular kind of bird, no bird of any particular color or size. It was nothing more significant than *something about a bird*. And yet this dream filled him with such a profound sense of urgency and foreboding that he immediately left his bed, dressed himself and fled his home in the middle of the night. By the time he came to his senses and realized that there was nowhere for him to go, he was already standing in his driveway with the door of his silver PT Cruiser wide open, ready to climb in and drive away.

He was confused, of course, and a little unnerved. After all, he wasn't exactly known for being impulsive. It wasn't like him to do anything without a reasonable amount of thought, much less jump up in the middle of the night and go running out to his car, inexplicably convinced that he desperately needed to be somewhere. But more than that, he was embarrassed. He closed the vehicle's door as quietly as he could and gazed around at the darkened windows of his neighbors' houses, very nearly convinced that at least one of them must be watching him, wondering where he thought he was going at a quarter past one in the morning, laughing at his ridiculous antics.

He was a reasonable enough man to know that this was utter nonsense. Even if someone *was* up and wandering around in their unlit home at this hour *and* just happened to be looking out the window as he hurried out the door, they'd have no reason to suspect that he was behaving strangely. Perhaps he'd lost something, his wallet, maybe, and was checking to see if he'd left it in his vehicle.

Still, he hesitated to lock the car for fear that the brief sounding of the horn would alert every nosy neighbor on the block to his presence and somehow instantly let them know that he was acting as if he'd utterly lost his mind.

He left the PT Cruiser unlocked in the driveway and returned to his house and his bed.

He was not crazy. He did not have a history of insanity in his family. He had no excessive mental or emotional stress in his life. He was also intelligent. He'd earned a Masters Degree in education and literature. With honors. He was a respected high school English teacher and he had never in his life poisoned his mind with drugs. He didn't even drink that much. Only seldom in his life had he drank enough to qualify him as being drunk, and never so much that he couldn't remember what he did the next morning.

And yet here he was.

Karen was waiting for him when he returned to bed. She was concerned, of course, and wanted to know what had happened, why he had risen and dressed, where he had gone. He told her the truth. He always told his wife the truth. And of course she laughed at him and told him how silly he was because she was always equally as honest with him and it was, after all, a funny and silly thing that he had done.

But long after Karen had drifted off to sleep again, Eric remained awake, staring up at the ceiling in the faint glow of the street light that filtered through the curtains and the nightlight that shined through the open bathroom door. He kept thinking of the dream he couldn't remember and the odd compulsion that had driven him out of his bed and into the cool August night.

The following day was no better. He couldn't stop thinking about the dream (something about a bird…) and that feeling of desperately needing to be somewhere (*now*). In fact, he still felt this compulsion. It gnawed stubbornly at him. His eyes kept drifting to the windows and doors. His thoughts kept returning to the parked PT Cruiser in the driveway. It was like an itch.

He very much wanted to get in the vehicle and drive down the road. Yet he remained unable to say *where* it was he wanted so badly to go.

That night, the dream returned. Like the first time, he recalled nothing but a bird (or birds, or something bird-like…he simply couldn't remember) and like the first time, he awoke utterly convinced that there was somewhere he very much needed to be, that he was, in fact, desperately *late*.

He did not make it all the way to his car this time. When Karen switched on her bedside lamp, he stood frozen and bewildered, his pants only halfway on, squinting into the blinding glare and trying to remember where it was he thought he was going.

Soon after, he was back in bed, the lights back off. Karen did not laugh at him this night. She did not tell him he was silly. She urged him back into bed and he came willingly, ashamed of the concern he saw in her sleepy face. The desperation he had felt was overpowered by the simple logic that he *did not have anywhere to be.* He returned to his pillow without a word and she snuggled against him as if determined to anchor him to the bed until morning.

Again, he lay awake, that feeling of being late still stubbornly refusing to release him and let him rest.

The next day was much like the one before it. He remained constantly distracted, his thoughts and eyes inexorably drawn to the parked PT Cruiser and the unknown roads it promised to carry him down.

Each time he forced his eyes away from the windows and doors he caught Karen watching him. She was no fool. No matter how many times he told her he was fine, she knew something was troubling him, and he felt terrible for worrying her. But still he could not shake the urge to get up and go.

The third night inevitably arrived and Eric awoke once more from the same mysterious dream with the same maddening desire to rush out of the house.

This time, he did not bother returning to bed. When Karen came downstairs and switched on the kitchen light at a little before three in the morning, she found him sitting at the table, fully dressed, a steaming cup of coffee in his hands and his car keys sitting in front of him.

For a moment she stood watching him and for that moment he watched her back, admiring her. She was considerably heavier than she had been ten years ago when he married her, but still as lovely as the day they met. In fact, he rather preferred her a little plumper. She'd been too skinny back when they dated, far too preoccupied with her weight. Now that she'd accepted that there was nothing wrong with being larger than a size zero, she'd filled out her figure with magnificently sexy curves. His eyes washed over her bare legs as she stood leaning against the doorjamb, clothed in only her favorite pajama top, her arms crossed over her chest as if chilled.

"You know," she said finally, "there's bound to be an easier way to sneak off and see your mistress."

Eric smiled up at her. "I know. She told me to stop waking her up at two in the morning."

"No girl's horny at that hour."

Still smiling, still admiring her lovely shape, he sipped quietly at his coffee.

"How far did you get this time?"

"Pretty well right here."

"Same dream?"

"Far as I know. Still can't remember it."

She stared at him and said nothing.

He kept smiling. "It's just a stupid recurring dream."

She was silent for a moment longer. She would not admit that she was worried about him. That simply wasn't her way. But he could see it in her eyes. And he didn't blame her for feeling at least a little concerned. These dreams were troubling. They were interfering with his life. Neither of them had ever dealt with anything like this before.

Finally, she spoke: "What are we going to do?"

"I'm going to go," Eric replied.

This surprised her. She stood up straight, her pajama shirt falling open a little at the bottom, where she'd left it unbuttoned. There was no force on earth that could stop his eyes from being drawn there. "Go where?"

Eric shrugged. "I'll just drive. See where it takes me."

"Okay...but there's nowhere to go. It's just a stupid dream. You said so yourself just now."

"I know. *Believe me*, I know. But this is the third night in a row I've had it and for some reason it's really getting to me. I've been so distracted. I *constantly* feel like there's somewhere I need to be."

"But there's not. You know that."

"I *do* know that," he assured her. "But apparently some part of my brain *doesn't*. That's why I'm going. I'll open myself up to it, do what it wants me to do. I'll just get in the car and drive. After a while, I'll prove to myself that there really isn't anywhere for me to go. Then I can come home and finally sleep. I mean, why not? I'm already awake."

She stared at him, studying him, considering what he'd said. He didn't know what else to say to her, so he took another sip of his coffee and let his eyes slide down her naked legs while he waited for her to speak.

"I guess that makes sense," she replied at last.

"*I* thought so."

"Show that messed up little brain of yours it doesn't know what it's talking about."

"Put it back in its place, right? That's what I'm saying."

She shifted her weight and continued to stare at him. He could almost see the thoughts swirling behind her lovely eyes.

"I'll be fine," he assured her. "And I can finally get this weirdness out of my system."

"But what if it doesn't work?"

"Then it doesn't work. At least I'll have tried, right? If I'm still having the dreams after this, I'll call the doctor."

Karen nodded. She knew there was no reason to be concerned. It was only a dream. It was irrational. So why not embrace the irrational and see what happened? Maybe then he'd at least be able to sleep through the night again.

And even if it didn't work, he wouldn't be any worse off for trying.

"I guess gas *is* cheaper than therapy," she reasoned.

"Just a little, I think."

"Just a little."

Eric took another sip of his coffee and found his eyes drifting to the door again. He felt impatient to go, but he refused to simply rush out the door.

"It'll be a fun little adventure for you."

Eric returned his eyes to his wife and smiled again. "I'll bet it will."

"No picking up sexy hitchhikers."

"But those are the best kind."

"I keep telling you, you don't know where they've been."

"If my adventure has a serious lack of romance, it'll be your fault."

"I'll just have to live with the consequences. How long will you be gone?"

Eric shrugged. "Long as it takes, I guess."

She didn't like this answer. She chewed thoughtfully at her lower lip. He loved it when she did that.

"Probably only a couple hours. I mean, really, where am I going to go? I'll be fine."

"Do you have your cell phone?"

Eric pulled the phone from the front pocket of his khaki pants and showed her. He hated cell phones, saw no value in them whatsoever, but she insisted that he carry one in case of emergencies. She was utterly unwavering about it. She'd even wanted to get him a high-dollar one with more functions than his laptop, like the one she carried, but he'd put his foot down. He carried nothing fancier than a cheap, pre-paid model from Wal-Mart. Even so, it had an obnoxious amount of extras built into it that he had no idea how to use. He didn't even know how to add minutes to the ridiculous thing. Karen took care of that for him.

He returned the annoying device to his pocket, finished his coffee and then stood up and rinsed out his cup in the sink. When he turned back around, Karen was right next to him, slipping her arms around him.

"It's okay," he promised her. "I'm just driving around. I *can* drive at night, you know."

"I just don't like being left alone. You know that. You won't fall asleep, will you?"

"I'll stay caffeinated," he promised. "Just go back to sleep. I'll be home before you know it."

"I won't be able to sleep. I never sleep well when you're not here."

"Try."

"You and your convoluted schemes to sneak off with your women."

"I like to keep it interesting. I'll tell your sister you said hi."

She gave his arm a gentle smack. "Pushing it," she warned him with an amused grin.

Eric smiled and kissed her again. "What've you got going on today?"

"Birthday cake for Joss."

"Oh yeah."

Karen was a talented baker and a freelance cake decorator. She'd earned an impressive reputation here in her home town and regularly earned fairly decent spending money.

"Toni's coming by to pick it up this afternoon." Toni was Karen's cousin. Joss was Toni's son, whose first birthday was tomorrow. He was an exceptionally adorable baby.

"That'll be fun for you."

"I know. Also, I'll probably get started on those pies for Lana." Lana was one of Karen's oldest friends. They went to grade school together. Lana often organized social events for the church, a responsibility she inherited from her mother when she was diagnosed with cancer several years ago. Karen made various pies, cakes, cookies, whatever recipes she wanted to try out, and Lana regularly earned her new customers.

Eric had tried to talk her into starting her own website, but she wasn't interested in expanding her hobby into an actual business. She was convinced it would take all the fun out of it.

"Maybe I should just get started now," she said, glancing at the clock on the stove.

"I think you should at least *try* and get more sleep. You don't want to be too exhausted when you're decorating that cake."

"I guess so."

"Go back to bed. I'll see you in a little while."

"Okay."

"Love you."

"Love you too."

Eric kissed her one last time and then collected his keys and walked out of the house.

Karen watched him from the doorway as he climbed into the PT Cruiser and backed out of the driveway.

Now he had only to convince *himself* that this wasn't completely insane.

He settled back into the seat and again tried to remember the dream. But like always, all that came back to him was the bird. It wasn't even an image of a bird. It was just the *idea* of a bird. As if that made any sort of sense.

He drove away with no idea where he was going, confident that he would find nothing waiting for him in the great open world and hoped to soon return home satisfied and back to normal.

Chapter Two

At this time of morning, Creek Bend, Wisconsin was peaceful and still. It was difficult to imagine that almost nine thousand people lived in the city when only a handful of vehicles roamed the quiet streets.

Most of the time, Eric liked being out when it was like this, but today there was a peculiar eeriness to the silent city. Something about the empty sidewalks and darkened buildings made him uneasy. It was as if he were walking through a graveyard instead of driving beneath bright streetlamps.

Although he told Karen that he might be gone a couple hours, he'd expected to be home in no more than fifteen or twenty minutes. He thought that he might merely circle the block a few times, or at most make his way across town to the shopping center and turn around. Unable to find whatever his troubled mind was seeking, he assumed he would quickly be resigned to return unfulfilled, though hopefully much less obsessed with traveling. Instead, being behind the wheel felt remarkably *right*. And soon he found himself driving south on the highway, leaving Creek Bend behind him.

He assumed the feeling would simply dissipate as he drove, that it would fizzle out as mysteriously as it had come to him, and then he'd be able to return to his home and his wife and be done with it. But the urge to drive only grew stronger as he made his way south, passing one town after another, until he came to the interstate. There, he felt compelled to take the onramp and proceed west.

It was about now that he began to wonder what he would do if this strange compulsion to drive overcame him to such a degree that he found himself irresistibly drawn right out of Wisconsin and into Illinois or Iowa or Minnesota. What if the approaching day found him cruising through Missouri or Nebraska or Indiana? What if wherever his subconscious mind was trying to take him wasn't even in the Midwest? Or what if it didn't exist at all?

A chill raced through him as he imagined himself helplessly driving on and on and on. He supposed that, eventually, Karen would kill his credit cards and he'd run out of money for gas. But would he then simply get out of the car and walk?

It was an eerie thought, and one he promptly pushed out of his head.

He was *not* crazy.

It was just a damn dream. That was all.

It was probably something psychological, something that he'd forgotten, perhaps, bubbling up to the surface through vivid dreams that were too complex for him to remember upon waking. The result was an irrational compulsion to seek something that wasn't really there.

That sounded reasonable. He guessed. He was no psychologist, but it seemed like a fairly sound explanation. It was at least *something*. It was better than crazy.

One exit sign after another passed by in his headlights as he made his way ever farther from home. Even long after he made up his mind to forget this ridiculous nonsense and turn around, he kept passing perfectly good exits. On and on he drove until, more than three hours after leaving Karen and Creek Bend behind, with the sun peeking over the eastern horizon, he at last switched on his turn signal and drifted into the exit lane.

Yet he still did not turn around. Instead, he cruised on down a little two-lane road that wove through countless acres of cornfields and cow pastures, ever farther from home.

After a while, he turned off this road, onto a narrow strip of blacktop that was far overdue for resurfacing, and drove for several more miles before turning onto yet another two-lane country road.

A loud buzzing rose from his lap as his cell phone began to vibrate enthusiastically in his front-left pocket. He didn't often get calls on his phone, and as such, the vibration usually surprised him, sometimes provoking him into using some of his favorite expletives. But it did not startle him this time, as he was just thinking that Karen should be calling to find out exactly where the hell he'd gone. Instead, it was the physical act of wrestling the phone from his pocket as the seatbelt fought to hold it in place that made him curse.

Like countless times before, he swore that one of these days he was simply going to throw the stupid thing away.

"You need to wrap up this booty call and get your ass back home," Karen said when he'd finally freed it from his pocket and pressed it to his ear.

"Sorry. You know how I like to snuggle after."

"No, you like to *snore* after."

"Right. I always get those two mixed up."

"Where are you?"

"Not sure, to be honest."

"You're not sure?"

"I'm not sure," he said again. "I see cornfields and a lot of cows."

"Quaint. Did you get lost?"

"Nope. I know the way home." Or he *thought* he knew the way home, at least. "I just don't know where I am, exactly. I'm pretty sure I'm still in Wisconsin."

"*Pretty* sure?"

"Yeah. *Pretty* sure."

Eric checked his mirrors to be sure he was still alone on the road. He didn't like using the cell phone any time, but least of all while driving. It pissed him off when he saw other drivers using theirs. But there was no shoulder and he had no intention of parking in somebody's driveway just to talk to his wife.

"You do know you're acting like a complete nut job, don't you?"

"Yes I do."

"You know a lesser woman would be really freaked out by now."

"I know she would. I'm so lucky."

"Yes you are."

"I'm probably just having the world's weirdest mid-life crisis or something."

"You're too young to have a mid-life crisis."

"Third-life crisis?"

"Besides, aren't you supposed to buy a motorcycle or an expensive sports car or something? I was looking forward to shopping for the car."

"We still can. We can *both* have mid-life crises."

"Don't be ridiculous. You know the women in my family stop aging at twenty-nine."

"Oh yeah. I keep forgetting about that. Funny math in your genes."

"It's called 'aging gracefully.'"

"My mistake."

"So are you coming home anytime soon?"

"I hope so."

"When?"

"When I'm done. Just trust me, okay?"

"You know I do."

"Good."

"But I warn you, if I have to eat lunch by myself I'm ordering delivery."

"Knock yourself out."

"Ooh. Fun."

"I can't explain it, but this feels right somehow. I think it may be working."

"'Nut job crazy' is working?"

"I think it is."

"Cool."

But if he were to be *completely* honest, he had no idea if this was really working or not. He'd assumed that he'd find himself with no idea where he wanted to go and therefore the compulsion would fade, but the farther he drove, the more it seemed to pull at him. He was beginning to wonder if there might be some specific place he was being drawn, though he could not fathom why he'd have any kind of subconscious desire to come here. He'd never been in this part of Wisconsin before.

"If nothing else, maybe it's the road that's good for me. Maybe I'm just overdue to take a nice long drive to clear my head."

"If you say so."

"I do. Did you start the cake?"

"I did. It's cooling. I'm starting my pies while I wait."

"What kind?"

"Strawberry."

"Yum."

"I miss you."

"I miss you too."

"Call me soon?"

"Sure. Love you."

"Love you too."

Eric said goodbye and ended the call. Ahead of him, the country road stretched on and on, ever deeper into the open farmlands. Cornfields turned to soybean fields and then back to cornfields again. Cattle herds occasionally shared the fields with horses and sheep and goats. Little patches of forestland cropped up from time to time, along with neatly planted apple orchards and even a Christmas tree farm, all punctuated with various farmhouses and barns and silos.

As the PT Cruiser's driver's seat began to grow uncomfortable beneath him and he realized just how far he'd strayed from home, he began to dread the long drive back.

And yet, he continued to pass driveways instead of turning around.

Finally, as he drove over a bridge, he spotted a perfect place to pull over. It was a little graveled drive at the far side of the small river, where fishermen could park and unload their gear.

Eric pulled off the road, but instead of turning around and starting home, he nosed the vehicle into the shade, put it in park and killed the engine.

He opened the door and stepped out into the morning sunshine, stretching his back and legs. The fresh air felt good and he realized that he needed this break.

He closed the door, then quickly opened it again and retrieved the phone that he'd deposited in the cup holder after his conversation with Karen. (He had barely won the battle with the seatbelt to get it *out* of his pocket; he wasn't about to try and wrestle with it to put the stupid thing back.)

When she first started making him carry the phone, he had a bad habit of forgetting it. And Karen had a bad habit of getting mad at him when that happened. It wasn't an ideal situation. It led to more than a few trivial fights. Over time, one of them had to give.

It wasn't her.

Cell phone properly deposited in his front pocket again, he locked the PT Cruiser's doors and strolled down to the river's edge to enjoy a few minutes out from behind the wheel.

Suddenly, and for the first time since waking from the dream that first night, he had no pressing desire to drive. He thought for a moment that he had beaten it, that he had finally driven far enough or long enough to have his fill of traveling.

But now he found himself being drawn along the riverbank and under the bridge.

Within minutes, he was around the bend and the rational part of his mind screamed at him to turn around.

This was far worse than his compulsion to drive. Now he was out in the middle of nowhere, utterly exposed and unprotected from the elements and in danger of becoming hopelessly lost. And yet still he walked.

At least he still had the phone. But how useful would it really be if something happened to him out here? As far as he knew, there was nothing for miles and miles but farmland and forests. How far could he go into this wilderness before he wandered out of the service area altogether?

A path appeared in the trees along the river bank and he found himself drawn there as surely as he'd been drawn to the river from his car. Leaving the water behind him, he made his way up a hill, through some thick brush and onto the neatly mown lawn of a modest, Victorian-style house.

His first thought should have been that this was private property and he had no business being here, that he'd be lucky if the owner didn't mistake him for a burglar and shoot him dead where he stood. Instead, he was compelled to walk to the back yard. Specifically, he felt drawn for some reason to a large, metal gate in the fence.

He walked up to this gate and rested his hands on the topmost bar. Beyond it, a narrow dirt path, little more than two dry wheel ruts in the tall grass, led away a short distance and then turned and disappeared into a field of tall and healthy corn.

"Ah. You finally showed up."

Startled, Eric turned to find an elderly woman hanging laundry up to dry just a few yards away. Even with his attention fixed on the gate and the path beyond, he was surprised that he didn't see her before now. "I'm sorry," he said.

"No reason to be sorry," the woman told him. "At least you showed up. Better late than never, right?"

He wasn't sure how to respond to this. He'd meant that he was sorry to be trespassing on her property, yet this woman acted as if she'd been expecting him. But that wasn't possible. Even *he* didn't know how he came to be here.

"But we *did* think you'd show up two days ago."

Two days ago? That would've been right after his first dream. "I'm sorry, but show up for what, exactly?"

The old woman turned and looked at him. She was very skinny, with long, silver hair that was neatly tied back, deep creases around her mouth and an ugly blotch beneath her right eye. "You're going out there, aren't you?" She gestured at the corn behind the gate.

Eric turned and gazed out into the field for a moment. Somehow, he didn't like the idea of going out there, but she was right. The same strange compulsion that had lured him into this woman's back yard was definitely pulling him toward that field. Looking back at the old woman again, he said, "I honestly don't know what I'm doing here."

She stood looking back at him for a moment, considering him. Then she went back to her laundry. "Ethan always knew you'd come. Ethan's my husband, by the way. He always believed."

"That's impressive. *I* didn't even know I was coming until I got here."

If the woman heard him, she made no attempt to acknowledge it. "I can't say for sure that I ever believed it. Not until yesterday. Not until I saw *him*."

415

"Him?"

She didn't look at him as she hung a man's work shirt on the line. "The other one," she replied as if this made any more sense than "him." "I saw him with my own eyes, walking into the corn there. Scariest damn thing I ever saw. It was like he was only half there…all faded…like somebody standing in a thick fog…except there wasn't any fog. He just faded into the sunshine. Damn scariest thing…"

This conversation was only getting stranger. Eric turned and looked out at the little road again, wondering what was waiting out there.

When he looked back, the old woman was staring at the work shirt she'd just hung on the line. "Ethan fell the other day. Hurt his back. His hip, too. Doctor thinks he might not be able to walk so good anymore. Probably need a cane. I hate to see that. Once you get as old as us, you have to keep moving. When you stop moving, that's when you die. That's what my daddy used to say. He lived to ninety-eight. Made sure he walked at least a mile every day while doing his chores. Went out of his way if he had to. Then he hurt his hip and he couldn't walk anymore. Pretty soon, just like he always said, he never walked again."

Cheerful. He'd wager she was a laugh a minute at bingo night.

"You said you were expecting me?" asked Eric, hoping she would give him some sort of answer as to why he was here…or at the very least not tell him how she lost her mother.

"Oh yes. Definitely." Then she fell silent again as she withdrew a flowered housedress from her basket and hung it on the line.

"Okay." Apparently that was all he was going to get. Again, he turned and stared off past the gate. It was hard to look at the woman.

There was something terribly sad about her.

"I gave him a red ribbon before he went in. That's good luck. Did you know that?"

"No. I didn't."

The old woman finished hanging her clothes and then picked up her empty basket and began walking toward the back door of the Victorian house. Without looking back at him, she said, "You should get going. I haven't been to the cathedral in a lot of years, but I remember perfectly well that it was a real long walk."

"Cathedral?"

But the woman was apparently done with their conversation. She entered the house and left him standing alone in her back yard.

Eric stared out into the cornfield for a moment. This was beginning to get spooky. He'd assumed that these urges to get in his car and drive were all in his head. He thought this even as he found himself getting out of his car and walking along the riverbank. But this woman had just told him that he was expected, as if he had been drawn here intentionally.

She also told him about "the other one." The one who looked like he was shrouded in fog, but without the fog. As if that made any kind of sense at all.

And she told him he was supposed to be looking for a cathedral.

It was beyond crazy. Either he just imagined this whole conversation, or she confirmed that he was here for a reason and not just because his brain was short-circuiting.

Or maybe they were both completely crazy.

He could still feel that strange pull, as if the cornfield were calling out to him. He did not want to go out there. Something was terribly wrong about all this. But he was fairly certain that he would find no peace by turning around and going home. And he certainly didn't want to converse any further with Mrs. Sunny Disposition.

Preparing himself for whatever weirdness awaited him on the other side, Eric lifted the latch on the gate and stepped through it to the other side.

ABOUT THE AUTHOR

Brian Harmon grew up in rural Missouri and now lives in Southern Wisconsin with his wife, Guinevere, and their two children.

For more about Brian Harmon and his work, visit

www.HarmonUniverse.com

Made in the USA
Middletown, DE
01 September 2019